THE SAVIOR OF WAR

THE
Savior
OF
War

M.E. SHUGERT

*For my Grandma.
I always dreamed of seeing
my book on your shelves.*

· PROLOGUE ·

Thea; 1983

Thea was jerked awake, sleep still clinging to her eyes, making the world around her look like a blurry picture. She blinked once to regain her sense of reality. Twice to realize that she was being held in her mother's wispy arms, being cradled with almost bruising strength against her mother's chest. A third blink and she could finally make sense of her mother's panicked whispers.

"…outside and I'll come back in to get your father. Thea? Baby? Are you listening?" Her mother's voice was scratchy and had an underlying tremor, a sure sign that something was wrong. It was the same tone that she used when Thea's father had drunk too much and she would escort Thea to her room, dragging her by the arm. She would then lie Thea on the bed, tuck the sheets to her chin, and sing *"My Little Sunshine,"* trying to be louder than the pounding and banging downstairs. Her mother had been an aspiring singer and poet in her youth but had never left the small town in Virginia where she grew up. She got pregnant at nineteen, never pursuing her dreams. On the nights her husband started drinking, she would stay with Thea, stroking her tangled, russet hair as she repeated the same song over and over, voice hitching and trembling with every loud crack that echoed through the house.

"Did you hear me Sunshine?" Her mother jostled Thea in her arms.

"What's going on? Mommy?" Thea's eyes were already watering because, even though she didn't understand what was happening, she could sense the fear. She sniffed, trying to hold back the tears and smelled the haze of smoke that wafted through the house. Her mom set her down and held onto her shoulders, forcing Thea to look her in the eyes.

"There's a fire. Oh baby, don't be scared. No, no. It's going to be alright." One of her mother's hands went to her cheek as soon as the whimper left Thea's lips. "I'm going to take you outside, okay? And then I'm going to come back in for your father. Just hold on to me," she said as she picked Thea up again. "Put this over your mouth and keep your head down. Can you do that for me?"

Thea did as instructed and took the dish-rag out of her mother's hands, keeping her head in the crook of her neck. She felt the searing heat crawl over her skin as soon as her bedroom door opened. Her mother crouched down, pulling Thea even closer to her body as she began to move throughout the house.

Thea's bedroom was the only room upstairs because it was meant to be the attic. Her parents had turned it into her room just a month ago, after she got too old to sleep with them. According to her father, too old was five.

Thea tried to follow her mother's instructions to keep the cloth over her mouth and head down but curiosity got the best of her. It always did. She lifted her head just enough to see what was happening. Her gaze was met with a mixture of reds, oranges, and yellows swallowing the walls and furniture. The couch in the living room was lit up, the green-turned-black fabric being overpowered by the fire's bright, searing dance. Nothing was safe from the flame's touch. That was the only thing she saw before her mother whisked her outside, set her on the sidewalk, and pushed the knotted mess of hair away from her face.

"I'm going to get your father. Stay here," she said, staring at Thea as if she was trying to commit her face to memory. She kissed her on the forehead before setting her shoulders and making her way back into the house.

From the shadows across the street, the cloaked woman watched as the child stared into the house. She watched as the girl's mother sat her down and gave her a kiss; the last one the child was ever supposed to get. The little thing hadn't been waiting long before she would take a hesitant step forward, clenching her fists and then taking a step back once again. The girl had been fearful, but she'd also noticed the spark of curiosity in her large hazel eyes. It reminded her so much of Andre's.

She'd taken millions of lives but she'd never been the cause of any deaths before him and the guilt still remained. She knew Andre, a boy of seven, was supposed to die on March 15, 1928 at 3:02 in the afternoon of a car accident. She'd been there that exact moment, waiting for him; appearing in the shadows as she had so often done before. Her job was to relinquish his soul from his body the moment it happened and guide it to its resting place. He'd seen her appear though, and that spark of curiosity had caused him to halt in the street with his eyes locked onto her and his head tilted just so. His mother didn't notice him stop. Neither did the oncoming driver. The car had sent his little body flying, folding over itself, until most of his weight had been forced onto his neck and it snapped under the pressure. She knew when and how the boy would die but she didn't know it would be her fault.

She knew the same thing about the little girl she was watching now. October 3, 1983; 4:32 a.m. Fire.

She watched as Thea's legs shook; as she willed herself to take another step.

As soon as her foot hit the pavement, she was running through the front door, past the green-turned-black couch that was still burning, and down the small hallway that led to her parents' room. The door was closed. She coughed hard as she stood in front of her parent's door.

The beams from the ceiling above her emitted a loud crack, a warning to move and move now. She looked back the way she had come. She could go back outside, wait like she said she'd do. Instead, she reached her hand toward the door and clasped her fingers around the golden, metal handle. It was hot to the touch but she flung the door open anyway.

The woman watched her as she did so. The parent's room had gotten the worst of the fire; the walls and floor were scorched. The room was in the ropes of destruction but the bed was where the true horror lay; where the parents were sprawled, trapped under a fallen beam, bodies ablaze.

The ceiling above Thea let out another pop, loud enough for her eyes to jump up. The woman saw only Andre in that moment. It had been her fault. Her fault one was dead and her fault one would live. What could it hurt?

As the ceiling above her began to fall, the woman ran to the girl pulling her close to escape the danger.

Thea felt as if she was being ripped in all different directions, as if every cell was separating from one another. Her vision swirled around her and she couldn't seem to catch onto reality quick enough.

She blinked, forcing her world to return to some sort of focus. Outside. She was outside, on the sidewalk, where her mother had set her down what seemed like ages ago. She searched around her. Had it all been a dream? It had felt so real. She backed into something, almost knocking herself over as a hand came to rest on her shoulder. Thea spun around, and the hope that had soared through her body, that maybe it was her mother, was squashed. The person behind her was a woman, but not one she recognized. She jerked away and fell to the ground.

"Easy, child. I will not hurt you," the woman's voice whispered, deep and soothing. She was cloaked in black with strands of blonde hair that fell down into her face as she watched Thea. "You remind me so much of him."

"What did you do to my mommy? You hurt her," Thea accused as she scrambled back to her feet, face red with anger and grief.

"I didn't do anything to her. It was her time," the woman said.

"What about me?" Thea's voice broke. The woman hesitated.

"I couldn't save her but I thought, maybe, I could save you." The woman reached for Thea's shaking body.

"Who are you?" Thea asked, taking a step away. "What are you talking about?"

"I am Death but you, you will live," Death replied, then softer added, "the other three will not like this. Balance should be maintained."

Thea took another step away, fear guiding her. The woman, Death, looked as if she would say something else, but Thea had already heard the sirens. She knew what they meant. Her mother taught her that they were safety, protection, and that the people who came with the sirens were superheroes. They would help her, help her mother, and take the woman away.

So she ran, bare feet slapping against the sidewalk, hands waving in the air as she saw the bright red truck. It went right past her and stopped at the house. The ambulance came to a halt next to her. One of the men picked her up, shushing, and speaking to her. She kept asking for him to get rid of the woman, that she had started the fire, and when he asked her what woman, her head snapped up. Death was no longer there. She had left just as swift and silent as she had come. The man loaded Thea into the truck, putting a mask over her face that helped her breathe through the coughing.

She wasn't sure when or how they had known but her aunt and uncle arrived after what seemed like forever. Her aunt tried to quiet her sobbing. They insisted she ride in the ambulance to the hospital, and her aunt rode with her, holding her hand and thanking every God she could think of that Thea was safe and alive.

· CHAPTER ONE ·

Finn. 150 years later

The world fell apart in a sudden onslaught of flames and anguish. Bombs ruptured the Earth as political tensions reached an all-time high. No longer able to contact other countries and afraid for his life, the President, with agreement from the legislative and judicial powers, relinquished his position to four trusted five-star generals who promised to restore the United States. Each general agreed to take control of one section of the country. The big question on everyone's mind is: will America truly ever be restored?

ANONYMOUS JOURNAL ENTRY; DATED AROUND 2023
SHORTLY AFTER THE WORLD FELL INTO CHAOS

Of all the things he had learned over the years, the one that Finn could never get quite right was controlling his anger. He'd tried everything to keep the outbursts at bay but no matter what he did, the end result was always the same. He rubbed his thumb over the sore knuckles of his left hand, scratched and bleeding because the only thing that helped was hitting something so hard that pain overrode the anger. Usually this was after he stocked away from whatever caused his irritation, away from prying eyes. A tree, a wall, a house—it didn't matter what it was, as long as it got the job done. He could hold the rage back for a few moments; enough time to get to a safe place, alone, where he couldn't see the fear his explosive anger caused. Fear that manifested in widened eyes and a less-than-discreet flinch, which always filled him with so much shame that he felt like he was drowning. The shame was there now, as he slowly walked back home. No one had seen him but there was always a little bit of disgrace that lingered.

He knew his new job would lead to constant anger, but Lydia McDonnell, commander to General Leander and overseer of Essex, had placed him in the position and he couldn't fight her authority.

Finn shoved his hands in his jacket pockets as he passed by a few people, who he assumed were also on their way home. They stared at him, moving as far away on the path as possible. That wasn't because of the anger. It had been like that since Declan left. Nobody knew where his brother was now, but it was whispered that he'd joined the rebellion.

Finn ran a hand through his chestnut hair as he came up to his house in the median district. He'd let it get shaggy since Declan left, much to the protest of his mother. She'd wanted it to look clean cut, but he didn't see the point now that he was no longer a counselor's apprentice. He took the front steps two at a time, stopping before the door as he tried to swallow down the shame that still churned inside him. The sun was just beginning to set. He was later than usual.

Finn pushed the door open and was met with a familiar sight. A group of kids his grandma watched sat huddled on the floor by her feet, listening to her tell a story, like he and his brothers used to do. Finn leaned against the door frame. At eighteen, her stories had lost most of their magic for him but he could still see it alight in the eyes of the children.

"You see, a long, long time ago, things were different. People who got very sick could sometimes be cured and when someone had a serious wound, a death blow, they never got back up again. No spirits lingered."

"But what happened?" a boy, Joey, asked, hands curled into fists against his knees in anticipation.

"Well the story goes that there was a woman who suffered a great loss, one so great that she couldn't bear it. She tricked herself into thinking she could stop the loss from happening but by doing so she unleashed the demons and angels that controlled the balance of the world." Little gasps rang out through the room. Finn tried not to smile.

"The angels were sealed away, and she allowed the demons to use her body as a host. She was lost to the madness of those demons." Lillian was one of the elders of the community who had offered to spend some of her time watching the children whose parents were working. Many of the older generation did this when they could no longer work, before they were taken to isolation and phased out of town.

"Why would she do that if things were going to end up like this?" Joey piped up again. He was seven and always the most enthralled with Lillian's tales.

"She didn't know things would turn out this way." Lillian leaned back against her favorite chair, a large brown one that swallowed anyone who sat in it. Her long white hair hung past her waist and swayed whenever she moved. She had deep brown eyes that would widen during the climax of one of her stories, as if she was living in the tale herself. Whenever she laughed, her round belly would jiggle with mirth. It was hard not to get caught up with her.

Finn glanced outside. The sun was nearly gone, casting a dark orangish glow across the sky. He pushed away from the doorway

"Grandma, it's time for everyone to go home," Finn said as soon as she'd paused, for dramatic effect, as she would say.

"Oh, is it really? Okay, okay. There will be even more stories next time. Maybe about her oldest son." Lillian clapped her hands as a chorus of groans resounded throughout the room.

"None of that. Go with Finn and Liam. They'll make sure you get home safely."

The room was thrown into chaos as little hands and feet scrambled to pick up their toys.

Lillian hobbled her way over to the staircase in the front room with the help of her cane. It was just a long stick that Liam had found and carved for her, which was sturdy enough to hold her weight. Still, she refused to use any of the others she had, which had all been made by one of the town's woodworkers. She called for Liam from the bottom of the steps. Finn lined the kids up at the door as they waited for his brother. His serious, seafoam eyes roamed a final time around the house, making sure no child was forgotten.

"Hey Finn, what happened to your hands?" A little girl asked, tugging on one of her pigtails before tucking the end of it into her mouth. His hands balled into fists at the mention of it. He reminded himself to relax and sent her a strained smile. Bending down to her height, he gently pulled the hair from her mouth.

"It's nothing to worry about. Just an accident at work." He tapped her on the nose as she giggled.

"Is everyone ready?" Liam called in excitement as he jogged down the steps, almost tripping but catching his balance. His clothes were still covered in wood shavings. He opened the front door and the wind picked up some of his sandy blond hair. With his deep, walnut brown eyes, he was the one who looked the most like their grandma. Everyone followed him. Finn walked a couple steps behind them, making sure there were no stragglers. They followed the road away from the center of town and toward the intersection that led them to the beggar's district which was hidden from sight by the forest.

"Hey Finn?" The little girl with pigtails had slowed down to walk with him.

"What is it Delilah?" He put a hand to her back, to keep her from slowing down even more.

"When do you think my mommy's coming home?" she asked, wringing her dress between her fingers. Finn squeezed her shoulder. Everyone in town was talking about how she'd been deemed an untouchable. Delilah still didn't know. Untouchables, they were the people who were either fatally wounded or who had a sickness that should have killed them. They were all but dead, living on borrowed time. Anyone who was deemed an untouchable was taken to isolation, away from everyone in town. Being an untouchable drove people to madness because of how painful it was. You could feel your body rotting. People who went to isolation were phased out of town. Nobody knew what happened after that.

"I don't know, I'm sorry," was all he could say. How could he tell a little girl that she'd never get to see her mother again? It was her father's job to explain that the government took away people who were severely sick, dying, or even too old to keep going. Isolation was on the outskirts of town, past the beggars district. There was a special exit there for those who were pushed outside the walls, forever deemed an untouchable.

Finn could understand the turmoil Delilah must have felt. The same thing had happened to their family when Finn's grandfather got sick. He couldn't remember much; he'd been four at the time. What he could piece together was the guards slamming open the door during dinner time. His father had shoved him under the table and Declan had followed, holding onto him and the screeching three year-old Liam. Their grandma had begged and pleaded with the officers to leave their grandfather, even as they heaved him up from the seat with his dinner spilling across the floor. It was the only time Finn had seen her cry. Liam didn't remember any of it but he'd always been afraid of the officers since then. Declan, being nine, had been the most affected by those events. Despite that, his parents still pushed him to become an apprentice strategist, one of the most honored positions you could land. He'd succeeded but he was never happy about it.

"The way they do things isn't right. Someone has to stop them from walking all over us," he'd always say. No one in his family took a serious interest in his words, not until he'd snuck out of Essex, one of the only towns still standing in Vermont. Rumors had spread faster than Finn could have predicted—that his brother had joined the rebellion, a group hell bent on taking down the government.

"But you think she might come back?" Delilah forced him to stop thinking about his brother.

"You never know, I guess." He did know, however. If you went to isolation, you would never come back. No one ever had.

"Hey you two, keep up. Deli's house is the next stop," Liam said. Delilah, as most of the other kids that needed to be watched over, lived in the Beggar's District. Most people there worked twelve hours a day. Once you ended up in that kind of poverty, it was almost impossible to get out. Employers paid you less, and most people considered them second-rate citizens. The government just looked the other way. The only exceptions were children who were smart enough to land a better job. Of course, if that happened, they'd be making enough to help their family but most were too ashamed to do so. They would take residence in a house closer to the capitol building, pretending their family didn't exist.

"Can I show you something?" Deli asked, wringing her hands. Finn nodded. Deli reached into the pocket of her dress and pulled out something wrapped in a dirty, white cloth. She opened it with careful fingers. Inside was a knife. The handle of it was black and the blade was dull, still, Finn snatched it from her. She made a whine of protest, reaching for it again.

"Deli, this is dangerous. You could get hurt," Finn said, repeating the things his mother had told him whenever he did something like that as a child. A pout began to form on her lips and he sighed. "Sorry. I didn't mean for it to come out that way. I was just worried. Why do you have this?" he asked her, tone softer this time.

"I found it. I know it's bad but I thought it would be good to have if the officers came back." She pulled her hair into her mouth again.

"Deli—" Finn ran a hand over his face, trying to sound disappointed in the same way his mother did when she tried to force him to realize he made the wrong choice. "These aren't toys. You could really hurt yourself or someone else."

"I just wanted to help," she said.

"I know but this isn't the way." He pocketed the knife. "I'm going to keep this but I won't tell your dad as long as you promise not to pick up dangerous stuff anymore. Deal?"

She gave a small nod, eyes downcast. She hadn't let any tears fall but her face was red and splotchy. He reached for her hand and squeezed it, waiting for her eyes to meet his before smiling in encouragement.

"Come on, let's get you home." They walked fast to catch up with the rest of the group.

Delilah's father was waiting for her on the porch of his crumbling, wood cabin. It was small and cracked. Finn remembered Deli saying that there was only one bedroom, despite her parents, her, and her dad's parents all living together. It was a lot of people for such a tiny place.

"Deli." Her father bounded toward them with his arms open. He and his daughter both had fiery red hair and a spatter of freckles across their cheeks. She gave Finn a quick hug before she was scooped up. She chattered on about her day but Finn could see the relief behind her dad's exhausted eyes.

Most of the other parents had come out to collect their children. Houses were small with almost no room between them in this part of town. Like Deli's family, everyone had multiple people crammed into one building. With each person's meager wages, it was all they could afford.

"Thank you boys for walking them back." Deli's father clapped Liam on the back.

"It's really not a problem, right Finn?" Liam's eyes were screaming for help. He was terrified of getting sick and knowing that Deli's mother had been taken for that very reason made him a bit jumpy. He chewed on his lip.

"It's really not," Finn replied, sticking out his hand to shake

Deli's dad's, relieving Liam who took a few steps away, toward their home.

"All of us prefer you walking them over the officers. They can't be trusted. What they do to our families just isn't right. My poor wife wasn't even that sick." His voice trembled with anger. "We think what your brother did was incredibly brave."

Finn bristled. Sure, his brother was fighting for what he believed in, and, yes, that was honorable. However, nobody cared how that had affected Finn's family. His father was almost fired. He was one of the overseers of the farm district, which was on the opposite side of town, near the normal entrance. There was enough undamaged land there to work the fields.

Finn and Liam lost all of their friends because everyone was too scared to be seen with them. Finn's girlfriend, ex-girlfriend, started to just ignore him. They were being watched by officers all the time, no matter where they went. Any hope for Finn landing a good job had all but disappeared. He'd been stripped of his internship as a counselor and forced to find something that wasn't linked to the government. He'd always wanted to become a counselor like his mother. Her job was to help place kids on the path to their future jobs based on their natural abilities and learned skills. That way everyone was participating and pulling their weight in the community. He wasn't good with his hands the way Liam was so becoming a carpenter or blacksmith wouldn't do. Instead he'd been pushed into becoming a gatekeeper and deciding who would and would not enter into Essex.

"Thank you, we appreciate it. We need to head back, though, don't want to miss curfew," Liam interjected as he began walking away. Curfew was another thing imposed after Declan's escape. They waved as they were leaving.

"I'm going to get sick. I think I can already feel a sore throat," Liam started as soon as they were out of earshot, clearing his throat.

"You're not going to get sick. No one else in their family was." Finn watched in amusement as Liam rubbed his neck.

"You don't know that." There was almost no stopping him when he got to this stage of panic.

"If you get sick, it's going to be your own fault." Liam sent him an accusatory glare.

"Nobody asked you anyway," he muttered. Liam never got into heated arguments with Finn and it wasn't just because of Finn's lack of control. He was maybe an inch or two smaller than his brother. He was lanky and skinny with next to no muscles or coordination. Finn's shoulders were broad and he ran two miles every day. He would lose if they fought and he knew it.

"Oh, so you weren't just complaining to me then?"

"No, I was talking to myself, and it's rude to interrupt someone's conversation," Liam said. Finn was going to make another comment as he pushed through the thicket of trees to get back to the main path until he noticed some of the officers leaning against the modest, wooden fence that separated the Beggar's and Median Districts. It wasn't them slacking on their duties that caught his attention. That was an everyday occurrence. It was the fact that they had mentioned the Douglass's. Finn's family weren't the only ones with that last name in town. Although it was a common last name, the officers were almost always referring to them nowadays.

· CHAPTER TWO ·

Finn

"What is it? Why did you stop?" Liam glanced at Finn but before he had the chance to say anything else, Finn grabbed him and pulled him behind one of the large trees. The tree was leaning slightly to the left, a crack running down its trunk.

"Be quiet and listen." Finn leaned over. Liam propped himself against the trunk, crossing his arms, an annoyed expression on his face. He didn't want to listen. He wanted to go home and finish looking over the plans for the new wing that was to be added to the infirmary.

"We're going to miss curfew, and that's the last thing we need," Liam started, but Finn shushed him.

"You know those boys are trouble. They could be feeding their brother information from the inside. I swear as soon as we catch them at it—" the guard let his sentence trail off but his hand circled the sword he kept at his waistline.

"What about the father? He works for the capitol building," the other man suggested.

"Winston? We're thinking of the same man right? He's a coward. There's no way he'd try something."

"Are they talking about us?" Liam's voice reached a new octave as he pushed against Finn's side to get a better look at the men. "They know we're not doing anything right?"

"Liam, can you be quiet for two minutes? I'm trying to listen." Liam bit his lip to keep himself from saying anything more.

"I bet it's that old crone. She fills all the kids' heads with nonsense. She no doubt leaks secrets all the time and no one suspects her." The officer pushed off from the fence. "I think it's about time she was sent to isolation. The bitch is a waste of space."

Finn clenched his hands, shaking. Rage pulsed through his body. They had no right to speak about his grandmother, not when she gave back to the community. She spent her days helping those who lived in the beggar's district. She'd give the families old clothes or extra food, things they would need to survive. And his father. To call his father a coward was unthinkable. His father believed in everything the government stood for. Anytime he was questioned about the rumored methods of Leander's interrogations, he always said they weren't true and even if they were, there must be a reason. The rumors were gruesome. He siphoned information out of people by torturing them. His father was the perfect champion to a broken system. He couldn't take listening to how the officers were speaking anymore. Gritting his teeth, he stood to his full height. He couldn't let them talk about his family like that.

Liam jerked him back behind the tree. Finn shoved his brother away from him, trying to get his anger under control so he wouldn't take it out on him. Liam stumbled back a few steps, almost tripping over his own feet, before catching his balance again. Although fear was etched onto his features, he still tried to stop Finn.

"Calm down. We need to get home soon or we'll be late," Liam said, voice low.

"I don't care. They shouldn't be saying those things about us." Finn clenched his hands, the scars a burning reminder of the last time his anger got the best of him.

"Do you think getting yourself in trouble is going to make things easier on us? If you try and attack them, they really will think we're helping Declan. Is that what you want? Mom would be devastated. Our whole family could be taken and locked up because you can't control yourself." Liam was weary, afraid of pushing Finn too far and making him more angry.

Finn started counting down from ten, forcing himself to relax. He didn't want to be the reason his family got in anymore trouble. Liam waited as Finn tried to recollect his composure.

"We still need to figure out how to get past them." Liam glanced over at the path that led to their district. Finn nodded, bringing one of his scarred hands to his lips, and drumming his fingers there as he thought. Allowing Finn to take a moment to regain his composure meant that they were late for curfew, as the sun was almost completely set.

"Get behind that tree and be prepared to run." Liam let out an annoyed groan but didn't protest as Finn pointed toward the last tree on the street. He made his way, careful about where he was stepping so the officers didn't see him. His heart hammered in his chest.

Finn grabbed a couple rocks, big enough that they carried some weight. He tossed one after the other into the woods, where the brush was thickest. A loud crack echoed through the area.

"What the hell? Come on, let's go check it out." As Finn had hoped, the guards moved from their post at the fence, rushing toward the forest. He went around the other side of the trunk as they passed by him, catching up with his brother and motioning for him to follow. They moved away from their cover and over to the fence. Finn pushed Liam to climb it, instead of going down the main road, knowing they would probably run into more officers.

"If anyone's there come out now," a gruff voice called as they struggled over the fence. Finn had to give Liam a boost. Liam landed on his knees while Finn stumbled but managed to stay on his feet.

Finn dragged Liam up and sprinted toward their house. They ran through people's backyards, the houses getting bigger and nicer the closer to the center of town they got. There was nothing separating one property from the other. The only fences in town were there to split up the districts. General Leander wanted to keep everyone accountable by taking away some privacy, to make sure there were no rebellion spies in town.

Finn thought they were going to make it. He could see his house. The wooden cabin at the end of the street wasn't quite as big as the other houses in the area. He heard a loud snap behind him. Liam had stepped onto a wooden board, breaking it in two. A guard was always posted somewhere near their home and there was no way he wouldn't have heard that. Finn grabbed Liam as heavy footsteps came their way. He pulled his brother in between two houses, ducking down to get past the windows and pausing at the end of the house to make sure the guard wasn't in front of their cabin. He pulled Liam with him as he dashed toward the door, jumping over the first squeaky step and shoving his brother inside.

Finn slammed the door and leaned against it. Blood pounded in his ears. Liam was on the floor, on his hands and knees, breathing hard. Somehow they had made it, by the thinnest strand of luck.

"What on earth do you two think you're doing? It's past time for you to be home. I thought you had gotten into some kind of trouble." Their mother stood in the doorway to the kitchen, her long, toffee hair in a braid over her shoulder. She was wearing an oversized, white shirt, tucked into brown pants.

"We didn't mean to scare you mom but—" Finn said, pushing away from the door.

"Didn't mean to scare me? Of all the times to be late, you've chosen now? When General Leander is coming to town? Security is twice as strict." General Chase Leander was one of the four powers that now controlled the country. He spent most of his time in Vermont. Out of the four generals, he was by far the biggest, nearing seven foot at least. He was the one who gave Lydia McDonnell the title of Commander. She was a woman built like a house, broad and harsh. Her hair was the same color as the dirt on the ground and cut just below her chin. She would do anything General Leander asked of her. The general, with his buzzcut and charcoal eyes, was often considered handsome in a dangerous kind of way. He had a chiseled jaw and a long scar that started from his eyebrow and neared his ear.

"Liam off the floor. I want you to look at me while I yell at you." Finn's mother, Arlette was typically a quiet person, until she became worried.

"Mom, please, you've got to listen to us." Finn offered a hand to Liam, helping him up.

"We're sorry, we didn't mean to make you worry." Liam coughed, still trying to catch his breath. Finn's grandmother sidled close to Arlette, patting her on the shoulder.

"Now, now, Ari, let's hear them out. Come, everyone to the living room." Lillian ushered them forward, hobbling over to her chair and dropping her weight into it. "Tell us what happened."

"We're doomed," Liam said, pacing behind the couch.

"What is going on with you, calm down." Arlette grabbed Liam's hand and pulled him into her, rubbing his back. She was a thin, small woman but her hugs were warm, all-encompassing.

"The officers are going to find a way to get grandma phased out." Liam started to bite his fingernails.

"How do you know this?" Arlette asked.

"We overheard them. They're spreading rumors that grandma is giving information to the rebellion." Finn sat down on the couch, bouncing his leg. His grandma didn't seem too worried.

"They've been saying that for years. There's no proof." She shrugged.

"Declan left. What other proof do they need?" Finn crossed his arms, digging his fingernails into his skin, trying to tamper down the anger that came with thinking of his brother.

"They need more than that." Arlette dropped her arms from around Liam. "I'm going to finish dinner. We're done talking about this."

She had still looked worried. Everything had felt wrong since Declan had left like things were still simmering below the surface. Now it felt like everything was just about to reach a boiling point.

· CHAPTER THREE ·

Finn

*We must retract our soldiers and cut ourselves off from
the rest of the world. We must stop anyone from entering
the country from this point forward. It's being reported
that soldiers who have been shot down, littered with
bullets, are standing up again. There is leaked footage
of this circling around online. Many are taking refuge
in churches, praying to God that they will be saved from
this horrible fate.*

NEWSPAPER ARTICLE DATED OCTOBER 28, 2026

Winston Douglas maintained a brisk walk from the
farm district and up to the door of his two-story
cabin. The home wasn't nearly the biggest one
in the median district, with three bedrooms upstairs and a
small storage space downstairs that had been converted into
his mother-in-law's room. Many who worked within the Capitol building had houses in their district. They were the nicest
houses in Essex and smaller only to the ones in the farmer's
district, as it took many people to tend the crops.

Winston heaved a sigh as he entered his house. Despite his

large physique, he didn't have a very commanding presence. He often kept his movements small and precise. Everything in his life was nice and tidy, from the way he managed other people to the way he did his hair. Like Finn, he had dark, chestnut brown locks that were parted more to the left side and cut in such a way to hide his slightly too prominent forehead. It was styled the same way every morning.

He could smell dinner cooking and hear Finn talking to Lillian, trying to get her to tell him one of her stories. Liam, he assumed, was either in his room drawing up new plans or working with the planks he brought home to build a shed in the backyard. His youngest was turning into quite the carpenter.

Winston passed the living room, where Finn sat, chewing his bottom lip and staring at Lillian.

"Finn, go tell Liam it's time for supper," Arlette said from the kitchen as Winston leaned down to kiss her cheek. He was tense, nervous about the conversation he needed to have with his family. Arlette lived in fear about losing the people she loved like she'd lost her father. More and more it looked like that possibility was becoming a reality.

Finn sent his grandma an exasperated look as he left the living room and bounded up the stairs. The narrow hallway had a door on the left, one on the right, and one at the end of the hall. Liam's room was on the left. Finn knocked twice before pushing the door open, a hard feat considering the piles of abandoned things spread across the floor.

"You should really clean this up, Lee." Finn squeezed through the door, glancing around the almost uninhabitable room. Papers and books were piled against the west wall, stacked in no particular order. Liam's "notes," as he liked to call them. Really they were unfinished plans for projects he had given up on and never completed.

"Don't step on that." Liam flung himself away from his desk, grabbing a paper from under Finn's foot.

"What's so special about it?" Finn eyed it. Everything was scratched out anyways, it wasn't anything important.

"It's a part of my process. I need to remember what doesn't work." Liam stood up.

"So, nothing?" Finn asked. Liam scoffed. "Mom says dinner is ready. Come eat." Finn, despite thinking Liam's things were trash, was careful of where he stepped on his way out.

The Douglass family sat around the table with food spread out so everyone could help themselves. Finn's father seemed on edge, more so than usual, and he couldn't quite pinpoint why. Every so often his father would put a hand on his mother's back and place a quick kiss on her temple. It was something he always did when she was stressed or worried, when she felt like things were falling apart. Guilt showed itself in Finn's tapping fingers and shaking leg. Had he caused all this by what he overheard?

Liam tried to ease the atmosphere by speaking about his recent project. He spoke fast, leaving barely enough time to breathe between some words and stuttering over others. He pushed at the food on his plate, rolling carrots from one side to the other without really eating. Winston rubbed a hand down his face, noting that he would need to shave soon. Arlette had told him what the boys had heard earlier. The news didn't bode well for their family.

"Dad is everything okay?" Finn asked, cutting Liam off mid-sentence.

"Your mother told me about what happened this evening," Winston said, "I have something of my own I need to say."

"Winston, now?" Arlette placed a hand on his arm, scrutinizing him.

"They need to be ready, just in case. They're grown men. They can handle it." He patted her hand. "I happened to stop by the Capitol building earlier than normal today to submit my report. Two senior strategists were there, discussing how they were going to handle the next raid and planning the official story."

"What does that have to do with us?" Liam asked after his father had paused for a minute. Anxiety settled heavily in Finn's stomach.

"The raid's on us, isn't it?" Finn asked, meeting his father's apologetic eyes.

"No, that's not right. We haven't done anything and none of us are sick." Liam stood from his chair.

"It has to be for us." Finn glanced at his dad, watching the nod of confirmation.

"It could all just be a misunderstanding. Your father's going to speak to McDonnell about it tomorrow." Arlette squeezed her husband's arm. "Liam you're making me feel restless. Sit down."

"Nonsense. They don't want people figuring out the truth, that the generals are the ones who caused the world to become like this." Lillian waved an ear of corn at her daughter.

"Mom, please."

"You know the truth. I never lied to you about it and you shouldn't lie to your boys," Lillian responded.

"That's enough. The government is doing what has to be done. Population control and isolation are necessary to the way we live." Winston slammed a hand on the table.

"Mom, don't. Winston is going to talk to them tomorrow and everything will get sorted out." Arlette looked at Lillian with pleading eyes. The fights between her mother and husband always took a lot out of her.

"If they only do what's necessary then why are they planning an attack on us?" Lillian ignored her daughter's plea. Focusing, instead, on the blindness of her son-in-law.

"Because you filled Declan's head with appalling dreams. He's gone because of you. We're being watched because of you, and you don't have the decency to care." Winston's face was blistering red.

"Boys take your dinner to your rooms, please." Arlette looked as if she would cry at any given moment.

Liam grabbed Finn's arm, already seeing his temper flare. Finn swallowed his words and followed his brother. He punched the wall outside of Liam's cluttered room. Declan had made his own choices. His father had no right to put the entire blame on their grandma. More than that though, he wasn't sure how much more his mother could take. She'd always been the peacekeeper, the one who mended problems whenever anyone got into a fight. Since Declan had left, tension between his father and grandmother had reached new levels. Both of them were unwilling to listen to anything his mother had to say. There were days he'd hear her crying to herself, trying to remain quiet. Things were harder on the days she worked late. On those days, Finn's father would take care of dinner but something always went wrong by the time Arlette came home and she was forced to do it.

Finn and Liam ate in silence, half listening to the argument downstairs. Words spewed out that had already been said, things that should have already been forgiven. They had instead been turned into even deadlier ammunition, intended to wound.

Only when Finn heard his parents walk to their room and shut the door did he move from his catatonic state on Liam's bed.

"Come on." Finn grabbed Liam's arm.

"Wait it's going to fall." Liam tried to save the pile of notes that he had accidently hit with his elbow. They spilled onto the floor. "Now I'm going to have to clean."

"Be quiet." Finn ignored him for a moment and then, "Your room's a mess anyway, why does it matter if they fall or not?"

"It's an organized mess and those papers don't belong there." Finn dragged Liam down the stairs. "What are we doing?"

Finn didn't answer, just continued until he was in front of his grandmother's door. The door swung open before he could even knock. Lillian stood to the side as the boys came into the small room. Finn sent her a questioning look.

"You're not as silent as you think you are," was all she said. His grandmother's room was bare. It had a twin sized bed, an end table, and a dresser that was missing two drawers. It still felt cramped with only those three things. She sat down on the bed.

"Finn, can you get into that little crawl space and hand me

out what's inside?" She motioned toward the end of the bed. There wasn't a lot of room for him to shimmy down but he managed. He dropped to his knees and pried the small door open with the tips of his fingers. Inside was a small wooden box. Carved on the lid was the shape of an eagle standing with its wings spread out. It's head was turned to the side, so the profile was visible. He stared at it as he handed it over to Lillian's waiting hands.

"What is it?" Finn asked. Liam had settled himself on the floor as Finn sat down next to Lillian.

"It was your grandfather's. This is the rebellion's symbol." She traced it with her finger before opening the box. Inside was a small pendant carved into the shape of the same eagle and a notebook.

"What do you mean it's the rebellion's symbol?" Finn grabbed the necklace.

"Your grandfather was an infiltrator for the rebellion for years. When we decided to settle down, the leader of our camp asked us to stay within the city walls to pass on any information we may learn." She grabbed the notebook that was inside. "He wrote down everything he learned in this."

"Grandpa wasn't part of the rebellion." Liam shook his head in disbelief.

"Your father said the same thing. That man is so blind," Lillian muttered. "He was raised here though, so I'm not surprised. Even after they phased out his own parents, he still believed Leander was doing the right things. Both your grandfather and I had these tokens. Declan took one when he left."

"You really did convince him to leave." Finn couldn't believe what he was hearing. He never actually thought his grandma was working for the rebellion. He just assumed she hated the government because of the way they took his grandfather. His father had been right.

"I didn't. He'd already made up his mind before coming to me. At the time, he didn't know that I'd ever been a part of the rebellion, but he suspected, I think."

"Declan wouldn't choose to leave without a reason," Finn said.

"He did have a reason, and if he had never become privy to Leander's plans, he would have stayed here." Declan had been working with Lydia McDonnell for years. Becoming a strategist was one of the hardest and longest apprenticeships to complete. Finn's parents had been ecstatic when he was one of three chosen for the job. Finn had been jealous that Declan could get it and he couldn't. His anger made him too impulsive. Finn wasn't stupid by any means and always lasted the longest in the family against Declan when they were playing in-depth games, but Declan was always one step ahead of him. Finn was still smart enough to get a government job before Declan's betrayal. Even if it wasn't as high up as his brother's.

"Why didn't you ever tell us?" Finn asked. He felt betrayed but curious too.

"Your mother didn't want to hear anything more about it after she married your father. I've never hidden anything from her, but she didn't want you to know. What could I do?" Lillian asked. "I'm only telling you this now because if something happens, you need to be prepared."

"Prepared for what?" Liam asked.

"Prepared to fight."

· CHAPTER FOUR ·

Thea

Sweat accumulated on Thea's brows and above her lip as she bent over her latest find. It left a salty taste in her mouth every time her tongue swiped across the chapped surface. She'd been working nonstop for a couple of months excavating a cave with her team, hoping to find the artifact she'd spent years looking for. She was so caught up in her whirlwind of thoughts that she didn't notice her husband coming up behind her until his hands were placed on her shoulders. She let out a gasp as she straightened.

"Don't scare me like that," Thea said, spinning around to face her husband who wore a mischievous smile. He took every opportunity to frighten her. Aiden, doing everything in his power to get under her skin, had a way of keeping things light-hearted, which a desperate part of her craved—not that she would ever admit that to him.

"Sorry, but how could you expect me to hold myself back?" he replied, holding his hands up in surrender. She tried to keep a haughty look but he was unfazed. "What do we have here?" He asked as he bent down next to her, drumming his fingers on his knees. His slightly shaggy, blond hair fell into his eyes. Thea always tried to tell him it would look more professional if it was slicked back or cut but it did capture the carefree, boyish attitude he still had.

She picked up the tablet she had been looking at. They had been in Palestine for almost two months now. Thea was sure they had gotten a false lead. There was very little information on the four horsemen after all, except for a small paragraph in the bible. She'd been researching for years to prove that they weren't some silly story. It was something she had focused on in her career—maybe to a point of obsession, as told to her by many friends and family.

The four horsemen had represented the end of the world. They were destruction and fear. At least, that's how they were written to be. It wasn't something she believed. She was still looking for solid proof that they represented something more.

Aiden always asked why it was so important to her. Why was she so concentrated on the four horsemen when it was such a small, almost insignificant story? She had told him about her past, about the fire and therapists but never about the woman who claimed to be Death; the woman who changed Thea's entire life. The memory had stuck with her since she was a child; vibrant and unmarred from the destruction of time and age.

"We'll have to call Clark. He should be able to translate this. I just wish we could go over it now. It looks important," Thea said, slow to speak as she tried to wipe off some of the dirt. Clark was a translator and close friend of the family. He and Aiden had grown up together. He was short and stout but had a smile that could warm the coldest hearts. He and his wife were their oldest son William's godparents.

"Ah, a mysterious tablet, just what we needed," Aiden said, taking it out of her hands and squinting his eyes, as if that would allow him to magically understand the foreign scribbles. "It's right up Clark's alley."

"It's important. I can feel it." Thea snatched it back as he continued to grin at her. She turned on her heel to keep the scowl on her face from slipping into a small smile.

"Alright, then how about we go to dinner tonight to celebrate? I mean, we're leaving in a week. It'll be one last freedom before we return to the kids." Aiden pulled her back by the arm.

"You know you miss them," Thea replied. The kids had visited for a couple of weeks about a month before but their time had felt rushed. Thea and Aiden always did digs during the summer, and they taught classes during the fall semesters. They called and video chatted with their family as much as possible when they were away. Doing digs in the summer was a compromise. They could have a career and family. So far it had worked.

"I do," Aiden replied with a great sigh. "I really do. Even when they're fighting."

"Let's go to dinner tonight, have some wine, get a little drunk, and wake up tomorrow with a hangover," Thea said, straightening out Aiden's shirt and pulling him closer.

"Hungover on the job? Am I hearing correctly? How many times have I heard you nag me whenever I want to have one little drink? 'We're working, you can't be drinking that.'" Aiden's voice shot up in pitch while he was mocking her. She scoffed. "The apocalypse must be happening."

"How old are you?" Was the only dignified response she could come up with and then, "That's not how I sound." The high pitched, almost baby voice he produced was nowhere near her actual voice, she assured herself.

"Don't be sour. How long have we been together? Too many years, it seems, because I've honed my impression of you to perfection, my dear." Aiden threw a hand over her shoulder and began to lead her out of the cave, rubbing the side of her arm with his thumb.

"You should keep your day job," Thea answered, eyeing one of the workers on their way out. It was an older man who was loading supplies into one of their trucks. He was struggling to lift up one of the boxes. Aiden followed her gaze and left her side to help him.

Despite being forty-five, Aiden had kept in shape. They both had because their job could be very physically demanding. He had a lean frame, more of a runner's body, but he was strong. To his dismay, he had slowly developed wrinkles. Crow's feet ghosted the sides of his eyes and he had laugh lines around his cheeks. Sometimes, she could see him poking at the skin, a slight frown clouding his features. She didn't think he believed her when she said she loved them. They proved that he had had a good life, one filled with laughter and joy. She was a part of that life and had the same type of wrinkles, as well as one beginning to show in a line on her forehead. According to her husband, it was from every time she frowned at him. She couldn't find a reason to care though. She was happy, had always been happy with him, even through the rocky moments. They had somehow found a balance, and once they got into their rhythm, they were unstoppable.

She watched as Aiden shook hands with the older man, warmth radiating from him. Thea was proud to say she married a kind man. She'd realized that about him the first time they met. Aiden might be a bit childish but no matter how irritating he got, no matter how many fights they had, she was proud to say they chose each other. They always would. They worked just as hard on their marriage as they had their careers. Aiden, being a child of divorce, always respected the importance of their union—sometimes more so than she did.

"What's with that look?" Aiden asked and Thea realized she had been smiling. She shook her head at him, not wanting to explain the thoughts as they began walking back to the car. "I don't think I'll ever fully know you." It was said in an offhanded way but she still felt the small twinge of hurt.

"What?" His words weren't harsh, and they weren't meant to be taken as an insult, but they did sting, just a little bit.

"It's not a bad thing. That's not what I meant," he said realizing how he must have sounded. "It's one of the reasons I love you. You have so much going on in that mind of yours that

I'll never understand. That's what I was trying to say." Aiden tried to cut off any insecure thought he might have caused her. His wife over thought, over analyzed everything. It was one of the reasons she was so good at her job but also why she was so bad at handling people. She could never just let loose. That was his strong suit.

Thea didn't answer him. Her brows were furrowed, and she was biting her nails, a bad habit he'd tried to get her to stop a million times. He'd made her wear nail polish to see if that would help. She'd glared at him the entire day because she'd felt so silly wearing bright red polish on her nails during a dig. It had been taken off that night, and he'd grabbed some caramel chocolate on the way home to earn her forgiveness. He'd given up that fight to save her sanity.

"Hey, come back to me." His voice grew softer as he started the car. It was what he always said to break her of her inner turmoil. When she looked at him again he said, "See, you go off in that little world of yours but you voice a quarter of the thoughts that roll around up there. You can find ten conclusions to an outcome where most people only see one."

Thea laughed and tapped her temple twice when Aiden looked over at her. It was something her mother used to do. A gesture that meant this was something she wanted to remember, like a snapshot. She wasn't sure if she would actually remember any of the moments she'd chosen when she was older but it was a comfort. She glanced out the window as the world passed them by. She was ready to go home, but she would also miss all the history and culture.

"From the entire dig, that's what you want to remember?" Aiden asked. He was teasing her again.

"You don't get to choose my memories," Thea responded in turn, a little reminder that even though they were a unit, she was still her own person.

"You pick the strangest things sometimes." He took her hand. He had developed her habit as well, but his moments were the big ones, the celebrations.

They sat in silence the rest of the way to the hotel. Thea had a hard time concentrating on anything other than her thoughts while in a car. It was something Aiden had a hard time accepting at the beginning of their relationship. He wasn't used to being alone with his thoughts for long periods of time, but she'd taught him how to be comfortable with his own company. She hummed along to the music, staring out of the window but not seeing the scenery in front of her. All she could think about was the tablet. It was important. She just knew it was. It was like a puzzle piece had slipped into the right spot.

She was so lost in her thoughts that she barely noticed when the car stopped. Aiden tugged at some of her unruly hair, getting her attention. He was the only one she allowed to touch her hair. She stepped out of the car and stretched, feeling the pull of her muscles, knowing the aches were a sign she was getting older. Aiden held the door open for her as they discussed the dig, their actions and gestures mirroring each other's excitement.

When they got to their room they busied themselves with getting cleaned up. Gathering clean clothes and showering together. They learned early on that having four kids didn't always leave them with time to just be together. The shower was their time for that and even when they were away from home, they didn't break the routine.

"I get bathroom," Thea said as she dried herself off. If they attempted to get ready in the same room, it would take twice as long, thanks to Aiden.

"You always get the bathroom," Aiden replied, his argument half-hearted.

"That's because I'm the one who wears make-up. If you decide you want to be the one to put on all this junk then you can use it." Thea straightened up, wrapping her hair in the towel.

"No, thank you. I doubt I could figure out where to put half of that stuff," he said as he walked out but not before a last glance at her as she began dressing. She knew he was watching her, or at least her backside, so she turned around and sauntered closer to him. She shut the door in his face, laughing at the offended sound he made.

"We're married, you don't have to play hard to get anymore," he called out as she shimmied into an ankle length brown skirt and billowy shirt. She kept all of her clothes as modest as possible to follow the customs of the area. She began putting on her make-up, not a lot, she didn't have the skill to do it like some women she'd seen, but just enough to highlight her features. It helped mask some of her age.

When she was satisfied she walked out. Aiden was dressed in a nice shirt, a white button down with the top button undone, and a pair of dark jeans. He was sitting on the bed looking down at his phone. That was as nice as she could get him to dress. He often complained that jackets were too restricting.

"Ready?" She asked as she put on her white sandals. He stood up and pulled her into his arms.

"How am I supposed to walk around with someone as beautiful as you?" He kissed the top of her head before moving to her lips, as she rolled her eyes.

"Easy, you put one foot in front of the other. Now let's go." She pulled him toward the door. They walked to the little restaurant that was on the corner. They had found it early on, and it was one of their favorite places to go.

The door to it was open as the breeze cooled off the inside of the building. Thea nudged Aiden in the ribs, nodding down at the ugly ceramic toad that propped the door open. He bugged his eyes out at her, trying to force the same shocked yet disturbing look the offending amphibian had. They were seated in the front of the restaurant, near the door, which was nice because the wind cooled them off in the sweltering heat.

The waiter came over while they were in a deep conversation, discussing what they were going to do when they got home—maybe take the kids to an amusement park and have a real family day before school started. They ordered a bottle of wine and some appetizers, planning on spending a couple of hours just with each other.

The night was going well. Thea already had a nice buzz going and time was slipping by. For those few hours, she had felt like nothing could ruin her night. How wrong she could be.

Neither she nor Aiden had noticed the man, twitchy and unsure, come into the restaurant. He was invisible to them and everyone else who seemed to pass by him without any concern. After a few moments, he pulled out a gun, firing it toward the roof to garner attention.

He yelled out instructions. Customers and servers dropped to the floor.

Thea watched as the man demanded money, waving the gun toward the cash register. Aiden had pulled her down to the ground, putting himself between her and the man. She looked toward the door and tapped her husband on the arm. When he looked at her from the corner of his eyes, she jerked her head toward the exit, pleading. He looked between her and the door and nodded. They began scooting backward, eyes locked on the man. Thea was so close, her hands were outside, they could have gotten out in a few more seconds but Aiden, kind Aiden, couldn't watch the man as he aimed the gun at a girl who was begging for her life. There was no thought in his actions. He stood and hurtled his body at the man dropping them both onto the floor.

"Aiden," Thea screamed as she watched the men struggle for control. "Someone help him." She was already running toward them, but Aiden had lost control of the situation. The gun was pointed at him. When the shot rang in her ear, she was frozen, dread hanging in the shocked silence. Thea screamed lunging at her husband, who lurched toward the ground. His movement had broken some kind of magic over the people in the restaurant. They rushed to the door, the need to escape greater than that to help. One of the patrons used the chaos to his advantage and wrestled the gun away but all Thea could see was Aiden. The blood on his crisp white shirt pooling out from his abdomen.

"No. No, no, no. Aiden, God, no." She pressed her hands onto the wound even as her body heaved with sobs. Blood was coming out of the side of his mouth as he tried to smile at her. It was more of a grimace.

"I love you," he wheezed out, coughing up more blood.

"Don't say it like that. Don't say it as a goodbye," she cried. "We're going to get you help, and you're going to be fine. Then we're going to go home and see the kids." He took in a shuddering breath. "You promised to stay by my side, always. You can't do this to me."

He had tried to tell her something, in those final moments, with his mouth open and golden eyes filled with meaning. All that came out was a strangled gurgle before he closed his eyes—before he was lost to her forever.

· CHAPTER FIVE ·

Finn

People aren't dying anymore. I shot a man point blank through the chest, and he didn't die. He fell to the ground, screaming in pain, hand placed over his heart as blood poured through the open wound. He looked just as shocked as I was that his lights hadn't gone out.

FROM A LETTER WRITTEN BY US SOLDIER
PETER HATFIELD TO HIS FAMILY

Finn ran, his feet pounding against the ground. The sun was just beginning to set. He tried to run in the mornings before he was needed at the gate but he'd slept in since he spent the night before tossing and turning. He didn't remember much from his dreams other than blood and a feeling of unease.

He slowed down to a meandering pace as soon as his house came into view. He'd hoped that going for a jog would help clear his mind.

Finn's neighbors stared at him as he walked by. They were sitting on their front porch, as they did most evenings. He tried to avoid their looks of pity and confusion. Shame bubbled up inside his chest, sending his heart into a painful cadence. The need to escape had him sprinting inside despite how tired his legs were. He could feel their eyes on him even as he shut the door and leaned against it.

"Finn?" His mother called from the kitchen. He didn't answer but followed her sorrowful voice into the room. Lillian had her arms around his mother who had red rimmed eyes. A new wave of tears began sliding down her cheeks the moment she saw him. Liam was on the floor, knees tucked to his chest, hyperventilating as Finn's father leaned down and rubbed his back. Finn was used to his brother's dramatics but he had never seen the terror on his father's face before.

"I talked to Lydia today. She told me that what I had heard must have just been rumors." Winston pulled Liam up. "Go to your mother."

"You didn't believe her?" Finn wasn't shocked by the news.

"I did at first but later I saw those two strategists being arrested for what I assume was carelessness. I'm thinking we still have two or three days before they come." Winston ran a hand down his shirt trying to smooth out wrinkles that weren't there.

"What are we going to do about it?" Finn asked.

"There's nothing we can do," his father replied, defeated.

"What do you mean nothing? We can leave. We can go right now," Finn said, throwing his hands up in the air.

"Finley, stop it. Stop it right now." His mother pulled away from Liam. "I can't handle this anymore. There's nowhere to go."

"We can go to the rebellion. Grandma can get us in." He raised his voice. "Declan can vouch for us."

"Declan left us. He caused this." Arlette stood up crossing her arms.

"So we stay here and what? They're not just going to listen to our side. We've heard the rumors about what they do to prisoners." Finn slammed his hand down on the table. Liam winced and moved to sit back on the floor with his knees to his chest.

His mother screeched in fury, and Winston was quick to take her out of the room before she could become even more upset.

"We'll talk about this later," was all he said to Finn in passing, shooting him a look of disappointment.

"Don't worry boys, I'll talk to your mother when she calms down." Lillian sighed. "I want to speak with her about you two leaving tomorrow."

"What? What about you? And our parents? We can't abandon you," Liam said.

"We'll follow the day after. I want you to get a bag packed. Be prepared, just in case." Lillian eyed Liam. "Just important things." She stood up and hobbled to her room.

"We'll be okay, right?" Liam turned toward Finn with wide eyes. The "yes, of course" was right on the tip of his tongue, an automatic habit to Liam asking that question. This time though, he wasn't sure. He knew the odds weren't good. Their grandma was slow moving. She'd never be able to escape if she got caught. He wasn't even sure how they would leave. He knew the schedule for when the gatekeepers would switch out but even then the gate wasn't left unattended. Liam made a strangled sound at Finn's lack of response, his chest heaving.

"Calm down, nothing's set in stone. Dad said we've got time to figure it out," Finn replied, kneeling on the floor next to Liam. "You've got to get your breathing under control."

"He said—" Liam started in between gasps, "There's nothing—"

"We can do. I know but do you really think they'd let something happen to us without at least trying to escape?" Finn started taking deep breaths, motioning for Liam to follow his lead. Liam copied him and once he calmed down, Finn stood. "Let's pack a bag, like Grandma said."

He could still see uncertainty in Liam's eyes, but he didn't know how to fix it. Liam followed after him, muttering about what he would have to take with him. They could hear their mother's cries from the top of the stairs. Liam paused before entering his room. Finn could see the same anguish that their mother had reflected in his face. Liam sent him a worried look as he went inside to begin packing.

Finn's bedroom was larger than Liam's and still furnished with two beds. He and Liam used to share it. When Declan left, Liam decided he wanted a space of his own. Finn never complained because it meant he could keep his room clean and clutter free.

Finn sat down on his bed, the royal blue blanket still tangled up at the end of it. His mind wandered to Declan. He was still angry. He still blamed him, but those feelings were mixed with a tinge of jealousy. Declan always had a choice, and Finn never did. He was smart enough to have his choice of any job. He got to choose to leave Essex. Finn would have been content staying in town not caring about what the general did or didn't do, if his family had never been targeted.

He focused his attention on the task at hand and looked over his room. There were some small, wooden sculptures that he liked. Ones of skyscrapers that used to tower among cities. He'd never seen one before but from what he'd understood there weren't many left. Most cities had been abandoned when the ruination first came about, not all of them but a good majority. They were the primary target during the war. At the time, there were those who fought against the transition of power from the president to the generals and those who fought for it. Those who were against the generals having power later became what was now known as the rebellion.

Did he need the sculptures? He didn't think so. He picked one up from the shelf, turning it over in his hands. His grandfather had made them. Finn had flickers of memories; sitting at his feet and listening to his stories as he worked on his carvings. He had grown up at the tail end of the war. When he hit seventeen, he left home, left the south, to see what the world had become. The skyscrapers were his favorite things to talk about. The few that had somehow remained, he used to say, were stunning. Even though Liam could barely remember him, his grandfather had inspired his love of woodwork.

Finn held on tight to the small carving and decided taking one wouldn't hurt anything. He gathered up some extra clothes, enough to last him a week or two, rolling them to make sure they took up as little space as possible. He stuffed each one into a bag that his grandmother had sewed. It was plain but could hold a decent amount of things. He placed the wooden structure on the very top. He sighed and made his way back over to the shelf where a small, folded paper lay next to the knife he had confiscated from Deli. Finn had never opened it. It was something that had been left for him by Declan the night he escaped. Something to remember him by, Finn had always assumed. He'd been too bitter to ever read it, despite Liam's constant nagging at him to do so. Liam held a lot less resentment than anyone else for Declan's actions. His parents never read the message that was left for them either.

He stared at it before a heavy sigh left his lips. He reached for the note and opened it.

Writing this is a lot harder than I thought it would be. Finn, I'm sorry. I really am. Liam was easier, because he never holds a grudge. And because I know he won't look at me leaving like I've wronged him. That's probably not a good way to start an apology and you might not want to keep reading. Trust me, please. I didn't do this because I don't care. I want the world to be better. Ask Grandma about the rebellion. Keep asking her until she tells you the truth.

Do you remember when Grandpa was taken away? When the guards came crashing through our doors at dinner? They tore through so many things. You were so upset and it was my job to hold onto both you and Liam. I was doing a good job until they struck Grandpa down. I was so scared at that moment. None of us could believe that they had hurt him. None of us could move. None of us, except you. Your temper has always been something to watch out for. I could see the instantaneous change in your face and before I could grab you, you were already running for them, your little fists beating against their legs, screaming at the top of your lungs.

Dad tried to stop them but they had already decided that you needed to be taught to "mind your manners." That's what they said. I thought that they would hit you but I never thought they'd throw you down, right into the shattered glass. There was so much blood.

I couldn't do anything to save Grandpa, and I couldn't do anything for you either. You must have realized the way things have been going. They treat citizens who are sick like they don't deserve any kindness. They treat them like monsters to hide the fact that underneath the masks of protection, the true monsters are the ones in control. Ever since that day, all I wanted was to help those who couldn't help themselves. That's why I left. I know you probably feel worse because I didn't trust you enough to tell you I was leaving. You need to understand that I wanted you as far away from danger as I could keep you. If you had known anything, they would have found a way to extract the information.

I really am sorry, Finn. I hope you understand. I know Mom and Dad probably won't but please try.

Declan

· CHAPTER SIX ·

Finn

The end of the world is upon us. We have angered God with our selfish deeds and no person from this point forward will be allowed past Heaven's gates. Hell has come upon us and we will suffer for an eternity.

RELIGIOUS PROPAGANDA DATED SEPTEMBER 15, 2023

Finn was sprawled out on his bed, one leg sticking out of the royal blue blanket. He stared at the ceiling, both his arms propped beneath his head as he listened to Liam's faint snores. His mind was reeling, and there was nothing to distract it. Declan's note was sitting on his dresser. He couldn't stop staring at it and wondering why reading it couldn't just fix the inner turmoil he felt. Maybe Declan did have a good reason to leave. Maybe he was doing the right thing, but Finn was still angry. Still hurt. If his brother was so smart, how didn't he realize his absence would break the family? Why didn't he know that their mother would spend every night for months crying? That their father would always be too tired to handle anything? That Liam's anxiety would get worse? Why didn't he know that Finn, already an outcast because of his anger, would feel even more alone?

Liam mumbled in his sleep while kicking his own sheets off the bed. Earlier in the evening, Liam had walked into Finn's room, packed bag in hand, and sat down with a block of wood and his knife. After a few hours, he had become tired and fell asleep. Finn didn't really mind. He'd rather have his brother's snoring than the intense silence of the night.

What felt like hours later, he fell into a restless sleep. His dreams came in quick flashes. Cities being torn apart. Skyscrapers crumbling. Soldiers being shot or impaled but still rising to their feet despite the pain on their faces. The dream shifted from broken images to fluid, clear ones. Instead of a war he saw his home. He watched as officers moved toward it, silent on their feet. Dread coiled in his stomach as they moved closer and closer to his unsuspecting family.

Finn startled awake. His breaths came in shallow waves that he forced to even out. Dreaming, he had only been dreaming and yet shuffling sounds filled the once muted night. It was too loud to be his grandma. He shot out of his bed, shaking Liam and dragging him out of his slumber.

"What?" Finn slammed a hand over Liam's mouth before he could say anything else, putting a finger to his lips. He bent down and grabbed both of their bags and shoved the knife that was on his shelf into his pocket. They slunk across the hall to their parents room.

Liam stumbled behind him in a confused daze. His parents room was the smallest one upstairs. The mattress almost didn't fit and their clothes were piled to the side.

Finn gripped his father's foot, rousing him with a start. "There are people in the house." That was enough to propel Winston into high alert. "I woke up and heard them downstairs."

"You're sure?" Winston put a hand against his wife's cheek, waking her up as well.

"I'm sure," Finn answered. Winston filled her in and fear danced across her features.

"Mom's downstairs. Winston, my mother is down there." Arlette moved to get up.

"I'll go down." Winston grabbed her. "Stay with the boys." He sprung from the bed and nudged the boys forward until they settled down next to their mother. Arlette put an arm around both of them watching the door as Winston left. Yelling broke the silence. Crashes and bangs echoed throughout the house.

"Mom?" Liam questioned as they listened.

"Finn, you were right. We should have tried to do something." Arlette squeezed him. "I want you to listen to me. I love you both so much. I couldn't have imagined having better children in my life."

"This isn't a goodbye." Liam cut her off before she could say anymore.

"It is, just for a little while." She rubbed his back and took a shaky breath."I'm so proud of both of you." She released them, pushing them away from her. "Sneak out the window. You should be able to drop down onto the porch's roof from here. It's not a long way down to the ground from there. You should be fine."

"We can't," Liam said.

"Please, sweetheart, please do this for me. I couldn't live if something happened to either one of you."

"We'll come back for them," Finn said, misery coating his tone.

"We can't. Finn, we can't leave them." Liam shook his head. Arlette pushed Liam toward the window despite his protests.

"You have to hurry." Finn scrambled across the mattress, dropping their stuff out the window. Liam gripped Finn's arm, a silent plea, a question. Was this really happening? Finn's answer was a nudge forward. Liam pushed back and wrapped their mother in a tight hug before staggering out of the window. He landed on the roof with an ungraceful thud. Finn followed his brother. He turned back when he was half out.

"We'll be back for you, okay?" His voice cracked. He needed her to know that he wasn't forsaking her, like she felt Declan had.

"I know you will."

Finn dropped down. Liam had already thrown their things to the ground below and was looking over the edge of the roof. "The ground looks pretty far away. We could break something."

"I'll go first then. That way if I break something, at least you'll know what's in store for you." Finn spun around, slipped to his knees, and slid himself down, holding onto the edge of the roof. Letting go seemed daunting. It took him three tries before he could will his hands to let himself fall. He landed on his feet and lurched forward, catching himself on the side of the house. His ankles throbbed in protest. He could hear the officers bounding up the stairs. Liam hung down from the edge.

"Just let go. We don't have a lot of time." Liam listened, and with his eyes clenched shut and lips sealed, he let himself fall. He landed on his back.

They could see into the kitchen window. Their dad was bent over, clutching his stomach. Bruises were forming on his cheeks and neck. His nose was bloody. Their mother rushed into the room and toward her husband to hold him up, tears slipping down her cheeks. Their grandmother was sitting at the table and an officer was at her back. They were asking again and again where Finn and Liam were.

Finn ground his teeth together so hard his jaw ached. How could he just run away after seeing his family beaten and bruised? He knew that they should listen to what their mother said and go. It would be safer but he didn't want to.

"Finn?" Liam asked, looking toward the forest. The only chance they would have was by hiding amongst the trees in the beggar's district.

"Hey! The boys are back here." An officer had come around the building, spotting them. He was one of the ones who was always stationed outside their house. Finn recognized him because of the deep grooves in his face, like the craters of a rock. Three men came from the front and two from inside.

Their family followed them, begging and pleading to let their children go.

"You boys aren't very good at keeping yourselves out of trouble." Crater Face spoke to them. "Round 'em up. We've gotta take 'em to Leander. We're gettin' our rewards tonight."

"You can't do this." Arlette grabbed his arm, but he struck her, sending her to the ground. Finn howled in anger, slamming his shoulder into the officer that was closest to him. Crater Face grabbed his machete. He took several swings at Finn, forcing him to back up. The other men just watched, leering. Finn dodged another swing, one aimed for his neck, and remembered the knife that Deli had found. He pulled it out of his pocket. It was dull and ancient, but it was better than nothing.

Anger pulsed through him, the intensity of it made his skin crawl, as if the emotion itself was trying to claw its way out of his flesh. As Crater Face came closer to him, he thrust the knife forward, focusing all of his fury in the strike. The knife elongated, the steel rippling, pulsing with energy. A red aura wrapped around Finn as the sword he held sunk into the officer's chest. Outraged cries rang out amongst the others.

Finn's fingers wrapped around the red hilt. Carved into it was a circle with two horizontal arrows inside it, one above the other. From all around the circle, tridents emerged with three lines through each of their bases. Finn let out another yell and charged into the midst of three other men, swinging the sword in broad arcs. Two of them were able to scramble back but the metal sunk into the third man's skull with a sickening crack. Finn was grabbed by the shoulder and thrown on the ground, his sword still in its cage of flesh and bone.

"The horseman's sword." His grandmother hobbled down from the doorway.

"You're going to pay for that boy," he was told as a rough kick landed on his ribs.

"Don't kill him. I think that's the sword Leander wanted. Grab it." The burly blond went after it, but Winston was already trying to stop them.

Finn pushed off the ground, shoving aside the officer that had kicked him in the stomach and ran toward the sword. He tugged it free and staggered back as it returned to its original form. Liam grabbed him, securing him as he held onto his side.

"Go, both of you. Get away. We'll distract them." Arlette rushed to stand in front of them, putting herself between her children and a guard.

"I'm sorry," Finn said but she shook her head.

"You need to leave. Right now."

"Finn. Take care of your brother," Winston said. Finn and Liam stumbled away, moving as fast as they could into the forest behind their house, toward the beggar's district. They made it to where the trees opened up to houses before Finn's shock wore off. He pushed away from Liam and fell to his knees, throwing up.

"I marked someone as an untouchable." He remembered the satisfying way the sword felt as it punctured the officer's chest and the shock that rolled across Crater Face's features. He trembled at the thought. The moment the knife began to grow, so had his rage and his bloodlust. He'd been powerful, and, in the moment, he was riding high. He vomited again, his whole body retching with it. He emptied out his stomach until bile was the only thing left. He dry heaved until he got control of himself. He wiped his mouth, hoping he would be able to keep himself from spewing anything else.

The adrenaline that had kept him going was out of his system. All he wanted to do was lay down and sleep, forget everything that had just happened. A strong hand gripped his arm and pulled him up. He groaned, trying to move away.

"Finn, you need to hold on just a little longer." Deli's father put an arm around his shoulder and Liam took his other side.

"What? What's going on?" He looked to Liam for answers but Liam only shook his head, confused.

"Your Grandmother sent me a note, warning me about the raid. She knows I work for the rebellion. I've been walking around the woods waiting for your family." Neal led the boys back to his house. "I'm guessing you're the only ones that got out?"

Liam nodded.

Neal let Finn lean against him all the way to his house. Delilah was pacing on the porch, her hair a wild mess of curls and tangles around her head. The moment she saw her father, she called into the house and ran down the path to meet them.

"You're going to cut your feet if you go everywhere barefoot, Delilah. How many times do I have to tell you?" Neal sighed.

"I was so worried. I couldn't help it." She gazed at Finn with sad eyes, wrapping her arms around his waist. "Are you okay?"

"I will be in a little bit." His speech was slurred with exhaustion.

"Inside. Go." Her father nodded to their house.

"Grammy made some food." Delilah took off back toward the porch where an elderly couple now stood. They were both very thin. It seemed as if every ridge of their bones could be seen through their skin. The man was tall, even hunched over, with a wrinkled bald head. The woman's hair was knotted and as white as snow. She opened the door for the group.

Although the house had always looked small on the outside, it felt so much smaller on the inside. There were a few chairs and a table as soon as they walked in and on the other side of that was a small kitchen space that held two counters. Neal helped Finn sit down on a chair. Then offered the other one to Liam as Delilah's grandmother brought them food. It was dark brown and watery. Delilah had scooted her way close to Finn and, as soon as her father took his eyes away from her to speak to his parents, she crawled onto his lap. He stifled a groan as she elbowed him in the ribs, and he adjusted her to lean on his good side.

"Deli," Neal said, preparing to take her away from Finn.

"It's okay." He reached down to take a spoonful of his meal, despite the fact that his stomach was churning in protest.

It had no flavor to it. For a family that had next to nothing to their name, feeding him and Liam was making an immense sacrifice. Not being able to finish the soup himself, Finn shared small bites with Deli.

"Once you've finished eating and slept for a little bit, we'll talk about getting you boys out of the city," Neal murmured to them as he watched his daughter's crestfallen face.

"I don't want them to go." Her eyes teared up and she leaned her head against Finn's chest.

"They can't stay. They need to be somewhere safe."

"Finn will you promise me something?" Deli asked him around a mouthful of food. He nodded. "If you see my mom, will you tell her hello and that I love her?"

"I promise I will." He gave her the most serious look he could manage.

"Is there a way to leave without getting caught?" Liam asked.

"Yes, you're going to leave the same way I showed your brother how to."

· CHAPTER SEVEN ·

Thea

Thea laid in a fetal position on the bed, the white sheets stained with makeup and tears. The small room with its bright yellow walls and wooden floors seemed to be closing in on her. She had lost the light of her life, the beauty, the magic of it. How? How could she go on? Thea curled her knees even tighter against her chest. At forty-three, she should have everything figured out. She should be able to be strong for the children. That's what she had been told for the past couple of weeks. No matter how hard she tried to pull herself together, she always ended up being a weepy mess, a shell of the woman she once was. She didn't feel anything except the intense grief as it pressed its weight against her ribs.

There were times when she really didn't think she could go on. She barely slept anymore and whenever she did she saw him, Aiden, with blood spilling out of his mouth as he coughed and sputtered, trying to take wheezing breaths to fill his lungs with air. Her sweet husband, her best friend, the love of her life. Two weeks and she still couldn't function. She hadn't gone to her office once to look at the artifacts they had recovered from the dig. That used to be their favorite part, discovering what exactly they had found and learning about a culture that had long since passed.

Thea quieted her cries when a knock on the door sounded. She wiped her eyes with the heels of her hands, pushing them into her sockets, as if willing the evidence of her tears away. Zoey peeked her head in. She was the baby, at seven years old and had a likeness to Thea's mother with her wispy frame and flaxen hair that curled around pink cheeks.

"Mommy? Can I come in? I can't sleep," Zoey whispered, small hazel eyes red-rimmed.

"Of course, sunshine," Thea replied, opening her arms wide. It had been three years since Zoey had felt the need to crawl into bed with them—her. Zoey flung herself into her mother's arms head against her chest, sobs tearing out of her so violent that they rocked Thea. She held on to her daughter, afraid of letting her go.

"I miss daddy," Zoey said through the tears with a hiccup. Despair welled in Thea's throat. She tried to force the painful lump down by swallowing a couple of times but it only seemed to get worse.

"I miss him too," Thea said, pulling Zoey with her as she scooted back to lean against the bed's headboard. "I miss him too."

She hoped her arms were a safety to Zoey. She hoped they felt strong because she didn't. She felt weak and numb and like giving up, but she couldn't do that.

"Why isn't there a way to bring him back?" Zoey asked. As Thea was about to answer, another knock sounded and she glanced up to see three more heads peeking their way into her room.

"Come on, all of you. I think we all need each other tonight," Thea said as they scrambled onto her bed. Bennett first, her ten-year-old with the chubby, round cheeks and eyes as golden as her late husband's. He nestled underneath the crook of her right arm, auburn head leaning against Zoey's. Next was William, the oldest at seventeen, who had grown so fast Thea wasn't sure what to do with him. He was taller than Aiden was. He settled himself on her other side, wrapping his arm around her shoulder, hand resting against Bennett's. Will gathered Eleanor, who was fifteen and a carbon copy of Thea, in his lap. Will's curly blond head slipped against Thea's own, seeking as much comfort as he was giving.

Will had his father's heart, his compassion. Even in his own pain, he was taking care of his siblings and of her. She cried because she lost her husband, because her children lost their father, and for the burden she had put on her oldest son. The five of them stayed like that, until each child had eventually fallen asleep and Thea questioned, why wasn't there a way to bring her husband back?

Her mind wandered back to when she was a little girl, to the night of the fire, and to the woman who called herself Death. Death who she had been told over and over again wasn't real by her aunt, uncle, teachers, and therapists. None of them could explain how she had gotten out of the house except to tell her that her memory was faulty due to excessive trauma.

They were all wrong. That was something she had believed with every fiber of her being. That woman had shown up and saved Thea.

It hadn't been Aiden's time. Thea was sure of that. He was too good to be taken from the world so soon. She needed to find the woman, somehow, and make her bring Aiden back. Her aunt and uncle were morticians by trade and she could ask them to preserve the body of her husband, late husband, just a little longer. It would take her a month, at best. She could do it; could bring him back and prove it wasn't his time yet. Thea fell asleep with those thoughts lingering in the back of her mind.

When she woke up the next day, she was sore but with a new resolve. She was going to save her husband. Her kids were still leaning against her and she could smell her aunt cooking downstairs. Since Aiden had passed away, her aunt had been traveling back and forth from her house to help out. Thea's uncle was very sick, so he often had a nurse to help take care of him when Aunt Liv was out.

Thea maneuvered her body, trying to get away without waking anyone up. She slid Zoey off her lap and gently brought Bennett's head to lean against the headboard. She got off the bed and went downstairs. The house was one that Aiden had loved because of how modern it was. The living room was open and large windows surrounded it. They had decorated it with whites and grays which seemed to just fit. She loved being able to see outside and feel the sun shining in the room.

She padded into the kitchen. Her aunt was flipping pancakes, humming the same tune that her mother used to sing to her. Her aunt was a smaller woman than Thea was. Thea had gotten her tall frame from her father but her aunt had always been on the shorter side. Her gray hair was tucked into a low ponytail.

"I thought about waking you, but when I went into your room I just couldn't bring myself to do it," her aunt said without looking up. She placed the pancakes on a plate and turned around smoothing out her white shirt and pants in the process.

"Thank you, Aunt Liv," Thea replied. She felt a little bit guilty about the fact that Liv had taken on so much of the work since Aiden's passing.

"How are you feeling today?" Liv asked moving to get Thea her morning coffee and sit by her niece at the island.

"Better, I think. It still hurts," Thea answered sipping at the hot drink.

"I know, dear. We have to have the funeral soon," Liv patted Thea's shoulder, a gentle reminder. It was something she had done since Thea was a little girl. At first it was an awkward thing. Her aunt and uncle never had wanted kids. When Thea would cry, Liv never knew what to do, hence the patting. It had turned into something that was welcomed and gave her a sense of security.

"Just a little bit longer, please? Just give the kids a little longer before they have to face reality," Thea replied, not saying that she needed a little more time and not telling her aunt that she thought she could bring him back. Liv gave her the look, the one that meant that she saw right through her excuses but didn't say anything else on the matter.

Thea sat caught up in her own thoughts as Liv began making pancakes for the kids too. She was going to go to the office today and look at the artifacts that she and Aiden had found during their last dig. She decided she might as well start there and do more research on the subject. Thea wrapped both hands around her coffee mug, the one that had a silly picture of her family, all of them making the craziest faces they could come up with. It had been taken the year before, on their family vacation. Aiden and the kids had surprised her with it for her birthday. She gently ran her thumb over Aiden's face and her throat constricted. Her first thought was that she was never going to have another moment like that with him but she shook the tears away before they could start. She would have that again, she just had to.

"William, dear, have a seat. I've made pancakes." Liv wagged the spatula toward the chair at the island without looking away from her cooking. When Will sat down, Thea ran a hand through his tangled hair, feeling the scar on the top left side of his head. When he was a toddler he had fallen down a set of concrete steps. Thea's back had been turned, just for a second, and she sprang into action once he had started wailing. His hair had been the color of blood that day as she drove him to the emergency room.

"How are you feeling sunshine?" She asked.

"Sore. We should have at least laid down last night," he replied, rolling his shoulders in discomfort. She smiled, running her hand down his angular jaw before bumping his shoulder with hers.

"I hear that. It's going to take a couple of days before I feel back to normal." Thea tried to make her voice light but even she could tell that it sounded fake. Will dug into his food as soon as it was set down. Liv slapped the spatula down on the counter in front of him.

"Slow down and eat properly. We are a civilized family." Liv gave him a firm look and he sent her a sheepish smile.

"Sorry, Aunt Liv," He replied.

"I was thinking about going into the office today, to look over the artifacts we brought back. Would you be willing to keep an eye on the kids?" Thea asked, tapping her hands on the mug. Liv turned around, surprised from the change in Thea overnight. When Liv and Teddy had first seen Thea after the incident, she swore she would never step foot in her office again.

"Of course, I would be more than happy to. They can come grocery shopping with me today," Liv answered. Will groaned. "Hey, none of that either."

"Actually, I was hoping that you would come with me today Will. There's some boxes that I need help moving from the basement to my desk. There's a twenty in it for you too." Thea had learned early on that offering her kids money worked better than just forcing them to do whatever work she needed done.

"Anything would be better than waiting hours for Aunt Liv to choose between two percent milk and soy milk," William replied with a shrug.

"That was one time. I'm an old woman. I need to take care of these bones, you know," Liv said. Thea chuckled. It had been the first time she'd laughed since Aiden. She stared hard at her mug, feeling apprehensive. Will wrapped one of his hands in hers and she squeezed his fingers.

"Maybe we can stop by that Chinese place for lunch?" Will asked. It had been one she and Aiden often went to during late nights and where they went for their anniversary. It wasn't anything fancy, but it was where they had their first date. They had never stopped going and the kids loved it.

"How about we bring some home for dinner instead?" Thea asked so that all of them could share the meal together.

"I've just fed you and still the only thing you can think about is food? You might just be a caveman," Liv said, sending Will the hairy eye.

"Go get ready and wake up the others so they can eat." Thea cut Will off before he could reply. The last thing she needed to do was to break up a verbal war over Will's possible Neanderthal status.

· CHAPTER EIGHT ·

Finn

*To become a strategist, you must be able to pass three
sets of tests. First is a standard test to assess what your
skill set is best suited to. The second test analyzes your
knowledge of previous battles, including but not limited
to specific wars and their dates, who was fighting, and
how the battles were won. The third and final test is a
simulation where the candidate will have to plan out
a strategy for a fake battle. Less than three percent of
candidates pass these tests.*

EXCERPT TAKEN FROM THE COUNSELORS GUIDEBOOK

Finn had spent the past two hours laying on the hard
floor, a thin sheet wrapped around him as he tried to
sleep. His body ached from his chest to his legs. Every
time he closed his eyes, he saw the way his sword stuck into
the officer's head, blood spewing over him.

He left his family. Guilt pooled in his gut at the thought.

His grandmother had recognized the knife, calling it the
horseman's sword. The name was familiar to him and he tried
to recall her stories. He couldn't remember a lot but what he

could remember was that there was a host for the demons—a woman who couldn't let go of the past. He knew she had four children; four children who had learned of what their mother was doing but couldn't fix it. In a moment of clarity, the host had given them the cursed weapons, where the angels were sealed away, and demanded they be kept hidden.

He knew the horsemen were legends that were actually two beings of good and evil, working together to create balance. That was it. Years spent listening to his grandma's tales, and that was all he could remember. He gnawed at his lip. Those were all stories, though, myths. They weren't meant to be true. He didn't want to believe they were true.

He just wanted to survive, for his parents and grandma to be safe, and for everything to go back to the way it was. But Finn didn't know how to fix it.

Declan would know. He would have a plan because he always had a plan. If Neal knew how his brother escaped, then they'd be able to find him and once they did, he'd find a way to fix this.

"Are you still awake?" Liam rolled over to face him.

"Yeah." Finn rubbed a hand down his face.

"What are we going to do?" Liam asked.

"I guess we're going to the rebellion." What other choice did they have? They couldn't fight Leander. They couldn't save their parents without help.

"What if they choose not to help us?" Liam asked.

"They have to." Finn tapped the knife, still safe in his pocket. It sent shocks through his skin and once again he could feel the rage and power pulsing from it. "We have this. We can use it to bargain. They help us save our family and we give it to them."

"They could just take it from you and then what? They don't have to care about our family," said Liam.

Liam was right. If they knew about the knife, there was nothing stopping them from just taking it. He would have to keep it a secret until he could figure out a way to use it to his advantage. The sooner he figured that out the better. He didn't want it. He could barely control his own anger, let alone the power that was coming from the knife. All he wanted was to make sure his family was safe. The knife was the only thing that would ensure that happened.

"It did something to you, Finn. It's like you wanted those officers to be untouchables." Liam pulled his sheet farther up his body, trying to untangle it. Finn flinched.

"I didn't want that." What else could he say? He couldn't take back what had happened no matter how much he wanted to.

"You couldn't control yourself," whispered Liam. "More so than usual."

Finn sighed. He was well aware that his first response to most things was anger and that he had a hard time keeping it under wraps, but he didn't know what he could do about it now.

"Finn?" Liam waited for him to say something.

"Go to sleep, Lee. We can talk more about it in the morning." Finn rolled over refusing to speak anymore.

Three restless hours later, Neal came into the room. He stepped up to the boys and sent Finn a small nod, noticing he was awake. He walked into the kitchen and began making breakfast. Finn kicked his brother. Liam turned over, still sleeping. Sometimes Finn felt as if his brother was such a heavy sleeper just to spite him. He kicked Liam again, this time letting his foot dig a little into his ribs.

"Ow, what? What do you want?" Liam snapped trying to hit Finn with the wide arch of his arm. Finn rolled out of his reach.

"We need to leave soon." Finn stood from his spot, stretching his aching muscles.

"Oh. Right." Finn could watch as each thought processed across his brother's face. Confusion, realization, fear, defeat, and acceptance.

"I would offer to let you wash up but we actually need you to look even dirtier," said Neal. Finn stared down at his clothes, covered in dirt, blood and vomit, wondering how they could look any worse. "Around the side of the house is a mud pit. Go roll around."

Finn and Liam said nothing, waiting for the joke but Neal looked very serious.

"I don't think I can do this," Liam said but still stood up with sleep-heavy legs and walked out the back of the house. Finn followed him outside.

"Don't think we have much of a choice here." The mud pit was hard to miss. It took up the entire space between Neal's home and his neighbors. Liam started shaking his head, taking a step back. Finn placed a hand on his back and shoved him forward. Liam stumbled, trying to right himself and Finn pushed again, sending him straight into the muck.

"What's wrong with you?" Liam hissed, trying to stand up while reaching for Finn, only to slip back down and splash them both with grime.

"Had to." Finn shrugged and offered his hand, knowing what was coming next. Liam pulled him down hard and he landed on his knees. Liam, wanting to make sure he was covered, pushed him and he toppled over to his side.

"Asshole," said Liam standing up and shaking his arms. Mud flung everywhere.

Finn was thinking with more clarity now than he had been the night before. Neal was one of the ones that had helped Declan leave last year. That was why his grandmother had warned him about the raid. She trusted him. How long had they planned for Declan's escape? How long had he been working for the rebellion? Did someone find out? Was that why he left? The questions just kept adding up.

He stood and walked back around the house. Neal set down two bowls of soup for each of them on the back porch. It was still steaming. They sat on the steps as Neal came out, another bowl in hand.

"Let's talk about how you're going to get out of here." Neal leaned against the wall across from them as they sat down.

"Just like Declan?" Liam began eating the soup, shoveling it into his mouth, despite making faces because it was too hot.

"Just like Declan." Neal nodded. "My family is one of the few here who work for the rebellion, sneaking people in and out of the town."

"Then how did your wife get taken?" Liam asked. Finn elbowed him hard in the stomach as a look of pain crossed over Neal's features.

"She had stopped going to work because she got sick. They took notice and came after her. She was sent to isolation, and we couldn't get to her in time. " Neal paused. "That's where you're going too."

"No. Absolutely not. No. I'm not going. Finn, there's no way." Liam stood, shaking his head.

"You don't have another choice." Neal was calm, trying to speak in a soothing manner.

"Do you want to stay here?" Finn asked. Liam shook his head. "Do you want to turn yourself in?" Another shake of the head. "There's really no other choice." Liam still looked reluctant but didn't say anything more.

"I have a contact there, also a member of the rebellion. He works as a disposer and will make sure you get out okay." Neal shut his eyes for a moment. "My wife was too sick for him to help, despite trying. She couldn't sneak away and was thrown into the pit."

"What's the pit?" Finn had never realized how close the rebellion had been his entire life. How many people did he know that were working for them?

"It's a chasm where they dump those who have been sick or wounded. They just let them pile on top of each other." Neal's disgust showed in his down turned lips.

"Why don't they climb out?" Liam asked.

"First, it's very deep and every so often they burn the bodies that are in there. Second, even if they didn't do that, the sick are too fatigued to do anything, the old don't have enough strength, and the wounded, the ones who should be dead but aren't, live a painful existence. Their bodies are rotting, and they feel every second of it."

"I think I'm done." Liam pushed the half-eaten bowl of soup away from him.

"Life as an untouchable is painful. It's wrong. It shouldn't exist," Neal said with conviction.

"What happens when they burn you?" Finn asked. This was something they were never taught to think about. All they had ever been told was once you went to isolation you never came back.

"Your spirit lingers, released from physical pain but unable to go anywhere. Death is not there to guide them anymore. Most spirits will not bother you. Some, if they have unfinished business, will find an untouchable because they are weakened and take over their body. There is more pain in that because the spirit will feel wrong taking on a body that isn't theirs on top of being able to feel the ailment of a broken body."

"Great." Liam slumped down farther into his chair.

"Why aren't there any here?" Finn narrowed his eyes trying to understand exactly how everything fit together.

"We assume that's because of General Leander. What you're not told, what the rebellion believes, is that he's the counterpart to the Angel of War. A demon lives inside him but he's not the original host. We think he ingests souls to gain power. It's the only explanation for the town being so safe." Neal ran a hand down his face.

Liam pushed his food even farther away from him. Finn stared at the ground.

"The rebellion's fighting to get rid of the generals."

"So isolation?" Liam leaned forward. Apparently being in the same place as a demon was enough to force him to deal with the sick.

"Isolation." Neal nodded. "I'll give you something to cover your face with. That way they won't recognize you."

"What's the plan? How do we get there?" Finn drummed his fingers against his knees.

"I'm going to take you there," Neal answered.

"We're just going to walk in? That seems a little crazy." Liam's brow furrowed.

"No, I'm going to walk in. It's different here than it is in your area. Here, people will kidnap or turn in untouchables to get extra food." Neal's lips twitched in a sarcastic smile.

"So we escape and you get extra supplies." Finn crossed his arms. "It's a fair trade."

"I'll give my contact the signal to let him know you're joining the cause when we get there."

"What's the signal?" Liam wondered aloud.

"I tell all of them that your faces are covered in boils. No one will bother looking at it because they'll think that you're contagious. There was an outbreak when I was a boy that created more untouchables than we'd ever seen before. Isolation's borders were pushed into our district."

Finn wanted to ask more questions but Liam already looked nervous enough. Neal reached into his pocket and pulled out a pendant shaped like an eagle.

"Don't lose this," he said as he grabbed their bowls and stepped into the house.

"Lee," Finn began. "You're not going to get sick."

"How are we supposed to do this? It feels like we've already lost everything," Liam said. He had been holding in his fear for so long that now it spilled over with his tears. "It's impossible. Even if we make it to the rebellion camp, if we find Declan, what then? How do we win against a demon?"

"I'm not sure. We're not doing it alone though. There are all these people that believe it can be beat. Remember what we were taught, most wars end in stalemates because the horsemen were sealed away. If they're right, then the reason the rebellion can never get a leg up is because General Leander controls how the wars go," Finn responded.

"So the only way to win is with the knife?" Liam asked.

"We don't know anything for sure. We've been lied to our entire lives." They fell quiet into a miserable silence.

· CHAPTER NINE ·

Finn

FROM WILLIAM'S JOURNAL, DATED JULY 17, 2032

"It's just a little farther," Neal pushed against a low hang-ing tree branch, letting the boys through. They were deep in the woods, farther than either had been before, heading to the Southern border of Essex, where isolation lay. The area was largely untouched except for the unkempt path they were following. The ground beneath them was just a little bit more manageable than the overgrown expanse around them. Neal led them through the thicket of trees as if he had traveled this path many times. Walking behind them was Gordon, one of Neal's neighbors.

Gordon, like Neal, helped house those entering or escaping

the town. It was better to have two men escorting them, so the story that Neal dragged them all the way to isolation seemed real. Gordon was a big man. Taller than Finn by three or four inches at least. His head was bald but he had a scruffy white beard with sprinkles of black here and there. He was one of two disposers that were members of rebellion. They took their shifts in turns. One week Gordon was in isolation; the next week it was Mac.

"Put on the masks," Gordon said, sending them a sharp look with his dark eyes. If Finn had learned anything about Gordon, it was that he didn't speak much, but when he did, you listened. The boys threw on the black masks they had been carrying. Neal set a hand on each of their shoulders. The masks covered their faces enough that they were unrecognizable.

"Don't speak to anyone, not even Mac. You need to keep up the appearance that you're sick. Mac takes the ones that seem the most sick. Most disposers are too afraid of getting the boils, so they never question it." His fingers dug into their backs. "We have to carry you the rest of the way."

"What about our family? Will they be okay?" Finn asked.

"There are a few members of the rebellion working in the Capitol Building. I'm sure they'll keep your parents and grandmother safe for as long as they can." Despite Neal's words, Gordon looked skeptical, which didn't sit well with Finn. It did seem to calm Liam down and Finn needed it to be the truth, so he didn't push any further.

"Good luck, boys." Neal brought them in for a quick hug before grabbing Liam and tossing him over his shoulder. Liam let out a grunt.

"Does this really need to happen? Because I don't know about you, but I'm uncomfortable," Liam said. Finn was going to tell him to shut up but didn't get the chance before he was tossed over Gordon's shoulder.

"Yes." Gordon spoke as he began walking again. Finn and Liam tried to remain as still as possible as the forest opened up to a towering gate. It looked just like the main one to the town, but the iron was rusting and it was poorly kept.

"Who's there?" A creaking voice called down.

"Neal Drevon. I've brought Gordon too. I noticed a couple of untouchables in the woods behind my house and brought them to trade for extra food." Neal and Gordon dropped the boys on the ground. Liam hissed in pain under his breath, and Gordon nudged him in the side with his foot. A man stood outside the gate staring down at the boys, a malicious smile on his face.

"We need to check 'em out. You know, we got wind of two boys tryna escape. Extra rewards for the ones that find 'em," The man said.

"I already checked them over. Don't you think if they were the boys I would have gotten myself that reward?" Gordon shot back with a bored tone. The man looked unsure as he circled around them.

"Maybe I want to see for m'self." That same grin returned but now that the man was closer Finn could see that his bottom teeth were all missing. His tongue swiped along the gums.

"Fine with me. If you get sick and cast out because you don't normally handle these types, don't come crying to me."

"Shit. That bad? You sure?"

"No, I'm not. Why don't you come take that second look." Gordon's aggression broke him. He started shaking his head.

"Look, I don't want none of that around me." He held up his hands, covered in dirt and calluses before turning around and calling, "We got some bad ones, Mac. It's all you. Open the gates."

The gates came open with a loud creak, being pushed outward by two other disposers who were about the same size as Gordon. When Finn was little, he remembered being worried that his job would be in isolation. His mother had reassured him that only a certain type of person could do the job, and he would probably never fit into that category. He'd never really understood what she meant before.

Another giant man came out, his long black hair tied back at the nape of his neck. It lay halfway down his back. Unlike Gordon's scruffy beard, he had just a little stubble. He walked up to the boys and nodded at Gordon.

"It's the boils, Mac. Biggest ones I've ever seen," Gordon stated.

"Great. Boils are my favorite." Mac bent down and threw one boy over each shoulder, grunting under the weight. "Les can take care of your food. Ain't my job."

Finn's stomach dropped. He hadn't realized until now that he and his brother were going to be alone. There was no one to help them if they got in trouble. They hadn't been told much about Mac, but he doubted that the man would give up his cover just to make sure they got out safely.

Mac threw them on the ground. Finn rubbed his back as he sat up, glancing around the area. It shocked him how many people there were. If he had to guess, he would say there were at least fifty people, most huddled together, watching the disposers in fear. Everyone talked in hushed whispers. Disposers walked around, ignoring the people around them. They weren't cleaned up much better than the untouchables. Finn wasn't sure what he'd expected isolation to look like, but he never would have thought it was just a giant clearing in the forest.

Finn and Liam were sitting close to another gate on the opposite side of the area. It was a large wooden door that looked too heavy for just one or two people to push open. Along the wall, near the gate, were carts. They were crudely made. Neither brother said anything or even moved, too terrified of being caught to do so. They watched as children played games in the dirt with somber faces and parents cried. Older men and women tried to move but with difficulty. They limped or dragged their legs, some fell because the muscles could no longer support their bodies.

They were kicked or hit if they didn't follow the orders given to them. Some, the ones that couldn't move, were dragged by their hair to wherever they needed to go. Finn had to turn his head away from the screeches of pain.

Liam shuffled closer to him so that their shoulders were touching, close enough that they could speak without anyone noticing or listening in. Finn waited but Liam didn't say anything. His entire body was shaking. There was no way they could back out now, and he knew Liam was heading straight into a panic attack. There were times, if they were able to catch the panic attack soon enough, that they could avoid the whole thing, but that was very rare. Finn had been expecting this to happen ever since the raid.

"We're going to be fine. We're not going to get sick," Finn said.

"It's not that simple. After Grandpa, I used to have nightmares about being phased out. Or about Mom or Dad or Declan or you being sent to isolation. This is my worst fear." Liam took a few deep breaths, but Finn could still hear the tremors in his voice.

"Try to focus on something else," Finn said. Their mother always knew what to say when Liam got like this

"Like what?" Liam shot back. Finn tried to rack his brain for something. He didn't understand Liam's fear. He didn't want to get sick or hurt, that he could sympathize with, but he didn't understand the immobilizing distress that Liam felt. He sighed, uncertain of how to help his brother.

"Do you remember when Grandpa would tell us stories about the outside?" Finn waited for his brother to shake his head before continuing. "He would always tell us how amazing it was to discover more than just the small patch of earth you lived in. He saw the Earth's scars from battles that had been fought long ago and abandoned towns and cities." Liam's breath was slowly becoming more even. He had started focusing on Finn's words instead of the turmoil he was feeling.

"Now you're going to see all of that. We're going to go out there. We get to see the same things that Grandpa did, and one day you can tell your own grandchildren about it." Finn watched as a woman got shoved out of the path of a disposer and winced for her as she fell.

"I'm not sure I'll have grandchildren. It would be nice to see more than just Essex, though," Liam agreed.

"You'll have grandchildren one day." Finn picked at the grass under his fingers. He didn't want Liam's self-doubt to bring on another attack. Liam just gave him a small smile in return. "Feel better?"

"Enough to keep myself under control for a little while," he answered. They spent the night restless and tense, neither one of them being able to fall asleep. Finn was just starting to nod off when the sun began to break through the trees. Liam nudged him, snapping him out of his drowsiness. The disposers were on the move, rounding up some of the untouchables.

"What are they doing?" Finn sat up a little more as everyone was lined up.

"It looks like they're inspecting them," Liam answered. He was right. They were only rounding up the ones that had trouble moving and speaking.

Some people, the ones who weren't going to be phased out, were directed to go back to the small camps they'd made or were pushed into a sitting position on the ground. This group was made up of the younger ones ranging from kids to thirty somethings. The others were left standing so they could be double checked. There were a few children in that group, too, but they were obviously sick with coughing fits and shaking legs. The disposers ran their hands along every part of their bodies, making sure there was nothing hidden under their clothes. Bit by bit people were directed over to where Finn and Liam were, some of them needing to be carried. The people who were able to stay looked at them with pity.

"Please don't take my baby away. Let us stay together. I'll walk beside the carts. I'll even help carry one, but please, please don't take him away from me." A woman cried holding onto her son who was trembling. The boy tried to raise his arms to grip onto her but was too feeble to do even that. Finn couldn't hear what was said to her, but gazed at the scene as her son was ripped from her arms. She let out a wail, beating her fists against the disposer. It was only a matter of seconds before she was taken away, jerked back onto the ground and held there. Finn looked away as the men began kicking her. He tried to ignore the cracks and screams that followed. Liam's breathing had once again picked up, ragged and heavy as he watched what was happening.

"You need to calm down," Finn said, pulling Liam's attention away from the brutal scene. Liam didn't reply, but he did try to even his breathing out.

The man carrying the boy came over to them and dropped him close to their feet. The other untouchables who had come over to their side had stayed far away from them. The man glared at Liam before walking away and telling one of the other disposers that they needed to evacuate soon.

The boy was staring at Liam with worried and wet eyes. His copper hair stuck to his forehead. His cheeks were hollowed and tearstained and his bones jutted out of his body as if pulling and stretching against the thin skin. He was small. Fragile. Tints of blue lined the skin around his lips and eyes. He moved one of his hands, so it rested on Liam's leg. For a moment, Finn thought this would send him into another panic attack but it seemed to do the opposite. Liam began to get everything under control.

"What's your name?" Finn asked the boy.

"Henry," the boy said, his voice hoarse and cracked.

"My name's Finn and this is Liam." Finn introduced both of them. The boy must not have realized why nobody else would get near them or he didn't care.

"Is my mom going to be okay?" Henry asked in a despondent tone.

"I'm sure she will be. I think she's more worried about you than she is about herself," he replied. The woman was curled into a ball on the ground whimpering for her son.

"I want to stay with her. I don't want to be taken away."

Henry tried to sit up but he didn't have enough strength. With how skinny he was, Finn wondered if he had any muscles left or if his body had eaten away at all them.

73

· CHAPTER TEN ·

Finn

If you see any suspicious activity from neighbors, friends, or family, you are under obligation to report it. Traitors working for the rebellion are to be apprehended immediately upon suspicion and brought to the capitol building for questioning. The rebellion is an organization of savage heretics who will stop at nothing to see the world torn farther apart.

FROM A POSTER TACKED TO THE OFFICIAL MESSAGE
BOARD IN THE MIDDLE OF TOWN, ESSEX, VIRGINIA

"They're going to take us to the pit, aren't they?" Henry curled even closer to Finn, his body trembling. Finn didn't answer. The disposers made their way around isolation three times, jerking people around, trying to decide who would be taken to the pit and who was lucky enough to survive another week.

"Let's get this over with," Mac said, walking over to them once everything was finished. Two others followed behind him with a small cart. "Those of you that can walk get to the gate." The man began pushing people forward before coming toward Finn, Liam, and Henry. "Let's load them up."

He grabbed Liam first, picking him up and dropping him into the cart. Liam let out a grunt of pain. Next the man grabbed Finn. Finn was dropped on top of Liam. Henry came last. Finn expected him to take up the empty space next to them but he was tossed straight onto their backs. The boy's elbow collided with Finn's head, and it took everything he had not to let out a string of curses.

"Sorry." Henry took a shaky breath, and Finn was quick to squeeze his arm, trying to convey it wasn't his fault.

Anyone who wasn't put in the carts were being pushed toward each other to form a tight group. They cowered away from the disposers, wanting to avoid being assaulted for not moving fast enough.

"Let's move, come on. Pick up the pace." Orders were being yelled out. From what Finn could see, there were two men directing the group of fifteen and Mac was wheeling the cart they were in. One of the disposers banged on the wooden gate with two quick hits. It began to open bit by bit. Four guards were pulling on ropes that attached to the door.

He wasn't sure what he expected things to look like outside of town. His entire life, he'd been told that outside was unsafe and uninhabitable, that people from the rebellion were crazy for even attempting it. From what everyone was told, the world was still damaged from the old war. He thought, at best, the world would just be ash and chaos.

How wrong that was. He saw green—lush trees and overgrown weeds. It wasn't uninhabitable at all.

They walked for a long time until the sun was about to set. The trees began to thin out and moans of pain broke through the silence of the forest. They were at the pit. How was Mac going to get them out of here?

"Start jumping. We don't have time for your crying," one of the disposers who was leading the group said, as he began pushing people in. Their screams of terror echoed.

"I'll stay to burn 'em," Mac called over the screams.

"Why are you always doing this? You're as sick as they come to enjoy the burnin'." Mac bristled.

"Last time you stayed behind what happened? Not all of 'em got taken care of did they? They came back beating against the gate. I'm sure General Leander will be happy to hear that something like that happened again. I'm covering my ass," Mac said and then jerked his head, a sharp signal to get them to leave.

"It was only a joke man, lighten up a little, will ya?" Nonetheless the three other men began walking back. The rest of the untouchables looked like they wanted to run, to escape, but doubt was clearly etched into their faces. Mac was stronger, and he was in peak condition. There was no way they would be able to escape.

"Alright boys, out." Mac had waited five minutes before finally speaking. Finn and Liam crawled out of the small cart. Confused murmurs traveled among the group. "I'm with the rebellion. We're going to get you to safety."

Most of the people looked scared, unsure whether they should actually believe him or if this was just some cruel joke.

"We're waiting on two more, a couple of scouts who will lead you to the camp. They should be arriving here soon." Mac reached into his pocket, pulling out a wooden token in the shape of an eagle, its wings spread out. Excited chatter broke out.

"This is real? We're not going to be burned?"

"We'll finally be able to have a real meal."

"All of those poor people down there."

Finn and Liam reached up and took off their masks and the heavy coats they were wearing. Everyone watched them with curious eyes. There were no boils on their faces. They weren't fatigued in slightest and didn't seem to be in pain. They were obviously not meant to be in isolation.

"You aren't sick?" Henry voiced everyone's question.

"We're not. Our house was raided." Finn pulled Henry up

from the cart, being as gentle as possible, and let the boy lean against him. "Our parents stayed behind so we could escape."

"You have a good family." Henry's eyes filled with tears. "I wish my mom could have come with us."

Finn understood. He wished his family was with them too. "His mom, do you think you can save her too?"

"I can try. I'm not going to pretend like—" Mac's words were cut off as he howled in pain. His arm reached out to grab his right shoulder where an arrow stuck out of him. "Scatter. Run away now!" He coughed up blood as a group of officers came running into the clearing.

"Grab the boys." The group split in three, four of them focusing on Mac who, despite having an arrow stuck in his chest, had grabbed a knife that he'd kept hidden. Seven of them turned toward Liam and Finn, ready for the fight. The two with bows stood at the back, ready for attack.

"Get out of here. Don't hesitate." Mac grunted moving away as a man lunged at him. Mac grabbed his arm, flinging him toward the ground, his knife slipping into the officers back and slicing upward along his spine.

Finn pushed Liam forward, picked Henry up in his arms, and took off into the sea of green trees, away from his home. He just wanted to survive. It was the second time he'd let someone else sacrifice themselves for him. The knife felt heavy in his pocket. The horsemen's weapons were supposed to belong to heroes, to people who would return balance to the world.

He was not a savior.

He was a coward.

· CHAPTER ELEVEN ·

Thea

Thea tugged at her greasy matte of dark hair. When she looked in the mirror that was hanging on her right, she didn't recognize herself. Dark circles outlined her green eyes. She hadn't been home in almost three days. Trying not to think about her appearance, she once again focused on the ancient tablet in front of her. She'd sent Clark images of it, and he'd been able to decipher enough of it to tell that it was a ritual of some sort. Three days and that was all she had. Clark had never been quick to reply and, although it usually didn't bother her, she was consumed with the need to know more.

She placed her head in her hands, heaving out a sigh. Her desk sat in the middle of the room with papers scattered across it and her laptop open and in front of her. Her back was toward the only window, which was open to let in cool air. She used to love her office. It was small and had once been comforting with its gray walls lined with pictures of her family. Now it was just a painful reminder of her husband's absence.

She stood up and paced around the room. Riddled with frustration and nerves, she knew she wasn't getting anywhere. She sighed again and leaned against the window sill. The town was busy, setting up for one of its annual festivals. She had lost count of how many they had in the summer but it always seemed excessive. The kids enjoyed it, and she couldn't really complain because they lived only an hour away from where she grew up. She never wanted to be far from home. Sometimes, she would leave work early and swing by the now empty lot where her old house had once been. When she was in college and met Aiden, she had told him all about her parents and the fire one drunken night. She hadn't meant to. It was just something that slipped out because she felt she could trust him. She knew he wouldn't look at her with pity because of it and he hadn't. He had rubbed a hand down her back and pulled her closer to him. He didn't apologize or try to make it better. He let the memory settle between them, another fact of Thea's life. It had been the first time they had gotten drunk together, even though Thea had sworn to never drink again after the embarrassment of their first meeting.

That night she had been celebrating a finished project and she had stumbled to her dorm, what she thought was her dorm in her drunken haze, but the key wouldn't work. Aiden opened the door, and she accused him of trying to steal her things. It had taken him a few minutes to get her to calm down and for her to realize that she had, in fact, not made it to her room. He was kind and offered her water and a place to wait until she sobered up enough to get herself home. She spent three hours just talking to him and when she decided it was time to go home, he walked her.

She had woken up the next morning ashamed, praying to every deity she could think of that she would never run into that man again. Fortunately, she did. They had some classes together because they were both studying to be archaeologists. Most of the classes were so big that she couldn't have possibly known everyone. He waved to her that morning from his seat with a sly grin as heat rose to her cheeks. She'd spent a month avoiding him until one day he had cornered her and asked her on a date.

Now, she stood in the remnants of their life together. Aiden's maps hung on the walls; ones that depicted ancient Rome and Egypt. There was a picture of her and Zoey in the hospital, right after she had been born. He had kept it because it reminded him that miracles did exist. Zoey was born two and a half months early, and the doctors hadn't expected her to live but their little fighter had survived. Thea smiled and picked up the picture. If Zoey, as a baby, could beat the odds and live, then Thea was sure she could bring her husband back.

She was pulled from her revere when she heard her children as they chatted in the hallway, boisterous voices carrying down the corridor. Louder than them though, was the click clack of Liv's heels, which seemed to be more aggressive than even Zoey's squeals of delight. Thea ran a hand through her hair, trying to tame it. She stretched her back, working out the kinks and stiffness in her muscles and bones. She opened the door before Liv could. Liv looked surprised at the suddenness of the gesture.

"What a wonderful surprise," Thea said, wondering if her voice sounded too high-pitched.

"We brought Chinese," Zoey said, throwing her arms around Thea's waist. Thea shuffled under the intense look from Liv. She knew what it was asking. Why hadn't she come home? The kids needed their mother, especially after the passing of their father.

"That's exactly what I needed. How did you know?" Thea rubbed Zoey's back. "I think I have a blanket somewhere around here. Why don't we go have a picnic by the lake?" She asked, unlocking her clinging daughter's hands from around her.

"Really?" Eleanor asked. Out of the four children, she was the one most in love with nature. She enjoyed growing flowers so much that Aiden had decided to let her have full control of the garden with the occasional help from Liv. Her love of the Earth had ignited a passion in her earlier that year. She had strode into the living room, hands clutching her pink polka dotted nightdress, fire in her eyes, and announced that she was done eating meat. At the time, Thea had been tucked into Aiden's side while they watched television. It had been late and instead of focusing on what she was saying, they asked her why she was still awake.

She had gone into an ill-tempered tangent then, complaining that no one listened to the things she was saying. Aiden had opened his arms to her, telling her they didn't care if she ate meat or not. If that's what she wanted to do, she could do it. Elle still grumbled but not quite as loud and Aiden pinched the small birthmark on the left side of her jaw before telling her she needed to get to bed.

"Do you have everything mom?" Elle called over her shoulder as she began herding everyone toward the door.

"I think so," Thea replied. She took one last look at the tablet before leaving her office.

When they arrived at the lake, Thea took a deep breath. She hadn't realized it before but a break was exactly what she needed. She felt refreshed.

"What's going on with you, Thea?" Liv asked as they watched the kids playing near the lake's edge.

"I'm not sure I know what you mean," Thea replied, glancing at Liv.

"You haven't been home for days. The kids have been worried about you. Bennett's been sleeping in your bed because he's been waiting up for you to come home." Liv expected an answer, an honest one, and Thea knew she couldn't do that.

"I know. It's just, I don't want the last thing I ever did with Aiden to be for nothing. He wouldn't want me to just ignore my job. He'd want me to do the research," Thea replied, careful of her words as her attention focused once again on the kids. Ben gave her his dimpled smile.

"He wouldn't want you to ignore them either." Liv nodded to her family. William had thrown Zoey over his shoulder, threatening to drop her into the lake. She was yelling, reaching her small hands toward Ben to save her.

"I'm not ignoring them Liv, I promise. This is just something I need to do. For myself," Thea said. Liv pursed her lips. Her aunt had always complained that Thea was too much like her mother. She would shut herself up and instead of asking for help, would try and accomplish everything by herself.

"Mom? Mom, help me please. Don't let him throw me in the lake," Zoey called, flailing her arms in the air. Thea laughed and stood up, jogging over to all the commotion.

"Alright, I guess it's time to show you your brother's kryptonite," Thea replied. Her fingers lightly brushed the back of William's neck and his body convulsed as he dropped Zoey. She landed on her back as William tried to keep Thea away from him.

"Get him," Thea said. Ben was the first there, reaching his hand up but Will ducked away. Zoey and Eleanor tackled him, sitting on his back as he tried to roll from underneath their weight.

"Stop. Stop," Will yelled grabbing Ben by the feet and tickling them until the boy was screeching, begging for help. Thea grabbed Ben's arms, pulling him away from his brother, just out of reach. "Okay, I surrender. I surrender." The girls leapt off of Will and he rolled onto his back panting.

"I think it might be time to head back. The rain's coming," Liv called as she began to fold the blanket.

"How does she always know?" Zoey asked her mom.

"I really don't know, but she's never been wrong," Thea replied as Will and Ben raced toward the car.

"Slow down," Liv called after them in exasperation. "Your children are heathens," she told Thea as soon as she was close enough to take the blanket from her aunt's hands.

"I know. You keep reminding me," Thea replied. Elle glared at her brothers, yelling that it was her and Zoey's turn to sit in the middle section of the minivan, since Ben and Will had got to on the ride over. She stalked over to them and pushed them both out of the way, waiting for Liv to unlock the doors. Zoey followed her sister and tried to match Eleanor's intense scowl. Her round face wasn't quite as intimidating.

"Guys, calm down. The girls get the middle this time," Thea said.

"Are we dropping you off at the office or..." Liv asked.

"No. No. I'm coming home. I think taking my mind off the work might help me. I'll go back in the morning," Thea answered. Liv seemed satisfied with that, and Thea was glad. She didn't need her aunt to be suspicious of what she was really doing cooped up in her office.

· CHAPTER TWELVE ·

Finn

Isolation isn't the end; it's the beginning of a new phase. Although the old, sick, and wounded are well loved, we must let them go. No one deserves to suffer more than they already have in this world. Please do not fight officers who have come to escort your loved one away. They are being well looked after and are beginning preparations for their new life.

NOTE ON ESSEX'S MESSAGE BOARD
SIGNED BY LYDIA MCDONNELL

Finn was faster than Liam, even with Henry clinging to his neck. He didn't think of how far his brother could fall behind until he heard the thud as Liam was tackled to the ground. He spun around at the cry of pain. An officer sat on Liam's stomach with his fist slammed against Liam's nose. Finn dropped Henry, and the boy wailed.

"Stop. I'll give you the knife, just let him go." Finn stepped closer, holding his hands up. He had no tricks, no way to win. He was afraid of wielding the knife, of what it did to him.

"You're in no place to bargain with us," the man replied. He still had his fist raised, poised to strike.

"Don't," Finn begged, staring at the blood that covered Liam's face. Three men crowded around him. The one to his right grabbed his hair, forcing him to his knees.

"Not so high and mighty now, are you?" The man kneed Finn in the chest. The firm strike knocked the wind out of him. He gasped for air, and the officers laughed as he did so. He felt humiliated. That humiliation planted a small, white hot kernel of anger in his belly.

He hated them for what they were doing to him and his brother, for what they had done to his parents, and for every unfair assumption they ever had about his family.

"Give us the knife and maybe the general will show you some mercy," the officer said. It was a lie. Everyone knew the general would never show mercy. Liam let out a cry of pain. Finn couldn't see him, not with the three officers standing in front of him.

The kernel of anger unfurled, spreading more and more as the officers tormented them until he couldn't contain it any longer. He ripped his head away from the officer's grasp, ignoring the stinging pain and the strands of hair still caught in the man's fist. Finn tackled him, slamming the back of his head into the dirt. That's all he could do before he was grabbed around the waist and flung back to the ground. He rolled out of the way as one of the officers tried to kick him in the ribs. Another one came up from behind him, hoisting him up from underneath his elbows and locked his hands behind Finn's head.

He was aware of the knife in his pocket and even though he hated how uncontrollable he felt when he used it, he knew it could have given him a chance in this fight. If he could only reach it. One of the officers punched him in the gut. He bent over with the force of it. The man was going to hit him again, had his fist curled and was pulling it back when a long sword pierced through his chest. It was jerked out and blood sprayed over Finn. In the time Finn had looked away and back again, the man's head had been severed from his body. A woman with long, charcoal hair and a deep scowl stood behind the fallen man with her bloody sword held in a defensive position. The other officers let out cries of outrage. The one not holding Finn sneered.

"You're going to pay for that, you bitch." The officer pulled his own sword from its scabbard on his back.

The woman let out a deep sigh, as if the man in front of her was a minor annoyance and not a dangerous threat. He swung wide and she dodged, stepping in close to him and thrust her sword through the bottom of the man's skull. He fell to the ground, screaming as red poured out of the wound, coating his neck and chest. Before the man behind Finn could even let him go and pull out his own weapon, she sprang into action, moving fast and driving her sword into his skull too. Finn was drenched in blood.

He looked for Liam out of instinct, shocked but ready to fight. A dark skinned man gripped Liam's shoulder, standing him on his feet and checking him over for any wounds. The man towered over everyone and had to bend down to wipe the blood off of Liam's face.

"Rushing in really isn't your style," the man commented, glancing at the woman with amused, blue eyes.

"I knew we would win. There wasn't any reason to wait," she said. Her voice was deep and raspy.

"What?" Liam backed up, putting space between him and the man. "Who are you?"

"I'm Lucian, that's Celeste. We're part of the rebellion." Lucian reached for the string around his neck, pulling out a token shaped like an eagle. "We went to the pit to meet Mac, but he was in pretty bad shape. He was able to cut down some of the officer's, but it cost him. He told us to leave him behind and find you. Strange that so many officers are after two boys."

Finn reached into his pocket and pulled out the token Neal had given him.

"Where did you get that?" Celeste was rubbing some of the blood off her face. She had a long, slightly crooked nose, as if it had been broken, and full, chapped lips with a small, vertical scar right above it. Her skin was bronzed from being outside so much.

"Our house was raided…" Finn began.

"And our parents helped us escape," Liam added, voice muffled as he held his hand over his mouth and nose. Lucian offered him a cloth. Liam stared before deciding the man was okay to trust. He grabbed it, leaning his head back to stop the bleeding.

"Neal gave it to us," Finn said. Celeste nodded but said no more.

"Your nose is definitely broken." Lucian bent over to peer at Liam's face.

"Great. Couldn't tell." Liam glowered. Lucian let out a boisterous laugh.

"I like this one."

"Do your parents work with the rebellion too?" Celeste turned to Finn, not expecting much from Liam in his condition.

"No, but our grandma did and so does our brother, Declan. Do you know him? Declan Douglass?" Celeste and Lucian shared a knowing look. "You do know him."

"We might," Celeste answered.

"You might? What does that even mean?" Liam brought the cloth away from his face. It was beginning to swell and purple marks were showing up underneath his eyes. Henry whimpered from the ground, and Finn moved to grab the boy. Guilt flooded through him when he remembered that he had just dropped him.

"That they don't trust us." Finn bent down to Henry who had been watching the entire exchange and held out a hand to pull him up, letting the trembling boy lean against him.

"We have to take all possibilities into account. It's nothing personal." Celeste shrugged.

"For all we know you could have teamed up with the General and staged everything," Lucian said.

"Makes sense. I would definitely let myself get punched in the face for nothing," Liam said under his breath.

"A rebellion camp in the West was infiltrated like that. I wouldn't put it past any of the Generals to fight dirty."

"What about the others? There were more untouchables who ran," Finn asked.

"Scouts will find them or maybe the free people will," Celeste answered.

"Free people?"

"It's what they call themselves. They don't belong to a town or the rebellion. You have a lot to learn," Celeste started then narrowed her eyes. "Do either of you know how to hunt?"

"No. How would we know how to do that?" Liam threw his hands up. "We're going to starve. We're going to starve, and we can't even die to be put out of our misery."

"Is he always this whiney?" Lucian asked, amusement catching in his voice.

"Every day," Finn replied as Liam scoffed.

"I'm not whiney. I'm just the only person who sees how irrational this whole thing is." Liam kicked a stick at Finn's feet. Finn laughed.

"I'll be back with some berries. It's not going to be much, but it'll be enough to hold the hunger off until we stop for camp," Lucian said walking away.

"What about Henry? We need to get him somewhere safe." Finn adjusted the boy's weight against him. Celeste glanced back with a glare that sent a spark of fear all the way down to his feet.

"We have people at camp who can help him," she replied.

"I don't like her, Finn," Henry whispered, and Finn could swear he saw Celeste tense up.

"How long will it take for us to get there?" Finn asked.

"Two days if we're quick," said Celeste. "I have a feeling we won't be though."

· CHAPTER THIRTEEN ·

Finn

> *I'm getting too old to keep running. I've gone from town to town along the East coast, from Ohio to North Carolina, trying to avoid the demon. The knife has stayed with me the entire time. I try not to touch it anymore, not after what happened last time. I was hoping when the nukes went off that I would be blown to bits and the knife too. It turned out to be just wishful thinking. I need to find a safe space to hide the knife. I wish I could die.*

WILLIAM'S JOURNAL DATED AUGUST 6;

THE YEAR IS TORN OFF

Celeste set a daunting pace toward the rebellion's hideout, a small cave that was used often by rebellion scouts without Leander's knowledge. They'd been walking for most of the day, taking a few breaks here and there when Liam started to complain about his nose. Finn followed her, carrying Henry on his back. The boy couldn't walk by himself, and Finn didn't trust Celeste or Lucian to carry him. Despite being used to running long distances, Finn was still struggling to keep up. Huffing and puffing after him was Liam. Taking up the rear was Lucian, who would suggest taking small breaks every time it seemed like Liam was going to pass out. Neither brother was prepared to do the amount of climbing they did during the trek. Henry had fallen asleep halfway through the journey, letting out snores every so often, and Finn envied him. Celeste led them up faint mountain paths and through giant thickets of brush. Most of what they saw was overgrown trees and rocky terrain, but there were times when they got close to the edge of the forest where Finn could make out craters on the Earth's surface. Rubble and debris covered the ground in those places. An ashy desert.

Liam had noticed it first and had grabbed Finn's arm, forcing him to look at the carnage. He hoped they wouldn't have to walk across the barren, scorched land anytime soon.

"It's just a little farther," Celeste said as night began to creep on them. "We can restock on water once we're there and get some dinner."

"This better not be some kind of joke because I don't think I can go on for much longer." Liam panted, leaning over. Finn was afraid he was going to vomit for the fourth time, but he just wheezed.

"I can carry you if you want." Lucian gave Liam a toothy grin. Liam looked like he was considering it but decided not to take him up on his offer and shook his head. Celeste had been quiet for most of the trip, walking at a fast, confident pace. Lucian, on the other hand, had no problem talking with them and laughing at Liam's constant complaints.

A terrible shriek echoed through the forest, catching all of them off guard. Henry clamped harder onto Finn, burying his head into the back of his neck. Liam flinched back, stepping closer to Lucian.

"Banshee," Celeste said. "Sounds like it's coming from the East."

"What's the plan?" Lucian asked, more serious than he'd been in the short time they'd known him.

"We're not that far from the cave. The opening is covered with brush but there's a couple of lines etched into the stone, right above the entrance. Wait for us there and make as little noise as possible." Celeste was already drawing her sword facing away from them.

"What's a banshee? What's going on?" Finn asked.

"Later, just go." Celeste set her shoulders. Liam wasted no time and began walking at his fastest pace yet, stamina be damned. They had never heard of banshees before. Celeste had turned to look at him, her face softening just a fraction. She nodded at him. He understood the message: follow his brother.

He jogged a little to catch up, keeping a tight hold on Henry. None of them spoke, not even Liam, whose face had grown pale. He was a rambler by nature. Words were a comfort to him, like silence soothed Finn.

"Lee?" Finn asked, uncertain about his brother's newfound quietness. Being only a little over a year apart in age, they'd always been close, always understood each other's quirks. Finn, although preferring quiet, never complained about Liam's incessant chatter, and Liam knew never to ask questions when he was rambling because Finn wasn't really listening.

"This is real Finn. Untouchables are just roaming around out here. How are we going to survive?" Words tumbled out of his mouth one after the other with barely a break between them.

"We'll be fine," Finn replied.

"We're going to become like them, Finn. We're going to be untouchables." Liam's voice was starting to rise in pitch.

"We're going to be fine if you just stay calm," Finn replied.

"How am I supposed to be calm? Do you understand what's happening?" Liam asked. He was still being too loud.

"Liam, shut up, for once in your life," Finn said.

"Is that it?" Henry pointed over Finn's shoulder. A great hill towered over them from the left. As Celeste had told them, there were trees and bushes covering the hill, and on a clear patch of rock, there were two thin lines carved deeply into the stone.

A loud wail sounded behind them. All three boys snapped their attention toward it.

"Is there another one? We have to hide." Liam went scrambling toward the brush, peeling it back quickly, searching for an opening. Finn used one hand to help Liam and one hand to keep a tight hold on Henry.

"Here, it's here." Finn's hand had gone straight through the vines. The wailing behind them had grown louder but they had all been so focused on finding the entrance to the cave that they hadn't noticed how close the banshee had gotten until Henry was ripped from Finn's grasp.

"Finn," Henry screamed as he was thrown to the ground. The woman who had grabbed him was so thin that some of her bones were piercing through the skin. Her abdomen was torn apart, as if it had been ripped open. It probably had been.

"I'll distract her. Get Henry." Before his brother could protest, Finn grabbed a large stone, throwing it at the woman. She turned her attention to him with another cry and snarl. He ran away from Henry and Liam and away from the cave and its safety. Despite the fact that she seemed so frail, the woman kept up with his pace.

He reached for the knife in his pocket, pulling it out. He wasn't going to make the same mistake he had with the officers. He was going to survive.

He was tackled from behind, falling hard onto the ground, his chin catching the brunt of the force, enough to make his head spin. The knife slipped from his hand. He felt the woman's nails sinking into his skin, ripping across his shoulder blades. His body bucked, a harsh movement that gave him enough time to twist around. Adrenaline and anger pumped through him. It was bubbling just below the surface but the more the woman fought with him the less he could control it. He knew he had to incapacitate this woman, this thing, because whatever this was, it was no longer human, but seemed to be vengeance incarnate. He remembered Celeste beheading the officers and knew that was the best option to take. Her body would be useless

He failed to block another swipe as he tried to escape. Nails scraped against his cheek, not nearly as deep as the ones against his back but enough for him to snap. His fury felt volatile, uncontrollable. He threw her off and reached for the knife, knowing exactly where it was as if it called to him. It grew in his hands as it had before and a faint red glow encompassed him. He felt its power pulsing with his rage.

For the first time in his life, Finn wanted bloodshed. He wanted her to hurt. There was no guilt or shame.

The banshee was scrambling back toward him. He waited until she was close enough to reach him before gripping the sword with both of his hands and swinging. The woman jerked back but the tip of his sword still caught her throat, ripping it open. She tried to release another vicious scream but all that passed her lips was a gurgle. She didn't stop; it was like she felt none of the pain. When she ran at him, he twisted his body moving out of her way and catching her leg with his foot. She fell to the ground but was quick to push up on her knees. He didn't hesitate to swing the sword down on her. Her head rolled, teeth still gnashing at him.

"Finn. Where are you?" Liam called, desperate. All Finn could think about was how he wanted another fight. Incapacitating the woman had been so satisfying.

Liam staggered upon Finn who stood over the woman. It was as if the person in front of him wasn't his brother. Finn didn't even recognize him.

"We need to get back. You don't want Celeste and Lucian to know about the sword right?" Finn made no acknowledgement of Liam's words. He started advancing. Liam backed away.

"Finn? This isn't funny." The words came out as a whisper. The only thing Finn could focus on was the anger that he felt still gnawing at the back of his mind. "I know you're still in there. What about Grandma and our parents?"

"That temper is going to get you in trouble one day. If you don't learn how to control it, you're going to hurt someone you care about." His grandma had told him once, after he'd become so angry he threw his fork at Liam. They had been really little at the time. Finn was maybe seven and he had been ignoring Liam. To get his attention, Liam decided to throw a block of wood at him, hitting him in the back of the head. He'd seen white fury and had thrown the utensil without thinking. It missed his brother but stuck in the wall behind him.

Now those same words crashed over him bringing him back from the brink of rage. The sword slipped from his fingers, returning to its normal form. He dropped to his knees, gasping for air and avoiding his brother's eyes and the terror they held. Fatigue made his limbs feel heavy.

"Put it back in your pocket," Liam said, stepping around the knife to grab Finn and help him up. After the knife was hidden away again, they made their way back to the cave. Each step for Finn took a great amount of effort and he knew Liam was struggling under his weight despite not saying it.

"Shit. Lucian, I found them," Celeste called grabbing Finn's other arm, relieving Liam of some of his burden. "What happened?"

"Another banshee found us. Finn led her away. I found him like this." Liam managed to spew out the words between labored breaths.

"Watch out kid, I'll take him." Lucian seemed to materialize out of thin air, hoisting Finn over his shoulder.

"He took out a banshee by himself?" Celeste's tone was cool and inquisitive. Finn never heard Liam's answer.

· CHAPTER FOURTEEN ·

Finn

The four generals were quick to discuss their rules and regulations for the new world. The most controversial of these was the removal of all guns. A statement went out saying, "Guns are useless in the world we now live in. If people can stand back up after getting shot, what's the point?" Riots broke out across the nation, but they stayed true to their word. They offered rewards for anyone who turned in neighbors or friends that were illegally carrying these firearms. Guns started popping up in black market trades, but those were swiftly taken over by the general's forces.

JOURNAL ENTRY FROM AN UNNAMED CIVILIAN

Finn woke to a crackling fire and overcast shadows along the cave wall. He stretched and sat up, feeling the new aches and pains in his muscles. He was still exhausted and felt like he could sleep for a few more hours at least, but he needed to check on Liam. He needed to know that both he and Henry were okay. Finn blinked a few more times, waiting for his eyes to adjust to the dim light of the cave. Liam was to his right, curled on his side a few feet from him, close to the flames. He was using his pack as a pillow and had one of the sheets from home tugged around him. Lucian was close to him, sprawled out on the floor, snoring a little. His sword was next to his hand. Henry was on the other side of the fire, eyes open and watching Finn with a relieved expression. He leaned against Celeste's side. She was sitting crossed legged and wide awake. She had her long hair pulled up, and she was rubbing Henry's back. Her eyes were also on him.

"Are you okay?" Henry asked him in a whisper, eyes darting over to Lucian and Liam.

"I'm fine. A little sore but fine." Finn rubbed a hand over his face, collecting his thoughts. "Are you okay?"

"I'm better now." Henry cast his eyes down, cheeks coloring. "I was having nightmares."

"It happens to everyone." Celeste leaned forward, putting her head in her hand. "Banshees are awful and powerful if you're caught off guard. Pretty hard to defeat."

"I just kept seeing her face in my dreams." Although Henry visibly relaxed, there was still shame in the way he hunched in on himself, afraid to take up too much space.

Finn winced at Celeste's words, knowing they were less to comfort Henry and more to make her suspicions known to him. "It was terrifying. I'm having a hard time remembering everything that happened, but all I was thinking was that I had to make sure you guys were safe. I just reacted."

Celeste regarded him as Henry tried to sit up a little straighter, eyes big and round and pleading. "You saved our lives Finn. I was so scared. I didn't know what to do. One day I want to be able to save people too."

"I'm sure you will." Finn smiled at him as he let out a yawn.

"Why don't you lay down and try to get some more sleep. We'll be right here." Celeste helped Henry lean back, careful not to jostle him too much. She looked to Finn. "We checked you over for wounds. I know a few things about medicine but not very much. Your cheek should be fine in a few days but the scratches on your back may take a while to heal."

Finn knew she didn't trust him and he understood why, but he couldn't tell if she thought he was a threat or not. Her words were still cold, matter-of-fact, and she kept any opinions to herself. It wasn't something he was used to dealing with and it put him on edge. Everyone in town had an opinion and most people made it known, whether that was outright or through subtle hints. Even those who worked under General Leander had their opinions. Celeste was closed off in a way Finn had never seen before.

"Thank you." He wanted her to trust him or at least give some indication of what was going to happen to him and Liam. "Liam and I lost everything in a day. I just couldn't lose him too. I don't want to be alone."

Speaking his fears out loud made him feel small but he needed her to believe him. They might not ever find Declan. They might never see their parents again. He couldn't lose Liam too. His entire world had fallen apart, and he wanted to hold onto the one piece of normal he had left.

It could have been just a trick of the light, but he thought he saw Celeste's face soften, just a little bit. She sighed and crossed her arms. "The camp is about a day's walk from here. It's going to be just as difficult as today was, but once we get there, you'll be able to have a full meal and maybe get those scratches looked at if you want." That seemed like a good sign, maybe things would be okay and maybe she was doubting them a little less. "Are you hungry? You haven't eaten anything in a while and you'll need energy for tomorrow."

"Food would be great." She stood and brought him pieces of meat and a few berry's that had been sitting next to her on a flat rock.

"It's not a lot. Animals are getting harder to come by because Banshees keep getting hold of them." She tended to the fire, making sure it wouldn't go out in the chilly night.

"What happens to the animals? When they get wounded?"

He scarfed down the food, wondering why he had never thought about it before. It wasn't something the town talked about. They bred animals in the farm district for meat, so there was almost always plenty.

"Same thing that happens to us. They're just as stuck as we are unless someone takes care of them. We almost never get meat from an animal who hasn't been wounded in some way. We cut off the head, hope that most of the animal hasn't rotted too much and cut off those chunks of it. Eat the rest." Finn must have made a face because she went on, "It sounds gross but you do what you have to do. They're suffering, and they can't do anything about it. It's better to think that you're helping them, taking away the agonizing pain they're in."

Finn looked at the meat she had given him, now thinking about the animal it came from and how much it could have been in distress. The thought made his stomach roll but in the end his hunger won out. He still ate everything Celeste had given him.

Celeste leaned back against the cave wall and started drawing something in the dirt. He couldn't tell what but he imagined keeping watch was boring. He let out a big yawn.

"You should get some more sleep."

He nodded. Now that he had eaten, he was realizing how tired he still was. He laid down, aware of the scratches on his cheek and back. The ground was uncomfortable and cold but he was too exhausted to care. He fell back asleep with ease.

Lucian woke them all up in the morning with a hefty pile of berries. He whistled while he went about getting everything ready for another day of hiking. Celeste gave half of her berries to Henry when he wasn't paying attention and then got up to help. Liam sat bleary eyed for a few minutes before he seemed to register what was going on. He tossed handfuls of food in his mouth at a time. Finn ate at a much slower pace. His mind was still reeling about everything that had happened. He wanted to just forget, to stay in the cave, and not face a single thing that had happened in the last few days.

"Time to move out," Lucian said, after getting everything packed. "We should be there by dusk."

Liam stood up and stretched only to wince and bring a hand to his face. "How bad is it?"

Underneath his eyes were bruised dark purple. His nose and cheeks were swollen like a deformed chipmunk.

"It could be worse. You look like you've seen battle." Lucian clapped a hand on his back and Liam hissed in pain.

"Looks like he lost the battle." Celeste slung her pack across her back, holding out her hand to take Finn's as well. "I'm guessing you're going to carry him?

Finn handed her his bag as Liam groaned. "You could lie to me. I'm fine with people lying to me to spare my feelings."

Finn picked Henry up, letting the boy rest on his hip. It would be much harder to carry Henry like this but the boy didn't seem comfortable with Lucian or Celeste still. His back still ached enough that he didn't want anything near it. Henry wrapped a hand around Finn's shoulders, mindful of his back. "It's not a big deal Lee; I'm sure no one will notice."

"I don't think I'm made to live outside Essex," Liam said.

Lucian took his bag out of his hands, slinging it over his own shoulder. "You should really focus on walking. The extra weight won't be good for you."

Liam looked like he was going to protest but thought better of it and shut his mouth.

"Okay let's go. We should have been back late last night, so I'm sure Arran's getting impatient." Celeste made her way out of the cave and the boys followed. Finn wanted to ask who Arran was but she didn't give him a chance to.

They hiked in the same line they had the day before. Celeste went first, leading them and pausing every once in a while to give them a break or just listen to her surroundings. Finn followed her, keeping up with her quick pace with some difficulty and chatting with Henry whenever he wasn't focused on his breathing. Liam walked behind him. Liam had thrown up less times today. Lucian brought up the rear, yelling to Celeste to stop whenever he felt the hike was getting too strenuous for either of the boys. Finn had expected Celeste to be more annoyed by the need to stop so often, but she never was. It was almost like she was unaware of them.

They stopped near a brook at midday for lunch and to refill their waterskins. Both Lucian and Celeste shared with the boys whenever they asked but that meant that their water was running low. Celeste made a small fire to boil the water, to purify it, and explained to them the steps she was taking. Lucian went to hunt, hoping to find something to sustain them. Henry talked to them about how weird it was being outside the wall. He'd been in isolation for a year with his mother and had almost all but forgotten what things were like in town.

Lucian managed to find them deer meat; thick cuts of it that impressed Celeste. Finn didn't ask why he would only bring that much and not anymore, afraid of the answer he would get. He was thankful for the food regardless. Liam turned away from the food afraid if he ate it that it would just come back up in an hour.

"You need to eat something to replenish what your body has lost." Celeste handed him a piece of cooked meat. "Trust me."

"Celeste used to puke too when she first had to make the hike up the mountain." Lucian laughed at her obvious annoyance and shrugged. "It's true."

"The more you do it, the easier it gets." Her face was set in a scowl, but it wasn't very threatening. If anything, it seemed more like this was how her relationship with Lucian was. He teased, she bristled, and they both enjoyed the interaction.

"I don't ever want to do this again." Liam took a small bite of his food. "I'll become an untouchable."

"You probably won't have to for a while, at least, but you might not have a choice." Celeste sat back to eat, moving her waterskin closer to Liam in case he needed it. Finn wondered what she meant. Neal had given them his token and that must prove that he trusted them. They would take that into consideration, they had to. They ate in silence until Lucian and Celeste decided it was time to move on.

"Only a few more hours and we'll be there." Lucian pulled Liam up, making sure he was steady on his feet.

A few more hours and they would be at camp, and they would find Declan—if he was indeed there. Then they wouldn't have to worry about becoming untouchables or look over their shoulders at every sound. The rebellion camp would find a way to save their family. A few more hours and everything would start to work itself out. Finn wouldn't have to worry about it anymore.

· CHAPTER FIFTEEN ·

Finn

There are a few key characteristics a person must possess to become an incinerator. First, they must have absolute loyalty to the general and their mission. Second, they will exhibit a restlessness, a need to travel that most of the population seems to lack. Third, they must not be hesitant. Their job is gruesome and not for the faint of heart, but their service is immeasurable. If a person shows these characteristics, the counselor must recommend them for the position as soon as they are of age.

EXCERPT TAKEN FROM THE COUNSELORS GUIDEBOOK

The rebellion camp stood at the top of a mountain, hidden by a forest; a place no one would find if they didn't know where to look. One moment they were walking up the steep mountainside, sweat dripping down their backs from the exhausting trek, and the next they were surrounded. The men and women around them held tight to their weapons, ready to strike if necessary. There was a tense, slow second before the weapons had been lowered, where Finn thought the general had somehow found them.

"Hey Celeste, you're a little late this time," a boy, no older than Liam said with a teasing smile crossing his features as he looked her over. He was short, even smaller than Celeste.

"We ran into some trouble but we've found some new recruits." She paid him no mind, moving past him without a second look. Lucian nudged Finn forward. The brown haired boy limped after them.

"Scrawny. At least this one looks like he can be taught to fight." He stepped up closer to Finn, not in the least concerned about the height difference. His distinct lack of fear was appalling. He didn't think Celeste or Lucian would ever hurt someone for the comments the boy was making, but it had been common knowledge in Essex not to piss off someone who was more powerful than you.

"Leave them alone, Dex. We need to get through." Lucian stepped in between them. Dex didn't seem at all fazed by Lucian. Nonetheless, after a small staring contest, he backed off.

"I wasn't trying to cause any trouble. Have you told them anything about Arran *the undead*?" he asked, glancing back and forth between the group. Whoever Arran was, he was important, the way Celeste and Lucian both paused told him as much. In the two days they'd been travelling together, Finn had never seen Lucian look as annoyed as he did at Dex; even with all of Liam's complaints. Finn had expected the rebellion to be more cohesive, a more tight-knit community than Essex was but it was just the same. Fighting for the same purpose didn't make you friends, just allies.

"What does that mean?" Finn demanded. Dex laughed at Liam's anxious stutters. Liam looked to Finn, horror mapped across his face, in the widening of his eyes and tremor on his mouth. Finn reached an instinctive hand to wrap around Liam's elbow, giving it a squeeze. He gripped Henry a little tighter too, the boy having gasped in fear.

"We'll explain later," Celeste answered waiting for Finn and Liam to catch back up to her. Liam had been rendered immobile at Dex's words and it took a gentle pull from Finn to get him moving again. Dex and the rest of his group broke away from them, back into the hidden depths of the forest. "After we meet your brother," she said in a quiet voice so just Finn and Liam could hear.

"We're going to see Declan?" Finn let go of Liam to try and match her fast pace. It was the first real confirmation that Declan was at the camp, that his brother had escaped and done so unscathed. The feeling of relief and betrayal was bittersweet. He was here, safe, and he would help them. There was no doubt in Finn's mind that Declan would do whatever necessary to fix what he broke.

Declan was here, safe, while Finn and his family had suffered. Living his life without needing to worry about the consequences of his actions. Unsuspecting of the turmoil he'd left in his wake and maybe not caring at all.

"I knew you had a soft spot in there. Can't just let your partner's family be subjected to Arran without a reunion." Lucian ruffled her hair. Celeste shot him a glare so deadly it would have stopped anyone else in their tracks, but Lucian just laughed.

"If you were anyone else, I would have maimed you for that," she said, sidestepping his large palm to keep him from doing any more damage.

"Partner?" Finn asked. It was clear Lucian and Celeste were partners. A light blush rose on Celeste's cheeks, enough for Finn to gauge what the term meant in this context, but she didn't elaborate.

"Keep quiet. It's not something we want to get out yet," Celeste snapped back. "It would have been reckless for us to trust you at your word. For all we know, you're being planted by the general."

Despite wanting to protest, Finn kept his mouth shut. He couldn't blame her for being cautious. He had his secrets as well and despite how surly Celeste seemed, she was still taking them to Declan.

Walking through the small forested area, they came upon a bustling camp. Tents covered the vicinity placed very close together. To the left, a small crowd stood watching two men fight.

"That's the training grounds and over that way is where we keep our sick or injured until they get better." Celeste pointed opposite of the fight. It was a smaller grouping of tents, placed away from the others. "That's where Henry will stay for now."

Lucian placed a large hand on Henry's back, offering to take the boy. Henry clung to Finn's neck a little bit tighter, burrowing closer to him.

"We have people who can help him, or can try to," Celeste said sensing the reluctance. "It's the best chance he's got."

Finn had grown attached to Henry, a fierce need to protect and comfort the boy had risen in him that he couldn't tamper down. It made knowing Celeste was right even harder. Henry needed medical attention, which neither Finn nor Liam could give him. Finn ran a soothing hand down Henry's back.

"Lee and I will come see you after we talk to our brother. I promise." Finn said meeting Henry's eyes. Henry nodded, but the despair that showed on his face made Finn feel guilty. Although she was rough around the edges, he didn't think Celeste would let anything happen to the boy. She'd been taking care of him too, in her own way.

"Don't worry, they're going to stay in a couple of tents that are close to yours." Lucian nodded to Finn and Liam as he scooped Henry into his own arms. Henry looked so small and weak compared to Lucian's bulk.

"Really?" Henry asked, a shred of hope daring to peek through his mask of sadness. His eyes darted to Finn and Liam, a small smile, shy around the edges, broke across his face.

"That's where a lot of new recruits stay. We keep them between our wounded and the normal camp while they're in training." Lucian cradled Henry, giving Celeste a nod good-bye. Henry mustered up enough strength to wave at Finn and Liam as Lucian carried him away. Finn waved back.

They watched Lucian walk away. Liam turned back to Celeste. "Where's our brother?"

"On other side of camp. There's a small clearing where Declan and I meet when one of us returns." She indicated for them to follow her. People stared at them as they moved through the crowd. "Just act like you belong here. They're not going to question it." She sent a pointed look at Liam; his nervous fidgeting was getting a little out of hand.

"Sorry. I'm not good at lying. Or being stealthy. Or hiding."

"Really? I never would have guessed." Celeste rolled her eyes. No one questioned them though some looked like they wanted to. Celeste's authority and unwelcoming aura was enough to deter them.

"Was that a joke? Finn, I think she likes us." Liam seemed pleased by the small upturning of her lips.

"You have to be serious when you're out there. If you're not, well, the worst could happen." Her tone turned somber.

"Except die," Finn interjected.

"There are fates in this world worse than death. Before the ruination, things seemed easier." Celeste halted and her arm shot in front of them. "Wait a minute."

Two men came up to her, looking the boys over. They both had scars along their faces and down their arms. Celeste held her chin higher. She didn't say anything. They stared at each other for a couple of seconds and then they backed down, despite seeming reluctant to do so.

"You're lucky Arran trusts you," one sneered as they walked past them.

"What was that?" Liam's eyes followed them as they disappeared through the crowd.

"They think because they're big, they can do whatever they want," Celeste replied. They were coming to the other side of camp now. There were less people around and she ushered them into the forest.

"But they won't actually challenge you?" Finn didn't blame them. He wouldn't want to be her opponent, not after seeing her take down the officers. She had earned the confidence that she wore wrapped around her like armor.

"I do a lot of the training here when I don't have scouting duties. We recruited those guys a little while back and they thought bigger meant better. They were insulted when I told them they'd better both fight me at once." She shrugged.

"I would be too. Two against one isn't a fair fight," said Liam with a shake of his head. He seemed to realize how that could sound a second too late. "Not that you're not threatening. I would never want to be pitted against you. I'd rather fight anyone else. Not that I want to fight. I'd lose to everyone."

Finn elbowed Liam, thankful when Liam clamped his mouth shut. Celeste didn't seem offended but Liam would have found a way to insult her if he'd continued on.

"That's how they've survived—by being big. They've never had to be anything else." She pulled a thick layer of brush hanging down from a tree, letting each one of them go through it. "As you can see, size has never been on my side. I learned from my father to be smart first. Then use my size to my advantage and be quick."

Behind the vines, a small clearing opened up. In the middle of that clearing sat Declan with his hazel eyes turned toward the sky. His features were harsher than either of his brothers with an angular jaw and the same straight nose. His lips were fuller and turned up naturally as if he had a small smile on his face. His dark brown hair had also gotten longer. It was tied neatly in a small ponytail at the nape of his neck.

"You're running a little late," he said but shock overtook his features as he noticed Liam and Finn. He stood. "What are you doing here?"

"Declan. I can't believe it. I mean, I know we were trying to find you, but I didn't think it would happen. He's alive, Finn. No offense, Celeste. It's not like I didn't believe you when you said you knew him… I just didn't think this was going to happen-"

"Lee, you're rambling." Finn was quick to cut him off.

"Right, sorry." Liam looked at his feet. Declan laughed, pushing himself off the ground and grabbing Liam in for a hug.

"What about mom and dad? Grandma?" He turned to Finn who shook his head. Celeste leaned against one of the trees, giving them some space.

"We were raided." Finn's throat tightened at the reminder of his family. His fists clenching at the horror of it all.

Declan remained quiet. Of course he did. He really hadn't considered how his actions would effect anyone else. He had just done what he wanted.

"You're not going to say anything?" Finn asked, anger rolling off him.

"I'm going to figure something out. I promise." Declan moved to place his hand on Finn's shoulder, but he jerked back.

"That's it? This entire thing is your fault. If you didn't leave, then the raid would never have happened." He knew he should stop, but once he started, the words tumbled out. Everything he had wanted to say could no longer be bottled up. "You've had your choice of everything, and we end up stuck in your messes. You got to choose what job you wanted because you tested high enough. You got to choose to leave because you decided to fight for the rebellion. After you left, I couldn't work in any government jobs because they thought our family were spies. I couldn't choose to leave or stay in Essex. I was forced out. Every choice you've made has taken one from me." All the stress Finn had felt since Declan had left began to bubble up to the surface. He reached into his pocket and felt the power of the knife surge, searing hot and uncontainable.

"Finn you need to calm down." Liam's warning fell on deaf ears. Finn's focus was on Declan and Declan alone. Celeste had a hand placed on the hilt of her sword, ready to stop Finn if needed.

"Finn, I don't want to fight you," Declan started but Finn was already vaulting forward to tackle him. They hit the ground with a hard thud. Finn punched him, a hard hit to the cheek that had Declan's vision swimming. It wasn't enough. It didn't stop the hurt of betrayal that had sunk into Finn's skin. Finn attacked, and Declan blocked the best he could. Celeste stood back, itching to step in but giving Declan time to stop it himself first.

"You left us and you don't even care how it affected us," Finn said gripping his shirt and jerking him up, just to slam him back down again.

"Of course I care. I didn't want to hurt any of you. I didn't think it would come to this." Declan made no moves to fight back. Finn raised his hand again.

"Alright. I've had enough." Celeste pushed Finn with more strength than he thought she had. He stood and faced her, but she danced away from every punch he threw. She grabbed Finn by the arm, twisting it and bringing him to his knees. He fought against the hold but she was unrelenting. He took deep breaths, steadying himself. "Just because you don't want to hurt him doesn't mean you should let him hurt you."

"He's right. It's my fault," Declan said, sorrow seeping out of him as he sat up, regarding Finn with compassion that felt like pity.

"That doesn't mean you should just let him attack you." She sent Declan a scathing glare even as he tried to shush her.

"You're right, Finn, and I'm sorry. I didn't think everything through." Declan kneeled beside him. "I can't change what I already did but we can try and save them."

Finn nodded, feeling some of the rage ebb away now that he'd hit his brother. He'd been waiting for so long to confront Declan over how he'd ruined their life and part of him felt deflated that Declan had admitted Finn was right with such ease.

"We need to take them to Arran. He's already going to be pissed that I brought them to you first," Celeste said.

"It's going to be hard to convince him they're not working for Leander." Declan groaned running a hand over his face.

"He won't just take your word for it?" Liam questioned.

"He likes to be sure of the people we let in. It took me three months to earn his trust before I left Essex." Declan put a hand around Celeste's waist. "He'll hate that Celeste let you in without vetting you."

"But Neal helped us escape. That has to count for something, right?" Liam interjected.

"We haven't heard anything from Neal for a couple of days. He usually dispatches a message by hawk when he's sending people through even when we're expecting them." Declan took quick notice of Liam's rising anxiety and met it with a comforting hand.

"Do you still have the pendant?" Celeste asked. Finn nodded, pulling it out. "I don't know if it'll help, but it's worth a try."

"Is he really called Arran the undead?" Liam asked. Celeste nodded. "Why?"

"Arran's soul has been around a long time. He saw the ruination happen. He lost his body when it was burned in the war that broke out between the people and the military. So he's been taking control of other people's bodies, ones who should have died. It's a painful process. He not only has to deal with whatever wounds or illness that comes with the body but also the excruciating torment that comes with inhabiting a body that's not meant for him," Declan explained as he led them back through the camp. He met the rebellion's suspicious eyes with a charming smile.

"It hurts to be in a body?" Finn questioned.

"Yeah. It's like his soul is being pulled in every direction, as if it could just snap apart at any given second." Declan squared his shoulders. "It's one of the reasons why he's so difficult sometimes.

"Great. Let's go meet the ghost with an attitude problem," Liam all but groaned.

· CHAPTER SIXTEEN ·

Thea

Aiden's hands were gripping hers tightly; blood stained their interlocked fingers, sticky and warm and unforgiving. She tried to pull her hands away but he wouldn't let go. She struggled in her seat—the brown, wooden chair that was a little too hard to be comfortable.

They were in the restaurant, sitting next to the door that was being propped open with an ugly, ceramic toad. It's eyes bulged out of its head like it was being squeezed. She was thankful to be by the door because a breeze lightly brushed against her sweating legs, ruffling the fabric of clothes.

"Aiden?" Thea asked, panicked and glancing around. Nobody was paying any attention to them.

"You did this," he told her, voice filled with spite where once was compassion.

"Aiden, you're bleeding. We need help. Someone call the police. Please, please, help us," Thea called twisting in her seat. His hands jerked her back, nails settling into her skin around the knuckles. No one looked their way. Her heart constricted in fear.

"You can still save me," he said. "There's still a chance." The blood was on his face now, oozing out of his mouth and dripping down his chin.

"What can I do? Please, tell me what to do," Thea begged. He

stood abruptly and she saw the red against his shirt. "Aiden," she called as he turned around and began walking outside. More frantically, she added, "Aiden, don't leave me alone again." But he didn't stop.

*

I will love you
Through every fight
Through destruction and despair
Because you are my sunshine

*

The dream changed. She walked down a hallway. She was home, but it wasn't the same. It was broken. Windows cracked, pictures laying on the floor, holes in the walls. She knew her children were here, somewhere in the dying, rotting house because she could hear them. They were reciting some kind of poem.

*

For without the sun
There would be no peace
There would be no cure
There would be no satisfaction
There would be no life
The sun shines for us all.

*

"William?" Thea called as she stepped over glass, aware of her bare feet. She was still wearing the same clothes, with blood lingering in vivid stains and crusted under her nails. Her dark, curly hair was still tucked into a bun, the only way to keep it manageable in the sweltering heat. "Eleanor? Bennett? Zoey? Anyone? Answer me."

*

I will love you
When you are hungry
When you are too thin and weak
Because you are my sunshine.

*

She got no answers as the words whispered inside her head, seeping into her skin. She followed her feeling of dread, knowing that she couldn't go back. She tried to open the door to William and Bennett's room but it wouldn't budge. She slammed her hands against it. Why weren't they letting her inside? Why?

*

For without the sun
There would be no peace
There would be no cure
There would be no satisfaction
There would be no life
The sun shines for us all.

*

"William, open this door right now," she demanded, trying to force the authority in her voice to overpower the fear.

"We can't let you in mom," William whispered.

"Are you going to bring him back?" Bennett asked. "We can let you in if you bring him home."

"Who? Who am I bringing home?" Thea screamed, pounding against the door. She didn't get a reply but their voices no longer joined the chant. She knew they weren't there anymore.

*

I will love you
When you are ill
When you're coughing and wheezing
Because you are my sunshine

*

She set her sights on Eleanor and Zoey's room. There was still a sign on the door, a pink and purple flower that insisted you knock before entering. She sighed, leaning her head against the frame and did just that as she listened to the hollow sound reverberating throughout the hallway.

*

For without the sun
There would be no peace
There would be no cure
There would be no satisfaction
There would be no life
The sun shines for us all.

*

"Mom, is that you?" Eleanor asked.

"Yes, I'm right here. Are you okay?" Thea responded with the same urgency.

"Mommy? Are you going to bring Daddy back? I miss him." Zoey said.

"Oh baby, I'm going to try. Now please tell me you're okay. Let me inside." Thea tried to get into the room, but no matter how hard she pulled against the door it wouldn't open.

*

I will love you
After you are gone

When the world has taken your soul
Because you are my sunshine

*

"We have to go now. We're not supposed to talk to you anymore," Eleanor said.

"No, not you too. Zoey? Open the door, please." Once again she got no answer, and she was swallowed in silence. She slid to her knees, the uneven wood of the floor pressing into her skin as she sobbed. Her shoulders shook with the weight of her grief. She pulled at her hair until she could almost hear it tearing from her skull as she tried to finish the chant herself.

*

For without the sun
There would be no peace
There would be no cure
There would be no satisfaction
There would be no life
The sun shines for us all.

*

It wasn't the pain that made her stop repeating it, the shuffling sounds hidden in the darkness, or the impatient clicking that seemed urgent but was dulled by the headache she had developed. It was a scream, shrill and loud.

When the silence returned, she got to her feet. Whose pain was that? Who could feel so much, so intensely? She moved forward, terrified and curious, but could not stop herself. There was only one place for her to go. Her room. The door to it was slightly ajar, and she pushed it all the way open, careful in her actions, not wanting to draw the attention of whoever was inside. Thea stared into the room, as fire danced around it. In the middle of the room she stood, back turned, hair wild, clothes shredded, nearly falling off her body.

"Who are you?" Thea asked, standing her ground despite her trembling legs. The woman turned. She held the tablet. The woman's hand was held over it as blood dripped from between her clenched fingers.

"This is what you must do," her voice was low, deep. Not Thea's own. "You must solve this riddle to save him. You must be the host." The woman's head snapped up, and a scream caught in Thea's throat. Where her eyes should have been were two holes and crimson seeped down her face from the sockets. She scrambled back in horror,

falling,
        falling,
                falling,

down the hallway, past the now open doors where her children stood, eyeless and chanting,

*

You are the balance
You are the way
You are the balance
That brings light to the day

*

She fell back into the restaurant where Aiden no longer was and farther still. She felt like a statue, watching the world pass her by. Right when she was sure she was going to hit the ground, it all stopped.

*

Thea woke by knocking her head against the nightstand as she plummeted to the floor. Her heart was still racing. It was only a dream, only a dream, she repeated to herself, willing the fog of sleep to recede.

Thea picked herself up from the floor, sneaking down the hallway to check on William and Ben. They were each curled up in their beds, on opposite sides of the room. Will's blue comforter was halfway off the mattress, tangled around his legs. His side of the room matched him; messy, clothes piled on the floor, books in stacks underneath his bed, and papers scattered across his desk. She had given up on asking him to clean his mess because every time she did he replied with, "It's an organized mess, mom. I wouldn't be able to find anything if it wasn't like this."

Ben, although younger, was far neater. He had inherited Thea's obsession with making sure everything had its place. He'd gotten so exasperated with William and his mess that he had marched into the kitchen, snatched the duct tape from the cabinet, and continued to create a line down the center of the bedroom. "Keep your stuff on your side," he'd said. William had looked to her and Aiden for backup but they were too amused by the situation to do anything. They had laughed about it for weeks.

Thea creeped into the room, pulled the red blanket off of Ben's face and kissed his forehead. She then moved to Will's side, avoiding piles of things and did the same to him. Her breath was coming a little easier. She made her way back to the hallway, and toward the pink and purple flower. She ignored the command written on it and went straight inside.

The room was illuminated by Zoey's ladybug nightlight. Zoey's side of the room had a jungle theme. Her bedspread, her pillow cases, and everything was trees and cute animals. Clutched in her hands was Hercules, a small, stuffed puppy with white spots.

Thea kissed each one of the girls and slipped back outside into the hallway. She stared at the pictures on the wall. She grasped the one in the center of a cluster. It was of her and Aiden, the day of their wedding. She traced his face with the pad of her thumb. His smile was wide and his eyes crinkled with joy pouring out in the way he held himself. Thea's grin and posture was a little more reserved, more shy, but pleased nonetheless. She had been so stressed out before the wedding. She had been worried about the seating placement. Two of her great aunt's couldn't sit next to each other because it always ended up in a yelling match over how one of them had stolen another's boyfriend some fifty years before. Aidan's grandmother couldn't sit next to his grandfather because they were divorced. The rumor had been that he had cheated on her but it was never said out loud.

The moment Thea had walked down the aisle and looked at Aidan, she didn't care anymore. He was hers. She didn't care about her aunts or his grandparents or the fact that her heels were a size too small. All she cared about was him. That feeling had progressed into the reception, where Aidan had convinced her that she should just go barefoot by taking off his own shoes and socks and flinging them across the room. It had been far from perfect but it was hers.

She sighed and placed the picture back on the wall, glancing at the other ones. William at two, covered in blue paint that was meant for the living room. Eleanor at six, who had fallen asleep at the movie theater, and was being carried out by Aidan. Bennett at seven, who stood proudly in front of the Mothman statue in West Virginia. He had been hoping that the rumors were true and that Mothman would touch his shoulder but it hadn't happened. There was one of Zoey, one year old and standing up for the very first time, head turned and mouth open to reveal pink gums and a small scattering of teeth.

Thea stood back, wide awake, and itching to get to the office. A frequent thing for her through the years. She had an idea, a desperate one, and the inspiration of it overwhelmed her, like waves in the ocean dragging her under. The nagging feeling was impossible to ignore. It didn't matter what time of day or night it happened, she would drop whatever she was doing and get to work. There were many nights when Aiden woke up, glanced at her frantic motions as she got dressed and jumped out of the bed to go with her.

"Your muse is at it again, I see," he would say. When the children were born, Aiden would wake up with her, but stay home with a cup of coffee, asking that she call him if she needed to or just to let him know what her "crazy genius" had figured out.

She walked to her room changing from her sleeping shorts and into a pair of jeans. She thought about waking Liv up and letting her know what was going on but settled for a bright green post-it on the black fridge that said, *Went to office with idea. Be back ASAP.*

She grabbed the keys and almost forgot to turn off the alarm before heading out to the garage. She jumped in her jeep, slamming the door.

When she got to her office, she grabbed the tablet and stared down at it, running her hand down the front and feeling the rigid groves of a language long forgotten. Someone had spent time on this, had labored over it, had created it for the world to see. It was part of a person that had been left behind. That's what she loved about her job and about the things she found. They were an extension of a person, a lifestyle, a culture. The tablet was a way to remember and to understand those people, those cultures.

She placed it on the desk and opened one of the drawers, taking out a small knife that she kept around just in case. She opened her hand, palm up, and just stared. Was this really what it had come to? This strange madness that her dream and the blood was a clue from the universe? She placed the knife against her wrist and squeezed her eyes shut. Taking a deep breath, she pushed in and felt the pain as the tip of the knife slid inside her skin. She dragged it across. Pain throbbed at the open wound and she held it over the artifact, watching as the blood dripped down, falling into the crevices of the words and settling there. She waited. Nothing happened. She dropped to the floor in defeat wondering why she had thought that that would work. She screamed and threw the knife. It clattered against the floor.

"Hush child, all was not for nothing," the voice spoke in her head, as if she'd had the thought herself.

"What?" Thea asked, bewildered, eyes darting around the room. What had just happened? Had she reached the end of her rope? Was she going crazy?

"You can save him, but you must release me, release us."

"Who are you?" Thea asked, still looking for someone in the small room.

"I am half of the entity you call war. We were sealed away to bring balance to the world, but that balance has shifted with your existence."

"If this is some kind of joke, I'm calling the police." Thea forced herself up from the floor.

"Death was not supposed to save you when you were a child. You were meant to die with your parents and it has created an imbalance, one that cannot yet be seen."

"I just want my husband back. Tell Death to give him back," Thea replied.

"I know what you want. I know that it was not his time. To get to Death, you must release us and the other horsemen."

"Won't that mess everything up? Won't I just do more damage?" Thea asked.

"Only if you do not seal us away. You must be host to half of us, the side that brings good, and the other half must be sealed away."

"Aren't the four horsemen supposed to be a sign of the apocalypse?" Thea tried to keep her wits about her.

"We are balance. Half is an angel. Good. Half is one of the fallen. Bad. Together we create harmony. That was thrown off by Death not following the design. We must follow the design. You must be the host for good so we can right the wrongs that have been done since your existence."

"How do I know that this is real? How do I know I'm not crazy? What if you're lying?" Thea questioned.

"What would you do to get your husband back?"

"…Anything. I would do anything," Thea admitted.

"Then what other choice do you have?"

She didn't answer, but for the first time she thought that maybe she should give in. If she was crazy then so be it. She would rather live in an imaginary world where her husband was than in a reality that brought only heartache.

"Good. There are three things you must do to break the seal. They are not easy things. They are things only someone with conviction can do, things only someone who is brave can do. Do you understand."

Thea nodded.

"The first thing you must do is sacrifice that which is in the bible that frees us."

"That frees you?" Thea asked herself, going over in her head what she knew of the bible. What started breaking the seals? "A lamb? You want me to sacrifice a lamb?"

· CHAPTER SEVENTEEN ·

Finn

Leander doesn't suspect a thing. He has no idea that the rebellion has infiltrators in his precious town. It took years of careful planning, but my wife and I were able to enter Essex and get jobs. Very few outside people are allowed the luxury of being let into the town.

FROM THE FIRST PAGE OF FINN'S
GRANDFATHER'S JOURNAL

Arran Granville stood in one of the only wooden structures inside the rebellion camp. It had one room big enough for a large group of people to gather in. There was no floor, just dirt, making the place seem unfinished and messy. Arran was in the middle of the room, back rigid and deep, wet breaths escaping him. Clear, emerald eyes watched as the group walked in, studying their every move. Arran looked just like Lucian. There were small differences and where Lucian's eyes held warmth, Arran's were cold, distant.

"I heard you were back. Why didn't you come straight to me, Celeste?" His eyes never left Finn's as he spoke, appraising him. Finn felt, not for the first time, like prey. Arran held himself like he was the most important person in the room, as if all eyes should be drawn to him. As the leader of the rebellion, some of that arrogance was deserved but the man had an inflated ego.

"I wanted to see if their story was true. They said they were Declan's brothers. If they were lying, it would have been an easy call." Her voice was as calm as ever but her shoulders were hunched close to her ears. While Celeste had never looked relaxed per say, she'd also never seemed anything but calm, unbothered. There was doubt in the way she met Arran's gaze.

"And since they're here, I'm assuming that it was true." Arran walked closer. His right side seemed to follow the rest of him, lagging behind. Finn zeroed in on it, making note of it, in case he would need to fight his way out of this situation. He doubted Arran would be merciful and just let them leave if he deemed them unfit for the rebellion.

"It was. Is." Declan was standing as close to Celeste as possible without touching her. His confidence never wavered, as if the only possible outcome to this situation was that Finn and Liam be allowed to join.

"We haven't had any time to watch them, you know. You can't just bring outsiders into the camp without being aware of their full intentions." Arran stepped into Celeste's space, looking down at her, unblinking. The smell of decay encompassed him. She held her ground, unflinching at his intimidation.

"I know. I know it was wrong but Mac wanted us to get them to the rebellion. I trusted his intentions," Celeste replied. He didn't move for a minute, waiting to see if she would say anything else, but she had nothing more to add. The tension in the air made Finn uncomfortable. He couldn't leave like he would have in any other situation, before the raid. Liam shifted beside him, antsy in the same way Finn was.

"What is so special about them that you would go against me? You've always been one of my most loyal, ever since I found you and your sister." Arran walked around Finn and Liam, looking them over. Celeste's impassive façade broke, a minute scowl on her face. She either didn't like the reminder or was insulted by the implication that she was anything but loyal. Finn wasn't sure which it was.

"Nothing. Like I said, I thought I could make things a little easier on you." Celeste shifted her weight from foot to foot. She knew he called her the most loyal to guilt her. From Arran's peacocking, it was clear most people bowed to his tricks, maybe even her when the fight wasn't worth having. He needed to win. Always.

"You know we can't have someone going against our orders, our rules, without being punished. The system is very fragile. I'd hate to see it disrupted." He grabbed Finn's chin, pulling his face up and to each side. Finn took a deep breath, trying to school his features when all he wanted to do was jerk away from Arran. He had no right to threaten Celeste like that, as if she was a traitor. The surge of protection, although small, still surprised Finn. When had he started seeing Celeste as an ally?

"Maybe there's no reason for that disruption. She's our best fighter. Everyone trusts her. There isn't anyone who could replace her. Like you said, the system is fragile," Declan rationalized as Arran let go of Finn. He put emphasis on everyone. Maybe the rebellion wouldn't stand for Arran hurting Celeste. Losing a fighter like Celeste could cripple the rebellion.

"Maybe I should have the both of you watched, seeing as you've decided that you two know what's best for the rebellion." Arran grabbed Liam like he had just done to Finn but his words were for Celeste and Declan. It seemed Arran didn't care about the repercussions of his actions. The rebellion was, after all, his. Liam was trying to pull away from Arran without anyone noticing. Arran gripped his jaw tighter, too rough. Liam inhaled in pain, trying to control his reaction. Finn couldn't watch anymore.

"We bargained with her," Finn said. His mind was already moving, trying to draw Arran's attention away from his brother and maybe help Celeste along the way. "For information."

"She could have just killed you. We don't bargain unless we're sure of the information." Arran sent him a chilling look but his grasp on Liam had loosened and Liam relaxed enough to take a deep breath.

"The knife Leander's been looking for; someone found it," Finn said remembering the way his grandma reacted to it. The knife could give anyone the power they craved and power was the biggest bargaining chip you could have. It did what was intended and caught Arran's attention enough to release Liam. He appraised Finn once more, face impassive. There was a thin line between bravery and stupidity and Finn wondered if he had crossed it.

"And how do you know this?" Arran asked. Finn could feel everyone staring at him. Liam with panicked confusion. Celeste and Declan with intense interest. Finn kept his eyes locked on Arran. He couldn't flounder, not now.

"My father overheard a couple of strategists talking about it." Finn thought on his feet. The lies spilling from his lips felt natural.

"He's more secretive than you ever were." Arran glanced between Declan and Finn. "We don't have use for secrets here."

He had a lot more negative traits than Declan. Declan, who was often looked at like he was golden, who could smile and charm his way into everyone's good graces like it was as natural as breathing. Finn, on the other hand, had never had any of the charm his brother did. He was rough around the edges; more secretive, more sensitive, more angry. Just more. He always had been.

"What was I supposed to do? You have no reason to trust anything we say, so what other option did we have?" Finn asked, letting some of the desperation seep into his voice. Arran hummed, a hint of curiosity peeking through his neutral façade. It was a truth, not the whole truth, but enough of one.

"Smart too. A dangerous combination." Arran sent him a cold smile. It wasn't enough. He didn't need Arran to trust him, he just needed a chance. There was no going back, there never had been, not since Declan left Essex.

"There were rumors about a knife, one that Leander wanted because of how powerful it is. We only learned about the horseman recently. Leander will probably be combing the whole city looking for it," Finn pushed on. There was a harshness to Arran that Finn didn't trust and Celeste's earlier words of doubt came back to him. He would never let Arran know about the knife. Arran would want it for himself at any cost.

"Then I'm assuming whoever had it escaped the city?" Arran asked, bending forward to be eye level with Finn. The smell of rotten flesh became stronger and Finn fought the urge to take a step back.

"I don't know. " Finn shrugged. Arran stared at him, expression unreadable. Whatever he had been looking for, he didn't find it. "We were more focused on leaving instead of finding out more information." Finn paused and then dug in his pocket. "Neal gave us this and our grandma had one just like it. Lillian Plumber. Do you know her? She asked Neal to help us escape."

"I do know of Lillian, of course. I also know that we haven't received any messages from our infiltrators for two days. There's no one to corroborate your story," Arran mused, but Finn had him. Arran didn't believe him about not knowing more information but that was okay. If he wanted more information, he'd need to keep both Finn and Liam around.

"They're not working for Leander. I'd stake my life on it." Declan stepped up grabbing Arran's attention.

"Well, it looks like you just did. Show them around. I need to think about this." Arran waved a hand, dismissing them. Celeste jerked on the back of Finn's collar and pushed him out of the cabin. She didn't let go once they were outside and all but dragged them over to a group of tents, choosing one that was uninhabited and shoving both Finn and Liam inside.

"What in the hell were you thinking? You can't just lie like that, not to Arran." She ran a hand through her hair. Declan wrapped an arm around her, trying to reassure her. Finn wasn't a good little soldier and that's what she had wanted him to be. It wasn't something he could be. She'd wanted to handle the situation herself. It could have kept Finn out of Arran's direct ire, but it could have also ended up with them being kicked out. Finn wasn't going to take any chances.

"I just wanted to help. Did you have a better idea?" Finn asked. Liam looked between them, biting down on his lip. Finn was frustrated, his hands clenching and unclenching.

"I didn't ask for help, did I?" Celeste snapped. Finn wondered how much of her cold attitude was just talk. She was worried, scared even.

"So, they walk into camp and the first thing they do is lie to the big man?" A girl popped up beside Celeste. Celeste groaned.

"Senna, why are you here?" Senna was smaller than Celeste by a couple of inches and much smaller than Finn. She had a thin, lithe frame. Her hair was the same inky black that Celeste's was but cut short. It messily rested on top of her head, touching the middle of her ear. Her round eyes were a little too big for her face but held an awkward charm to them. Her features lacked the harsh edges of Celeste's.

"I was helping in quarantine when a little boy came in and began talking about how you had helped him and was going to save his mother." She shrugged, then added, "He was also talking about two boys that saved him. So are you the hero or the complainer?" Finn and Liam looked at each other.

"That's how he described us? The hero and the complainer? Really?" Liam threw his hands up. Senna winked at Finn. She had broken the tension that was radiating from Celeste, who was now more focused on waving Senna away than fighting with Finn.

"I guess that answers the question." Senna had a sly smile as she ignored Celeste.

"I'm Finn. This is Liam." Finn gestured. Celeste ran a hand through her hair, giving up on trying to make Senna leave.

"Everyone's talking about you, you know? Getting out of the city is tricky business." Senna spoke fast, waving her arms and seeming to have no sense of personal space. Finn had to pay close attention to understand what she was saying. "How did you do it?"

"It's already getting around?" Celeste asked. When Senna nodded, she let out a curse. "You guys stay here for a minute. We need to figure out what's going around and try to control it."

Celeste grabbed Declan and pulled him away. Declan looked troubled but not surprised. Senna hadn't taken her attention away from Finn, waiting for him to answer her question.

"It just took some careful planning and a lot of luck," Finn said. "Have you always been part of the rebellion?"

"Technically no, but I don't remember the time before being here. I was really young when Celeste got us out. I don't have many memories of before. She wasn't that old either." Senna shrugged. "I think she was eight. She doesn't talk about it."

"You're a lot more talkative than Celeste is." Finn stumbled around his words, trying not to offend the girl. She didn't look at him like an outsider, something he wasn't used to, not since Declan left Essex. She'd talked to him without any judgement in her words. He liked that. She laughed, open and loud, her large eyes closing with the full burst of it.

"You're a lot less charming than your brother is," she retorted but was far too pleased to hide it.

"You're not wrong," Finn replied in amusement, glad she wasn't offended. She was rough around the edges too, lacking elegance and tact in a way that felt familiar to him.

"I'm never wrong, Hero," Senna mock saluted him. He cringed at the nickname but didn't correct it. He doubted it would stop her. If not even Celeste could force her into something, Finn doubted that he, a stranger, could. Instead, he turned his curiosity to her. She was more open than anyone else he'd met here. She could give him answers.

"Can I ask you something?" Finn questioned. Senna nodded. "Arran and Lucian; are they related?"

"Oh, that." Her face dropped. "Arran has taken over a couple of bodies since I've been here. The ones that have been wounded like that often expire quicker and become almost impossible to control after a while. It used to belong to Carson, Lucian's twin. They had been Celeste's partners since they all started training. We were all really close, like family."

Finn swallowed thickly, his mind already beginning to piece together how Carson's story came to an end.

"Arran's last body was an infiltrator who had an unfortunate infection that should have killed him. Arran doesn't like weakness, especially in his spies, so he took over the body. He had it for a few months before the infection spread too far and rendered the whole body useless. Carson got hurt pretty bad around that time. He was trying to save a group of sick kids, and an officer got him on his right side. Like I said before, Arran doesn't accept weakness." Her jaw clenched. It seemed anytime she spoke Arran's name, it was spewed out of her mouth in disgust. She had to stare at a man she once considered family every day, and realize it wasn't him anymore. The person she had known, had loved, was physically there but mentally gone.

"Maybe a day will come when we won't have to worry about things like that," Finn said, not knowing what to say but feeling like he should offer some kind of comfort.

"Maybe," she replied. "I'll see you around, Hero."

She waved as she left the tent. Liam sat down on a pile of blankets, rummaging through his pack.

"We're in over our heads," Liam said grabbing out a small block of wood and one of his knives, starting to carve it. Liam was angry with him.

"We can handle this. We made it here. That's what matters," Finn replied. He sat next to Liam. Close but not touching.

"And the knife? You didn't tell them you had it," said Liam.

"I didn't trust Arran. Do you?" Finn asked. Liam shook his head.

"Of course not." He stilled his hands. "You didn't tell Declan either."

There it was. Liam wanted him to trust Declan, wanted everything to be back to normal as much as it could be. Finn couldn't do that yet, couldn't open himself up like that, reveal all his cards, if it meant he would be betrayed again.

"What if Declan told him? Sure, he's our brother, but he left us for them first." Finn wanted Liam to understand. He wanted someone to look at him, just once, and understand him, to read him like a book.

"He put his life on the line for us." Liam met his eyes. Less angry then.

"If Arran gets it, there's no way to save our parents. He wouldn't care. I just want to make sure we can get them out of the city." Finn slumped down. "Please don't say anything yet, Lee. I'll tell Declan soon. I promise."

"Do you want to keep it? You know what it does to you." Liam began working again but he was getting less short. Finn knew he would give in. The reluctance was wearing down.

"Imagine what it would do to Arran. I just want it to make sure we get our family back. I don't care who gets it after that." Finn wasn't a hero, no matter what anyone said. He didn't want to be a hero. He just wanted to live his life, ordinary and maybe a little boring. Boring was always more appealing than fury.

"I'll keep my mouth shut for now," Liam agreed, still reluctant, still upset but Finn knew he wouldn't say anything. They sat in silence until Celeste and Declan returned. They both looked uneasy.

"What's going on?" Finn pulled his legs closer to him as Celeste sighed.

"The whole camp already knows about you two. They don't trust you. We'll have to convince them that you're not any trouble and get them used to seeing you around camp." Declan rubbed Celeste's arm.

"We'll need to start training you soon. I don't think Arran will kick you out since he hasn't already, but we can't be sure." Celeste looked deep in thought. Finn didn't believe that. He didn't know much about the rebellion, but there was no world where Arran let them stay if he wanted them gone. He didn't let those thoughts be known though.

"Does that mean you'll teach me how to fight?" Finn asked. "I want to learn."

"I don't," Liam set down the block of wood before Celeste or Declan could say anything. "I can't."

"You have to learn the basics. Everyone needs to know how to defend themselves," Celeste said. Liam, for the first time, met her gaze. Although he often times was agreeable, there were certain things that he refused, that no one could force him into.

"He's really good at woodworking and building things," Finn replied. "Maybe he could stay away from most of the fighting and do that instead?"

Celeste looked him over, a thoughtful expression on her face. "I guess we could convince Arran to let you apprentice with our blacksmith. He's been shorthanded for a while now. If Arran does let you stay."

"He has to. Where else would we go?" Finn asked. "And if he wants to know more about the knife, Lee and I are his only choice right now."

· CHAPTER EIGHTEEN ·

Finn

Subject 0708 seems to be in immense pain the longer he is alive. The bullet wound in his chest has started to rot. It has started to affect his heart. He has limited mobility and seems to be spiraling into insanity.

FROM A FILE RECOVERED FROM AN UNDERGROUND BASE; THE DOCUMENT IS NOT DATED

Two days after first coming to camp, Finn and Liam were summoned to have another meeting with Arran. They once again stood in the small cabin. Liam was shifting his weight, keeping a hand around his pack of things, afraid they were going to be kicked out. Declan was next to him, a comforting hand on his shoulder. Celeste stood behind them leaning against the wall, hands in her pockets. Her shoulders were tense.

Arran stared at each one of them but did not speak. Liam was unable to be still, despite Declan's attempt to calm him. The nerves were eating him up from the inside. He breathed through his mouth, hoping that would keep the stench of rot from seeming as strong.

"This one seems guilty," said Arran. Liam kept his eyes trained on the ground. Finn was exhausted, they'd been being questioned for what felt like hours. Retelling their journey from Essex to the rebellion camp over and over again. Liam, the whole time couldn't meet anyone's gaze.

"That's just his personality," Finn replied, never looking away from Arran, who met his obvious contempt with indifference.

"Let's go over your story again." Arran ignored him. Finn had decided he disliked Arran from the first moment they met and this was only cementing that fact. Not for the first time, Finn found himself wishing that death was a viable option.

"For fuck's sake," Finn rolled his eyes.

"I don't want to hear from you anymore." Arran forced Liam to look up, hand cupped around his chin. "Let's hear it, boy."

Liam glanced at Finn who tucked his shaking hands behind his back. "We were raided?"

"Are you asking me?" Arran hadn't let go of him. Declan's hand was still on Liam's shoulder. He was biting back his own annoyance at his leader. Finn and Declan both knew Liam hated being touched by strangers.

"No. No, we were raided. That's a fact, not a question. It was in the middle of the night, after our father overheard strategists say there would be a raid, and Finn woke me and our parents up because he knew there were officers in the house and our dad went to save our grandma—"

"Hurry it up, boy."

"We ran, Neal found us, got us to isolation, which is a disgusting, awful place, and I'm never going back." Arran's face hardened and Liam pressed forward once again. "Neal told the disposers we had boils. And we were taken to the pit by Mac, who was going to let everyone go, us and the untouchables, but we were attacked and he told us to run and then Celeste and Lucian found us and brought us here."

His story was the same as Finns. They'd been over it twenty times in the last hour they'd spent with Arran.

"And?" Arran prompted.

"And what? Do you want more details? You told me to hurry up." Liam floundered, not sure what else he could say.

"I want the truth."

"I gave you the truth."

"Your brother said something about the knife yesterday. How do you know about it?"

"I saw it." Liam knew he had made a mistake but he always had a hard time controlling his words. Finn squeezed his eyes shut, jaw clenched. Liam surged through, "When Mac was attacked, we saw that another untouchable had it but we were told to run and we were afraid of getting caught so that's what we did. Run, I mean."

"And you don't know anything else?" Arran stepped closer and Liam almost gagged at the smell of his decomposing body.

"No. There were a lot of officers though. I can't imagine he got away," Liam said. He drew his pack closer to his body, in part to stop his need to fidget and to provide a barrier between him and the untouchable before him. He tapped his foot on the ground.

"Your stories do match up," said Arran as he let go of Liam and moved away, focusing on Finn once more. "But I still don't believe you."

"How are we supposed to prove to you we're not working with Leander? He raided our house and took our family. We don't want anything to do with him." Finn squeezed his hands together, until pain shot from his knuckles into his arm, trying to gain some levity.

"He could also be using your parents as bargaining tools to force you to do what he wants," Arran snapped.

"Why would he send Liam if that were the case?" Liam made a sound of protest. "He's terrible at this."

"Amusement," Arran replied. Declan reached behind Liam to grab Finn's arm, pressing down hard. "This is what's going to happen. I'm going to let you stay. You'll have an escort with you at all times, and you won't be allowed outside the camps perimeters for now."

Finn wanted to argue, but Declan spoke before he had the chance. "That sounds reasonable. If Leander is, and I don't think he is, but if he is using our parents as bargaining tools, they would have to send him information soon."

"You're not going to be the one watching them." Arran scoffed, like he could read Declan's mind. Finn knew Declan would never suggest something so reckless. He had loyalty to both his family and the rebellion. He wouldn't choose between them if he could help it.

"I didn't think I would be. I'm too close to the situation for that to be a logical choice," Declan replied, smooth, easy, like Arran hadn't suggested Declan was in some way trying to deceive him.

"Lucian and Jonas will be watching over you. Jonas is on the night guard, and you two will join him, as well as begin your training. Celeste will handle that." Arran waved him off.

"I don't want to learn to fight." The words burst from Liam. Even he looked shocked by the outburst but his mouth was set in a stubborn frown. He wouldn't take it back.

"If you can't fight, then what use are you to the camp? Everyone contributes here." Arran shifted closer to Liam. He almost looked surprised.

"He was a carpenter's apprentice and Celeste said your blacksmith could use the help. He's good with his hands," Finn said. "He also knows the town's plans, he's studied them."

Arran eyed Liam, not speaking for a long moment. "You'll spend most of your time creating a map of the city then, in exact detail. Make notes of anything helpful. You'll work with our blacksmith. If he doesn't think you're up for the task, then you will learn to fight and you will serve on the night guard." Liam let out a relieved breath. "You'll still need to learn the basics of fighting. Everyone here does."

Liam nodded. He was thankful that he wouldn't be put on

the night guard, but apprehensive that now he had to design a map of the town.

Arran turned toward Finn. "If you have any objections, I would keep them to yourself." He didn't leave Finn any room to respond before waving them away.

Celeste led them out of the cabin and to the center of camp where food was being distributed. Finn's stomach rumbled at the smell.

"When am I supposed to start helping the blacksmith?" Liam broke the silence.

"Tomorrow, I would guess. Arran will have someone come for you and escort you to where you'll need to be," Declan answered as they waited in line.

"At least Lucian will be watching us," Finn said. Lucian was easy to get along with. Friendly and at ease in every situation Finn had seen him in.

"Lee. He'll be watching Lee. Jonas is part of the night guard, so he'll be with you, Finn," Declan said. Finn felt pensive at the thought that he wouldn't be with Lucian but if he and Liam had to be split up, it was better his brother was with someone they already knew.

"What's Jonas like?" Finn asked. Declan and Celeste shared a look as they shuffled forward.

"Quiet."

"Gruff."

Declan cleared his throat. "We don't really know much about him. He keeps to himself, and he likes working during the night." He shrugged. "When you become of age to train here, you always start out on night guard before transferring to something else. Jonas has always liked it, so he's never left."

They were handed wooden bowls filled with a dark brown stew. People stared at them as they walked by, curious about the boys who escaped Leander, and, although Finn didn't welcome the attention, it was far better than the ones of contempt or pity he received from the villagers of Essex. The more he learned of the rebellion, the more he realized it wasn't so different from his home. There were a lot of moving parts to keep things running. People here weren't quite the savages that Finn had been taught to believe. It had always been understood that the rebels were the people who attacked first, showed no mercy, and would stop at nothing to destroy the general and the towns that he controlled. Arran didn't seem friendly, but he hadn't killed them yet either.

From what Finn could tell, they didn't just send people away here either. Untouchables weren't forced out of the camp. Family members could still visit them whenever they had free time.

There weren't any districts here either. No one was better than the next person. Everyone contributed and everyone got food and shelter. The living situations weren't as nice as in Essex, but nobody was scrambling just to survive either.

They found a place to sit in the far back of the area. The conversations around them continued on. Nobody moved away from them, not like they did in Essex. Most gave Celeste and Declan a nod of acknowledgement, but didn't pay much attention to Finn or Liam. One man, sitting across from them, pulled Declan into a conversation as soon as the group sat down. Finn listened until Senna plopped down by his side, knee brushing against his as she made herself comfortable.

"I see you're still here." She began shoveling food into her mouth.

"There wasn't anywhere else for us to go," Finn answered, eating at a much slower pace.

"I didn't think he'd just kick you out, but you never know." She talked with her mouth full, and Liam stared at her with distaste.

"Has he kicked other people out before?" Finn asked. He'd never met someone quite as tactile as Senna, who didn't seem to notice if she was in someone's personal space.

"Yes, but only if he's sure they've been working with Leander. Or if they've been consistently not doing their job, but that's only happened once." She spilled some of her stew and wiped her hands on her pants. "No one says it but we all know we need the people to defeat the general."

"We're not," Finn said, mind still focused on the first part of her words.

"Not working for Leander or not doing your jobs?" She asked.

"Working for Leander. Why would you even ask that?" Liam said. A few heads turned to look at them, not with open hostility but the mistrust was evident. He dropped his gaze. Senna laughed, and that seemed to help break the tension.

"Senna, please." Celeste groaned. She was always most expressive when talking to Senna, although that came from annoyance more than anything else.

"I was answering their questions. Since when is that a bad thing?" Senna held her hands up in mock surrender but a sly grin remained on her face. Celeste sighed. Still, Senna sat back and opted to change the subject. "I'm guessing you're joining the night guard?"

"I will be, but Lee is going to be making maps and working with the blacksmith," Finn answered. Senna set her empty bowl to the side and leaned forward to get a better look at Liam, fingers tapping on her knees.

"I'm surprised you're not on watch too." She smiled and waited for him to meet her gaze.

"I don't want to fight," he said, quiet, as if she would laugh at that.

"I don't either. I refused to learn, except for a couple of lessons with a bow. I'm still not very good at it," she said with gentle encouragement.

"Really?" Liam asked, tilting his head to assess her. She nodded.

"I don't want to hurt anyone." She shrugged as if it wasn't a big deal, but Finn could see the seriousness of the statement in her eyes. "Better get ready, Hero. Night guard is the worst."

· CHAPTER NINETEEN ·

Thea

Thea hurried around her room, throwing on a purple button-up shirt and a black blazer, matching it with dark wash jeans. She needed to look semi-presentable to convince her aunt that she was going to a meeting. She felt like a teenager lying and sneaking around. She picked up her boots, the black ones with the golden heart-shaped clasp, but realized they were a bad choice as she sat down on the bed. She dropped them and let the stress wash over her. Was she making the right choice? Was this really what she needed to do?

She stood up, grabbed her sneakers instead, and slipped them on before walking out of the room. There was no going back. She slipped down the hallway, past her kids' room, and down the stairs into the open foyer, the large glass windows allowing the sun to brighten up the room. Coffee, Thea resolved, was just what she needed. She made her way into the kitchen, where Liv was sitting at the island with a crossword puzzle.

"Thea, I'm glad you're up. I need to speak with you about something," Liv said, placing the crossword down, still lying open. Thea didn't look at her as she made her way to the still full coffee pot. She didn't see then how tired Liv looked with dark circles underneath her eyes and her normally tidy hair thrown back in an unkempt bun.

"Sorry. Can't. I have a meeting I need to get to," Thea replied, striding out of the room, trying to get out of the house before she changed her mind.

"Thea, please, we need to talk," Liv said in exasperation, following her to the door.

"I don't have time right now. This meeting is very important," Thea replied, grabbing her black jacket from the coat hanger.

"Don't have time for family? Are you listening to yourself?" Liv asked, right behind her. Thea stopped in the doorway halfway onto the steps with her head down.

"You're right. I'm sorry. I'm just nervous, I guess. I want to get the day over with." Thea turned around. "It can wait if it needs to. Let's sit at the table."

They walked back through the house, Liv with her head raised but shoulders slumped low enough to concern Thea. Her aunt was a proud woman who almost never asked for help. She took on burden upon burden without complaint. After Thea's parents had died, she'd taken Thea in, caring for the young girl while in her own state of grief. After Aiden had passed, she did it all over again. She was also caring for a husband who had Alzheimer's and grew confused and agitated at the drop of a hat. Thea didn't know how her aunt was able to handle so much. How could she keep going when her life seemed to be falling apart at the seams?

They sat at the table, and Thea waited while her aunt gathered her bearings. She wondered what was so important it couldn't wait until she came home. She knew she hadn't been very helpful and that her all-encompassing need to focus on her work didn't look good. There was a reason she did it though. Her husband needed her. Her kids needed him.

"Teddy's getting worse. I don't think he's going to be around much longer. I wanted to tell you, give you some kind of warning." Thea reached out and grasped Liv's hand. Tears sprang to her eyes. She knew he was sick, but she hadn't realized it was this bad. Guilt washed over her. How many signs of distress had she missed? She hadn't spoken to her uncle in a long time. The last time she had gone to see him was right before she and Aiden had left.

Uncle Teddy had been her saving grace more than once. Liv was oftentimes strict with her rules when Thea was growing up. One year Thea had snuck into their kitchen and opened the candy drawer, which held all of her prizes from Halloween. She ate the entire drawer without thinking of the consequences. When she was finished her hands and face felt sticky, but she knew she had to get rid of the evidence.

She pushed the candy drawer closed with as little pressure as possible, to keep it from making a loud creak. Then she washed her hands and face, scrubbing until her skin felt raw. She crept into her room with all the candy wrappers and stashed them under her bed, as close to the wall as possible.

The next morning, she was woken up by Liv's yelling. Thea's stomach dropped as she listened to the words spewing out of her aunt's mouth as she made her way down the steps. When she entered the kitchen, Liv's nostrils were flared, her curling hair wild. The first thing she did was motion to the candy drawer where little, chocolate handprints exposed her crime.

"I can't believe you ate it all. Every. Single. Piece. Every one," Liv said, eyes harsh with anger.

"Olivia, dear, calm down. She's only seven," Uncle Teddy spoke, brown brows creased in concern.

"Don't tell me to calm down, Theodore," Liv snapped back. "Thea Marie you have some explaining to do."

"I'm sorry. I'm so sorry. I won't do it again," Thea choked out, guilt and fear quaking in her voice.

"You're right; you'll never do it again. There will never be candy in this house after today. That means none from the store and none from trick or treating." Liv slammed her hands onto the counter in a fit of rage.

"But Aunt Liv—"

"Olivia is that really—"

"Yes, it really is necessary. She did something wrong," she stated first to Teddy and then to Thea. "You need to be punished."

"Please don't do this. I promise, I pinky swear, it'll never happen again," Thea pleaded wringing her pink nightgown in her hands.

"And I'll make sure it doesn't. Now go to your room." Liv pointed a hand in the general direction of the stairs and turned her back toward Thea. Thea looked at her uncle, guilt pooling in her gut. He gave her a reassuring nod, and she backed out of the room. Instead of climbing the steps, she stayed behind the wall.

"She's only a child, Olivia," Teddy said after a moment of silence, and Thea peaked her head around the doorframe. Liv stood at the sink frantically scrubbing at the dishes.

"But she did something wrong. She needs to be punished," Liv argued.

"Yes, I understand that, but she doesn't need to be punished for the rest of her life. You can't take away a holiday from her when everyone else on the block celebrates it." Teddy gripped Liv's hands to stop her from rubbing the plate into oblivion.

"I know. I'm just so angry. Why would she do that when she knows she shouldn't?" Liv turned to face him, still mad but simmering down.

"She's a child. Her job is to be selfish. It's ours to teach her not to be and to teach her about the consequences of her actions." Teddy wrapped his arms around his wife, setting his chin against the top of her head.

"I was never meant to have kids, Teddy. I don't have a nurturing bone in my body. You're more motherly than I am." Liv let him hold her, comfort her.

"You're doing fine. No one expects you to just magically understand how to take care of a child. You're trying, that's what counts," Teddy replied.

"Is that enough?" Liv asked on a sigh.

"I think so." Teddy grinned at her and turned his head

toward the kitchen door where Thea was still spying. When she realized she had been caught, she bolted up the stairs and into her room, tripping over the steps.

Later that night, Teddy had come into her room explaining that Thea was grounded for two weeks. No candy, no radio, no nothing. She would be helping out around the house more, and she could have access to the library. That day would lead to her spending hours in the library where she had first picked up a book about Ancient Egypt, their customs and cultures. It was that book that first piqued her interest in archeology. Now, Thea was an archeologist who had followed her dreams but was still struggling.

"What do we do?" Thea asked, hands still grasping Liv's, trying to feign strength.

"We continue living. We give him our love, we help, and we keep moving forward. That's what Teddy told me when your mother passed away," Liv, with tears in her eyes and a waiver in her voice, replied. She was still trying to hold everything together.

"Do you want me to stay today? I don't have to go," Thea said thinking maybe this was a sign. Maybe going to the farm was a bad idea. Maybe she should just accept the hand that fate had given her.

"No. You need to go if it's important," Liv replied.

"Are you sure?" Thea questioned.

"We can all take a trip to go see him tomorrow. How does that sound?" Liv suggested, standing up from the table, grabbing Thea by the elbow, and guiding her back toward the door. Thea chewed her lip as her aunt patted her shoulder. She had been so absorbed with herself that she hadn't even paid her uncle a visit since she'd come back. Tomorrow, she promised herself, tomorrow she really would go to see him with Aunt Liv and the kids.

"I'll be back later tonight. I'm not sure what time. Go ahead and have dinner without me." Thea took both of Liv's hands in hers and squeezed for a moment longer.

Liv sent her a tired smile and nodded. There were unspoken words behind her eyes but Thea couldn't read them. She'd never been any good at reading people. She'd found herself in more awkward situations than she could count because she'd mistaken flirting for just friendliness or anger for quiet. Aiden was better at understanding people. His eyes would flicker over their movements and emotions like he was reading a book that was laid open.

Thea released Liv's hands and strode to her jeep with false purpose.

She pulled out of the driveway, her foot like lead due to the nerves. The farm was an hour away. She could probably have gotten a lamb closer if she'd really wanted to but the thought of someone she knew seeing her was too frightening. She was nervous. Instead of butterflies fluttering, it felt more like there were spiders twisting around her gut, trying to burst free. On the whole ride over, she drummed her fingers along the steering wheel and reached to turn the music up one notch at a time until it couldn't get any louder.

The GPS in her phone alerted her to turn into a long driveway at what seemed like a moment too late. She jerked the vehicle, trying to keep the car on the road as it swerved.

The land was massive. A yellow house with a picket fence sat directly in front of her and the barn, large and pristine, was off toward the left. From where she parked, she could see the horses, cows, and pigs. An older man with a kind smile walked down the stairs to meet her. His walk was led by his gut. She dropped out of the jeep, plastering on a grin that felt fake.

"Hello, ma'am. You here for the lamb?" he asked her in the same voice she imagined he talked to frightened animals with. He eyed her jeep and it was only then that she realized she should have brought a trailer or something.

"Yes, I am." Her cheeks were heated with embarrassment.

"Would you like to come in and sit down for a bit? Maybe it'll help you relax," he said, pointing his finger over his shoulder. She knew he was trying to be polite but she wanted to get the day over with.

"No. No, thank you. I'm on a tight schedule actually. I hope you don't mind, but I need to be leaving soon." Thea clasped her hands behind her back, afraid he would notice them shaking.

"Where you gonna put it?"

"Just in the back is fine," she replied trying to grasp some form of steadiness.

"Are you sure?" He stared at her, but she'd already paid him so there was very little he could say to her.

"Yes, I'm sure." Her words were clipped, frustration leaking through her tone. He probably thought she was crazy. Hell, she thought she was crazy. He didn't say anything but nodded.

He walked around to the far side of the house, disappearing for a couple of minutes as she opened the door and shuffled around. When he came out, he was dragging the lamb by a rope. It tried to fight him until the farmer decided it would just be easier to lift it the rest of the way. He pushed it into the backseat before slamming the door and wiping his hands on his pants.

"Can't say I've ever seen one of 'em in a backseat like that before." He laughed, wrapping slightly on the window. "And I've seen a lot of things. Believe you, me."

"Sorry, this was a little last minute for me," Thea replied letting out a nervous chuckle.

"It's not a problem. Just be careful on your drive back. Don't know what could happen if it gets spooked." The farmer tapped again on the window before walking to the porch. He waited there as Thea got back in her car and left the property. The lamb let out a loud bleat that sent her already racing heart into overdrive.

"Just be quiet. Lord knows that would be best for both of us right now." Thea glared at it through the rearview mirror. She didn't want to get too attached to it, yet she couldn't help but think it was cute. Thea groaned, slamming her sweaty hands against the steering wheel. She drove back into town and toward her office with all the windows partially rolled down, because of the smell. Her fingers were once again dancing to the music. She made it back to her office at around noon and was thankful for the fact that it was a Sunday. Most people spent Sunday's as far away from the office as possible. It was the only day they truly had off.

Thea got out of her car and propped open the building's front door. She took a deep breath before opening the back seat and grabbing the rope to pull the lamb out of her car. It bleated at her as it tried to move away. She cursed at it, and climbed in the back to pull its front feet forward until it was out of the car. She pulled it close to her body, keeping hold of it as it struggled against her. She struggled to get the wiggling creature to come with her as she walked into the building, trying to hold onto it while she checked over her shoulder.

When she was in her office, she shut the door with her foot. The lamb moved as far away from her as possible, staring at her with frightened eyes. She set out a large plastic bag on the floor, which was used for covering furniture. She hoped it was big enough to keep everything clean. She rummaged around the office, looking for the cleaver she had just bought the day before. She had stashed it in one of the drawers of her desk without paying much attention. She pulled hard on the bottom left one. It always got stuck, and she always had to pull back with all her weight. When she finally managed to pry it open with a loud crack, the lamb bleated at the loud clattering.

Thea held onto the weapon with a white knuckled grip as she stared at the animal cowering in the corner. She felt sick. She couldn't do it. There was no way. Her eyes slid over to the tablet. People did this every day. Animals died every day. She looked over at the lamb and made her decision. If she had to give up a small life to get her husband back, she would do it. Her husband's life affected more than just hers, it mattered to her children, his family, his friends, and his co-workers. She was saving more than just one life.

She grabbed the rope of the animal and began to drag the lamb onto the plastic. It struggled but she tied it to her desk before it could get away again. The knot wasn't perfect, but it would hold. The lamb acted like it knew its fate. She tackled it, trying to hold it still as it fought back, its legs kicking her in the stomach. She almost lost her breath and with it her nerve. She had her knee on its belly and her free hand holding down its head. It watched her with terror in its eyes.

"I'm so sorry. This has to happen. I'm doing it for more than myself." She took a deep breath and stopped short of plunging the cleaver into its neck. It screeched, loud and terrible.

"I'm sorry. I'm sorry," she repeated as she closed her eyes tightly and thrust the knife straight down. She heard as the animal's cry was cut off and felt the way the knife scraped against bone.

God help her.

She pulled the knife free with a harsh jerk. Blood sprayed. It's eyes, dull and betrayed, were still watching her. It's breathing was ragged. It was choking on its blood. She wanted to end its pain, to end the torture. The knife fell from her grasp and she scrambled away from those eyes. The ones that seemed to know they were dying, the same look that Aiden's had. It wasn't supposed to happen like this. It was meant to be quick and easy.

She curled up against the back wall, bloody hands tightly pulling on her hair, smearing her face. It watched her and no matter how much she wanted to, she couldn't look away from it—couldn't look away from those eyes. Aiden's eyes. So she waited for ten minutes as it was slowly suffocated by its own blood.

When it stopped breathing, she crawled to it and placed a hand on its head. She brought the tablet over, pushing her fingers into the red pool that had formed. It was still warm. She wiped it on the tablet. The blood soaked into it, like it was made of sponge, not stone and then disappeared. What was happening?

"Good. You've done well," the voice whispered to her as if it was inside of her head. The tablet glowed, and new markings were added to the side of it, sketching over the older ones.

"What does this mean? What's going to happen now?" Thea asked, gripping it tighter.

"You'll get your next task soon."

"Tell me what it is now," she demanded.

"You are not ready yet. You will receive it when you are ready."

"I'll figure it out then. I won't stop until I know what it is."

· CHAPTER TWENTY ·

Finn

Finn rubbed sweat off his forehead before dragging his hands down his face with an annoyed groan. He sat on the ground, trying to catch his breath. Liam sat off to the side, watching him with anxious eyes. Lucian and Jonas stood beside him. Finn had been training with Celeste all afternoon, and he'd had yet to best her. He was exhausted and his body ached in places he didn't even know could ache. The past week he had been training with Celeste for at least two hours a day and during that time she had never let up. She wasn't even breaking a sweat.

"You're getting better," she said, handing him a canteen filled with water. He chugged it.

"I feel like I've gotten worse," he replied as Senna walked into the clearing with a wave.

"You're getting better at handling your sword, and I'm not going as easy on you as I was before." She offered him a hand and pulled him up.

"Hey, Hero, you've got someone asking about you." Senna grabbed the edge of his sleeve nodding her head toward the infirmary tents, where Henry was. Celeste sighed, knowing Senna would wait around until Finn was free, which wouldn't be a problem if Senna wouldn't go out of her way to annoy her.

"Come on, Liam. Your turn," Celeste said, handing him a sword.

"I'd rather not." His eyes glanced around them, refusing to even look at the weapon in his hands.

"You're not getting extensive training, just enough to make sure you can defend yourself," replied Celeste. Liam hesitated before taking a small step forward.

"We'll just be with Henry. Come find us when you need us." Senna tugged Finn forward as Celeste waved them away.

"Watch her back for me, Finn. She's a master at finding trouble," Celeste said to him, nudging his side with her elbow as she walked past him.

"Let's go see your greatest champion. He's telling everyone who will listen about how you saved him." Senna hadn't let go of his sleeve as she pulled him, and he made no move to take his arm back. He followed her, studying the back of her head. Jonas was a few steps behind them.

"I can't figure you out." The words slipped off his tongue before he could reign them in. She laughed, her head thrown back. She was prettiest in those moments, he thought.

"I'm going to take that to mean I'm not dull and predictable, so thank you." She smiled at him, her large eyes dancing with mirth. It was just another reaction he wasn't expecting. While Celeste reminded him of a river, calm and quiet but viscous when needed, Senna was more like wildflowers, as vibrant and loud as she was sweet and unexpected.

"You're definitely not predictable," Finn answered. They pushed past several people who were coming and going from the infirmary tents. The odor of rot was strong on this side of camp. He was sure he'd never get used to the smell.

"What happens to the people here when they're too far gone to be helped?" He looked around. Everyone that was being tended to didn't seem like they were that bad off. Not like some of the people he'd seen in isolation.

"It's difficult because they suffer no matter what. There isn't a solution where they don't unless someone can bring death back. If they truly can't stand it anymore, we try to release their souls. Sometimes that's done by people here called extractors." She must have sensed his confusion. "Extractors are spirits that have grown strong enough over time that they can possess another body, like Arran. I'm not exactly sure how it's done, but one body can't hold two souls for very long, so the weaker one gets expelled. When a person has been in pain long enough to warrant an extractor, they're ready to give up their body. The extractor will return to the original body they were using once the soul has been expelled."

"Afterwards, we create a pyre to honor our fallen and purify the body." She must have seen the look that passed over Finn's face because she settled him with a challenge in her eyes. "I know it doesn't seem much better than what Leander does, but it's the most humane way we've come across. We don't do it unless it's asked for."

"How many spirits are strong enough to become an extractor?" He wondered how many people he'd passed that were in the body of another person.

"We have about seven here. Spirits aren't able to be seen unless they possess a different body because they live on a different plane than we do. Essentially, extractors are like banshees, but they've been able to keep a rational mind throughout the pain and anger. I'm not sure why, but I always thought it would be rude to ask. They work with the sick because the bodies they use have already been compromised."

"Doesn't the possibility that they could become feral scare you?"

"No. It frightens everyone else though. It's why so few of the healthy work in this part of camp. I've talked to them and heard their stories. They're still people in those bodies, even if it wasn't their original one." She stopped for a moment, looking toward the sky, forming her thoughts. "I think doing this keeps them from turning. The pain of being in another body is excruciating, but they've always wanted to help. I think doing this gives them purpose."

"So why do you work here then?" He studied her, the contemplative look on her face was a rare sight. She grinned at him over her shoulder.

"Because I don't want to hurt people. I just can't. So I choose to do this instead. It's still dangerous. I could get sick, but we try to take preventative measures so I don't." She paused at a tent, listening for a moment before pulling it open and ushering him inside. She gave a small nod to the man who was tending Henry. Jonas opted to wait outside.

"Finn, you're here." The boy scrambled up from his position as best as he could, despite the protests of the dark haired man watching over him. The man pushed him back down by his shoulder with a gentle hand. When he moved back, Finn noticed the way his left shoulder and arm remained stiffly at his side. An extractor. Finn didn't get the chance to dwell on that thought because Henry began speaking, pulling his attention away from the man as he left the tent. Henry told him everything that had happened after he left in as much exaggerated detail as the boy could muster. Senna helped fill in any gaps that Henry may have left out, speaking just as fast. Between the both of them, he had trouble hearing an entire sentence.

Henry was cleaned up. His blond hair was less matted, and his face was flushed. Finn could almost forget the sickly sight of the skeletal boy he had met but knew under the still enormous clothes that he was all bones. He glanced around, aware that he had been staring at Henry's grotesquely thin arms. He made a mental note to ask Senna if his body would be able to heal, or if he was an untouchable.

"Finn?" Senna nudged him with her elbow. "Hey, come back to us."

"He did that all the time on our way here." Although he felt a twinge of guilt, Henry beamed at him, like it wasn't an inconvenience and instead something that he was fond of.

"Where do you go?" Senna's intense gaze was focused on him.

"Sorry. Nowhere. I was just thinking about everything. This is the first time I've been able to relax in a while." He felt like he was holding in too many secrets and too many lies. He had started to care about these people, about their thoughts and opinions of him. He enjoyed training with Celeste, even if it left him with a bone-deep exhaustion. He looked forward to seeing Lucian everyday, who would tease him about his form and was always ready to lend a hand for anything Finn asked. He liked Senna and seeing her laugh, who embraced herself fully and loudly where Finn tended to make himself invisible, trying to hide the parts of himself he hated.

"Of course. Should have realized. I need to start thinking before I open my mouth." She settled him with such a look of compassion that he would have told her anything in that moment if she had asked him.

"Don't," he started, then fumbled for a reason why before he could embarrass himself. "You wouldn't be you if you started doing that now."

She laughed and pushed against his shoulder. They continued talking, Liam joining them after a while, claiming with mock sternness that he needed to speak with Henry. Finn was surprised Liam had come out at all given his fear of getting sick. His brother sat as far away from Henry as possible and seemed to hunch into himself.

"Like you have any reason to look surprised," he began as he took a seat next to Finn. "The complainer? Really?"

"Are you complaining about your nickname?" Senna asked.

Henry began giggling and Finn tried to stifle a laugh. Liam sputtered before glaring at her.

"I don't like you very much," he said when he realized she'd gotten the best of him. It was an obvious lie. There weren't many people Liam didn't like after he'd gotten to know them.

"You're not the first person to tell me that," she answered, giving Henry a quick wink. She'd been trying to seem inconspicuous but the whole side of her face lifted with it—an accidental exaggeration.

They spent a couple hours just speaking about nothing, about Liam and Finn's family, some of their journey, and about hope for the future. He felt he belonged in that moment, more than he'd felt like he'd belonged anywhere else. When he was younger, he always felt out of place. He was quieter than both Declan and Liam. Declan seemed to just have the innate ability to understand how people worked. He could charm almost anyone if he set his mind to it. Liam was awkward but loud and always had the right timing to make an entire room laugh, even if it was unintentional. Finn was neither loud nor charming. What most people seemed to remember about him was his anger. Here, no one knew him as the kid who punched a peer for making fun of how his grandmother had limited mobility. To stay in control meant to stay around people that didn't anger him. So the group of people he had around him was always small. Being here, for the first time, he felt like maybe his rage wouldn't get the best of him. They could save his family, maybe save more people like Henry, and create a new life within the rebellion. He would play his role and live a quiet life with his family, away from the madness.

It wasn't long before Declan, Lucian and Celeste came to collect them for their progress meeting with Arran. They had meant to get in, grab the boys, and get out but Henry began speaking to Celeste to thank her once again for bringing him to the medics and asking for any news about his mom. His bashfulness was able to soften even her features as she bent down next to him. She ruffled his hair and tapped his cheek with her knuckles as she explained they hadn't heard anything yet. Although disappointment flitted across his features, he nodded in understanding. Jonas was still waiting outside when they left the tent. He didn't complain about the long wait and he hadn't interrupted them. He could have. If he had wanted to leave, Finn would have had to follow. Not toon far off, Finn noticed Arran. It was time to do their check-in.

They made their way to where Arran and another man were waiting.

"Let's hear it then," Arran said with disinterest. Celeste stepped forward first.

"Finn's picking up training fast. He's got the basics down. If he continues this way, he might become one of our best fighters." Arran nodded for her to continue. "Liam is reluctant to fight, so he's learning at a slower pace but is still making progress."

"You have to learn, boy. The next time you're here, I better be told that you're doing better." Arran motioned for her to step back. "Next."

The other man stepped forward. He was small and balding on the top of his head. His arms were littered with scars. "Liam's been picking up things at the smithy with more ease. He's a quick learner. It's good to have someone competent working with me."

He stepped back and Jonas spoke, "Finn's doing just fine on night guard. Also hasn't been corresponding with Essex. Don't see why I need to keep watching him all the time."

"Because that's what you've been told to do." Arran scowled. Jonas didn't seem bothered by him.

"Liam also hasn't been in contact with Essex," Lucian interjected. He gave Liam a little nudge, as if they had an inside joke. It did seem to make the anxiousness on Liam's face smooth out a little.

"Good." Arran looked them over. "Keep watching them. We'll meet again soon. Leave."

They did. Finn was beginning to feel the exhaustion hit

him again. He needed to lie down, to give his mind and body a break.

"I hate him," Senna said with her arms crossed over her chest after they got far enough away from the cabin to feel safe.

"Senna." Celeste cut her off, a harsh edge to her voice.

"Just because he's in charge, doesn't mean he's right. People can do good things for the wrong reasons. They can justify doing terrible things, just because they think they're helping. What he does isn't right and nobody will speak up because he has something over them." She gripped her arms so tightly that small, angry crescents showed up on her skin.

"There's nothing we can do about it." Celeste grabbed her. "Please keep your mouth shut. I'm not losing you because you can't keep your opinions to yourself."

"You wouldn't have to if Arran didn't rule with an iron fist." Senna shot back. Finn knew Senna didn't like Arran and had gathered that she hated being told what to do even more, but he'd never seen her look passionate, so enraged, before.

"Please Senna, I'm begging you." Celeste squeezed her tighter. He'd expected more annoyance from Celeste but she spoke to Senna with a soothing voice.

"Fine." She jerked away from her sister. "This is why I think the Exo Colonies are better. They at least have a council, not a wannabe king."

"Exo Colonies?" Finn asked.

"The Exonerated Colonies," Celeste said, not at all surprised that Finn didn't know what they were talking about. He wondered how much she had to teach Declan about the world outside of the walls. Less than Finn or Liam. Declan had to have been exposed to more while working with the rebellion when he was still in Essex.

"You don't know about the Exo Colonies?" Senna whipped toward him. Their lives had been so different. She had grown up in the rebellion and didn't know what Essex was like.

Didn't know about all the lies or the Beggar's District or isolation.

"We were taught there were only two sides. The cities under the horseman and the rebellion," Finn answered. "They told us that the rebellion was formed by a bunch of heathens. Our grandma always told us that wasn't true. Dad said she filled our heads with fanatic stories. I never believed the rebellion was that bad if Grandma was for it, but I didn't think there was anyone else either. I thought you had to be one or the other." Finn remembered the way his Grandma would tell her stories, her eyes lighting up and voice raising with excitement. They weren't supposed to tell their parents that she'd been telling them those things, though somehow they always knew.

"That's how they control us Finn, they tell us you only have two options: be on our side or be on theirs. They only tell you that after they slander the rebellion first, so you're actually just given one choice." Declan kept his voice low.

"There's still a lot for you to learn." Celeste put a hand on his shoulder. It wasn't shocking to hear that Leander had lied to the town, but it made Finn wonder. Just how much of what he knew about the world was actually a lie?

· CHAPTER TWENTY-ONE ·

Finn

I've found nothing here. No whisper, no trace. Nothing of the angels. The kids may have split up, but do we really think they would have made it as far as the West coast?

A LETTER FROM GENERAL NILSON TO GENERAL LEANDER

Finn was furious, pacing around the camp. Jonas sat not far from him, watching him with no expression. They had another meeting with Arran, who continued to imply that he and Liam were traitors, despite there being no evidence. They had spent close to two hours being questioned again, right after Finn's shift on the watch. Liam was now back to work with the blacksmith, after presenting as detailed of a map of the city as he could remember. The farm district was a little lacking but the boys had never been in that part of town. There was no need.

Declan had taken the map from Liam and was working with a few others to study it. He wasn't privy to what they were doing with it. He wasn't privy to a lot of what Declan did around the camp, but from bits and pieces he heard, he assumed it was similar to what he did as a strategist. He was surprised Declan hadn't made a map of the town yet. He'd made one of all the ins and outs of the capitol building.

Celeste and Lucian went back to their duties which seemed to change every day. Some days they went out to scout. They did this after Celeste was done training. There were times when her whole day consisted of training. Lucian, on those days, would either help out where he was needed or leave to meet with the free people and continue working on relations with them. Declan would sometimes go with him, but Celeste almost never tagged along.

Arran was doing who knows what in that little cabin. He sent for other people to come and meet with him quite often, but Finn didn't know what for. His job was kept the most secret and not even Celeste or Declan knew the full extent of what he was doing all the time. Finn assumed he was questioning people in the camp, asking if they'd seen either he or his brother acting in any way suspicious.

He clenched and unclenched his hands just thinking about it. He hated it here. It was supposed to be better. Yet here he was, still being watched over like a criminal.

He had thought Liam was going to break with Arran right in his face, edging closer with every question. It wasn't the fact that Arran had been almost screaming at them and threatening them, but it was the smell. That's what Liam hated the most. He was so afraid of untouchables and even more afraid that that would be him one day. Finn had tried to reassure him, but they all ended up as an untouchable in the end. Either the soul was released from the body or they existed with the unimaginable pain that comes with rotting.

Liam had stumbled over his words a few times, trying not to throw up anytime Arran got too close, but he kept telling him the same thing, over and over again. Finn wondered how similar Arran and Leander must be. Leander would question and torture people until they broke, even if they had never committed a crime. He was starting to think that, given the option, Arran wouldn't be so different.

"You're driving yourself insane, boy." Jonas crossed his arms, still watching as he paced. Finn didn't reply. He was too angry right now. He needed to hit something. Some part of Jonas must have understood that because he waved his hand. "Not lookin'"

He moved so his back was to Finn. This had happened once before where he could feel the anger buzzing just beneath his skin. He couldn't go running, and he didn't always have the option of sparing with someone, not if the training ground was already being used. He had just snapped one day and rammed his fist into a tree, just once, when he and Jonas were on watch. Jonas had looked almost shocked but the familiar shame settled in fast, and Finn turned away from him. Jonas was quiet but observant, and it didn't pass him by. He offered Finn no comfort, but he didn't treat him any different either—just acted like nothing had happened.

The anger was still there like pin pricks over his skin. That wasn't the person he wanted to be. He resumed clenching and unclenching his fists, digging his fingernails into his skin every time. It wasn't the same. It didn't give him the overwhelming numbness he'd get after hitting the tree, but it did take away the immediacy of his rage. He did that until he could feel the anger retract, still there but no longer swarming him.

"I'm okay." He was still clenching his fists when Jonas turned back around, eyeing him.

"Arran's a prick." Jonas shrugged. "Most can't stand him."

"By now, he has to have some idea that we're not here to spy on the rebellion." Finn pushed his hands in his pockets, hoping that would help keep the anger at bay too.

"It's happened before," Jonas said. Finn waited for him to go on. Speaking with Jonas was sometimes like pulling teeth.

"And?"

Jonas sighed, a full bodied one, like the entire conversation was taxing. "Rebellion got hit pretty hard. Lost a lot of good people. Lost some not so good ones too. Took years to rebuild to what you're seein' now."

The fact that Arran's mistrust, not his actions, was justified was insufferable because he could understand. Finn knew how terrible it was to watch the people around you become untouchables and not be able to do anything about it.

"Hey, Hero, got a minute?" Both he and Jonas turned to Senna, who seemed oblivious to the tension.

He squeezed his hands tight from inside his pockets and took a deep breath, trying not to let his irritation into his voice. "Yeah."

"Great, let's go." She grabbed his arm and pulled him along, waving at Jonas to follow. He heard Jonas mumble something under his breath. "I know you should be sleeping now, but you seem a little keyed up. Not that I blame you. Dealing with Arran is hard."

"Where are we going?" Finn asked.

"To the overlook." Jonas groaned again behind them. "It's on the other side of camp. Not a lot of people go there, but it's nice to just get away from everyone for a little bit."

"Should let the boy rest," Jonas spoke up.

"Do you mean him or you? Because he doesn't seem tired to me." She sent Finn a mischievous grin. Jonas didn't reply, accepting that this was his fate. Finn suspected that if Jonas wanted to, he could force him to go back to the tents.

The overlook was more impressive than Finn had expected. It was a large rock at the end of the forest that could fit maybe three or four people, but the view was what really caught his attention. The sky was blue with a few clouds rolling across it. He could see plush green stretched out for miles beyond him and a river much farther than that. There were some places, barren and gray, that were like giant holes in the forest—craters from the old war when bombs were frequent and frightening. He wondered how terrifying it must have been to live in that time, never knowing when a bomb or attack would happen on your town. They'd never been told which side the bombs came from. Was it people fighting against the generals or for them? The generals were in power, and that was maybe answer enough. How many people had been decimated before bombs became a thing of the past? He wondered what was lost to the people first—their guns or their bombs.

"I thought, since you've never really been away from Essex, that you'd want to see what your world really looked like." Senna squeezed his hand, and it was then that he realized he hadn't let her go. She didn't seem to mind.

It was beautiful.

It was devastating.

He didn't want to live in a prison like Essex ever again. Not after everything he'd seen and experienced. Not after knowing that this was what the world looked like.

"Thank you." He didn't know how to show her the all-consuming gratitude he felt for her. She stayed quiet as he took everything in. He wasn't sure how long they spent just soaking up the view, but neither she nor Jonas pushed him to hurry up.

Senna only spoke up when Finn released her hand. "I like to come here to remind myself what the rebellion fights for. I know I said I prefer the Exo Colonies, but when I come here I remember all those people in the General's towns, who don't know what the world around them looks like. That's what we fight for; what some of us fight for, anyways."

Finn thought that he wanted to fight for that too. Neither his mother nor his father had ever seen the outside world. His father would have loved it. As uptight as he could be, he loved nature. It must have been hard for his grandparents to leave this behind, even if it was their choice to do so. He didn't think he'd make the same one in their shoes.

"Does it all look like this?" He couldn't find a way to tell her the scrambled thoughts in his head.

"I don't think so but I've never left Vermont." She glanced behind them at Jonas.

He sighed. "It doesn't all look like this. If you go far enough west, there's a desert; far enough south, it doesn't get snow, not like we do."

"One day, I want to see those too." Finn wondered what else the world had to offer. What about places beyond the ocean?

"If I had to bet on anyone here getting that far, I'd bet on you." Senna smiled up at him, bright and captivating.

"Not your sister?" he asked.

"I think she wants to be here, where the people she loves are. If they left, she'd go too." Senna shrugged. "I wanted to go when I was little. Our mom and dad talked a lot about what the world had to offer."

Finn yawned, feeling the exhaustion hit him before he could say anything else to her.

"We might want to head back now. I didn't mean to keep you guys awake so long." It was the first time he'd seen her look almost bashful.

"I would stay here for longer if I thought I could, but you're right." He made a note to come back to the spot when he had a chance. Maybe he'd convince Liam to join him. He'd have to convince Senna to show him how to get back though, as he hadn't paid enough attention on the way there and he was too tired now to try and figure it out.

They walked back to camp in comfortable silence. They split when they got to his tent. "See you around, Hero."

She was gone as quick as she'd come, no looking back.

"You ready for some sleep?" Jonas eyed him. He looked far more tired than Finn felt and guilt swirled around in his chest. He hoped Jonas wouldn't be grumpier than usual tomorrow. He nodded. He was going to regret staying awake so long later, when he had to get up and stay up the whole night again. He hoped his time on watch would end soon, but given how Arran had been treating him it was doubtful.

· CHAPTER TWENTY-TWO ·

Finn

*There's one working train that goes from the West Coast
of the country to the East coast. The generals use it to
trade resources and send messengers to each other.*

EXCERPT TAKEN FROM THE COUNSELORS GUIDEBOOK

Finn, much to Jonas's chagrin, decided he would visit Liam at the blacksmith's after his shift. He wasn't sure what to expect as he'd never entered the small building before. He hadn't even known where it was until Liam described it to him as a small, two-room building that was built a little ways away from camp, hidden by the cover of trees. When Finn had asked Jonas why it was like that and not in the middle of camp, the man just shrugged.

Finn was curious what Liam did all day, and he wasn't tired enough to fall asleep yet. Jonas, although not happy about this turn of events, didn't try to stop him either. He followed along behind Finn. The building looked like it could fall apart any moment. He was surprised Liam agreed to work in a place like that.

The thick wooden door was hard to push open and it

scraped against the dirt floor. Both the blacksmith and Liam were staring at him. "Hey Finn. What do you need?"

He shrugged. "I just haven't been this way before, and I was curious."

The balding man got over his shock much faster than Liam did. "You came at a good time then. We're creating a few more swords for our soldiers."

In the middle of the room was a small metal cage where a bright fire was burning. Next to it was an anvil. The man handed Liam the sword he was working with as he brushed his hands on his leather apron. He held out a hand to Finn. "I'm Trent."

Finn shook his hand surprised by the hospitality.

"We've almost got this one straight, just need to iron it out a little more. Really got to put our backs into it." He took the sword from Liam as he was explaining, putting the metal part of it back into the heat and holding it there for a few minutes. When it was burning red hot, he pulled it out and began hitting it with a hammer, flattening it even more. Finn flinched at the noise, but it didn't seem to affect anyone else. When he was finished, Trent held it up, inspecting it. "Again," he said and put it back into the fire. He tried again and seemed to be happy with the results this time.

"Are you thinking about being a blacksmith after your time on the watch?" Trent seemed excited by the idea but Finn didn't think he'd like it very much. The place was cluttered, with a bunch of things pushed to the back wall and he could just imagine what the other room looked like. He hated how loud the work was too. He preferred the quiet, somewhere he could hear his own thoughts.

"I don't think so." He shrugged. "I've never seen what a blacksmith does though so I was curious."

He noted Liam seemed at home here. He had confidence in what he was doing. Better him than Finn.

Trent eyed Jonas for a minute. "Have you eaten yet this morning?"

Finn shook his head.

"We have some extras from breakfast if you want some. We eat and work throughout the day. I can bring him back to the tents whenever he's ready if you'd like to sleep, Jonas." Trent grabbed a plate of food and handed it to Finn.

"Not too long. You're wearing yourself thin," Jonas said to Finn and then turned to Trent. "Thanks."

He left the shop.

"Hard time transitioning to working at nights?" Trent asked after Jonas had left. Finn had shoveled the scrambled eggs into his mouth so he just nodded. "I had a hard time before I transitioned to this job too."

Trent motioned to a bench that was pushed all the way against the wall. Some clothes lay strewn across it. "Take a seat. Relax for a little while." He handed Liam the other plate and let him sit too.

"How long have you been here?" Finn asked after he swallowed.

"As a blacksmith, about fourteen years. I've been part of the rebellion since I was born though. My family has been serving the rebellion for generations."

Finn wondered how different his life would be if his grandparents had stayed here rather than opt to live in Essex. His life hadn't been horrible in Essex, except for the last year, but now that the veil had been lifted from his eyes, he felt like the whole thing had just been made up.

He spent an hour with Liam and Trent, listening to them talk about a new key design they'd been told to make. It was an idea Declan had come to them with for a master key, something that would allow their infiltrators to get into places they didn't have access to. He'd been working on the idea for a while, wondering if it would even be possible. It was a great idea but maybe not one that was possible right now. Not when they didn't have communication with their soldiers inside Essex.

"Let's get you back to your tent." Trent interrupted one

of Liam's long-winded stories. "You look like you could fall asleep any moment."

He was tired. He hated sleeping through the day. He felt like he was just wasting precious time. Still, Trent was right and both Finn and Liam followed him out the door. People were still waking up and getting ready for their duties. They passed the training grounds, where Celeste was standing, hands on her hips. She noticed them and walked over, confused to see Finn still awake.

"Morning Celeste." Trent waved.

"Hi Trent. How's everything going this morning?" She studied Finn for a moment before looking over to the blacksmith.

"Good, good. Finn had never seen our neck of the woods and wanted to know what it was all about." He clapped a hand on Finn's back.

"I'm still having problems sleeping." Even as he said that, Finn yawned.

"I imagine that's because you've gotten used to training after your shifts." She sighed. "I tried to tell Arran that the schedule he wanted you on was too much."

"How much has he been training?" Trent asked.

"A lot more than most people do after a shift." She put her hands in her pockets. "I think he wants to see how serious you are about the rebellion."

"He's not doing that to me." Liam shifted his weight, tapping his fingers against his thighs.

"Well, you're scared of him." She ran a hand through her hair. "Finn's challenged him. I think he's trying to break your spirit."

Finn took a deep breath and tried to calm the anger before it could get too far. He had known that, at least on some level. It wasn't a surprise, but the confirmation made the feelings worse.

"I don't agree with his tactics," she said. "I'm not the only one."

"Declan?" Liam asked.

She nodded. "And Jonas. I was confused when I saw him without you this morning. I was leaving Arran's cabin as he was going in. I didn't hear much, but I did hear him tell Arran to 'cut the shit.' Decided it was best to just keep moving along."

"You guys don't have to worry about me so much. I'm tired a lot, but I'm okay." Finn had never expected Jonas to speak up in general, let alone for him.

"You've been looking really pale. That's why you haven't had training for the past couple of days. I was afraid you'd pass out on me. It's not safe, and I wasn't about to let that happen." Celeste reached out to ruffle his hair, the way Lucian always tried to do with her. There had been a couple of times when he stood up that he felt dizzy but he didn't think he was that bad off. He felt tired most of the time, except when he needed to sleep, but he thought he was handling it well.

"I appreciate it." He did feel a little better today.

"Yeah well, I did it for you and to protect Senna. If I didn't, she would have tried to give Arran a piece of her mind too." Celeste ran a hand down her face at the thought of trying to keep Senna contained.

"She really does not like him." Liam was still tapping his fingers and sent them all a nervous smile.

"Do you?" Finn asked him.

"I didn't say I blamed her." Liam stopped his tapping to look at Finn. "I love you, but I'd never argue against Arran for you."

That made Finn laugh. Liam had a hard time with speaking up like that but he showed he cared in other ways. "I wouldn't expect you to."

"He could rip me in half," Liam whispered, tapping resumed.

"Why are you so nervous today?" Finn would have preferred to ask when they had a moment alone but he was starting to doubt they ever would.

"What if my map isn't good enough? What if it was wrong?

If something happens it'll be my fault and I'll be cast out or worse, he'll mark me as an untouchable." Liam's words spilled out so fast he had trouble controlling them.

"This isn't Essex. No one is going to turn you into an untouchable," Trent assured him. Celeste's mouth was set in a deep frown. Finn wasn't sure if it was because of what Liam said or if she thought Trent could be wrong.

"We haven't been treated much better here than we were there. Not by Arran." Finn grabbed Liam's arm and gave it a reassuring squeeze. He stayed close to keep Liam grounded. "He's not wrong for having that fear."

Trent looked like he was going to argue but Celeste cut in. "I know it feels like that and that Arran's been cruel, but there are people here who will fight for that not to happen."

"Are there?" Finn asked.

Liam put his hand over his heart, now gasping for air. Finn cursed. He should have been trying to ease Liam away from a panic attack, not arguing with Celeste and Trent to prove a point. He helped Liam to sit on the ground, sitting in front of him. "Follow my breathing okay?"

Finn had heard their mother ask Liam that so many times when they were younger. He wasn't sure he'd be any good at being soothing like she was but he tried anyways. It had been a long time since an attack had been this bad, even with everything that had happened. He assumed it was because of all the buildup. He started a slow pace counting to ten and had Liam follow along with his breathing. Celeste and Trent were crouched next to him.

"Back up a little and give him some space." Celeste reacted much quicker than Trent, taking three big steps back and pulling the blacksmith with her. He kept his voice quiet, like their mother had. "You're doing good. What do you need?"

"Still count," Liam gasped out, and Finn complied. It could have taken five minutes or fifteen for Liam to calm back down. Once his breathing was normal, he put his head in his hands. "Sorry."

"It's fine. You did really good that time." Finn put a hand on his leg. He wasn't sure if he still needed any grounding but he thought better safe than sorry. Liam's shoulders tensed, so Finn knew he didn't believe him. When Liam lifted his head again, Finn could see how exhausted he looked. He was always tired after. He wanted to say something reassuring, to help Liam believe that it was fine, but he didn't think he would say anything Liam would believe.

"I think maybe you should rest for a little while." Celeste had taken a few cautious steps forward, wanting to give Liam space if he needed it.

"I can still work. I just need a minute." Liam's voice was hoarse when he spoke.

"Trent can come back and get you around noon to finish your shift, but you should listen to your body and rest for a little bit." It was the first time Finn had seen her look so open. Liam was about to protest again. "It's okay. I promise you won't get kicked out because you need a small break."

Liam looked put out, like he had made the biggest mistake.

"I used to get panic attacks too. I know how hard it is to try and work after having one." She crouched down next to him. Both Finn and Liam stared at her with wide eyes.

"I was eight when we escaped. A lot of the memories are foggy, but our family was part of the beggars district. Our mom got really sick, and they were going to send our whole family to isolation but my dad told me to take Senna and run. So I did. Back then there was a hole in the wall at the very back of the beggars district. I was able to push Senna through and squeeze out." She pulled down the edge of her shirt, showing a ragged scar on her shoulder, like the skin there had once been peeled off. "Officers had been chasing us. I took us as deep into the forest as I could get. Arran found us a week later. I had panic attacks for years. Sometimes, I start to get the tightness in my chest, but I haven't had an attack for a long time."

Neither one knew what to say, but she was already turning to Trent. "Get them back to the tents. They both need to rest."

Trent didn't hesitate. He seemed too shocked by everything that happened to even question her. "Let's go boys."

Liam said a quiet thank you to Celeste as they were standing back up, eyes watering. They walked in silence back to the tents. Finn was surprised that someone like Celeste had ever had panic attacks. She seemed so unphased by everything but maybe that was her coping mechanism. A way to keep the feelings at bay. She wasn't as cold or calculated as he first thought and, even though a part of him already knew that, he was still surprised whenever she let another wall down in front of them.

He didn't think he'd ever know Celeste's or Senna's story. Senna said her sister hated talking about it. He took that to mean that it was something she would never speak about. He was starting to believe that maybe there were people in the rebellion that would fight for them, even if Arran hated them.

· CHAPTER TWENTY-THREE ·

Finn

The knife was found fifty-two years after William had hidden it. The man who found it thought he would be the one to stop Leander, but he fell into madness, attacking his friends and family, slaughtering them all.

EXCERPT TAKEN FROM THE REBELLION'S RECORDS

Finn scrubbed at the dirt that stuck to his skin. The sun was just beginning to rise, and its red-orange hue reflected in the river he stood in. It was waist deep. His shift with the night guard had finished twenty minutes ago. He was exhausted, still not used to being up so late, but more pressing was the suffocating need to escape. It had been three annoying weeks where Finn had no time for himself because he was being watched all day and night. Even now as he bathed, Jonas was there with him, washing off too. Jonas never said much, but Finn was aware of how observant he was.

He needed an hour away from Jonas's gaze. Not because he wanted to spill the rebellion's secrets, but because he needed to relax. He felt like he was tip-toeing around, trying to prove that he could be trusted. He couldn't go on his usual morning runs to clear his head. There was no time to sit down after a long day and just decompress. No time to make him feel human.

Finn had, of course, tried to talk to Jonas about it, but the man just grunted one word answers at him. What was he supposed to do with that? He never thought he'd miss Liam's ability to fill a silence. He gave up any hope of conversation and stewed mostly in what he thought were awkward silences that never seemed to bother Jonas.

Finn scrubbed at his arms until they turned bright red. He couldn't get time by himself to feel comfortable expressing his anger in his usual way. His knuckles were, for the most part, healed for the first time in years. He thought there were a few new scars on them, but it was hard to tell because of the ones he got when he was a child. Instead of punching something to feel the numbness he craved, he had taken to scrubbing his skin so hard he'd feel the sting for hours after. Jonas never said anything about it, but it was starting to get worse. Surface wounds were scabbed up the length of his arms from the day before and now he was reopening them.

Jonas let out a sigh before his hand covered Finn's. "You can't keep doing this."

Finn set his jaw. His anger still simmered beneath the surface. He could feel Jonas's eyes on him but wouldn't meet them. Jonas took his hand away. "Noon. I have something to take care of. Be about a half hour. I'll leave you at your tent. Be there when I get back."

It was more words than Jonas had ever spoken to him.

He'd never felt so thankful for anything in his life. "I understand."

Jonas remained quiet as they returned to their tent where Finn laid down on his cot to get some rest. Jonas stretched out on his make-shift bed, muddy boots laying over his blanket.

"I'll wake you before I leave." Jonas placed his hands behind his head, closing his eyes. He left no room for Finn's thanks.

A few hours later, Finn felt a sharp kick to his leg. Jonas left the tent without looking back. Finn waited, listening to others pass outside before deciding that he was going to leave for a little bit. He reached into his bag and grabbed out the small skyscraper carving and pocketed it. Most people weren't on this side of camp since it was the middle of the day. They were scouting or training.

His first thought was to go back to the overlook, but he'd have to risk getting seen. He'd have to go through the middle of camp. There was one other place he knew he could go. He kept his head down, shoulders bent forward as he walked toward the little clearing Celeste had first brought him and Liam to. He dropped down, hiding behind a tent as a group of people came near him, acting like he had dropped something in case he was spotted. They passed without noticing him. He prayed no one else would come.

He held his breath until he was hidden by the forest, where he finally relaxed his shoulders. There was nobody he had to worry about, nobody he had to answer to. He knew he had only a small amount of time. Jonas had taken a chance on him. For what reason, Finn didn't know, but he wasn't going to repay that kindness by not being there when Jonas returned. He still needed to prove he wasn't working with Leander and being caught by himself would get him, at the very least, banished from the rebellion.

He sat down in the clearing, and took out the little skyscraper, rubbing his thumb over its grooves. It was the only thing he had from his home and the memories it held gave him comfort. He wouldn't stay long, he thought as he leaned back against the tree.

He had a few minutes of peace before a voice rang out in the welcoming quiet. "What are you doing?" Declan's voice was pinched.

Finn pocketed the carving and pushed himself off the ground. "I'm not doing anything, I swear. I was just sitting."

"Where's Jonas? You think sneaking away looks good for you?" Declan's arms were crossed. Fire started to rise in the pit of Finn's belly.

"He saw how ridiculous this whole thing was and gave me a minute to myself." Finn's ears flushed, red hot.

"And you didn't think that it was a trick? That he and Arran hadn't planned this as a test?"

"Did you see anyone else following me?" Finn demanded.

"Not that I could tell," Declan started, "but that doesn't mean anything. Jonas could come back any minute. Then what?"

Finn clenched his fists, brushing past Declan. "Fine. I'll go back."

"Finn," Declan said, turning around. "I'm just trying to protect you."

"Did you ever think that I don't need protection? All you've done is fuck everything up." Finn wasn't trying to keep his voice level anymore. He shoved his hands into his pockets, brushing his knuckles against the knife.

Declan ran a hand through his hair. "I understand why you're mad at me."

"Do you?" Finn asked. "Because you abandoned us. You didn't tell us anything. You just left." His fingers wrapped around the knife, feeling the power surge through him.

"Finn."

"Do you know what it's like to wake up and your brother's just gone and then the entire world is watching your every move like you're the enemy?" He flung his hands out still clutching the knife. He was buzzing with energy. All he wanted was a few minutes to himself. He didn't need an interrogation from Declan. He thought he had been starting to let go of the resentment that he felt for his brother, but it had bubbled up to the surface so fast that he wasn't sure what to do with all the emotions. The knife began to grow emitting a dangerous red aura.

"It can't be," Declan whispered. Finn charged Declan before his thought could be finished. He drew his own sword and tried to block but as soon as he did, his weapon was ripped from his hands, flying to the ground. Finn had the sword. War's sword.

Finn had been training with Celeste but the knife's influence made him clumsy. Declan was able to dodge him without much worry, stooping low when Finn swung at his neck. The weapon was a legend. A sword that granted its master the strength of ten men and even premonitions of battle but it was uncontrollable. It sent its owner into a rage so consuming they would kill anybody until it's bloodlust was sated. The story was a common one told in the rebellion, passed down from one of the host's children. The child had learned to master it but it didn't help him when he needed it most. So he'd given up on it, on life. It had been found by a man who couldn't control it. As the story went, it had taken fifteen men and a lot of luck to stop him. They weren't able to hold him though, and he escaped. He hid the sword, and it had been lost for years.

Declan knew there was no way he'd be able to take the weapon out of Finn's vice-like grip. "You know I didn't mean for anything to happen to you guys. I would never put you in danger on purpose." Declan rolled out of the way of another strike. "Christ. I wasn't thinking about the consequences. I was just thinking about myself. Is that what you want to hear?"

Still Finn didn't answer. He stalked toward Declan. "Don't do this. If you kill me then you'll be doing the same thing I did."

"I'm nothing like you." Finn swung wide and Declan dropped to the ground. The blade stuck in the hefty trunk of a tree.

"If you mark me as an untouchable, Arran will find the knife and have you burned, no matter what I say."

Finn tried to pull his weapon from the tree.

"Who will save our family if I'm too wounded to do anything and you're gone?"

With a loud creak Finn was able to free the sword.

"Mom and dad will rot in Leander's prison if you do this. You know that."

It was like a fog had been lifted from Finn's eyes and he paused, conflicted. His parents. He knew Declan was right. No one would care about his family. If Arran got the knife, he would take down Leander. He'd start the true rebellion, but he wouldn't care about the people who sacrificed themselves for his cause.

Finn took a deep, gasping breath, feeling his mind begin to break free. The anger remained, pulsing just beneath the surface, present but no longer in control.

"You can't tell anyone about this," said Finn, fixing Declan with a glare.

"Do you really know what that sword means? We can finally win. We can beat Leander. You can't expect me to keep this a secret." Declan hadn't moved any closer to him but his face had filled with hope. He was already calculating a plan to use it.

"You have to. At least until we get our family back. It's the only way." Declan looked like he was about to protest. "Don't choose the rebellion over us again. Not this time. Please."

Declan was hesitant but nodded. "I'll put our family first, but after we save them, you need to take out Leander."

"Me? It should probably be you." Finn frowned. "Or Arran."

"You're already starting to control it." Declan held up his hand, ending the conversation. "I think it needs to be you."

Finn slumped forward as the knife shrunk to its original size. His breaths were labored. He was too tired to argue with Declan about whether or not he should have control over the knife.

"We should get back. Hopefully, Jonas is still busy. You need to rest." Declan stepped up and wrapped an arm around him, supporting his weight. There was no hesitation in him and a little piece of his resentment broke. His brother didn't see him as a monster, didn't fear him or the knife. He just accepted it, like it had always been a fact.

"I promised I would visit Henry today since I don't have a shift tonight." Finn struggled to carry his own weight.

"I don't think that's a good idea."

"I don't want him to be disappointed."

"I think he'll understand."

"I'm going."

"Why are you so frustrating?" They were nearing camp now, and Declan jerked him forward into his tent. Jonas was nowhere in sight. He helped Finn lay down.

"I already told Jonas that's what I was going to do. It'll look suspicious if I'm too tired to go." Finn's eyes were already starting to close. He could get a couple minutes of sleep before Jonas came back.

"Fine but be careful." Declan left but not before looking back at him with a frown.

When Jonas came back they made their way to the infirmary tents, running into Liam and Lucian on the way. Finn tried not to show just how exhausted he was but from their continuous worried looks he knew he wasn't doing a good job.

Liam started rambling about his work. It was easy for them to fall back into their usual routine with Liam's constant talking and Finn's muttered agreements as he focused more on his thoughts than he did the conversation. Jonas and Lucian opted to stay outside the tent as they went in.

"Finn, you're back." Henry sat up and Senna grabbed his arm to help steady him.

"You really need to announce your presence before you come in, Hero. He's going to topple right off the bed one of these times." Senna ruffled the boy's hair. Senna had been spending a lot of time with Henry, she had announced herself as his primary medic and wouldn't take no for an answer.

"I'm getting some strength back. I could probably get up by myself." Henry pouted.

"I'm sure you could but maybe we should try it out another time. It's almost time for dinner, anyways." Finn sat down. He tried to come often to eat dinner with Henry and Senna. It was a good way to begin his days when he was on duty.

"Are you doing your rounds tonight?" Henry asked Finn as they ate the soup that had been brought to them.

"No, thankfully not," Finn replied.

"This is your first day off? You should have had time off earlier." Senna set her bowl aside. "That ass just wants to make things harder for you."

"I'm glad Arran let me work with the blacksmith instead of doing that." Liam spoke through a mouthful of food.

"I think I'd rather stand guard over nothing than build anything," Finn answered. "Were you ever on guard at all, Senna?"

"No. I was always following around the extractors. They've always fascinated me." She shrugged but continued, "One day I started bringing them and the sick food during dinner. They didn't trust me at first. I don't blame them, even here, it's hard for people to accept what they are. They began to let me help after a while.

"Larissa, she's worked here the longest, went to Arran and asked for me to train under her. Since I refused to fight, he thought it would be beneficial for me to work here. I'm thankful for her. I told her that I preferred helping people to hurting them, and she took it on herself to train me, even though she's very busy. I've been able to learn a lot from her and help a lot of people that places like Essex would just throw out of the city."

"Arran didn't protest at all?" Liam set his bowl aside and sent her a skeptical look.

"It was right after he'd taken control of Carson, so I think he was trying to save face. A lot of people were upset with how he handled that. Plus, it's made relations with the extractors better. A lot of people feared them because of Arran. A few more people have stepped up and said they wanted to train with them after I was allowed to do so."

They continued talking until Senna decided it was time to let Henry rest for the night. The boys went back to Liam's tent. Liam was still full of anxious energy, but somehow Finn convinced him to lie down, instead of staying up late again. Liam was snoring as soon as his head hit the pillow. Finn made a mental note to make sure his brother was sleeping more before he fell into fitful dreams.

"Sir, we've discovered a rebellion camp about two days' journey from here. It's at the top of a mountain, but we can overtake it with the element of surprise," a stout man with a patchy beard said, glancing down at a map.

"You're that confident?" Leander seemed unimpressed, almost unconcerned about the plans.

"I am."

"And the boy? Is he there?"

"We don't know. It seems like the only place he would go. We have information stating that's where his brother went when he snuck out."

"Yes, that's where I would go too. Maybe we should try asking his parents again."

"I've already got my best man on the job."

"Tell me, how do you think you'll be able to take over the camp?"

"We've been scouting their perimeters. It seems they have a handful of guards watching at all times, but I'm confident we can take their first defense." The man paced back and forth around the length of the room. Although he had some idea of where this was taking place, all the details of the room seemed foggy and Finn couldn't get a good look at anything.

"How long will you need to prepare?"

"A couple of days. At most three."

"Fine. You have one shot at this. Don't fuck it up."

"We'll dispose of their guard and then take out the rest of the camp, or enough of it to damage their numbers."

"I don't care about their numbers. They'll never be able to defeat me without the sword. Bring me the boy."

"If all you want is the sword, why don't I just bring you that instead. You won't even need the boy."

"If he has control of the sword, taking him down won't be easy." Leander paused for a moment. "I want him for myself."
"It's just a weapon. I don't think he'll be that hard to defeat."
"You don't know what kind of power that sword holds."

Finn startled awake, covered in sweat, and trying to catch his breath. He took in his surroundings. He was still in Liam's tent. Liam's snoring calmed him down. It was familiar and a reminder that they were safe for the time being.

This dream felt similar to the one of the raid. The images weren't clear, and he couldn't remember anything except for the conversation.

"Liam. Wake up. Come on." Finn stood up and shook his brother.

"What, what's going on?"

"We need to get Declan and Celeste. The general's planning an attack on the rebellion." Finn hauled him up.

"What?" Liam questioned, still not fully awake.

"I'll explain everything soon, just come on." Finn threw on the shirt he'd been wearing the day before.

"Finn, are you sure about this?" Liam asked, scrambling around to find his own clothes.

"I wish I wasn't," Finn answered.

Celeste sat back, leaning on her hands, her face a careful mask of indifference. She'd kept the expression since Finn, Liam, and Lucian had shown up right as she was falling asleep. Finn, eyes wide and anxious, said they needed to speak to Declan. Lucian could only shrug, looking baffled. She waved them inside and spent the next five minutes trying to wake Declan. She tried to be nice about it, but he was a deep sleeper. In the end, she pinched his nose until he jerked awake.

Her eyes were on him now, assessing the way his brow furrowed while he was listening to Finn's story, as if he actually believed his brother's dream was true. It was impossible. Finn was under a lot of stress. His nightmare was just that. A nightmare. She'd thought Declan would put this delusion to rest, but instead he sat enraptured by what was being said.

"You're sure about this?" Declan asked once Finn was finished.

"You can't be serious?" Celeste cut in. She sat up leaning closer to Declan.

"I swear, it's true. I can't explain it exactly, but I was connected to Leander. I'm sure," Finn answered, ignoring Celeste.

"It was a dream. That's all it was," Celeste dismissed, gaining everyone's attention.

"No, it wasn't. You don't understand." Finn ran a hand through his hair.

"Then explain it to me because I've seen people go crazy, and you're sounding a lot like them."

"Celeste." Declan sounded horrified by how cold she was acting.

"Tell me I'm wrong," she said then gestured to Lucian. "We've seen people become delirious because of a strong bout of illness, and we've watched people turn into banshees. Some people just snap under the pressure." Declan looked like he was about to interrupt, but she continued on, "You never saw any of that huddled away behind Essex's walls."

"There's more to this than you're seeing right now," Declan said in earnest but he was doing what Finn asked, keeping his secret, no matter how much tension it was putting between him and Celeste. Declan was frustrated because he would have just trusted Celeste if their positions were reversed, no questions asked. Celeste wasn't the same.

"Then what am I missing?" she snapped. "Because you seem too close to this situation to make a judgement call."

The frustration began to show on his face in the way his lips turned down. Finn hated seeing Declan look like that, especially at Celeste, who his brother really cared for, who he was so obviously in love with.

Finn cut in before Declan could say anything else. "I have the knife."

"The knife?" She echoed in disbelief. She shared a glance with Lucian, one Finn couldn't read. He hoped they weren't agreeing to go to Arran.

"War's knife. I have it." Finn was watching her with a guarded expression. He trusted Celeste, and had ever since she'd brought him to Declan instead of Arran, but he still didn't know how she would react to this. He trusted Lucian too, he'd trusted Lucian first because the man had never doubted him or Liam.

"The horseman's weapons have been lost for years. It's not possible." Celeste kept her face impassive, waiting for more. Lucian was much of the same. For the first time, Finn couldn't tell what he was thinking. The nerves began flutter in his stomach. Maybe this had been a mistake.

"I've seen it." Declan reached for her hand. "You trust me?"

"Of course, I trust you." She let their fingers intertwine. Though she was still hard to read, Finn hoped that meant she was leaning more toward believing him. "But sometimes you follow people blindly."

Declan's face went slack in shock. "I don't follow blindly."

"Before you listened to Grandma's stories, you thought Leander was going to save the world." Finn shrugged. Celeste was right. Declan was an all or nothing person. He believed in you and your cause without any doubts or he didn't trust you at all. Nothing in-between.

"It's not a bad trait to have. You just have to be careful with it." Declan didn't respond to Celeste, still stunned. She turned her attention fully to Finn. "Prove you have it."

Finn grabbed a small piece of cloth, so as not to touch it, and took the knife out of his pocket. "It becomes a longsword when I'm angry."

"So get angry."

"That's not a good idea." Declan said with a firm voice. Celeste needed to see to believe but the consequences could be devastating. Finn didn't think he could hurt anyone in the room, except Liam, but someone could find out.

"It's hard to control," Finn said.

"Maybe someone else should try it." She eyed the weapon with doubt.

"No. He's close to controlling it. The legends all say that it took groups of people to overtake whoever owned the weapon. I was able to calm him down without it coming to that." Declan looked proud but not at himself, at Finn. At Finn, because Finn was able to be talked down, because there was still a part of him that could hear reason, even when in the clutches of the knife's power.

"I was too." Liam spoke for the first time since they sat down. He leaned away from the knife, eyeing it with distaste.

"I still don't know if I believe any of this," Celeste said after a moment's pause.

"But you'll help us?" Finn asked. She turned to look at Lucian. He met her gaze head on. There was no hesitation in his eyes. The choice was hers.

"Fine, but I don't know how you're going to convince Arran that we're going to be attacked. If he finds out you have the knife, he'll take it from you by any means necessary."

"We don't have to mention the knife," Declan said. You could see a plan forming in his eyes. He was always two steps ahead. "What if we send him a message?"

"From who?" Lucian asked.

"The horseman?" Finn sat up a little straighter. "We've already told him that someone has it."

"He wouldn't believe it. He'd be more likely to think there's a traitor in the camp." Celeste sent Finn and Liam a pointed look.

"We'll forge one from one of our infiltrators." Declan ran a hand over his face, still holding Celeste's with the other. "I think it's our only choice."

"How are we going to do that? All of our falcons are accounted for. We couldn't get past the trainers anyways." Celeste chewed her bottom lip.

"We won't have to," Declan looked at Lucian. "In two days,

Lucian's going to receive his own falcon from one of the Exo Colonies."

"Why from the colonies? Why not from the camp?" Finn asked.

"Ours are only used by the trainers, that way they're easier to keep track of. Infiltrators are the only ones in the rebellion that have their own," Lucian answered. "The Exo Colonies raise them and have them bond to their masters when they're babies. They're very picky about who they allow to take part in the bonding process. It took a lot of convincing for me to get one."

"Arran knows he's getting it though," Celeste cut in.

"But he's not expecting it to be trained fully yet. He's never bothered to learn the customs of the Exo Colonies." Declan squeezed her hand. "He'd never expect Lucian to do it."

Celeste stared at Declan. "If anyone finds out, we'll be branded as traitors. There's no going back."

"We can find another way if you two don't want to be involved in this," Declan said in a low voice. Celeste scoffed.

"I already said I'd help you." She turned toward Lucian. "Your choice, big guy."

"I'm in." Lucian put his hand on Finn's shoulder. "You better be right about this."

· CHAPTER TWENTY-FOUR ·

Thea

The office looked as if a tornado had come through it. Books and papers were scattered along the desk and on the floor. There were empty food containers and coffee mugs littered everywhere. The coffee had left stains on some of the papers from where it had spilled. Normally Thea would never be able to function in an environment like this. Everything had a place but it had been almost a week and Thea had heard nothing from the tablet. She needed to hear it, needed to know what the next task was. Crazy. That's how she felt. There had to be some way to make the voice talk.

She hadn't even showered in the past couple of days. She thought her dedication had to do something; had to show the angel that she was ready to take on whatever she needed to. Was this what crazy felt like? She needed answers, needed help but couldn't talk to anyone. No one would listen to her if she began spewing things about the four horsemen and disembodied voices.

What would Aiden think if he could see her now? She could almost see the way his brows would furrow in concern and feel the way he would take her into his arms, rubbing small circles across her back. Would he think that she was clinically insane?

Would he be proud of the fact that she was fighting so hard for him? She hoped it would have been the latter.

She slammed her hands on the desk, rereading the same paragraph of the book laid in front of her. She couldn't concentrate to save her life. She would make it halfway through the second sentence and her mind would begin to wander. She pushed it away from her at the sound of people coming down the hallway. It was late. She couldn't imagine why anyone else would be here. She listened to the brisk pace as it neared her office and stopped before the door swung open, slamming against the wall. Liv walked in first, fury radiating off of her in waves. The kids followed behind her. William was shielding his younger siblings from the wrath of his aunt.

"How could you?" Liv asked. They were all dressed in black, the boys in nice sweaters and the girls in dresses.

"What? What are you talking about?" Thea asked. She had seen her aunt angry plenty of times, but never like this. Liv let out a violent scream, making Zoey cry out. William brought her into his arms, letting her hide her face against his chest.

"I called you. I texted you. I did everything I could so that you would know. You should have been there." Tears were rushing down her face and Thea wondered if they were from anger or sadness. "Is your phone broken or do you really just not care anymore?"

"Aunt Liv, please calm down."

"Calm down? You want me to calm down?" A strangled cry, a hysterical laugh came from her throat. "Don't you understand what's happened? Teddy's gone. He's gone and you weren't even at his funeral."

Zoey's cries were the only thing that broke the silence. Thea opened her mouth to speak but didn't know what to say. The shock of the news felt like a boulder had been dropped onto her.

"Aunt Liv, I'm so sorry. You have to believe me. If I would have known. My phone did break. It's been broken for a week now. I'm sorry. What can I do? Please, what can I do?" Thea stood, stumbling over to Liv, gasping as if the wind had been knocked from her.

"There's nothing you can do anymore. Why wouldn't you come home? Why wouldn't you let us know?" Liv hissed stepping away from her niece. "After everything I've done for you, everything he did for you, you still couldn't be bothered. You're not the only one who has felt the effects of Aiden's death. You are selfish. The most selfish person I have ever met. The only person you think about is yourself."

"That's not true. I've been thinking of more than myself. You just don't understand." Thea tried to reason with her.

"Then make me understand. What could be so important that you couldn't come to your own uncle's funeral?" Liv yelled, throwing up her hands in exasperation. Thea just shook her head, knowing that if she tried to tell her aunt what she was doing, she'd likely be put away. "That's what I thought. You don't have an excuse."

"I promise I do. I just can't tell you yet."

"I'm leaving. I can't be here anymore. If you can't put your family first, then I obviously didn't raise you right." Liv tucked her shoulders back, reigning in what little composure she had left and turned toward the door. "You should know that I also buried your husband. I couldn't keep him from that anymore. Your children needed to say goodbye."

Liv walked out, turning her back on Thea's heartbreak, her screams, and her pleading. William set Zoey on the ground, going to his mother, who was on her knees, sobbing. He placed a hand on her back. There was no explanation, no reason he could come up with for the way his mother was acting but he assumed that's what grief did to a person. When he was little, he used to think his parents were superheroes. Now he understood they were only human.

His father, who was supposed to be invincible, who could do anything, was gone. His mother was losing herself, falling deeper and deeper into her despair. He didn't know how to fix it.

"Mommy?" Zoey asked, sitting on the floor in front of her. "Mommy, please be okay."

Thea took in a shuddering breath as Elle and Ben came to her side as well. She wiped her eyes and opened her arms to pull Zoey into her.

"I'm so sorry. I know I haven't been the best mother." She took in another gulping breath to try and stop the feeling that her throat was constricting.

"You are the best mom." Ben spoke up, desperation in his voice.

"We're all doing the best we can," Elle added, looking at Will and hoping she was saying the right thing.

"Oh god. This is backwards. I'm supposed to be the one helping you, comforting you, not the other way around." Still, she couldn't find anything comforting to say.

"We'll get through it together, Mom." William was still rubbing her back. He was so much like his father.

Thea nodded as she tried to pull herself together. She didn't want her children to see her like this. She didn't want anyone to see her like this. The realization that she had hit her lowest point washed over her. She had let everyone down. Her aunt, her uncle, her children, probably even her husband too. She pushed away the hurt and shame as she stood and looked around the office.

"I'm going to gather up everything I need and take it home. Then I'm going to take a shower and make some dinner. How does that sound?" She ruffled Will's hair as he stood up, brushing her hand against his scar.

"We'll help you carry everything to the jeep." He nudged Ben, who nodded.

"Yeah, I'll take the heavy stuff. I'm strong now, mom," he said, placing his hands on his hips—his Superman pose.

Thea began gathering things up and handing them to her kids. She gave Elle her laptop and Zoey some of her research papers. William had a large box of any books she might need, which Ben complained about.

"I said I could get the heavy stuff," he whined.

"I know, I know, but I thought I'd give you the most important thing. How's that?" She asked, handing him the tablet. "You have to be very careful with it. I'm trusting you with this, it's something I need for my research."

"I got it. Stop worrying mom," he replied getting ready to take off down the hall.

"Don't run with it Ben." Elle grabbed his shoulder, jerking him back in the room.

"But I want to be like the Flash," he told her as if that was information she should have already known. She rolled her eyes at him.

"Can you be serious for five minutes? Mom just told you she needed this for her research."

"Elle, attitude," Thea said, giving her a pointed look. "Ben listen to your sister. You can't run with that, okay?"

"Fine." He started walking in slow motion until Will lightly hit him on the back of his head. Ben sent him a dirty look but began walking at a normal pace. Thea had never felt more grateful for anything than she did for her kids at that moment. Things felt almost normal for the first time since Aiden had passed. Little things were different; like the fact that Elle had gotten quieter and even more serious. Will had lost some of his light-heartedness by trying to take on some of the responsibility of caring for his siblings. Ben had started to live more and more in his imagination, fighting off fake bad guys, and Zoey was always on the verge of tears, any little thing could set her off. Despite these little changes, they were all surviving.

When they got home, Thea had the kids bring her things to her room and started getting a late-night snack ready. She was determined to put them first and take care of them like she should have been doing all along. She attempted to give her kids a normal night. They played board games to pass the time like they used to do, and she tucked Zoey into bed with a story. She let Will and Elle argue over who had control of the TV until it was time for them to go to sleep.

She waited until all of them were in their beds to head to her room. Everything she had brought from the office was still in piles on her mattress. The tablet laid across her pillow where Ben had tossed it. Thea placed her hands on her hip, trying to calm her racing thoughts.

"I'm wasting my time. I should've been spending time with the kids," she stated out loud. It was sometimes easier for her if she voiced her thoughts. It helped her categorize them. She walked over to her nightstand and picked up the picture that was sitting there. The frame was pink with little yellow stars on it, at least, that's what she had always assumed they were. Eleanor had made the frame in art class when she was eight. She had presented it to Aiden and Thea, a wide smile on her face with no fear of showing her missing front teeth. Neither one of them had the heart to ask her what the yellow-green blotches were.

Some of the paint was chipping off and she ran her thumb across those spots. The picture was of her little family in the hospital. She was laying in the bed, baby Elle sleeping against her shoulder. Aiden was sitting in a chair next to the bed holding Will. The smiles on their faces were big and proud, although exhausted. Will wasn't looking at the camera but instead was reaching for his new, tiny sister.

"Aiden, I wonder where you are right now," she asked, staring at the younger version of her husband.

"It is time," a voice whispered in her head.

"After all this time? Now?" Thea asked. She gripped the photo harder.

"You had to see."

"See what? See how I was hurting my children by not being there for them? Or how I hurt my aunt?" Thea slammed the photo back on her nightstand. The glass cracked.

"You had to see how everything falls apart without him. You need him, your children need him. He was never meant to die. You were never meant to live."

"What does that mean?" Thea asked.

"You will know soon enough. You need to make things right. Are you ready for your next task?"

She was supposed to have died? Not him? He should have been the one to come home to the children? Was that what she was being told? Guilt thrummed through her, stronger than it had ever been before. She had always felt that she could have done something more, tried harder to stop Aiden, anything that could have kept him alive.

"Are you willing to accept his fate or will you try to save him?"

"I want to save him."

· CHAPTER TWENTY-FIVE ·

Finn

All lights will be shut down at 8 p.m. sharp, no exceptions. We must preserve the wind turbines to keep power.

SIGNED LYDIA MCDONNELL

"Come on Finn, we're leaving." Senna grabbed his arm as he was aiming the bow. He was practicing without Celeste today. Jonas stood nearby watching with a pained expression on his face. Jonas was an archer and had tried to teach him on the days Celeste wasn't able to train him but had given up after a while when Finn showed no improvement. Archery was much harder for him to learn than swordsmanship, but he wanted to be as prepared as possible for the upcoming battle. He missed the target far more times than he hit it.

"Leaving?" Finn asked as she pulled him away, toward the gates. He bent down to put the practice bow in its spot as she tugged him forward.

"That's what I just said, isn't it?" She didn't let go of him, despite the fact that he would have followed her willingly, even if to just find out what her plan was. Jonas remained a few steps behind them. Although he didn't say anything, Finn had become adept at reading his moods and knew by his raised brows and relaxed stature that he was amused.

"Leaving where?"

"You ask a lot of questions," she replied, bringing him to the opening of the camp. Declan, Lucian and Celeste were all gathered by them. "We need more herbs to make ointments. It's usually my job to go and get them. Unfortunately since I can't fight, that means I have to bring scouts with me."

"Where's Lee?" Finn questioned as the gates were being opened.

"He's still working. I tried to convince Trent to let him come with us, but he just grunted at me. That usually means no," Senna answered.

"I think I'll go rest a bit since you're here," Jonas said to Lucian. Then to Finn, "Meet me at the tent when you get back."

"Everyone ready?" Lucian asked, slapping a hand against Finn's back.

"Ready." Senna nodded.

"Come on, we can talk and move." Lucian ushered them forward. Celeste walked beside him shaking her head.

"Lucian is meeting with a falcon trainer from one of Exo Colonies, Ferox," Senna spoke fast, a large grin forming as she did. Finn shifted his weight trying to seem surprised by the news. She didn't know what the plan was. She wasn't even supposed to be here because Celeste didn't want her involved. He could still see that in the way Celeste clenched her jaw as Senna spoke. "So I decided to tag along since our stocks were getting low," Senna continued on, her large eyes cast downward in thought.

"Where are we meeting the trainer?" Finn asked

"There's an area we have not far from here where we meet. They keep their base hidden away from us. We've agreed on a couple of meeting spots that we use to trade items or information." Celeste moved to be closer to Declan, grasping his hand.

Declan led them deeper into the forest, following marks

that Finn had only just started to learn how to read. Every safe house where scouts sometimes needed to stay was marked like the cave was, three lines above the opening. Safe paths were marked with a small *X* on tree roots and the base of trunks. A circle meant there was a trap ahead.

When they first arrived at the rebellion, everything felt impossible. It felt like the whole world was against them. Things were different now that people trusted him, believed him about the knife. He didn't feel like he was quite so alone. He didn't feel as suffocated as he did before.

"Finn, are you all right?" Senna asked him, noticing him pulling away from the group.

"Just thinking," he answered.

"I'm not bothering you then, am I?" She sent him a small smile.

"No, of course not."

"Are you sure?" She narrowed her eyes at him, as if that would somehow tell her if he was lying or not.

"Very sure," he replied. "Can I ask you something?"

"Anything and if I don't know the answer, I'll make one up for you anyway." Playfulness creeped back into the quirk her lips.

"Why haven't you joined one of the Exo Colonies? You don't like fighting and you hate Arran." He put his hands in his pockets.

"Celeste wanted to stay in the rebellion. She wanted to fight for our parents, and I didn't want to lose her after losing them too." Senna shrugged. "When you've lost as much as we have, you tend to stick together. I can also help a lot of sick people this way. I'm not really sure how the free people deal with their sick and wounded."

"What were your parents like?" The question slipped past his lips before he could think to stop himself. "Sorry, you don't have to talk about it if you don't want to."

"How about you tell me a little about yours, and I'll tell you a little about mine?" She offered.

"My dad has always believed in the government until they raided our house that is. He's a little more tightly wound than my mom, but I think that's what makes him a good overseer for the farm district. He's always focused on the details and making sure we have enough to feed everyone in town and to trade. He hates when my Grandma says anything negative about the government, but she doesn't like being told what to do, so they don't get along. I think they put up with each other because of how much they love my mom." He paused.

"And my mom, she's caring and understanding. She's a counselor, they help kids find a job to start apprenticing based off of our skills. She's good at it too. A lot of people in those positions don't take into account what we want to do but Mom always did.

"For as understanding as she is, she's still got a temper when she runs out of patience. One time I got into a fight with another kid. I was maybe seven or eight, and he had been saying that my Grandmother was crazy and how my Grandpa had been too, before he was taken away. I've always had trouble controlling my anger, so I hit him. We got into a big fight and officers had to break us up and walk us home. My mother yelled at me for an hour because I had gotten myself in so much trouble." Finn smiled at the memory.

"It sounds like you have a really good family." She toyed with a strand of her short hair. "My dad was the opposite of yours, I think. He was a friend to everyone and would talk to anyone. He loved painting. We did a lot of that together as a family using clay and berries. Sometimes Celeste still paints. Not very much, just when she's stressed out and wants to feel closer to dad again. She's really talented. I still try sometimes too, but I'm not very good. She got the creative gene. My mom was the more strict one but only because my dad always caved when he tried to punish us, so she complained she always got stuck with that job.

"Both of our parents were carefree. They always told us

they wanted us to be happy over anything else. Celeste is so uptight, and she's always been serious. I don't know where she got it from."

"What are you saying?" Celeste asked them, turning to glare at her sister.

"Just that you don't know how to have any fun," Senna answered, beaming at Celeste.

"Ah, Mister Webster, it's good to see you again," Declan cut off their conversation before they could start the argument. They were a little way down the mountain, surrounded by lush trees and brush. Mister Webster leaned against a broad trunk, arms crossed.

"Hello, m'boy, come for a falcon, have you?" Webster asked Lucian. He was an older man with a crooked smile.

"He's been waiting ages for you to train one for him." Declan laughed as Lucian stepped forward, a hand outstretched to greet the man.

"Of course, of course. I didn't forget my promise. I've got a special one, just for you. The biggest one I've ever trained. It's a small thank you gift for my life." The man outstretched his arm, covered with a thick glove, and whistled sharply. A large bird flew down and onto his arm. It was dark brown with golden eyes. It looked at the group, tilting its head to the side. "I've had a special glove made for you, too."

"We're near the clearing that you wanted to go to, Senna. We can start collecting the things you need while they're doing this." Celeste gestured toward the south and Senna nodded, grabbing Finn once more to bring him along.

Celeste followed them, knowing what herbs to help Senna gather, as Declan and Lucian talked to Webster. Senna didn't speak as she gathered what she knew she needed. Every so often, Senna would hold up a plant or berry and tell Finn what she needed it for. He nodded along as she spoke, not quite understanding. Most of the plants looked the same to him. So he'd point to some and wait for her to shake her head or nod. They met back with Lucian and Declan when they were all finished. Lucian whistled, and the falcon swooped down, landing on his arm.

"Did you get everything you needed?" Declan asked as he slipped close to Celeste.

"For now. We should have enough for a while," Senna replied, glancing at the basket full of plants. Declan led them back up the path but turned off it ten minutes into their trek back. Senna followed, giving Finn a confused look.

"Is there something else we need?" Senna asked. Celeste walked over to her as Declan pulled a scroll from his pocket and attached it to the falcon's leg. Celeste stood in front of Senna and poked her nose.

"Trust?" Celeste asked, opening her palm. It was something they had done since they were younger. It was a way for Celeste to let Senna know that something was going on, but she wasn't able to tell her the full story yet. It was also a promise that she would when she was able to. Senna hesitated before grabbing Celeste's hand and nodding. "We're sending a message to Arran. We think there's going to be an attack on the rebellion soon. You can't ask me how I know."

"Why can't you just tell Arran?" Senna was still holding Celeste's hand.

"It's complicated. Please, I know you hate this. I know it's unfair, but I promise I'll explain it to you later." Senna didn't look happy, but she nodded nonetheless.

"How does it know where to go?" she asked instead.

"The trainer made sure it knew where its home was," Lucian replied, lifting his arm into the air and watching it take off. Celeste squeezed her sister's hand before letting it go.

"Now we wait." Declan sat down, running a hand over his face. "I hope this works."

Two hours later, Finn waited as the camp's guards spoke to Declan, Celeste, and Lucian. He couldn't hear what was being said, but he could see the rapid, jerky gestures of the shift commander and feel the air of anxiousness that seemed to surround her. Senna fidgeted at his side, twirling her hair around her fingers. He had expected her to be nervous or maybe even afraid, but she seemed calm, almost bored. Neither one of them spoke, both refusing to break the tension that seemed to linger as they tried to overhear what was being said. Finn couldn't hear much, just the murmuring of words.

When the guards began to disperse, Declan motioned them forward, and they continued the trek to camp.

"Arran didn't buy the note," Declan said at last, making sure the guards were out of earshot. "He thinks there's more to it."

"Like what?" Finn asked.

"Like Leander being behind it." Celeste ran a hand through her hair. "He thinks Leander got information from one of our infiltrators, and that he's setting a trap."

"Our camp is hard to find and we know this land better than anyone in Essex." Declan grabbed Celeste's hand. "Arran thinks Leander is trying to draw us out."

"What's going to happen?" Senna asked.

"We're going to maximize our defenses. Camp is locking down. As of tonight, the only people that are allowed to come and go are those assigned to watch the perimeters or those who are authorized."

"That's good, right?" Finn walked at a brisk pace, keeping up with everyone else.

"He still isn't convinced Leander will actually attack, but it's something," Declan replied.

· CHAPTER TWENTY-SIX ·

Finn

Las Vegas should be overflowing with spirits long forgotten, but it's not. We've never received any intel of banshees or extractors in the city or from a five-mile radius of it. We think the generals have something to do with this. Are they able to capture the souls? Or maybe ingest them?

A LETTER FROM EMILEE HARRIS, LEADER OF
A REBELLION CAMP NEAR LAS VEGAS

The sun was coming up over the mountain, sparking with shades of orange and red. Finn leaned against a tree, eyes toward the sky. Jonas sat a few feet away, sharpening his blade. Another night and nothing. It wasn't that he wanted an attack to happen, but the dream had felt so real—not like normal dreams. It wasn't clear, but he didn't think it was something his subconscious could even come up with. Embarrassment pooled in his belly, burning hot and uncomfortable. Had he made a big deal out of nothing? Had he been so stupid? He hated the feeling that he might have made such a senseless mistake. He hated that he might have made everyone worry for nothing.

"Alright?" Jonas asked.

"I'm fine." Finn shrugged, dropping his hand.

"You know you always begin to chew on your nail, the thumb mostly, when you're worried." Jonas started working again. Finn had not known that.

"It's nothing."

Jonas let out a hum of acknowledgement but didn't look like he believed him. He didn't pry though. Not for the first time, Finn was thankful Jonas was the one who watched over him rather than Lucian. He appreciated and trusted Lucian, but also knew the man wouldn't let it rest if he was worried. Jonas checked in on him but never pushed him, a rare occurrence in his life.

"You training with Celeste after this?" Jonas held his blade up to study it and seemed satisfied with his work.

"Yeah. I wish I had a break though. Even when Celeste isn't training me, I feel like I need to do more. I feel like Arran expects me to do more." The last few days he'd spend all night outside the camp partnered with Jonas and then he'd head to the training grounds straight after. Although it was exhausting, he had improved, with the sword at least. He was useless with a bow. Most soldiers were at least decent with both but trained more with one. Celeste had spent quite a few days just trying to help him hit the target before she decided it would be best to just focus on the sword and come back to the bow at a later date.

Jonas snorted as he stood up. "Never get breaks here, not really." He angled his head toward the camp. The others on the night guard were beginning to trickle back to the camp's entrance. The morning watch was already there, waiting to trade off. They gave Finn and the rest of the group nods as they passed by. Jonas walked with him to the training grounds where Celeste was waiting with Liam and Senna.

"I'll be at the tents. Have Celeste escort you back." Jonas raised his hand in acknowledgement to her and walked away. Finn was envious that Jonas got to go straight to sleep after a shift.

"You look rough, Hero." Senna was sitting on the ground, leaned back on her hands.

"Thanks." He shook his head as she laughed. He felt rough. "That's what no sleep does to you."

"Still having trouble sleeping in the afternoons?" Celeste asked offering him a sword.

"Sun's too bright." Finn took it.

"He's always been a morning person, if you can believe that," Liam said with a look of distaste and took a seat next to Senna, knowing that he would be training next. "He used to wake me up at dawn when we were little just because he was bored."

"I don't think it was that early. You just like to sleep in." Finn laughed as Liam sent him a withering look.

"That doesn't surprise me." Senna grinned.

"How come you're here?" He flinched with how brash the statement sounded and was quick to try and revise it. "I mean, you don't fight right?"

Senna looked amused as he fumbled over his words. "No. I don't want to but the compromise was that I at least learn how to use the bow, just in case. I get to be Liam's training buddy when you're done with yours."

"Speaking of which, are you ready?" Celeste was already waiting for him, sword at the ready. He yawned and nodded. "Don't be so excited. Really."

"Sorry." He stood in the middle of the area, across from her.

"I'm not going to go easy on you at all today. I think you're at a point where you can handle it. So don't let being tired distract you." She held her sword in front of her, her feet spread apart. One foot was in front of the other. Finn copied her position with a nod. Since he fought with a long sword, his position was more centered and squared off. Celeste fought with a one handed sword because it allowed her to move faster.

Finn and Celeste moved around each other but weren't attacking yet. Finn had learned the hard way that attacking Celeste first never worked. Celeste thrust her sword toward his side, lightning fast. He blocked her. He was too slow, like always at the start of a training, because she was able to crowd his space. His weapon was a lot harder to maneuver if the person he was dueling could get in close. She used that to her advantage, placing one of her legs in between his, just behind his right foot, and used her force to push him back. He tripped over her and fell to the ground.

"Don't let me get that close to you, you know this." She grabbed him by the arm and pulled him up.

"I'm just getting warmed up." He picked up the sword and got back into his stance.

"There's no warming up when you're in battle. You either survive or you're wounded." They circled each other again. Finn zeroed in on her, ignoring how tired he was and the fact that Liam and Senna were right there. Celeste shifted her weight from her left foot to her right, and he braced himself, knowing she was going to strike again. When she did this time, he not only blocked but used that to push her back. She didn't hesitate to strike again, and he let himself react, parrying her sword to the right and taking a step in the opposite direction to take up that space.

As she pulled back her sword, he took a swing at her himself. She jumped back, avoiding the tip of the blade. "Good." And once again, tried to get closer to him to take him off balance. She said she wouldn't go easy on him, but he knew she was still holding back. He blocked her again but was too slow. She crowded him in the same way she had before, but he was ready for it. He took one hand off his blade and grabbed her free arm to push her down. Instead, she dropped her weapon, turned so her back was to him, twisting out of his grip in the process, and grabbed him instead. She flipped him over her shoulder. He hit the ground with a thud and a groan.

"That was pretty good." She bent down. "You okay?"

He nodded, taking a few deep breaths. The pain always made him angry, and he needed to take a second to calm down. "You still took me out too fast."

"I did but someone less experienced, and believe me when I tell you Leander's officers are always less experienced, wouldn't have been able to do that." She once again offered him a hand. He took it. "I was surprised. People fight in patterns and if you figure out the pattern, you can figure out how to win. That was different than your usual pattern."

"You told me to fight dirty, so that's what I'm trying to do." He dusted himself off. Buying a little more time before they went again.

"I can't believe you encourage people to fight like that." Liam sat with his head in his hands, looking almost disinterested. "Isn't there supposed to be honor in fighting?"

"It's not about honor. This isn't a game. It's survival, and if you're smart enough to win with a trick, then you use that to your advantage." She stepped back. "I know you don't feel like you're getting any better but trust me, you are."

Finn stood his ground raising his sword again. He knew that she wasn't lying to him. She was too straight-forward for that. She never had any problem with telling him what he was doing wrong.

On the days that he still had a hard time falling asleep, he watched her train or spar with others in the camp who wanted to get better. She was harsh but fair and would dole out praise as easy as she would criticism. When he stopped by those days, she made no mention of how he should be trying to sleep, but the next day their lessons were always shorter. She also never mentioned it to Leander, nor did Jonas.

He waited for her to attack again, wondering how he could ever get the best of her. She swung high, so he ducked, throwing a hand in front of him to help balance. He grabbed a handful of dirt as she swung at him again and threw it at her face. She spluttered and coughed jumping away from him with her eyes closed.

"Shit." Celeste started to back away, eyes watering. He used that to his advantage and rammed his shoulder into her, knocking her down. Both Senna and Liam looked as shocked as Finn felt. He thought, for a brief moment, that he had managed to best her but she kicked out one of her legs and knocked him off balance as swift as ever. He fell down hard and she raised her sword with the tip pointing at his throat.

"Don't presume you've won until the enemy is incapacitated," was all she said but she was grinning at him in the way she did when she was impressed.

"I really thought I had it that time." He fell back, breathing hard.

"It looked good from over here, Hero." Even Senna sounded awed by what happened.

Celeste laughed. "Almost lost by the oldest trick in the book."

Senna walked over to them, a waterskin in her hand. "Up you go. Take some of this." She handed it to him.

"I can't believe you almost won." Liam, who was still shocked, had yet to move. "With dirt."

"It was a good move. A lot of people just don't think of it. They're too in their heads about what they need to do next." Celeste stood up and stretched. "I think maybe we do some shooting now. You're free to leave." She motioned Finn away.

Finn's gaze turned to Senna who was already watching him with a small smile. "I think I should practice a little more with the bow first."

Celeste snorted but didn't say anything. She handed each one of them a bow and began setting up the targets. Liam sighed as he stood up, grumbling under his breath. When Celeste was done she pointed to Senna. "You first. Let's see it."

Finn had never seen Senna use any kind of weapon. She stepped up, grabbing an arrow from the quiver that Celeste had set on the ground to mark the place they should be shooting from. Senna raised the bow and pulled the arrow taut. A long moment passed before she released. Bullseye. Finn was impressed. He had a hard time hitting the target at all. She aimed her next arrow at another target. Another bullseye.

"You're really good with that," Finn said as she was taking aim again. After she hit her third bullseye in a row, she turned toward him.

"I had a good teacher." She looked to Celeste. "She made me promise to at least try and master one thing."

"And you agreed to that?" Finn watched as she took another shot. This one was a little left of the bullseye.

Senna stepped back as Celeste collected the arrows. "Not at first. We used to fight a lot about it. I realized, a little too late, that she wanted me to learn more for her peace of mind than for me. It wasn't that she was expecting me to fight at all. She was just scared."

"Liam you're next." Celeste interrupted them.

"Do I have to?" he asked but took his place next to the quiver nonetheless. She didn't bother to respond, just waited for him to start. His form wasn't as sharp as Senna's was and Celeste was quick to correct him. He was clumsy with the bow, but still better than Finn. His first arrow hit the target, at the very top.

"Are you okay, Finn?" Senna lowered her voice so Liam couldn't hear, looking him over. He was surprised to hear his real name come from her.

"I feel like I may have messed up." He told her, matching her volume. He had said as much to Declan too the other day.

Senna looked thoughtful. "So what if you did?"

Liam's next arrow went too far right to hit the target. He groaned in exasperation.

"What do you mean?" When Finn had talked to Declan, his brother had put a reassuring hand on his shoulder, telling him that he hadn't. He was still sure that Leander would attack and it hadn't even crossed his mind that Finn could have been wrong.

"Just that, so what if you did?" She grabbed his arm, giving it a squeeze. "It's not a mistake that's hurting anyone. Security is more tight sure, but what if you hadn't said something and the general did attack? That would be way worse."

And she was right. Of course, it would be a lot worse but he still couldn't shake the feeling of shame that coiled around him. Maybe he wasn't as in tune with the sword as he thought he was.

"I know," he said. A way he could agree with her without really agreeing with her. Liam's third arrow hit the target, a little low but it still stuck.

"I don't think anything I say is going to help, but if you just need someone to listen to you, you know where to find me." He was glad she didn't try and reassure him anymore. In time, he was sure he would feel better about it but he needed to let himself feel the shame and embarrassment right now.

Liam's last arrow hit the bullseye. He snapped his head over to Celeste with a wide-eyed stare. She looked impressed.

"Good job. That's your first one," she said as she began to remove the arrows. "Finn your next."

Liam still couldn't believe he hit the bullseye as he traded places with Finn.

"Soon you're going to be just as good as me." Senna laughed.

"I hope not," Liam replied.

Finn tuned them out as he picked up an arrow and pulled it back. He looked down at himself, making sure his feet were in the right place. He lined up his shot, held his breath, and let the arrow fly.

It went into the ground in front of the target.

"You're holding it too low." Celeste pointed up.

He tried again but over-corrected. The arrow went soaring above the target. "I know, it's too high."

He felt a touch at his elbow as Senna guided him into place, lining him up with the third target. "You've almost got it."

He tried not to move an inch from the position. He released the arrow again and hit the target for the first time. Not anywhere close to the center, but much better than he had ever shot before.

"Try again. No help this time." Celeste sent her sister a pointed look. Senna just shrugged. She didn't look too apologetic.

Finn tried to match up his posture with what Senna had just shown him, aiming for the final target. When he let the arrow go this time, it hit the very bottom of the target. If he had aimed any lower it would have missed.

"Could have been worse." Celeste began to pull his arrows out. "Let's go again."

Finn yawned, exhaustion setting in. "I think I might go lay down now."

Celeste waved her hand, dismissing him.

"Good job, Hero." Senna gave him a thumbs up. "See you later."

He waved to them as he left. He wasn't ecstatic about how training had gone, but there was progress. He could at least go to sleep knowing that something had gone kind of right.

· CHAPTER TWENTY-SEVEN ·

Finn

Fog pooled around Finn and Jonas in the inky darkness of the night, settling over the mountain in thick tendrils. Finn was used to patrolling around the edge of camp in the dark, but the mist made even Jonas antsy. It had crept in three days ago and had yet to cease. Jonas and Finn were stationed on the main path to camp, while others were stationed around the outside of camp. They had many extra hands working since their scouts could no longer leave the camp and that allowed the guards to remain in one place rather than patrol the area.

The past week had been spent with everyone on edge, waiting for another letter or a sign that an attack would happen.

None had come but that seemed only to make anxieties run higher. Finn had felt so sure that his dream had been a vision, that he'd been somehow connected to Leander.

Jonas sat whittling away at a small piece of wood, eyes scanning the fog in front of them every so often. He hummed to himself while he worked. For the most part, that's what their nights had looked like. Sometimes, if Jonas noticed Finn was getting restless, he would start up a small conversation. It was a rare occurrence. Finn kept one of his hands in his pocket holding onto the little skyscraper. He'd been carrying it around for the last few days. It helped him calm down when he felt anxious about his dream.

Jonas paused his work, staring into the night. Finn straightened up to follow his gaze, but he couldn't see anything. Instead, he watched Jonas, who remained stock-still.

"What's wrong?" Finn asked, moving a few steps ahead.

"Listen," Jonas responded.

Finn looked toward the sky, taking in the sounds around him. The trees stirred with the wind. Crickets chirped. From farther away, there was a rhythmic rustling.

"What is that?" Finn squinted, trying to make out what was happening.

"Footsteps. Fuck." Jonas stood. "Run back to the camp and sound the horn. You're faster than I am."

Finn hesitated as Jonas began to ready his bow. "You can't see anything."

"Go." Jonas turned to look back at him once. "Now."

Finn ran.

They had only been about a mile outside of the camp, so it didn't take him long to find the horn that stood near the entrance. He skirted to a stop in front of it, took a deep breath, and blew. A loud rumble crescendoed through the area. He blew twice more and saw Celeste coming toward him. She had a sword in her hand and a slightly shorter one at her waist.

"Leander?" She gave him the weapon from her hand.

"How are you here already?" He watched as she took a few steps forward with a frown.

"I lead the army." She cursed at the fog. "We won't be able to use the horses. Do you know how many soldiers there are?"

Finn shook his head. "I couldn't tell."

Behind them, Finn heard panic as the camp came to life. Yells to hurry, to be at the ready were being hollered. He listened as hundreds of foot falls sounded, heading to the front of the camp. His heart hammered in his chest. Men and women began gathering at the gates, weapons at the ready. They all looked to Celeste.

"Finn." Lucian was waving him over to where he stood, off to the side of where everyone else was. Celeste nudged him forward. He walked over to stand by Lucian's side. "Stay with me. I'll make sure nothing happens to you."

"Where's Declan?" Finn searched through the crowd.

"With Liam." Lucian shifted his weight from foot to foot. "Declan didn't want him to fight. He'll stay with the sick and help the extractors with what they need. He's going to join us once he knows your brother is in good hands."

"And Arran just let that happen?" Finn watched as their soldiers organized themselves. No one else seemed to be speaking.

"Arran doesn't know." Lucian stood a little straighter as Celeste walked over.

"Ready?" She asked.

Lucian clasped a hand over her shoulder. "No point in waiting much longer."

She nodded and ran a hand over her face. "Be safe, Finn."

He didn't get a chance to respond before she was moving back in front of their army.

"What do I do?" he asked. They were still standing off to the side.

"You stay with me. I promised Declan I would watch over you," Lucian replied.

"Why aren't we with everyone else?" Finn's gaze once again fell on the soldiers, most of them stood rigid with their eyes trained on Celeste.

"I'm second in command here. If something happens to Celeste, it's my job to take over." Lucian rolled his shoulders back, trying to release some tension. Despite the rigidness of his back, he seemed otherwise relaxed.

"I feel like I'm going to throw up. How aren't you more scared?" Finn asked.

"I am scared. Everyone is, but, like Celeste, it's my responsibility to be the backbone. Every single one of those people need to see confidence from us. How well do you think they'd fight if I looked as nervous as everyone else?" Finn understood where he was coming from. "Keeping morale up is what's most important here. Remember that."

Celeste lifted her sword, catching the attention of those around her. "I know you're scared. I know this isn't what any of you wanted to happen, but here we are, in the very midst of battle, just like we were warned." Murmurs broke out around them as she paused. "They've come to our land, our home. We know this area like the back of our hands. We have the high ground. They can't win." She paused as she looked around at the soldiers before her. "They think they can beat us. Today you will fight against those who will see the world fall. Today, you will help change the world."

Yells erupted around them and the soldiers raised their weapons in the air with Celeste, as they stomped their feet and pounded against their shields. Finn found himself joining in, believing that maybe they could pull this off.

Celeste turned toward the mountain side, sword held in front of her. Finn understood now why she was so important to Arran. Everyone trusted her. They would fight for Arran if he was up there because that's what they were supposed to do. They fought for Celeste because they believed in her. They trusted that she would fight for them, so they fought for her. Despite all the pressure she seemed to be under, she never cracked. Her face had remained impassive through the entire speech. No fear or nerves breaking through.

"With me," she yelled, moving forward. They followed.

"Try to stay by my side, Finn." Lucian pulled out his sword moving with the rest of the soldiers. Finn muttered a quick prayer that his brothers would be safe. The soldiers didn't slow down or hesitate despite the fog until they came to where the night guard was. The small group still stood their ground, Jonas at the lead, firing arrows blind into the night. The enemy fired back. Jonas had an arrow lodged into his calf. He leaned against a tree to keep his balance.

"Those of you who are able, come with me," Celeste motioned them forward to where Finn could see the torches the enemy were using to light their way. Jonas met Finn's eyes, and he tapped his finger twice over his heart. A gesture everyone in the guard did when they split up. Be safe, it meant. He tapped back and ran with the rebels toward Leander's army.

Soon, swords clashed around him and adrenaline pumped through his veins. He fought next to Lucian, locked into battle, the metal clangs ringing in his ears. His arms grew tired, but he pressed on with Lucian taking the brunt of the fighting. He kept the advice Celeste had once given him at the forefront of his mind.

"There's a good chance a once-fatal wound will take some-one out of the fight because the pain can make it impossible, but don't bet on it. The safest option is to remove the head from the body, that way it can't be controlled," she explained to him when they'd been training. When she'd told him that, he'd thought it would be hard but standing face to face with people who were trying to protect their families and homes too, he found it next to impossible. Lucian always made the final blows.

Arrows flew above his head in both directions as he parried a sword aiming for his heart. He wasn't fast enough and the sword sliced his arm. His own weapon fell from his hand. He dodged another slash, looking for Lucian, eyes scanning the battlefield and wondering how they'd been split up. He moved right, trying to grab his weapon but was blocked by a man who raised his sword high. Finn dropped into a roll to avoid losing his head. Lucian, who he spotted a few feet away, was battling three opponents, trying to get back to Finn's side.

"Your friend's a goner. He'll be an untouchable soon." The man sneered, swiping at Finn's torso. "Even the biggest men fall." Finn stepped back, avoiding a lunge and tripping over a body. He hit the ground. "You'll just be another one that needs to be cleaned up."

Finn reached into his pocket, where the knife sat waiting to be used. As soon as he grabbed it, his vision swam with pulsing red. A promise for bloodshed. Anger wrapped around him, swam through him, until it was the only thing left he could feel.

His opponent lifted his sword above his head. Finn pulled out the knife, thrusting it as it transformed into a long sword, impaling the man through his chest.

He let out an echoing yell as he stood, cutting the man's head off. For a moment, the battle lulled with the realization that War was on the field. An aura of red surrounded Finn as another soldier ran at him. His moves were quicker, more precise but the biggest impact was the sheer strength he seemed to possess. He blocked the strike of another soldier and the power behind it sent the man's weapon to the ground.

"With the horseman," Lucian yelled, starting to fight once more. He heard Celeste echo the call and soon the rebellion was fighting with renewed vigor. Men came at Finn left and right, trying to bring him down, but he fought them off one by one, cutting through them as if they were only a nuisance. The bloodlust he felt was nowhere near quenched. It demanded more. It demanded everything and everyone. Yet when he looked to Lucian, sword ready to betray his friend, he stopped. Finn battled for control over the sword's influence. He wanted to fight, but not at the expense of those he cared about.

Pain blossomed from Finn's side. A sword cut deeply, right

under his ribs. He staggered back, dropped to his knees and held onto his fresh wound. The sword fell to the ground.

"Look out." Declan rushed in stabbing the enemy through the side. Lucian cut off her head. "Come on, we need to get you out of here."

Declan grabbed him by the arm and lifted him up. Lucian watching their backs.

"No. We need to win. I can still fight." Finn stumbled forward grabbing the sword off the ground. The pain ebbed away until the only thing he felt was a dull ache. A constant reminder not to lose himself to the power. The bloodlust was overwhelming still, but the slow throb of his side subdued it.

Declan held onto him tighter, doubt clouding his features. Finn pulled away, moving to help Lucian fight. He felt more secure with Declan near him.

The rebellion was pushing the enemy force away from camp. Celeste was still calling out orders from the other side of the fight. Declan kept an eye on her, his body angled toward where she was.

"Retreat. We can't win. Retreat." The soldiers at the back of Leander's force were able to get away, down the mountain. The rebellion fought off the stranglers who didn't break away in time.

"Jesus, Finn, I knew the horseman's power was strong, but I didn't know it was that strong." Declan clapped him on the back. Although covered in blood and exhausted, his older brother appeared to be okay. He hadn't been hurt too much aside from a gash on his leg from what Finn could see.

"Yeah, more than I thought too," Finn replied. It took every ounce of concentration he had to uncurl his fingers from the sword's hilt. It returned to its normal state. He gasped, stumbling into Declan as his side exploded with pain. His vision swam. Declan grabbed his arm before he could hit the ground. He closed his eyes trying to fight the sudden onslaught agony.

"Shit. I wasn't expecting it to take so much out of him." Lucian grabbed his other arm, helping Declan stand him up.

"We need to get him to an extractor. They need to disinfect his wounds and stitch him up." Declan threw Finn's arm over his shoulder.

"Grab the horseman and his accomplices."

216

· CHAPTER TWENTY-EIGHT ·

Thea

Thea danced around the living room, tugging on a coat while trying to help Zoey with hers. Toys were scattered across the floor. The brown carpet was hardly visible. The couch was in the same shape, but it also housed a mysterious stain that she hadn't noticed until that moment. Later, she told herself; she would have to deal with it later. She shot her youngest child a suspicious look, knowing that she'd had some hot chocolate earlier that day.

"Ben if you're coming with us we need to go now. Elle, are you sure you don't want to come?" Thea shouted from the bottom of the staircase.

"Mom, I can't find my other shoe. You've gotta help me." Ben appeared at the top of the steps holding out a sneaker. The heel of it was looking a little rough for wear, and she made a mental note that she needed to go shopping.

"Why didn't you tell me earlier?" Thea asked, glancing around the room. "Did you check the kitchen?"

"Because I didn't know it was missing until now," Ben replied as he ran down the stairs and through the living room.

"Eleanor did you hear me?" Thea yelled again.

"Yes, I heard you, and no I really don't want to go," Elle shouted back.

"How come I have to go?" Zoey asked, one hand reaching to take hold of Thea's and the other tugging softly at her pigtail.

"Don't you want to support Will?" Thea ruffled her daughter's hair. Zoey hesitated before giving a small nod. "Ben, did you find it?"

"Got it." Ben walked into the room with both shoes on. It was then that Thea realized he was wearing one black sock and one white one.

"Your socks." Thea groaned, running a hand through her hair, and wondering if there was time for him to change them.

"They're just socks, Mom, nobody's going to care." Ben sent her his toothy grin. It was his secret weapon to charm his mother into giving him what he wanted. She sighed knowing what he was trying to do, but she had also learned a long time ago that she had to be strategic when arguing with the kids or else she might spend the whole day dealing with bad attitudes for no real reason at all.

"Okay, fine. Let's get going, but if anyone asks, you're not mine." Thea ushered them all outside, ignoring the offended noise Ben had made and Zoey's laugh.

Thea drove toward the bowling alley, brown bricked and a little worse for wear on the outside. It looked as if none of the windows or glass doors had been cleaned in a long time. Will had joined a bowling team with his friends during the summer, and they had somehow made it to the championships. Thea hadn't been to many of his games because she and Aiden had been out of town. He had stopped going for a while after his father's death.

Will hadn't intended on even going that night, but Thea wouldn't let him miss it. He needed some time to himself, where he could hang out with his friends, and maybe forget the summer's tragedy for a little while.

"Do you think Will's going to win?" Zoey asked from the backseat.

"I'm not sure. I haven't seen him play yet," Thea replied, guilt sitting deep in her stomach. "What do you think Ben?"

"Yeah. Will's team is really good. Last time he played he got a turkey." Ben nodded excitedly. From what the boys had told her, Ben had gone to every one of the matches. Although he probably just went to play the arcade games.

"Why would they give him a turkey? Did he do better than everyone else?" Thea laughed, caught off guard by Zoey's question.

"Not the bird, sweetie. A turkey is when someone gets three strikes in a row. It's very hard to do," Thea replied.

"Right," Zoey said very solemnly, nodding her head.

There weren't many people in the bowling alley. William grinned and waved them over when he saw them. Her son never ceased to amaze her. At his age, she would have been mortified if Aunt Liv or Uncle Teddy had decided they wanted to show up while she was hanging out with her friends. His teammates acknowledged them with a small nod as they walked up.

"Are you going to get a bird?" Zoey asked him.

"If I'm lucky, I will." Will chuckled but didn't correct her. He pulled at one of her pigtails causing her to puff out her cheeks.

"Mom, can I have some quarters? I want to play air hockey." Ben was bouncing from foot to foot.

"I don't have any quarters, but here's a five. Don't spend it all right now because that's all you're getting."

"Got it." He ran off after she gave it to him, and Thea tuned back into the conversation between Zoey and Will.

"Are you going to win?" She asked.

"I hope so," he replied. "We're starting soon, so it won't be too much longer."

"You don't have very many answers," Zoey told him, her tone matter-of-fact.

"Come on Zo, don't you believe in me?" he asked, placing a hand over his heart. She giggled and threw her arms around his legs.

"Of course, I do." Her voice was muffled by his jeans, and he put a hand to her head. Thea's heart constricted for a moment. That was what Aiden used to do. She wondered if Will knew just how much like his father he was.

"It's time to start," one of his friends said, clapping him on the shoulder. Will nodded.

"Good luck. I'll get everyone some food." She let Zoey stay with him as she ordered a pizza, a basket of fries, and onion rings. It wasn't the most healthy dinner, but she knew none of the boys would complain. She and Zoey sat down at the table right behind the team's lane as they started. During the game, Ben would come and go as he pleased. He'd met some of his own friends and was in the process of beating everyone else at air hockey. Thea watched as Will's team took the lead at a steady pace.

"You did a great job." Thea ruffled his hair.

"Thanks Mom," he replied as his friends snickered behind them.

"Did you get a bird?" Zoey asked, slipping her hand into his.

"You bet I did. I got one just for you." He curled his fingers around hers as she started babbling to him about the pictures she had drawn that day. Most kids his age would be embarrassed when their mom showed too much affection, and she'd seen teenager after teenager ignore their younger siblings. Will waved goodbye to his friends, still holding onto his sister's hand and listening to what she had to say.

"Ben, it's time to go," Thea called over to him. He let out a small groan but made his way over nonetheless.

"Did you win?" Ben asked.

"Of course, we did. Are you doubting our skills?" Will challenged.

"Hey, you never know. You could have had a bad night." Ben shrugged. "Shotgun," he called out as they reached the jeep.

"Let Will have it. He's earned shotgun rights tonight," Thea said before Ben could open the door. He groaned again.

"Tonight I played better than ever." Will slid into the

passenger seat, sending a smug look over his shoulder at Ben. Then added, "I wish Dad could have been here."

The sudden shock of Will's words almost sent Thea into sobs. Her hands shook as she began to drive back to the house. The bitter sorrow that had accompanied Will's tone cemented the fact that she needed to bring Aiden back. She had spent three days trying everything she could. All she had been told was that she needed to give a part of herself to the tablet.

The one who wishes to free us must give a piece of themselves as sacrifice.

She wasn't sure what piece of herself she needed to give. Last time the lamb's blood was what triggered the tablet. She had thought hers would be enough too. She had tried cutting her palm, which was harder than she'd expected. The movies made it seem so much easier to cut yourself for the sake of someone else. She was no Indiana Jones. It had taken her at least an hour to finally slide the knife against her skin hard enough to draw blood. Nothing had happened.

Maybe the amount of blood she had given was too small. So she had tried to cut open her thigh next. She had made seven slices on her skin over the next two days but again nothing happened. Very slowly, she was reaching her wit's end. Thinking about it now sent her into another wave of anxiety. She had spent the past couple of days with the kids, but as soon as Zoey and Ben went to bed she holed herself into her room to concentrate on her work. She was only brought out of that focus when Will and Elle knocked on her door to say goodnight.

When they got home, Thea took Zoey to bed, and as was always requested, read her a bedtime story. She changed into more comfortable clothes. An old pair of Aiden's sweats and one of his shirts that had yet to be washed. She just couldn't find the strength to clean them knowing that they had touched his skin. She headed downstairs to get a bottle of water and a small snack. Will was flipping through channels on the TV, and Elle sat against the side of the couch, scowling.

"He beat you to the remote again? Weren't you here all night?" Thea asked watching the annoyance wash over her daughter's face. "Careful, with an eye roll that big you might just pull a muscle.

"I let him have the remote since he won, but I'm not happy about it," Elle responded. "It would be different if he'd just pick a channel."

"Hey, aren't you the one who said that you wanted to focus on your drawing?" Will switched the channel again. "It's not my fault there's nothing on."

"I'm not drawing, I'm designing." Elle's curt tone was a warning. Her plan, at the moment, was to go to school for fashion design. She'd taught herself how to sew and had bought fabric to make her own clothes. She hadn't made anything yet, but Thea had to give her daughter credit for her determination and discipline. Her other kids didn't have half the amount of ambition as Eleanor had. She'd always been like that. Her fiery personality and stubborn attitude had gotten her pretty far. She'd already won an award for her poetry, a small piece that took months of rewriting and editing, and she was the only child of Thea's that had a perfect GPA.

"Whatever," Will replied, settling on the history channel. "Are you working again tonight Mom?"

"Yes. I'm sorry. I can't just stop working though; I'm trying to balance it out a little better." Thea started up the stairs giving her children an apologetic look.

"It's fine, we get it." Elle elbowed her brother.

"Right." He slapped her thigh. Thea thought about telling them to knock it off, but they'd already stopped. She sighed and continued to her room. It seemed like she couldn't do anything without feeling guilty. When Aiden was still around, they would take turns in the evening. One concentrating on work, the other spending time with the kids. Wednesdays and Thursdays were the only exceptions. Those were family nights. Wednesdays were only missed if there was a special reason, and Thursdays were no exceptions. Those were the days Liv and Teddy came over and had supper with them. *I should call Liv*, Thea thought. Teddy was always the one that smoothed things over after a fight. Without him, she was afraid they would never speak again. Her aunt was stubborn and once she decided something there was no changing her mind. Thea knew she would have to be the first to reach out. Time always seemed to get away from her and whenever she thought about it, she would promise herself she would do it later. Later never came. She had to just suck it up and get it over with.

After she figured out her problem with the tablet, she would do it. She sat down on the bed, pulling the heavy rock onto her lap and staring at it with determination. Sacrifice a part of herself. She'd tried blood but maybe it wasn't something tangible. Maybe it was something that had meaning to her, something that had a piece of her soul in it. She hesitantly pulled on the chain around her neck. Aiden's wedding band was kept on it, as was hers. Looking down at her finger fifty times a day and seeing the blue sapphire and silver metal was too painful, so she put them on the necklace.

She slipped the chain off of her neck and stared down at it. It would be a small price to pay to have Aiden back. She kept repeating those words to herself as she set the jewelry down on the tablet. She reached for the bookend that was on her nightstand. The books toppled over, one slipping to the floor. She didn't bother picking it up. Setting the necklace on the stand, she held the book end over it, gathering the courage to smash her most prized possessions. There was no way she could do it. She dropped the owl.

"Please, I can't. It's a piece of our marriage, of our life. There must be another way. Help me," she said, desperate for any other solution.

"You said you would do anything to get him back." She was reminded. It seemed to be chastising her.

"But not that. Anything else, please." She had never expected to get help this time. Why now? Why not sooner?

"A piece of metal or a little bit of blood isn't enough. You must lose more."

"Like what?" Thea exclaimed in annoyance.

"That is your problem to solve."

"Stop speaking in riddles." She pulled on her hair.

"Humans always say things they don't mean. 'I'll do anything.' Do you know why? It's because you're selfish. You cannot, or rather will not, do anything unless it fits into your own needs. When the price becomes too steep, you give up."

"That's not true. My aunt took me in when she didn't have to. Aiden has, time after time, helped people without expecting anything in return," Thea argued. "There are people who do selfless things, no matter how high the price is."

"But you're not one of them. That's why you loved him so much. He was something that you could never be."

She had always considered herself practical, not selfish. Was she wrong? She had loved Aiden's ability to see someone and help. Even with their aspirations, no matter how far-fetched they could be. She always hesitated and asked them if they were sure it was something they wanted. She thought she had been helping people by making them see the more practical route. Was she really just being selfish by making people see things her way? By casting doubts into their lives?

"Make your choice. Do you want your husband back or not?"

"Of course, I want him back. Why wouldn't I?"

"Then you must lose something more."

Those words echoed in her head as she slipped downstairs once again. She hadn't realized how late it had gotten. Every light was turned off as she walked down the stairs, not bothering to turn them on. She placed her hand against the wall as she went into the kitchen, pulling out the first drawer she reached. She kept the sharpest knives in there. With a large knife in hand, she returned to where the tablet was waiting.

She felt numb. She had expected fear to be coursing through her but there was only a destitute resignation. There was nothing else she could do to save her husband. For the first time in her life, she was going to be selfless. She would gladly give up a part of herself for her husband. She hoped it would be enough.

She sat on the floor, bringing the tablet with her. She stared at it.

"If you're going to do it, it needs to be now. You'll never have enough courage again."

"I don't know if I can." It hurt to even whisper the phrase. Her throat was closing up, the familiar sensation of panic setting into her stomach.

"Do it."

She took a deep breath, trying to calm her nerves, and placed her hand on the tablet. All of her fingers were curled toward her palm except for her pinkie.

"Do it."

She tried to block out the voice that was screaming in her head. It never stopped its chant. She put the knife above her finger.

"Do it. Do it. Do it."

Anything. She would have done anything at that moment to make the voice stop pounding against her skull. With each sharp word, it felt like a mallet was cracking into the bone.

"DO IT. DO IT. DO IT, NOW."

She brought the knife down forcefully, closing her eyes at the last minute. Pain. Searing. White hot. Screaming. Who was screaming?

A hand grabbed her, and she was pulled into someone. Will? He was speaking to her, fear and horror creasing the lines of his face. He spoke to her and when she didn't reply he gripped her face, forcing him to look at her.

"Oh God, Mom. What happened? Mom? Please listen to me." He shook her. He wasn't prepared to handle this. All he could think about was whether or not he was about to lose another parent.

"Will? Why's there so much blood? Is she okay?" Elle hadn't been too far behind him. Ben was on his knees sobbing.

"Get Ben and Zoey back. Don't let them see this. I'll call an ambulance. See if you can reach Aunt Liv." Will tried to stand up with Thea, but she was in a catatonic state. "Elle, now. They can't see this anymore. Are you listening to me?" Will yelled, his tone harsh enough to get a screech from Zoey. Elle yanked Ben off the ground, supporting him the best she could while forcing Zoey back down the hall. She shoved both of them into her room, slamming the door and leaning against it. She took her phone from her pocket, dialing her aunt. Will was already on the phone.

"911, what's your emergency."

"Please help. Our mother cut off her finger. She's not responding to anything."

Will had turned his back to the room as he gathered Thea up, helping her get downstairs. He didn't see the tablet, abandoned on the floor as a bright light emitted from it.

"Soon. Soon, you will have your husband back."

· CHAPTER TWENTY-NINE ·

Finn

A counselor's job may be one of the most important in the territories. It is their job to work with people from the time they are children to adulthood, to analyze their skill set, and place them in the job that will most benefit the town.

EXCERPT TAKEN FROM THE COUNSELOR'S GUIDEBOOK

"That didn't go as well as you planned." Finn watched as Leander turned a cold stare to the man who led the attack on the rebellion. The world around him felt hazy, as if he had opened his eyes under water. The man, although looking somewhat nervous, held the general's gaze. Finn recognized him from how he was dressed as one of Leander's elite guards. There were very few of them. They were the only people the general trusted.

"It wasn't a complete failure, sir," the man responded, breaking eye contact. His fingers twitched at his side.

"Not a complete failure? War was on the battlefield. The weapon he had will give me the power I need," the general spoke, his voice was barely above a whisper. He was seated at a desk, back rigid. "Tell me why I shouldn't snap your neck right now? Why shouldn't I feed off your soul, like I have so many others?"

"We could attack again. We could win. The fog is the only thing that stopped us. You can ingest the new souls from the battle. They'll give you more power." Leander leaned back in his chair, prompting the man to continue. "Many people became untouchables. You'll be able to feed off of them once the rebels take care of them."

"When souls detach from the body, you never know how far they'll scatter." Leander watched him. "I suppose that's only something a demon would know, though, isn't it?" He grinned—a tight, malicious thing.

"Surely you should be able to find them."

"I suspect I could." The general stood to his full height.

"Sir?" The man asked as Leander made his way around the desk.

"It doesn't change the fact that you failed me." Leander put both hands on the man's head. They began to glow red, and the man let out a yell. In seconds, it seemed as if the life had drained out of him until he could no longer stand. His body dropped to the ground. For the first time in his life, Finn understood what death really looked like.

Finn groaned and his entire body ached, but he found himself unable to stretch out like his muscles needed. His hands were tied, the rope digging into his skin, leaving unforgiving, red marks. He gasped in pain, his right side throbbed.

"Finn, are you alright?" Declan asked from beside him as he struggled to sit up. Declan, Lucian, and Celeste were all with him, tied up as well. At least five guards were stationed near them. They were being held in the middle of camp, in front of the little cabin. People stared at him as they passed.

"My side." He adjusted his position, trying not to jostle it too much.

"It was bandaged after the battle. It was a deep cut but from the sound of it, but it wouldn't be classified as a fatal wound." Declan spoke in a hushed tone, trying to soothe away the frantic look that crossed Finn's features.

"You're sure?" Finn asked.

"You'd be a lot worse off otherwise," Declan said.

"What happened?" Finn tried to take a few shallow breaths to ease the pain but even that made his wound ache.

"Arran happened. He demanded we be neutralized, as he put it." Declan motioned toward their hands. "He wants the knife for himself. He doesn't care about anything else."

"No one will challenge him. Cowards," Celeste said, staring at a few people passing by them. The group tensed but didn't glance over.

"Celeste," Declan warned.

"It's true. Would you have seen this injustice and just stood by?"

"I might have if I had been able to convince myself it was for the greater good. I would have sided with Arran over a stranger," Declan admitted with a weary smile.

"Well that's why you've got me. I'll tell you when you're being too much of a blind follower." She pulled at the ropes, trying to free her hands. Lucian chuckled then groaned as he shifted his weight.

"I definitely have a few broken ribs." He took in a deep breath. Finn sent him a worried look.

"He tried to keep them away from you after you collapsed but too many ganged up on us," Declan said.

"I'm sorry I got you guys involved in this. I should have just told them I had the knife." Finn sent them an apologetic look. Celeste scoffed.

"You shouldn't be. He went for the knife without a second thought and used the excuse it could be dangerous in your hands." She rolled her eyes. "Like you weren't the reason we were able to win in the first place." Her face softened. "I don't blame you for not saying anything. I wouldn't have either."

"Where are Liam and Senna?" Finn asked, glancing around them.

"We don't know. The extractors wouldn't say anything to Arran," Lucian answered.

"Two scouts came to take them and the extractors held them off until Lee and Senna got away," Declan replied. "Hardly any of them had weapons and since they're already borrowing bodies, Arran thought it would be better to have them under watch. They're each being questioned by Arran one-on-one."

"What does that mean for them?" Finn asked. His hand went to his pocket, knowing if Arran had the knife, he might have the small carving too. He was relieved to find it still sitting in his pocket.

"I don't know," Declan replied, voice soft and strained. "It's not something that's ever happened before."

"I'm glad Liam and Senna were at least able to escape. Do you know where they would have gone?" Finn thought of all the banshees that they could possibly run into.

"Somewhere safe, I hope, but I don't know where that would be." Declan's brow furrowed as he thought about it.

"I'm sure they're fine. Senna doesn't like to fight, but she's pretty good at finding her way around out there. And she knows what berries they can live off of. I'm sure your brother could make them something to hide out in." Celeste seemed far less confident in his brother's abilities than she did Senna's.

"As long as she keeps him from panicking," Declan said.

"He's gotten a lot better than he used to be," Finn offered. "If she doesn't mind him talking nonstop, he can usually keep it under control"

"They've already got scouts out looking for them. I'm assuming they sent out Trent and Jazz. They're the best ones we've got." Celeste leaned forward, glaring at their guards. They remained silent as more people walked past them, giving them looks of pity or sympathy to varying degrees.

"How can all these people just watch him treat us like this? We haven't done anything wrong." Finn stared after a group of scouts who were keeping their distance, trying not to make eye contact.

"They haven't known you as long as they've known Arran, and you've kept the sword a secret the entire time." Lucian shrugged.

"But don't they trust you? You led them into battle. You've trained them. Why aren't they fighting for you?"

"People are afraid of change, Finn. The only reason you wanted the knife was to save our family. You didn't really want to be War." Declan nudged his shoulder.

"I didn't want that many people's lives on my hands." Finn swallowed hard. He wanted it now though. He was beginning to understand how to control it. For the first time, he wanted to help restore the world to what it used to be.

"I know but everyone here trusts Arran. He's led this section of the rebellion for thirty years," Declan said. Finn remained quiet, mulling everything over.

"Okay, so what's the plan?" Finn asked. Celeste sent him an almost defeated look, one he had never seen cross her features before.

"We can't figure one out." She tried once again to free herself.

"Can't figure one out?" Finn echoed.

"We're in the middle of camp, where people pass through all the time, day and night. Even if we could get out of these ropes, we wouldn't get very far." Declan turned to Celeste. "You're only hurting yourself."

"I appreciate your concern and that you've always worried for my safety, but right now it's getting on my nerves." She stopped trying nonetheless. "We've come so far, and we're just going to give up aren't we?"

"Can you think of a way to get out of here?" Lucian asked her. She sighed.

"Hopefully Arran doesn't figure out how to use the knife," she answered.

"He's got a lot of anger," Lucian responded. "When did we switch roles? Aren't you supposed to be the pessimist?"

"I'm just not an idealist like either of you are, but I guess you've rubbed off on me a bit," she said with a small, defeated smile.

"If the world wasn't already messed up, I'd say you admitting that would have started the apocalypse itself." Declan chuckled while Celeste fought hard to hide the upturn of her mouth.

They spent the day in the same spot, Finn relaying the dream he'd had. They were given water and a handful of berries throughout the day. Declan pleaded with the guards to at least listen to them, but they just shook their heads, never taking their eyes off the ground.

Finn tried to listen as the others figured out a plan of escape. Each time someone would come up with something that might work, a flaw was pointed out. It led to frustrated and constant bickering.

The hours passed, unhurried and sluggish. Declan did his best to keep everyone's hopes up, and even Celeste was trying to find a way to be more positive, despite being the one to point out the error in the plans Declan and Lucian came up with.

When night fell and the camp began to settle down, one of the guards came up to them, making sure there were no passerby's. He was stubby, short and bald with a full, unkempt beard.

"Laine?" Declan studied him as he shifted from foot to foot.

"I can't stay too long, but I don't like how Arran's been treatin' ya. Neither do they." He craned his neck at the other two guards who were on duty with him. He lowered his voice even more. "Be prepared. A group of us who support the horsemen," he broke off to bow his head in Finn's direction. "We got wind from the extractors that Senna and your brother are safe. They're with the Exo Colonies."

"What?" Finn asked, voice too loud. He was shushed by Celeste.

"Trent and Jazz, they're good friends with Celeste here. She saved their tail once when they made a mistake on a mission;

haven't forgotten that they owe her one. They sent a message to us. Our little healer allied with the Exo Colonies. They've never cared much for the rebellion or the general's towns, but they do believe in you. One of their people will be waiting for you in the usual meeting spot tomorrow night." Laine's gruff voice held determination. "They'll fight for you because all they want is to put the world back in order."

"Laine, I can't thank you enough for doing this." Declan shook his head in disbelief.

"You've done way more for the people of the rebellion than Arran ever has. You came back for me when you shouldn't have. I'm only alive because of you. Believing in you is the least I can do." Laine began pulling food out of his cloak, setting it down in front of them. "You'll need your strength for this battle. We're not finished yet." Laine walked away, returning to his post.

"It's the knife's power, not mine," Finn said.

"But you wielded it. To them you are the horseman," Declan replied.

"How did you save him?" Finn asked, grabbing a strip of meat.

"It was one of the first weeks after I left Essex. I was partnered with him, learning to be a scout. One of the first lessons you're taught is to not go back for someone if the situation looks hopeless. I never agreed with that." Declan shook his head. "We were investigating a place we were told the general visited often, trying to figure out why. Laine went in, and I was supposed to keep watch from the outside since I didn't have as much training. He was meeting with someone in secret. Banshees were gathered right on the other side of the clearing, shrouded by brush. They started wailing as soon as they saw him. There were too many for him to fight alone.

"He pulled out his sword to stall them while I escaped. He was already limping so he couldn't outrun them. In that situation, according to Arran, I should have gone back to camp because I could escape and deliver news that it had been a trap. Five banshees against two of us was too much of a risk." Declan gave Finn a sad smile.

"I don't blame the others who have followed that rule, but I just couldn't. I jumped in and fought with him. I expected him to berate me for not following the rules, but he was thankful. We've always watched each other's backs since."

"I don't understand why you wanted to be part of the rebellion, working under someone like Arran. He doesn't care about the people under him." Finn rolled his shoulders, trying to alleviate some of the stiffness in them.

"You don't have to agree with a person to fight for the same things. If I could save every single person, I would, but that wouldn't stop the general. I'd be so worried about everyone's lives that I wouldn't get anything done, and I'd always be on the defense. Arran might care less about individuals, but he wants to see the world put back to what it once was."

"And he wants to be the hero," Celeste muttered.

"And he wants to be the hero." Declan sighed. "Which means he wants you out of the picture."

"You can still lead and care about the people under you though," Finn said. "I'm not going anywhere without a fight."

"Maybe Finn will be a better leader than either of us." Celeste nudged Declan in the side, who grimaced in pain.

"I don't know about that." Finn said.

"I do," Declan responded.

· CHAPTER THIRTY ·

Finn

*Remember that the rebellion's efforts are more import-
ant than individuals. While none of us want to be
captured, or worse to be made an untouchable, it would
be far worse to lose a rebellion camp. We cannot let the
generals gain any more ground than they already have.*

EXCERPT TAKEN FROM THE REBELLION'S RECORDS

Sweat rolled down Finn's forehead. The sun's rays beat
down on him, bright and unforgiving. He was so thirsty.
Arran still hadn't let anyone bring them water, not since
the morning. He would give anything to wash himself off in
the river right now. He felt grimy, like dirt had caked itself
onto every inch of his skin. He tried to take his mind off
of how uncomfortable he was by talking to Declan, Celeste,
and Lucian but that didn't help much. He thought of Laine
and how, by tomorrow, they would be free. He thought back
to the conversation they'd had. How Celeste had said Arran
wanted to be the hero. That scared him. Not because he was
afraid of Arran using the knife, but because he had realized
that he liked that people thought of him as the horseman and

liked the power boost the knife gave him. Did that make him similar to Arran? Would he reach the point where being the hero was more important than the lives around him?

The thought of becoming more like Arran made his stomach churn—Arran, who had spent the day interrogating the extractors. They had been escorted into the cabin one by one, each with their shoulders squared back and a defiant tilt to their heads. They stumbled out, holding tightly to the wounds of their borrowed bodies, gasping and leaning against their fellow rebels who had the audacity to look on with guilt but say nothing.

Finn was sure that one of them would break and tell Arran where Senna and Liam were. It seemed as if none had.

"They're so used to enduring the pain of an already broken shell that Arran's methods don't matter. They're better at compartmentalizing the pain." Celeste bowed her head when one of them looked over, a silent thanks for protecting her sister.

"I don't think I could handle what they do," said Finn as the extractor gave a subtle nod back.

"There are very few who can."

No, Finn didn't want to be like Arran. A man so focused on remaining in power that he was willing to hurt the people he was supposed to lead.

It was the late afternoon when Arran emerged from the cabin, taking stock of the camp. Most people refused to meet his eyes. Instead, they walked by him at a brisk pace, heads bowed and bodies hunched. This didn't seem to bother him. Finn expected to see some kind of sign that the past few hours had been difficult for him, whether that was through tiredness or regret.

There was none.

The man who stood before them had the same hardened look of determination he always wore. There were no cracks in his impenetrable mask. When Arran looked at Finn it was with an expression of inconvenience as if he was a bug needing to be squashed, not a boy who had helped win a battle.

Although without the sword, maybe he was just a nuisance. Arran strode over to them.

"Please listen to us." Declan moved to stand up but Arran put a hand on his shoulder and forced him back on his knees.

"What's wrong with you?" Celeste struggled against her binds.

"What's wrong with me? You betrayed us. What were you expecting?" Arran squeezed tighter until Declan let out a hiss of pain.

"We weren't trying to betray you." Declan tried to move back, away from the iron grip of the undead man.

"Silence." Arran pushed Declan back and he fell to his side. Celeste leaned over him. "You're coming with me boy." He lifted Finn up like he weighed nothing with his large hands under his armpits. He cried out in pain, trying to pull away. His side burned with it. Arran dug his fingernails into his skin to quiet him.

"Stop." Lucian jumped up but was prevented from doing anything by rebellion soldiers who stood between him and Arran.

"As leader of the rebellion, it's my job to protect the camp from enemies. Traitors are enemies." Arran dropped Finn to his feet and began pushing him toward the cabin. Finn staggered forward.

"You're not a leader. You're a coward hiding behind glory," Lucian said, venom lacing his every word.

"I wonder, does it make it harder to say that to me, now that we have the same face?" Arran turned around.

Lucian's jaw clenched. "You might be using Carson's body, but I know the difference between you. He believed in people and the cause. He didn't care about being a hero."

Declan, Celeste, and Lucian all protested as Arran led Finn into the cabin. Even when the door was shut, he could hear their shouts. Arran pushed him to his knees but remained silent, as if he was waiting for Finn to fill in the blanks.

Finn could feel the familiar pulse of anger. The more his side ached the more the feeling grew. He squeezed his fingers together hoping the exertion would bring him a small reprieve from the overwhelming feeling. It did nothing. It only heightened the white hot fury he felt.

"I expected you to be smarter than this." Arran circled around him. "You've kept your secret well all this time just to give it away now."

"I was fighting for the rebellion. I was helping." Finn took a few deep breaths, trying to calm himself but it only made the pain in his side grow.

"You had no control over yourself. I know how the knife works." Arran pushed him down and kept him there with a hand in between his shoulder blades. Finn kicked his legs, ignoring his side to try and free himself. It didn't faze Arran. "You thought you could hide it from me. That was your first mistake."

Arran moved his hand from Finn's back to his head, pushing his face into the dirt floor. Finn was still unable to break free and yelled in frustration.

"Your second mistake was thinking you could betray me."

"Let me go," Finn said, feeling like the pressure against his skull would crush it. Arran ignored him and leaned in close.

"You didn't really think you'd take the rebellion away from me, did you?"

"What?" Finn froze.

"Don't play dumb with me boy. I figured out your plans."

"I'm not playing dumb. I never wanted to take over the rebellion. I wanted to save my family."

Arran's hand tightened in his hair. "You know I don't like liars."

"I'm not lying. I never wanted to be the leader of anything. I just wanted to get my family out of Essex. The knife was the best way to do that."

Arran lifted Finn's head and slammed it back into the ground. Pain exploded as a sharp crack sounded from his nose. He could taste the blood as it gushed down past his chin. Arran turned Finn around, digging his knee into his stomach. "What did I just say?"

"Fuck you," Finn replied, trying to push Arran's knee off of him. He gritted his teeth. His head was pounding.

"I can do a lot worse to you if you don't start telling the truth."

Finn spit in his face.

The blood and saliva landed against Arran's cheek and slid down. He wiped it off and stared at his hand. Finn recognized the fury that crossed Arran's face. Arran curled his fingers. His fist was the last thing Finn saw before it slammed into his jaw.

He was shaken awake by Declan.

"Come on, Finn." Declan hauled him to his knees as he tried to blink away the foggy feeling. His whole body throbbed. Declan slipped a knife through the ropes around his wrists, setting them free. He rubbed the angry, red marks that were left behind.

"What? Where did you get that?" Finn took the hand his brother offered him, touching his nose and flinching at the pain that blossomed there.

"Laine," Declan said. Lucian and Celeste were already up. "They're getting us out of camp."

"Are you ready?" Laine nodded his head toward the far side of camp. Finn sent Declan a confused look.

"What about the knife?" Finn turned toward his brother, panic rising up in him.

"We need to get out of here first. None of us are in any condition to fight Arran. We wouldn't be even if he didn't get a power boost from the knife." Declan shifted from foot to foot, anxious about getting out without being seen.

"He's not going to be able to control it. He's going to hurt someone." Finn, despite being in severe pain whenever he moved the wrong way, couldn't just let Arran have the knife.

"I promise you, you'll get the knife back." Declan grabbed his arm. "Please trust me. We don't have a lot of time."

Finn, as reluctant as he was, nodded. Declan had trusted him from the beginning, and it was time Finn started doing the same. He would get the knife back, one way or another.

They snuck through the camp as quickly as possible, avoiding the main trail and weaving through tents as carefully as possible. All Finn could think about was getting the knife back. His fingers twitched with want at the thought of it. It had become a comfort to him over the past month, knowing that he had a powerful secret.

"Who's over there?" Jonas was leaning against a tree right outside of camp as if he had been waiting for them. Lucian and Declan had been quick to step in front of Finn.

"Shouldn't you be off duty?" Laine called back.

"I've had this schedule so long, I can't sleep during these hours anymore. I gave the other guard a break." He pushed off the trunk, not putting much weight on his right leg, and beckoned them forward. "There's no point in hiding now, is there?"

Laine let out a long sigh. "The guard stationed was going to help us."

"Jonas, I'm glad you're alright," Finn said, relief flooding through him. He really wasn't sure the man would make it through the battle.

"You look worse than I do, boy and that's a hard feat," Jonas said. Finn grinned at him. It was very rare that Jonas ever made a joke. "I thought I might get some peace and quiet by working."

"I guess I showed up right on time tonight," Finn said. "Are you going to let us pass or do we have to beg you?" Jonas snorted.

"The horseman groveling would be something worth seeing. Let's go then." Jonas began to walk down the path.

"You want to go with them?" Laine looked him over with shock.

"Aye. I trust the boy, more so than Arran at least," Jonas replied. Finn was shocked. Although Jonas never seemed to like Arran, he hadn't shown a hatred of him either. He seemed indifferent at most to the way Arran ran things.

"Are we going or do you lot want to wait around until somebody notices you're gone?" That set the rest of them in motion. Declan and Lucian slapped their hands on Laine's shoulders, thanking him for everything he had done. Celeste and Finn joined Jonas until the other two were ready and they made their way down the mountain. Finn was surprised by how little Jonas seemed to care about his wounds, as his own were throbbing in protest over all the activity he was doing.

"Do you even know where we're going?" Celeste followed behind Jonas.

"Aye, to the clearing. Where else would we be going?" Jonas shot her a disgruntled look over his shoulder.

She scoffed then muttered under her breath, "What a smartass." From the way Jonas' shoulders shook, Finn guessed he heard her.

"What happened on your end of things during the battle?" Finn ducked under a tree branch, trying to ignore his pain as he did so.

"Arran stayed back with us, watching over things, but he was quick to join the fray when shouts of the horseman started sounding over the noise of battle." Jonas slowed down to match Finn's pace, letting Celeste and Declan take the lead. Lucian was bringing up the rear. "All of us archers were starting to lose hope, not much we can do in the fog except hope. When we heard the shouts, we started firing again. We just knew the horseman was fighting for our side.

We were pretty shocked when you were brought back to camp, tied up and unconscious, and these three as well. They were all fighting against it, of course." Jonas shrugged. "Not what I was expecting of you."

"Sorry." Finn grimaced. "I wasn't trying to lie to everyone."

Jonas shook his head. "If you didn't lie, you'd probably have been captured and questioned by Arran right away."

"Jonas, there you are." In the middle of the clearing stood a woman with bronze skin and russet curls. "I was afraid you'd have trouble getting out."

"What?" Celeste turned to him, hands on her hips.

The woman threw back her head and laughed. "Even the Exo Colonies have some spies. We were never sure if we could trust you or not."

"But Jonas has been in the rebellion for years. There's no way," Celeste said.

"And I've stayed on the night guard by myself for most of those years. My job hasn't been hard." Jonas shrugged. Lucian's booming laugh joined the girls. "I was sent a letter to make sure you got here safe. My time with the rebellion is finally over."

"He always hated that he had to join the rebellion, but he blends into the background better than anyone else I know. He was the perfect candidate." The woman walked over and put her arm through his. "Are you ready to go?"

"I think so." Declan motioned for them to lead, his face had been much more controlled when finding out Jonas' true alignment. "Can we get your name first?"

"I'm Beatrice, but everyone calls me Bee." She didn't ask for any of their names. Instead, she started the trek forward, taking them zigzagging through the forest. She didn't seem to be looking for any specific markings, she just knew her way.

They walked for four hours, through thickets of trees and brush. Bee kept talking most of the way there, her arm still looped through Jonas's. Finn almost ran into her back at her sudden stop. She cupped her hands around her mouth and mimicked a bird call. An answering sound returned.

Soon, the free people came from out of the trees, faces curious but solemn. Senna and Liam were right at the front of the group and upon seeing them, ran to greet everyone. Senna flung herself into Celeste's arms, laughing and holding on tight. Finn and Declan grabbed Liam, checking him for any injuries before Senna barged in, wrapping her arms around Finn's neck and squeezing him. He hissed one hand going to his side and the other wrapping around her. She adjusted so she wasn't touching his wound but didn't step back.

"I knew you could do it, Hero," she mumbled into his chest before letting go.

"I lost the sword. Without it, I'm just normal." Senna scrunched her nose in disagreement but didn't get the chance to say anything. A group of older men and women stepped up to them as the rest of the free people stayed behind. There were twelve of them.

"You must be Finn. We've heard a great deal about you from these two." A woman with graying hair spoke first. Her demeanor reminded Finn of his grandmother. "I'm Holly, one of the council members of the Exo Colonies." She gestured around at the people that had walked up with her.

"It's nice to meet you." Finn stuck his hand out. Holly took it in a firm grip. "I'm going to be honest. Arran took the sword, that's what has the power, and I'm just ordinary without it," Finn said, and for the first time in his life he understood what it was like to be Liam, nervous and rambling.

"Then we get the sword back," she replied. "For the record, I don't think you're just ordinary. There are people who are willing to risk being branded as traitors to help you."

"Not for me. For them." Finn gestured to those around him. "I'm only here right now because of them."

"That's not what I've heard. Not from Jonas, or these two, or the scouts that came by. You've inspired people. They fight for you because they believe in you." She looked over her shoulder, and Finn followed her gaze as more free people stepped forward. More people had come then he realized.

Holly looked him over, noticing how his hand stayed clutched against his side and seeing the wounds on his face. "Come, we'll have someone look you over. After you can rest. We can discuss more later." She turned to the people behind her.

Another member of the council called out, "Make sure the ladders are lowered. Hurry back, let's go."

Senna pulled away from Finn but grabbed his hand. They followed behind the free people past the trees they had come through and found at least fifty rope ladders hanging down from the trees. Among the branches, there were platforms and small buildings.

"Isn't it amazing, what they've done? They have an entire city up there and you wouldn't know unless you looked up." Liam grinned, excited by it all. "They keep the ladders up unless they hear a bird call. I can't believe this. They have a woodworker who let me see some of the plans they had for more buildings."

"It is pretty amazing." Finn smiled at him.

Climbing up the ladders was hard for Finn. Liam, Senna, and Celeste had gone up ahead of him. Declan and Lucian were behind him in case it was too hard and he needed a boost. Several times he had to take a break from pulling himself up. Declan put a hand on the back of his ankle, reminding him that he was still there. When he got to the top, Celeste helped pull him up, grabbing his arm as Declan put a hand beneath his foot to give him more leverage. His breathing was labored when he got to the top. He'd expected the platform he was on to be a little shaky but it held sturdy. Liam was right, seeing what these people had built was amazing. They had a small village up in the trees, connected by platforms and rope bridges.

"Get back to what you all were doing. Our guests have had enough to deal with. They don't need your staring," Jonas yelled out. He met Holly's curious gaze with an indifferent expression.

"This way, Finn. One of our healers can take a look at you. We have some salves to help numb the pain." Holly led him to one of the small buildings. A man was standing outside, holding a wooden bowl filled with green goop. "He's all yours Harry. We'll get the rest of you set up in a cabin to spend the night."

Declan and Liam refused to leave until Finn had been taken care of. Senna had wanted to stay too, but Celeste convinced her to give them some time. Celeste didn't want to be too far from her sister either, and it would be pointless for them all to wait outside while Finn was being tended to. Harry didn't speak to him. He focused on his task, checking over Finn's wounds and wiping off the dried blood on his face with a wet cloth. He rubbed on the salve with a gentle hand.

"You should be thankful none of your wounds are warm. That's the start of infection," Harry said as he cleaned his hands.

"What do I do if that happens?" Finn asked.

"Not much you can do other than hope for the best. Don't worry about it though. I haven't seen an infection happen, not when we've had the chance to rub this stuff on it. Smells terrible but works like a charm." Harry motioned him out of the cabin. "Go on now, get some rest."

Holly was still waiting for him outside, deep in discussion with Declan, who seemed to make it his mission to learn everything about how the free people ran things. She cut him off when she noticed Finn and took them to a cluster of small cabins. Celeste was sitting outside. "You three will stay here."

Once Holly left, Declan bid his brothers goodnight and slipped into a cabin with Celeste. Liam shifted his weight from one foot to the next. "You're sure you're okay?"

"I promise I'm fine, just tired. It's been a long day," Finn said. Liam nodded. They both slipped into their rooms.

Finn, wrapped tightly in a blanket, fell asleep as soon as he laid down.

· CHAPTER THIRTY-ONE ·

Finn

I hate being stuck in this town. I wished to stay in the rebellion with my little family, but Arran thought this would be best. I know I will be taken away soon. I'm getting too old and I have a hard time moving around. I will be phased out and suffer the consequences, as many others have too.

One of the last pages of Finn's grandfather's journal

Finn woke up the next morning to hushed whispers and giggles. He was confused by his surroundings until he stumbled outside, right into the midst of a group of wide-eyed children who dispersed as soon as he opened his mouth. He scratched his head as he looked around. It seemed as if he was the last one up.

"Hey, Hero, you hungry?" Senna was walking over from a bridge to his left, wooden bowl in hand. He took it from her as soon as she was next to him, scarfing down the scraps of meat that were in it.

"Where is everyone?" he asked, mouth full. Senna laughed.

"With the council. They're trying to figure out the best way to get the knife back." She leaned against the cabin behind her, kicking her foot. "I got bored, so I came to wake you."

"Why didn't anyone get me before?" Sudden fear shot through him. Maybe they would decide the knife belonged with someone else. He should be there.

"Relax." Senna put a hand on his arm. "They wanted to give you time to rest. Your injuries aren't going to heal overnight."

Finn still wasn't convinced, but he leaned back too. Senna was flush against his side. "How did you get here?"

"One of the extractors helped out the free people before. She knew the area their camp was in and told Liam and I how to get here. We still got lost. Your brother is terrible with directions." She rolled her eyes. "One of them found us anyway and brought us back here to talk to the council. Liam didn't want to tell them about you, but he coughed up the truth."

"And you're not mad?" He looked over at her. She was staring up at him, biting her lip.

"It's a pretty big secret. I'm a little annoyed I'm the only one that didn't know." She sighed. "I don't need to be protected from everything."

"I wasn't trying to hide it from you or make you feel like I didn't trust you." Finn took her hand in his free one. "I was thinking of myself. I didn't want to get caught with it. It was selfish, but the only person I was trying to protect was me. I wanted to keep the knife." He paused and shut his eyes. "I wanted to use it to save my family, but I also liked that I had a powerful secret, something that would keep me safe."

Senna turned toward him, squeezing his fingers. "You will save your family, Finn, whether you've got the knife or not."

He smiled at her. The sun shone down on her from between the tree leaves, lighting her face in a glittering pattern. Mischief danced behind her eyes, even though what they had been talking about was serious, and a grin curled at the edge of her lips. He wanted to kiss her then. The desire rolled through him, sudden and overwhelming.

"Finn, you're awake." Liam came barreling at them, and they stepped away from each other. He didn't seem to realize he was interrupting. "They told me to come find you two. The council wants to speak with you."

Liam was more at ease than he had been in months. He no longer seemed to be looking over his shoulder all of the time. Finn wondered if it was because they were with the free people, who seemed to just accept them or if it was because he was no longer holding onto Finn's secret. He belonged in an environment like this, where people were just living. They weren't always preparing for the next battle to happen here.

They followed behind Liam as he led them to a round, open platform. Benches were built into the wall. Declan, Celeste, Lucian, and Jonas were sitting on one end of the circle, the council on the other. Everyone was relaxed and greeted them with a smile.

"How is your side doing?" one of the men asked. He looked to be the youngest one there with delicate wrinkles and graying temples.

"Still hurts but it's much better than it was." Finn took a seat next to Declan. His brother sat with his elbows on his knees, leaning forward. He was still wrapped in a conversation with a council member who was telling him about how their colony had managed to stay hidden from Leander's watchful eye.

"It'll probably be that way for a while." The man stood up and walked over to Finn. Everyone else quieted at this action. He held a hand in front of Finn. "I'm Howard."

Finn shook his hand, unsure if the man was just being friendly or if there was an ulterior motive. Everything seemed too good to be true. He couldn't wrap his head around why everyone here was so willing to trust him. His confusion must have shown on his face.

"We're not trying to trick you," Howard said as he sat back down. "I can imagine it feels like that."

"I don't even have the knife anymore. I'm not sure what you want from me." Finn looked over at his brother and friends, wondering what they had been talking about before he arrived.

"It doesn't matter that you don't have it right now." Holly tapped her fingers against her thigh as she was speaking, a rhythm only she seemed to hear. "You'll get it back."

"Why don't you want it for yourself? The knife can be used by anybody. Anybody can wield it." Finn clenched his hands, his white scars becoming more prominent.

"But not anybody can be the horseman. That's the difference." Holly stood up and began to pace. "The truth of the matter is the people of the rebellion have already seen you wield it. You're the one who stopped Leander's surprise attack. I'm guessing most of the rebellion has figured out the tip came from you. It would take a truly incompetent person not to put anything together by now.

"Not only did you fight against Leander, you fought for those people, and you were able to control yourself. The knife creates more trouble than it's worth, everyone knows that. Yet, you were able to not only control yourself but you won the battle."

"Not alone." Finn was uncomfortable with the way everyone's attention was on him. His part of the battle was contingent on everyone else who had kept his secret, who had listened to him, and helped him. He wasn't the sole reason it was won.

"No war is ever won alone." Holly stopped her frantic pacing to direct him with an intense look. "People need someone to turn to. The horseman is powerful and the only person who has a chance at beating Leander, but he's also a symbol of hope. Our world is broken and the only ones who can put it back together again are the ones who are able to wield the horsemen's weapons. That day on the battlefield, you proved that was you."

"They're going to help us get the knife back. They'll help us fight Arran." Declan's leg bounced in place. Finn could tell he was already formulating a plan. "We can go in at night, like Leander tried to do. There are already people volunteering to fight for you."

"I don't want that." Everyone looked shocked. "I want the knife. I'll be the horseman, but I don't want to attack the rebellion."

"What are you proposing?" Howard asked.

"We can still sneak in. I think the night guard will just let us in, if Jonas and I talk to them." Jonas nodded at his words. They both had good relationships with the people on their watch. "I'll challenge Arran to a fight. Just me and him. We're already fighting against Leander, we don't need to be fighting against the rebellion too."

Howard laughed. "There might not be much of a choice. You'll still need an army with you, in case things don't play out as you hope."

"We might need the extra people if they don't let us in," Finn conceded.

"It might work," Jonas spoke up. "Not many people were happy with Arran's treatment of them, Celeste and Lucian especially, and they're not ready for another battle. Too many were wounded when they faced Leander's army. They're not going to want to fight."

"You actually think this will work?" Howard marveled at them. Some of the other council members looked skeptical. "You can't fight against the knife one-on-one."

Holly seemed impassive. "It's his decision."

"You're agreeing to this?" Howard asked.

"I have a feeling that they would just do whatever they wanted regardless of what we said. It's his choice to fight Arran." Holly didn't look happy about the conclusion, but she at least accepted it.

"Unbelievable." Howard sat back and stared at them. "And if you become an untouchable?"

"Someone else will have to fight Leander." Finn shrugged. He hadn't thought that far ahead. He didn't want to. If Arran beat him, then it was likely no one would try and take the knife away from him but at least he'd try and take down Leander.

Declan leaned over to him, dropping his voice to a whisper. "Are you sure this is the way you want to do things Finn?"

Finn nodded. "I need to be the one to take the knife back."

Declan nodded.

They decided to end the meeting there, not wanting to put too much pressure on Finn since he was still wounded. They were offered to be shown around by a few of the council members who seemed to side with Holly's disappointed resignation over Howard.

He knew Declan would still try to talk to him about this decision later, but it wasn't a reckless choice. He needed to be the one to confront Arran. He needed to be the one to get the knife back.

· CHAPTER THIRTY-TWO ·

Thea

"I promise, I'm really ok. It was just a slip of the hand. I was working late and was tired," Thea said from the front seat of Liv's lime green car. Her eyelids felt so heavy. All she wanted to do was sleep and forget about everything that happened. She leaned her head back on the seat and held in a sigh.

"You need to take a break. Do you realize the emotional trauma you've just put your kids through? They thought you were dying." If Liv's grip on the steering wheel got any tighter, Thea was sure it would snap in half. Liv was right. She needed to rein in her feelings and be strong for them. She needed to show them she was okay.

"I know. I know they were scared, but we handled it." She was thankful her aunt was there, but she didn't want to have this conversation. She felt like a teenager again. "Aunt Liv, I'm sorry. I can't express to you how sorry I am or how thankful I am you came as fast as you did."

Liv grumbled some words Thea couldn't quite make out, but there was no doubt that they were meant to be insulting. She'd been listening to her lecture the entire way back to the house. Will was driving everyone else in her jeep because Liv "needed to speak with her alone."

"It's just, I'm trying to work to keep the house over our heads and trying to take care of them. I'm used to being part of a team, not handling it by myself. Balance is tricky to find." It was the truth, just not all of it. Liv sighed.

"You need to put your children first." Liv sent her a strong warning look.

"I will. That's been the plan. It'll get better, you'll see," she said, determination dripping from her words. "I'm sorry for what happened with Uncle Teddy. He was such a big part of my life. I don't think I could accept him being gone either. For a long time, it felt like he was keeping me together. I know it probably doesn't take away the hurt, but I wish I could go back and be there for you like you were there for me."

"I appreciate that. I've thought about coming over to talk to you, but you know I'm bad that way. Teddy always said I was too stubborn." Liv turned into the driveway.

"I thought about calling you every day to apologize. I guess I got the stubborn gene too." Thea opened her door. "I really do appreciate everything you've done for me."

"Why don't I come inside for a little bit. I'll make some hot chocolate for everyone." She was already getting out of the car. There was no way she'd take no for an answer. Thea took a deep breath, steeling herself before opening the door. God, she was so tired. Her finger throbbed when she moved her hand. Now that the shock was wearing off, she was beginning to feel how awful the pain was. She held onto the prescription bag in her hand. She just needed to go inside, take the pain medication, and go to sleep. She should probably spend time with the kids before sleeping.

"Do you want to spend the night? The guest room is still decked out how you like it," Thea teased, knowing that Liv hated the color scheme—bright yellow walls with white trim. It was too bright to sleep in according to her. Liv laughed.

"Do I have any other choice?" she asked as Ben and Zoey ran toward their mother, throwing their arms around her. She lifted her bandaged hand to keep it from getting jostled. The doctors had put stitches over the wound. No one had thought to grab the finger to give it a chance to be sewed back. Her stomach knotted at the realization that she'd have to clean up. What do you do with a finger anyways? Throw it away?

"Aunt Liv, are you coming too?" Will asked as he walked up to wrap an arm around his mother.

"Yes, I'm going to make hot chocolate for everyone, like we used to." William looked up in obvious excitement. "And yes, I'll make a couple of snacks too."

"I'll set the table," Will said as they all walked inside.

"Does that boy think of anything except food?" Liv muttered under her breath as she made her way to the kitchen.

"Momma, are you sure you're alright? Do you need me to do anything for you?" Elle asked, shifting her weight. Thea wrapped her arms around her eldest daughter, rubbing her back softly. Elle took a deep breath and leaned her head on Thea's shoulder.

"I'm fine, sunshine, I promise. You don't have to do anything right now."

"Are you sure?" Elle hugged her a little tighter.

"I'm positive, but if you really want to do something for me, you could wash the dishes tomorrow morning." Thea laughed when Elle pulled away and scrunched her nose.

"I guess I can do that," she answered.

"I would really appreciate it." Thea nudged her shoulder as she made her way to the table, thankful to be off her feet. Liv set down a glass of water in front of her. She opened her medicine and took a pill, hoping it would kick in fast.

"I love you, Momma," Elle whispered as she sat down.

"I love you too," Zoey chimed in rushing over to wrap her arms around Thea.

"Don't forget about me! I love you too." Ben plowed into them, his arms open wide.

"Come on Elle, group hug," Will said as he pulled her up and squeezed her between Thea and himself. "I love you too." Liv laughed and took a picture of them on her phone.

"Send that to me, please?" Thea asked. Liv handed her phone to her niece.

"You send it. I still haven't figured out texting on this phone," Liv replied offering her phone to Thea.

"Do you want me to show you?" Will offered.

"Nope. I just want to serve this hot chocolate and have a nice night with my family. We don't want to ruin that by arguing about a phone." Liv smiled, handing out the steaming mugs.

"What about snacks?" William asked, grabbing his cup and taking a seat at the table. Liv sent him the hairy eye and walked back into the kitchen, grabbing a carton of frosted cookies and setting it on the table.

"Will that satisfy you?" she asked him and he nodded, opening the package.

"Zoey, Ben, why don't you grab a game we can all play? It's been awhile since we had a family game night," Thea told them. They ran into the living room, searching through the cabinet.

"You want to play a board game now?" Liv looked incredulous. "You should rest. You look exhausted."

"Are any of you going to be able to sleep?" Nobody answered her. "We could all use a little fun, don't you think, to take some of the stress away. I'll be fine to play one game."

Zoey and Ben ran back in, tossing the game on the table. They spent two hours playing all of their favorite ones just laughing and enjoying each other's company, like they used to do. Thea was running off an empty tank but was happy to be with her family and to see them laughing again. A part of her still hurt knowing her husband wasn't there to share this moment with them. There was nothing more in the world she wanted than to have him sitting beside her, winning every game. When they first started dating, that was something she had to get used to, losing all the time. The man's superpower was winning board games. That's what she used to tell everyone. It bugged the kids almost as much as her that their father almost always won. Ben had inherited a little of his father's good luck with games and had won a few times himself.

Being an only child, she used to get really upset when she lost, letting her attitude work its way into her voice. Aiden had started to throw games every once in a while so she could win a few times, hoping that would help. It only made her more upset. It was something that had caused a lot of fights in the beginning of their relationship. Thea would get annoyed, and Aiden's immediate response to that was anger and yelling. It was something they both had to work on.

Now, she'd give anything just to have another fight with him, another moment. Her life had seemed to go by so fast. There were so many memories that she cherished, but there were so many more she wished she got to have with him. Growing old, retiring, seeing their kids get married. He'd never be able to walk Zoey or Elle down the aisle. He'd never meet their grandchildren. All of the things that she had taken for granted, that she just assumed that they'd have.

"Mom, it's your turn," Will said, glancing up at her. "Are you okay?"

"Yes, sorry, I'm just tired." She tried to smile at him but it wasn't quite convincing.

"I think it's time for bed," Liv said standing up. "Come on, no complaining now. Your mom's tired." They all made their way upstairs, and Thea hesitated at the top.

"Mom, will you sleep with me tonight?" Zoey asked, taking her hand. "Please?"

"Of course, sunshine." She kissed the top of her daughter's head. Everyone said their goodnight's, and Thea curled up with Zoey on her twin bed. It was a tight fit but it was much better than being alone right now.

"Mom, tomorrow can we have pancakes for breakfast?" Zoey asked.

"And maybe a little whipped cream on top?" Thea replied.

"Yes, please." Zoey rolled closer to her as Thea wrapped an arm around her youngest. As she laid there thinking about everything that had happened and wondering if she was doing the right thing, a voice whispered in the back of her mind. Telling her what her third task was. Her heart dropped into her stomach.

257

· CHAPTER THIRTY-THREE ·

Finn

*Brother, I'm sending you a prisoner who we think has vital
information about where the cursed weapons are. I think
your interrogation style is more suited to siphon it out.*

A NOTE FROM GENERAL NILSON TO GENERAL LEANDER

The Exo Colonies were larger than Finn had first
thought. He'd spent the better part of the day just
walking around, seeing everything there was to see.
The colony itself was formed in a giant circle, miles long. They
had everything the rebellion camp had and more. There was
a large space just for falconry, and there was a long line of
mews where the falcons were housed. Finn was still surprised
Arran didn't have one in the rebellion, but it was, according
to Declan, something Arran didn't want to waste his time on.
The Exo Colonies had school for the children, who were split
up in age groups. They were taught down below most of the
time so they could get real training. It was amazing.

Liam had walked around with him pointing things out and
jotting down notes to ask their carpenters about later. He left
when they came to the sick buildings, still not comfortable

being around that many untouchables. Finn didn't linger there long either. It reminded him of Henry and that made his heart ache. He was desperate to know how the boy was. He didn't think Arran would do anything to him, and he doubted even more the extractors would let him get near Henry. He wished he could have let the boy know they were okay.

Senna, who had been helping out, caught his eye. She said something to the person she was working with before coming up to him. "Hey, Hero, how are you feeling?"

"Not bad, considering." He shrugged. She looped her arm through his and led him away. "Are you learning a lot from them?" He nodded his head toward the building.

"Some things. We do a lot in common because we all have access to the same herbs and plants." Her feet scuffed the wood as they walked. "They've taught me some, and I've taught them some."

"Do you like it here?" He kept his eyes on the side of her face. She, like Liam, was more relaxed.

"Of course." She met his gaze. "You don't though."

It wasn't a question but he answered anyway. "I just know this isn't where I'm supposed to be." He mulled over what he wanted to say next, wanting to make sure he was conveying his feelings the right way. "I think I understand now that there's more to life than just living it. Before, I would have been happy to just stay in Essex until I was phased out. I can't imagine doing that now. I know how I can help, and that's what I want to do."

"You're starting to sound like your brother," she said. That made Finn laugh. Maybe Declan had rubbed off on him.

"Sometimes, I think of who I used to be, and I don't recognize him," he said in a whisper, like a confession.

"I think it's the same for everyone. If we haven't changed then I don't think we've learned anything." They paused to lean against the railing. "I like it here, but I know I don't belong here."

"What do you mean?"

"Just that. Do you remember when I told you Celeste wants to be near the people she loves?" Finn nodded. "I do too. I like it here, but I'm not needed here."

Senna never stopped surprising him. She was loud and unabashed and seemed to always know what she wanted. She was also soft and, despite the fact she would defend anyone, she refused to be a soldier. She laughed hard and spoke with passion. She never held back any of her feelings. He admired her for it.

"Come back to me."

He blinked down at her a few times, coming back to reality and gave her a sheepish smile. "Sorry."

"Do you think you'll win? Against Arran?" she asked him in a quiet voice. He bent his head down, looking at the forest below them.

The truth was, he didn't know. How could he? The knife made the user powerful. It would be easy for Arran to overtake him. He had to try though, didn't he? In the end, he wanted the knife. He wanted to fight Leander. He didn't care what the price was of trying.

The thought of becoming an untouchable scared him. It was a deep, uncomfortable feeling that sat heavy in his gut. But the fear that he wouldn't get the knife back, that he maybe wouldn't see his parents—that was far greater.

"I have to try," he told her. She moved closer to lean against him and sighed. He wrapped his arm around her. "If I'm going to be War, then I have to."

"Alone?" she asked. It seemed she already knew the answer.

"Alone." He squeezed her tighter. If he brought in another army to fight the rebellion, they would resent him. They had to see for themselves that Finn was the horseman and that he alone was the horseman.

They stood there for what could have been fifteen minutes or an hour. It was the quietest he'd seen Senna. He was happy to have a few moments of privacy now that he wasn't under Arran's watchful eye. There were still people all around him, but he felt the freedom to come and go as he pleased. He got a few moments to himself here every day, just to collect himself, to think and exist.

"Come on, Hero. We need to get more salve on your wound." She pulled away from him, grabbing his arm to take him back toward the sick building. She laughed at the face he made.

"I hate that stuff." He let her drag him anyway.

"Everyone hates the stuff." She patted his arm. "It works though."

"But is it worth it?" he asked.

"I'm not going to justify that with an answer because you know it is." She shot him a playful glare.

He didn't protest when she brought him to the building. Harry was there. He tossed Senna a small jar. She motioned for Finn to sit. He did, taking off his shirt in the process so she could look at his wounds. They still hurt all the time, but so far, he hadn't had an infection. Senna touched him with gentle hands, careful not to apply too much pressure. He clenched his teeth. It was still painful.

"It's not warm; the redness is fading," she said to herself. "It's already starting to scar down here at the bottom."

She uncapped the salve and started spreading it around. He hissed at how cold it was and she murmured an apology. It always started so cold and then began to tingle until his whole side felt numb. Senna always made sure to put a decent amount on, just in case. There were a few times where he'd rollover on his side during the night and woke up because of the pain. He'd mentioned it to her one day, and she decided to switch the time he got the salve from the morning to evening.

"Okay, looks good. Let's go get dinner." She handed him back his shirt, and he slipped it on. They made their way to the canteen, where food was served to the free people. The cooks there were always busy as people came in and out throughout the day. Finn, and everyone else from their group, agreed to eat when it started to get dark. That way they could all go their separate ways during the day. Liam had spent the past couple of days splitting his time between their carpenters and blacksmiths. Declan and Lucian spent most of their time with members of the council, learning how everything worked. Lucian had, according to Declan, often sat with rapt attention while listening to them debate over things that would be best for the colony. Celeste was sometimes there too, but she didn't care much for the diplomacy of it all. She was often down below, learning how their scouts worked and watching them train. A few times, she had stepped in and offered to show them some of her training techniques. She was still the best fighter.

Finn bounced around everywhere, depending on his mood. He did like learning about the council but watching them debate back and forth for hours at a time grew dull. He would stay there for half a day before joining Celeste down below or just walk around to see how day-to-day life was in the Exo Colony. People still stared at him and whispered about him but he didn't feel judged or hated the way he had when he lived in Essex. Some people stopped him to strike up a conversation, about nothing more often than not. He could tell that they wanted to ask him about the sword and being the horseman but a lot of them seemed too nervous to do so.

People in the Exo Colonies were less confined than they were in Essex. There wasn't a Beggar's district. None of them were living in luxury either. Everyone was on the same level. Like the rebellion, everyone worked together in some capacity. They all had to contribute in some way. The council made that clear, but the rules weren't so cut and dry here as they were in the rebellion. Nobody was forced into a job that they didn't want. They could choose and seemed happy to do so.

In the rebellion what Arran said went, no questions asked. Here, Finn had seen people talk to the council members, whether that be to seek help or complain about a decision they made. They didn't get cast out for disagreeing with the council, but they still had to follow the laws that were put in place. Holly seemed to be the one with the most power but that was still checked by the other members. She was just a natural leader and people followed her.

The canteen was the largest building in the Exo Colonies. It was a giant wooden square but many people gathered inside, sitting on the floor to eat and relax. Finn wished he could have grown up here, away from the turmoil of both Essex and the rebellion.

Declan, Celeste, and Lucian were already sitting down with their food. They waved to Finn and Senna as they joined the line to get their own. The cooks handed them wooden trays with meat and berries on it. There wasn't much variety in the cooking, but Finn wasn't about to complain.

"You missed an interesting discussion today," Declan told him as they sat down. Finn raised his head to look at him. "They were talking about making an extension to the colony, building out from the circle."

"Do they need that much more space?" Finn popped some berries into his mouth.

"They're growing. They keep a census of everyone who lives here. I guess it's been increasing for years. They think in five to ten years' time it could become overpopulated so they're trying to find a solution for that."

"Five to ten years? Why are they worrying about it now?" Senna asked through a mouthful of food. Celeste smacked her in the thigh.

"You always have to think of the future when you're in charge." Declan smiled at her. "If they start worrying about it after this place is already overpopulated, it could take too long to figure out."

"I never want to be in charge of anything." Senna scrunched her nose. Lucian laughed. His voice carried through the building.

The doors to the canteen opened again and Liam scrambled in, looking frantic. He searched around until he met everyone's gaze and then got in line for the food. Celeste and Declan shared a look of confusion but Finn just shrugged.

"Is he okay?" Lucian asked, doing nothing to hide the amusement in his voice.

"Yeah. It's just his personality." Finn watched as Liam walked over to them. He looked more calm now.

He gave them an apologetic look. "Sorry, I lost track of time. The carpenters let me help with some plans today, and I didn't want to leave until we had most of it done. They're deciding whether it would be best to reinforce some of the older wood or tear it apart and replace with it new things. They've done both in the past."

"Slow down, Lee. Senna and I just got here too." Finn patted the spot next to him and Liam sat down.

"They let you do some of the planning for that?" Celeste looked doubtful.

"Well, they were asking for my opinion. I think they were just testing me but they looked impressed by some of my ideas, so I think I passed." He looked delighted with himself. "I really like it here. I'm going to be sad when we leave."

The others made noncommittal noises. Finn felt bad because he knew Liam would prefer to stay here and never go back. He would prefer to stay away from any kind of fight. He wished Liam could have that option, but he knew his brother wanted to save their parents just as bad as he did. The only way to do that would be to throw himself back into the fray.

"Things will feel better once Leander is defeated," Declan said. He had finished eating and clasped hands with Celeste.

"There's going to be new problems once that happens." Celeste leaned her head on his shoulder. Finn was surprised with how comfortable they were with each other outside of the rebellion and outside of their positions of authority.

"There's always going to be problems." Declan patted her hand. "That's just how society is."

"And there's no way to stop it?" Liam sounded wary.

"You could try like Arran and Leander have, but I haven't seen anything work so far. Every place has its own problems."

Declan kissed the top of Celeste's head. Liam made a disgusted face, and Finn wasn't sure if it was at his actions or his words.

"Have they decided when we leave?" Liam asked.

"No. They're still getting supplies ready and Finn needs to heal a little more first," Declan answered.

Finn sighed. He knew he wouldn't be fully healed when he had to fight Arran. He just hoped his side was able to heal enough that it wouldn't split open again after being hit once or twice.

· CHAPTER THIRTY-FOUR ·

Finn

We have currently come to a shaky alliance with the Exo Colonies here. One of our scouts and most trusted members has gained their trust over the course of two years. It was not the easiest way but perhaps the best. The goal is to send in one of your most charismatic scouts to help them out and put no pressure on the free people for anything in return.

A LETTER FROM ARRAN, SENT TO A
REBELLION CAMP IN SOUTH CAROLINA

A week later, Finn stood on the familiar mountain path that led to the rebellion camp. His hands were held up, palms out. Jonas stood beside him, arms crossed. Declan, Celeste, Lucian, Senna and Liam were behind them, ready to step in if needed. The free people who had decided to fight for Finn stood farther behind them. Holly was with them, standing at the front of their lines. A few other council members had come as well. The rebellion's night guard looked them over. They hadn't tried to attack yet, but they were wary.

"I promise I don't want this to be another battle. I just want the chance to fight Arran and get the knife back." Finn dropped his hands.

"If you just want to fight Arran, why are they here?" one of the guards asked.

Finn turned around to look them over. "Arran demanded that I be tied up after fighting for the rebellion and passing out. They're here because I want a fair fight. If I came here alone and he commanded the rebellion to capture me, people would do as he says. I need him to listen to me."

"It could still be a trick."

"We could also just overpower you and go in anyways," Jonas shrugged. Finn sent him a look, pleading with him to be quiet with his eyes. "We're not doing that though. Should be proof enough."

They still looked hesitant, but after glancing once more at the army that came with Finn, they moved to the side. There was no way they could win.

Finn walked back into the familiar camp, everyone following behind him. The rebellion's soldiers stumbled out of their tents, grabbing weapons but none attacked. Apprehensive eyes watched as Finn and the group made their way to Arran. They were far too fatigued and unprepared for another battle. However, they would fight if it came to it. The guards stationed at Arran's tent stood tall, gripping their axes tightly.

"I'm not here to fight you, I just came for what was taken from me," Finn spoke loud enough for the soldiers around him to hear. He took a deep breath to try and calm down his pounding heart. "Did you hear me Arran? Come out and return what's mine."

The flap of Arran's tent flung open. A scowl settled on his face as he climbed out, straightening his back to be at his full height. He held the knife in his hand.

"After everything we've done for you, you turn your back on us for a boy you don't even know?" Arran sneered at the free people.

"We do not follow you. We follow the horseman," Holly stated. "We would see the world put back together. That is something you cannot do."

"Why? Who says it has to be him?" Arran acted as if he was in control of the situation, but Finn could see the rage in his eyes, in the way he held onto his weapons, and the way he stood.

"The sword's already messing with you. You're barely able to control yourself." Finn tried to warn him but Arran cut him off.

"Shut up, boy. I wasn't talking to you."

"He's the one who saved your camp, is he not?" Holly left no room for doubt in her voice. Arran laughed, a quick burst of air accompanied by a mirthless smile.

"And what does that matter?" he asked her. Then turned to Finn. "You think you're ready to lead? You're pathetic." Arran paced in front of him. "You'll never be able to defeat me."

Declan was ready to step forward, to fight Arran himself, but Finn blocked him. As much as his body hurt, the knife was his and he would fight for it.

"If you want to fight, let's fight, just me and you. Nobody else needs to get hurt." Finn could feel the knife pulsing and see the faint red glow around it, but it didn't extend.

"Finn, are you sure?" Celeste's hand was on his wrist, forcing him to look at her.

"I need to do this, Celeste."

Declan looked unhappy with his decision but grabbed Celeste's shoulder, pulling her into his chest. He gave Finn a nod of encouragement.

"You better win, Hero. We need you around." Senna gave him an unsure smile.

"I will." He took a step forward, toward Arran. He felt like he was standing at a fork in the road. One path would turn him into an untouchable. The other would turn him into the horseman. Either way, his life would change after this battle, and there was no going back. He would be something or he would be nothing. He pulled his sword out from its scabbard on his back, holding it in front of him.

Arran's eyes were feral, darting from Finn to someone else and back, over and over again. Where Finn had discovered how to control the anger inside him, it seemed Arran was engulfed by it, so much so that his collected demeanor was lost. His movements were jerky and no longer expressed care for his injured side.

Finn remained on edge, unsure of what Arran would do but knowing how tempting a fight was with the knife in hand. Arran charged him, the knife extending to its true form. Arran held the sword over his head, but Finn moved left, letting the sword crash to the ground with a thunderous sound. He wheezed in a deep breath as his side flared in protest. Arran was already stronger than him when he wasn't injured but with the sword's added power trying to block him would be a mistake. The people around them watched with bated breath as Arran continued to swing the sword, chasing after Finn's evading form. The anger clouded his logic, and this coupled with his injured side caused his movements to be sloppy and predictable.

"You're fighting like a coward." Arran swung the sword at Finn's neck. Finn ducked, taking a step back to keep the distance between them. He tried to ignore the throbbing pain. He wanted Arran to overexert himself, knowing that once the knife's power wore off, Arran would be left in a state of exhaustion. He kept his own movements as small as possible, dodging a blow and taking a step or two away from Arran each time. Although his strategy was as predictable as Arran's, the bigger man was too overcome by the sword's power to focus on anything else.

The knife seemed to be boosting Arran's energy, as it had done for Finn. Finn weighed his options. At this rate, he'd be getting tired long before Arran would. He somehow needed to get the knife away.

Despite the sword's power boost, Arran's wounds were still affecting him more than usual. The injured side lagged behind.

The knife may have boosted his stamina, but it couldn't fix the stiffness or rotting that came from being an untouchable.

Finn evaded another blow, eyes locked onto Arran's weak side. He wasn't trying to protect it. If he could make the wound worse, it might be enough to shock Arran out of the knife's control. Finn took a deep breath. His own side was killing him. He wouldn't be able to carry on much longer, but knew he had to do something. The knife was dangerous in the hands of a man who only cared about glory. And if Leander somehow got the knife, it would be the start of the end of the world.

Finn still dodged swing after swing of Arran's furious strikes but took calculated shots at Arran's ribs whenever he got the chance. The first two didn't come close to connecting but the third one did, slicing open his skin just a little bit. It only made Arran's anger swell even more. Finn scrambled as the bulking mass of a man threw himself toward him, sword swinging at the object of his ire.

Finn was caught off guard, and Arran's blade slashed him across the chest. Pain erupted as he staggered backwards, hand against his open wound. It was painted red when he pulled it away. Arran laughed, a harsh sound coming from deep in his gut.

"This boy is who you want to be your savior? He's a coward. He's done nothing during this fight, and when he finally does, he fails," Arran said, meeting the gazes of those around them, chin held high. Finn clenched his teeth against the blossoming pain in his chest, breath ragged. He could feel his own rage build-up inside him. The same kind he felt when his grandpa was taken and when he heard the guards talking about his family.

He remained silent, taking deep breaths to calm himself down. He'd never be able to win if he lost control now. He rolled his shoulders, trying to ease the tension he felt and ignoring the sharp pain that protested the action. Arran didn't let him recover for long before he was attacking again. Finn still dodged the attacks but was moving slower, his chest and side flaring with every deep inhale. Arran fought as if he was trying to prove himself.

Arran flung his whole body into his next movement and Finn dropped to the ground, thrusting his own sword through the bigger man's side. Finn ripped his weapon out preparing to strike again. Before he could, Arran threw down the sword and pinned Finn to the ground, knocking the breath out of him. He punched Finn, who had gone limp under him from the pain of Arran's knee so close to his chest.

"You think you deserve to be the hero? You haven't seen half the things I have." Arran punctuated each sentence with another hit. Finn's vision swam and the taste of blood filled his mouth.

"Finn." Senna ran at Arran trying to tackle him to the ground, but he flung her off without much effort. "Leave him alone, you asshole."

Arran held his belly and laughed, a ragged sound that held more madness than joy.

"Senna what are you doing?" Celeste asked, horrified. Senna ignored her and searched for the knife. When she found it, she kicked it toward Finn, trying to avoid touching it with her bare hands.

"Grab the knife." She attempted to push Arran off again, but Celeste intercepted her. Grabbing her around the middle and hoisting her back to the side.

"This needs to be a fight between them." Celeste held tighter as Senna began to struggle.

Arran was still laughing. Even without having the knife in his hand, he was still crazed. Finn, disorientated, started searching for the knife. He felt the edge of it but couldn't grasp it. He steeled himself and used the last of his strength to push himself up just enough to grab it. The change was immediate. Instead of the pain, he just felt numb.

Red swirled around him as the knife once again extended. Arran was raising his fist to strike him, to get the knife back. Finn didn't hesitate to thrust it through Arran's chest. Blood sprayed onto Finn's face. He used the strength the sword gave him to fully push Arran away from him.

He stood up, staring at the horror and awe of the people around him. Senna freed herself from Celeste and stumbled forward. "Finn?"

He turned back to Arran who remained on the ground, blood pouring from his chest.

"I know there are a lot of things I haven't seen or even know about, but the knife is mine whether you like it or not." The knife began to shrink to its natural state and all at once he felt the energy drain from him and the pain return. Senna was by his side in a second, helping him stand. He pocketed the knife. "I want to return our world to what it once was." He turned to everyone who had been watching the fight.

"I understand what I need to do now. I'm sorry for deceiving you, but I need your help to defeat the general. I'm asking you to stay and fight. Not for me but with me. Please."

Liam was the first to move, throwing an arm around Finn's waist to help support him. Lucian was quick to follow. Senna let him take her place, but she remained close. Declan and Celeste stood behind him. Declan put a hand on his shoulder, a proud smile on his face. More people began to step up, joining him, accepting him. Some still turned away, remaining loyal to their fallen leader. Finn let them go. He didn't want to be like Arran. He wanted to lead with trust not fear. More stayed than he was expecting, and he knew it was because of Declan, Celeste, and Lucian, who had all in some way or another been leaders of the camp too.

"How are you holding up?" Lucian asked him.

"At least I'm still standing this time," Finn replied.

"We'll get an extractor to look you over." Lucian beckoned one of them forward. The man had his supplies ready. Lucian addressed the rebellion soldiers. "Get some rest, there's nothing more to see here."

People began to disperse, still looking over their shoulders at Finn as the extractor helped him sit. Arran began to move.

"Stay down Arran, you'll be out of that body soon enough." Lucian pushed him back.

Holly stepped up to them. "What would you have us do"

"Rest. Please. We'll need our strength. We need to attack the general before he has a chance to attack us again." Finn glanced around at the free people. "Will you help us fight?"

"The ones who came with us chose to be here. They chose you. We will see the world returned to its former glory, as long as we remain free."

"Of course. I don't want to force anyone to do something they don't want to," he answered

"We have enough room for everyone. I'm sure Liam can show you where you'll be sleeping." Declan smiled at Holly, nudging his brother forward. Liam looked unsure.

"It's okay, Lee. I'll be back at the tents soon," Finn said. Liam was reluctant but did as he was directed. Lucian grabbed Arran, hoisting him up.

"I'm going to honor my brother's sacrifice, the way it should have been long ago."

"Do you want the rest of us there?" Finn asked. Lucian shook his head.

"This is something I have to do."

Senna crouched next to him, trying to help in any way she could. Her hands were shaking. The extractor sighed, pausing his work and taking the bandages from her. "Go rest."

"I want to help." She didn't look away from Finn, but there was a tremble in her voice.

"Senna, you're of no help right now." The extractor didn't mince his words. "It would be better for you to get some rest. This will already take some time. If you're here, it will take longer."

She searched Finn's expression, waiting for him to decide. He tried to give her a half-hearted smile as reassurance. "Go. I'll be okay."

She hesitated but huffed and stood up. "I know. I'll see you in the morning, Hero."

Celeste wrapped an arm around her, and they both walked back to their tents, heads together as they whispered to each other. Declan took Senna's place at Finn's side.

The extractor started working again as soon as she left, cleaning Finn's wounds and bandaging them up. He checked him over four times before saying he was okay to return to his tent. He was given a walking stick to help alleviate some of the pressure on his side. Declan helped him stand.

"You really are the horseman now." They walked at a slow pace, trying not to cause Finn anymore pain.

"I don't feel any different than I did before," Finn said, then added, "Except everything hurts a lot right now."

"You'll heal in time," Declan said. "I know you don't feel different right now but you are. When you first came here, you were angry. You didn't even want the knife, and now you're going to fight against Leander. You're going to be part of the world's history forever."

"I don't care about that. I just want things to be better." Finn shrugged. He cut off whatever Declan was about to say. "There's something I need to do before I go to sleep."

Understanding crossed Declan's features, and he clapped him on the back. "We can talk more in the morning."

Before Finn laid down, he needed to check on Senna. He checked her tent, but when he called out he got no answer. He opened the flap of her tent but didn't see her. He stared at the empty space before realizing there was one other place he could look. He hobbled his way to the overlook.

Senna sat on the rock, looking over the world below. Her knees were drawn up to her chest. He could hear her sniffling. He cleared his throat.

"Senna? Do you want some company?" he asked. She jerked around to stare at him with red rimmed eyes.

"You need to be resting." Tears flowed down her cheeks, yet she still scooted over to give him room to sit.

"I wanted to check on you." He took great care to lower himself on the ground beside her.

"Your injuries are more important. If you don't take care of them, they could get infected and we can't treat that." She rubbed her hand across her face.

He ignored her. "I wanted to say thank you. I wouldn't have won without your help."

"I just wanted you to be okay." She crossed her arms and dropped her head, trying to make herself smaller, as if admitting that out loud was saying too much.

"I am okay. Still not an untouchable." Finn poked her leg with his walking stick. He shuffled closer to her, reaching out to put his hand on her knee and giving it a gentle squeeze. "I wasn't going to win."

She looked up at him. He moved a piece of hair out of her face.

"I didn't want to watch you rot away or burn on a pyre. I just wanted to help." Her voice was quiet, but it held conviction. "I've never seen anyone become an untouchable before."

He was going to tell her how much she meant to him, but she cut him off.

"You really need to get some rest." She moved away from him. His heart constricted. "Please."

He nodded, and she helped him stand. He leaned on his walking stick as he walked away.

"Hey, Hero?" He turned to look at her. "If I had to go back to that moment, I'd make the same choice again."

She sent him a sad smile before turning around and lifting her head to the sky.

· CHAPTER THIRTY-FIVE ·

Finn

There's no reason to bother with the rebellion. They're nothing. They could never hope to win against me. I know they have their spies in town, but without the knife, they'll never beat me.

A LETTER FROM GENERAL CHASE LEANDER
TO COMMANDER LYDIA MCDONNELL

Finn didn't go back to his tent. First he needed to see Henry and make sure Arran hadn't done anything to him. He doubted he would, but he couldn't be sure. He hobbled his way to the infirmary tents. The guilt was niggling in the back of his mind. They'd left Henry. The boy had no idea what was going on, and Finn wanted to make sure he knew it was because they had no other choice. They wouldn't just abandon him. He ducked into the tent, holding onto his side and trying to keep the pained noise to himself. He looked up to find Liam already there, halfway up from his sitting position.

"What are you doing here?" Finn asked at the same time Henry sat up and called his name. Excitement danced across his features.

Liam looked just as shocked to see him. "I just wanted to check on him."

"Me too." He walked over to where Henry was laying down and sat next to his cot. Henry started to cry, taking in big heaving breaths with his head in his little hands.

Finn reached out to put a hand on his back, shushing him. "I'm sorry we left. We were always going to come back. We wouldn't leave you."

Henry hiccupped. "I thought you were gone. They said Arran tied you up, but they were going to help you escape." He scooted to the edge of the cot to be closer to Finn and Liam. "I was so afraid you'd leave me here. I'm sorry. I'm so sorry but after my mom I—"

"You have to breathe. You're going to make yourself sick." Finn hated seeing him like this and knowing that it was, in part, his fault. Liam looked just as guilty. Henry took a few stuttered breaths, trying to calm himself down. "I'm sorry, Henry. I wouldn't have left you if I had any other option. I hope you know that. We wouldn't abandon you."

"Promise?" Henry's voice was soft and scared.

"I promise." Finn continued to rub his back.

"Me too." Liam moved closer to the cot, close enough to put a timid hand on the boy's knee. Finn tried to keep the surprise off his face. He didn't think Liam would ever touch someone who was sick. It was a deep-seated fear.

Henry wiped his nose with his hands. Liam tried not to show his disgust at the snot, but his face could never lie. Henry's breathing was more even now, but he was still sniffling. There were still tears. "Okay."

"What do you need from us?" Finn asked. He wished knowing Henry was as easy as knowing Liam, but the truth was, he'd had years to adjust to Liam's needs and not even an eighth of that time with Henry.

Henry wringed his hands together, looking distressed. His mouth began to form a little frown. "It might be too much."

"We'll tell you if it is and figure something else out," Finn replied without a second thought.

"Could you stay here tonight?" Henry asked, voice still small. "I know you probably don't want to because you're hurt, but I'm scared if you leave you might not come back."

Finn met Liam's eyes. He knew he would stay. The ground would be painful but he wouldn't refuse Henry this one thing. It was a much bigger ask for his brother. Liam met his eyes with a small amount of fear but gave a small nod nonetheless.

"We can do that." Finn gave him a reassuring smile.

"Really?" Henry pushed closer to him, like he expected Finn to be lying.

"Of course." Finn patted his back. "We'll have to grab blankets though."

Liam stood up. "I can do that. I'll be right back."

Henry squeezed his hands together. "He's going to come back?"

Finn nodded. "He's going to come back."

Henry gave him a shaky smile and started to lay back down. Finn grabbed his arm to help him. "I'm sorry. I'm really tired."

"Don't apologize. I am too," Finn told him.

"You do look pretty bad." Henry grinned when Finn made an offended noise.

"Go to sleep. Lee and I will stay here." He ran a hand through Henry's hair. Henry sighed and closed his eyes.

Finn kept his hand in his hair until Liam came back with a large bundle of blankets. He tossed them on the ground and handed some to Finn. He started to create a makeshift bed on one side of the tent, close to the opening. Finn struggled to get up so he could do the same. Liam grabbed his arm, helping him stand. Concern crossed his features but he didn't say anything.

Finn began to pile on the blankets to make a bed for himself. It would be smarter to go back to his own tent, less painful, but he couldn't bring himself to care. He at least owed Henry this. Liam waited to help Finn lay down, and then went back to his spot. Liam had laid down with his hands on his chest. He looked as exhausted as Finn felt.

Finn knew this was just the beginning. He had the knife. He was, at least somewhat, recognized as the horseman. He still had to defeat Leander and then try and figure out a way to merge the rebellion with the General's cities. It all felt impossible.

Defeating Arran had felt impossible too, but he had done that with Senna's help.

He hoped everything would work out. They'd be able to get into the city and take down Leander. He'd be able to find his parents and grandma again. They could all be together again and help Finn figure out what the next steps were. That's what he wanted, more than anything else—to have his family all in one place again. It wouldn't be the same, not after everything had been ripped apart, but it would be better than this. Maybe then he would feel like he had more control over everything that was happening.

· CHAPTER THIRTY-SIX ·

Finn

> *Arran Grandville; leader of the rebellion camp in Essex*
> *for almost ninety years. Cold and calculating, he is*
> *believed to be a real threat to Essex. From what we*
> *know, it is common for him to switch bodies as soon*
> *as the one he's currently using becomes too damaged or*
> *hard to control. Because of this, we have no accurate*
> *description of him. Please always be vigilant while on*
> *duty outside Essex's walls.*

NOTE TO ALL GOVERNMENT PERSONNEL WHO
WORK OUTSIDE THE TOWN'S WALLS

"Sir, we have a man here claiming he knows the rebellion's next move."

Leander sat at his desk, glancing over a stack of papers, eyes never looking up from the page.

"And you believe him? He's probably an untouchable searching for shelter." Leander crossed something out on the page.

"He says he was part of the rebellion." This caught Leander's attention and he gestured for the man to go on. "He has inside information about their plan of attack."

"You think he's credible?" The demon leaned back in his seat, focusing on his subordinate.

"He knows information about our shifts, sir. I'm not sure how he was able to attain it, and he says he can point out rats who are secretly working for the rebellion."

"Bring him in." The man left, returning with another, shorter man with a plain face and receding hairline.

"I'm Arran Ellis, former leader of the rebellion."

Finn woke up in a cold sweat, chest heaving in painful throbs. He took a couple of gasping breaths to calm himself down before lifting up, slow and careful. Liam lay along the other side of the tent, snoring. He thought about waking his brother, but the most Liam would do was sit around stewing in his anxiety. Henry was still curled up on his cot with one hand hanging over it, close enough to Finn that he could touch him if he wanted. Finn groaned as he tried to stand. He needed to speak with Declan. Fast. He shuffled around until he was on his knees and placed both hands on the ground. He paused to steel himself against the pain before pushing himself up. Finn staggered backward trying to catch his balance. He'd never thought about what the consequences of overtaking Arran would be or how much danger it would put the rebellion in.

His muscles ached in protest, but he pushed forward nonetheless. They needed a plan. They would need to send notes to those who were undercover in Essex and hope that it wasn't too late to get them out. There were rumors about how the general liked to punish traitors; of people being brought in from another area within his quadrant so Leander could siphon information out of them. Leander was seen as the most merciless of the four generals.

The moon was still high in the sky. He slipped toward his brother's tent, trying not to disrupt the stillness in the air. He was thankful that Declan's tent was closer to the middle of camp instead of being on the other side of the camp. When Finn reached it, out of breath and shaky, he pushed aside the opening flap. Celeste lay curled into Declan's side. She held herself with such confidence and stoicism that he often forgot she wasn't that much older than him. He shuffled his feet, feeling awkward about the whole situation.

"Wake up." Finn kicked Declan's foot. He didn't budge. He went to kick his brother again, but before he could Celeste was jumping up onto her feet, a knife pointed at his chest. He raised his hands, palms open. She blinked at him a few times, her face expressionless.

"What are you doing?" she asked, dropping her arm. Her hair was a tangled halo on her head.

"I had a dream about Leander and Arran." He put a hand to his chest, rubbing his wound.

"Shit. Okay. Okay, give me a minute to wake up." She bent down, grabbing Declan by the shoulder and shaking him. She wasn't being gentle at all. "Wake up. I swear one day I'm just going to start dumping cold water on you."

"I'm up," Declan said, rubbing his hands down his face. "What's going on?"

"Arran and Leander have teamed up." Celeste ran a hand through her messy hair, trying to untangle it.

"Arran was already able to take a new body?" Declan sat up, concern settling into his features.

"Apparently."

"What do you mean?" Finn asked.

"It's hard to transfer into a new body. It takes time to get used to it. It takes him around a day or so to get full control of one." Declan grabbed Celeste's arm, pulling her down next to him.

"Not this time."

Declan stretched his arms up before gesturing for Finn to sit down.

"Tell us everything."

Finn did just that, explaining the conversation that he'd witnessed. They both gave him their full attention.

"We need to get word over there and have all of our infiltrators pulled out," Declan spoke after a long pause.

"It's too dangerous. There's a chance that by the time we get a message to them that Leander will have already captured them. Any message we send would just confirm their involvement and could make it worse." Celeste spoke up.

"We have to try. If there's a chance we could save just one person from Leander, we have to take it." Declan's jaw clenched.

"If we do that, then the general will be aware we know what's going on. Right now, Finn's visions are the only thing we have against him. Sending a letter could tip him off if he's monitoring for future instructions." Celeste grabbed Declan's hand, squeezing it. "If I thought saving them wouldn't be detrimental to us beating him, I wouldn't be saying this. We need to keep sending our normal messages."

"So we just what? Let them become untouchables? That's what you want us to do?" Declan shot her a sharp look.

"No. I don't want to leave them." Finn was surprised about the amount of patience she had in that moment to keep her voice so calm. "You know I don't want that. If we send that message, then there's a good chance all of them will become untouchables. Every single one of them. If we don't send that message, they'll be locked up, yes, but we may have a chance of breaking them out."

"I think Celeste is right," Finn said, thinking of their parents and how they stayed behind to fight, knowing that Finn and Liam needed to escape. He felt a pang in his heart. He'd left them. He told himself over and over again it was because that's what they wanted, but he knew fear was a large part of the decision. He hadn't wanted to be captured, fearing what would happen to him. He would keep his promise to return and save them. He would do the same for the rebellion soldiers. He wouldn't just leave them behind.

"You can't be serious." Declan glared at him in disbelief.

"Declan, you know this is the right way. This is war. There's no such thing as no man left behind. You can't save them all," Celeste spoke before Finn had the chance to. She put a comforting hand on his back. He clenched his fists but didn't push her away.

"I don't agree with it. I want you both to know that, but if that's how you want to handle this, then that's what we're going to do. We need to put up a united front." Both Finn and Celeste nodded.

"Okay, now that we've got that settled. We need a plan, something Arran won't be expecting." Celeste sighed, leaning back on her hands.

"We could send carts to the front of the building with our soldiers in them. We could take them by surprise. Traders come into Essex from time to time. It wouldn't be that strange." Finn thought back to his time guarding Essex's gates. Most small towns didn't get a lot of trade business, but Essex was different. Since Leander liked to spend most of this time there, traders decided it would be best to bring the business there as well as the bigger cities across the East coast.

Declan hummed in thought but looked doubtful. "Arran would expect something like that. It's an obvious choice. Arran would figure it out."

"What if we used that as a decoy?" Celeste turned to Declan, her mouth pulling up at the corners. Finn waited for her to continue, but Declan understood what she was hinting at right away.

"We can have the extractors drive them with some of our soldiers." Finn looked between them, waiting to be keyed into the plan. "They're already untouchables. Like Arran, they'll be able to find a new body easier since they've already been through the process before."

"We'd have to find three or four of them to agree, but I don't think that will be a problem. They hate Leander more than we do." The look on Celeste's face began to sharpen. It was the same look she had whenever she began training with someone.

Excitement began to make its way into Declan's tone, the same way it always did when he knew he was about to win a game. "The rest of the army will go in the back way. We'll have a group of infiltrators attack the exterminators when they try to dump the bodies. Since nobody goes back that way, I doubt anyone will notice."

"They would let us in the back, and we can surprise Leander from behind," Finn said, putting the last piece of the plan together.

"We should send a note to the Beggar's District. Warning them about the attack in front. That way all of Leander's officers will be there," Declan said.

"Shouldn't we just take them by surprise?" Finn asked.

Declan shook his head. "Think about it. Arran knows you have the knife. He knows you have the support of the rebellion and the free people. He knows there's going to be an attack. What he doesn't know is that you're aware that he went to Leander."

He should have known Declan would already be three steps ahead of him.

Declan ruffled Celeste's hair. "We make a good team."

"I want to take a small group in before everyone else comes through. Not too long. Give us twenty minutes. I want to get our parents and our infiltrators out of the capitol building. Leander won't have any leverage that way."

"It's too dangerous to do that, Finn. If he sees you or knows you're there, the surprise attack will be in vain." Celeste took in a sharp breath looking at Declan.

"You know how I feel about this so don't look at me."

"This is something I have to do. I won't negotiate it. I can't leave them in his control when I have this chance."

Celeste's lips were drawn in a thin line, but she didn't protest it.

"Get Lucian and Liam. Lucian will be able to lead the infiltrators. He's broad enough to pass as an exterminator. Liam might have some ideas of how to break into the cells they have in the capitol building," Declan spoke to Celeste.

"He hasn't seen the cells though," Finn interjected.

"But I have. I can explain them to him and together we'll be able to figure something out." Celeste was already moving to leave the tent. "Get Senna too. The extractors trust her the most."

"I think she needs more time," Finn said.

"We don't have more time." Celeste looked distraught.

Finn turned to his brother. "This is it, isn't it?"

CHAPTER THIRTY-SEVEN

Thea

Thea spent the next day curled on the couch with her children, having called the school and telling them that everyone in the house was sick. It was obvious they didn't believe her but didn't push it. Her children, although not top of the class, had always done well in school, missing only a few days here and there.

Elle had been the first one awake in the morning, panicking when she realized it was 10 a.m. She came downstairs in a flurry, pausing to see Thea sitting at the table and Liv cooking a feast for breakfast—pancakes, eggs, toast, sausage, the works. Thea was humming, doing a crossword and still in her robe.

"I thought we all needed to take a mental health day," Thea explained once she noticed her daughter's confused expression. Elle heaved out a sigh of relief, sitting next to her mother and stealing a sip of her coffee. Liv set a stack of blueberry pancakes in front of her, knowing it was her favorite. It had been Aiden's favorite, too. Elle sat down, still in her pajamas, dark hair sticking up all over the place.

"Can I have some orange juice?" she asked as she began digging into her food.

Ben was the next one up. Her middle children were definitely the early birds of the four. He took a seat to the right side of his sister, eyeing the food. Liv set a stack of pancakes in front of him, too. Chocolate chip this time. Thea had told her each one of the kids preferred morning meals. Thea grabbed the whipped cream from in front of her with her good hand, giving it to him. She noticed the questioning look he sent to his sister, who just shrugged in return. Ben piled his plate with food, and Elle grabbed a few pieces of toast and some of the strawberries that had been set out.

Thea was still tired. She'd taken a pain killer as soon as she'd woken up. It was just starting to kick in, but it also made her eyes feel heavy.

"Momma, what's going on?" Zoey asked from Will's arms, one hand rubbing at her eye and the other wrapped around his neck. He sat down with her still in his lap, and she made no move to leave. Liv slid them their pancakes.

"We're going to spend some quality time together today. I thought we could all use a break," she replied ruffling the little girl's hair.

"Don't question a good thing, Bug." Will grinned as he began filling the rest of her plate. Zo hummed in response, jamming as many pancakes into her mouth as she could. Bug, as he sometimes called her, was the nickname he gave her when he saw her for the first time in the hospital. She had been such a little thing; he'd compared her to one and the name had stuck. She never seemed to mind it. They were ten years apart, but she was always glued to his side.

After breakfast, they sat around the TV watching Ben's favorite movie. They decided a movie marathon was the best choice for the day. Each kid would get a choice. Will chose an action film full of giant explosions and a lot of car chases. Elle chose a documentary about space; she'd always been fascinated with astronomy. Ben's choice was an animated movie that everyone in the family enjoyed, and she guessed Zo's choice would be the same. It was the first time none of them complained about what the other picked. More times than not, Will and Elle would bicker about each other's taste in movies but neither one of them made a peep.

Thea fell asleep five minutes into the first movie and woke up a few times during it. A blanket had been thrown over her legs, and Zoey snuggled into her side. She'd woken up to her daughter's intense stare a few times, like she was afraid Thea would disappear if she looked away even for a moment.

Thea needed a family day. A reminder of why she was going through the trials the tablet gave her. She was beginning to second guess everything. She no longer knew if she was making the right choices.

What would you do for your family?

It had asked her. Anything. She had always thought she would do anything for them without hesitation, but here she was questioning everything. When the voice had spoken to her, told her the third task, she had almost thrown up.

You must take what you wish to receive. And when she refused to believe what that could mean it added, *a life for a life. When you were spared, another was not taken and the balance of the world shifted. You cannot let that happen again.*

She didn't know if bringing Aiden back was worth taking another life. Guilt sat like lead in her stomach. If she had died the same day as her parents, like she should have, then Aiden would still be alive. Her being spared had taken away the life he should have, so she owed it to him to try. Her kids deserved to have their father.

When she woke up that morning, she paced her room trying to think up a loophole. She had almost decided to trade her own life for his. That should be enough. She didn't want to die and what if there was something that she would still have to do, another task. She had started this by herself, not wanting her kids involved, and if there was still another step Aiden wouldn't be brought back. She'd be gone too. Her kids would lose two parents. She was trying to keep that from happening.

She pulled Zoey against her, laying a soft kiss on the side of her head. Zoey hummed in acknowledgement, not taking her eyes away from the screen. Will sat sprawled out on the floor, phone in hand, not really paying attention. Elle was sitting on Thea's other side, with her notebook out, scribbling down ideas and looking up at the TV so she could still have an idea of what the movie was about. Ben kept inching closer to the screen. If he got any closer, nobody would be able to see the movie.

After Zoey's movie finished, Thea sent Will to pick up some food for dinner. They'd eat and maybe play another board game before bed. Tomorrow the kids will go back to school.

After dinner, Thea, claiming she was exhausted, which was true but not the full truth, made her way to her room where the tablet sat on the dresser. It was still filled with her husband's clothes.

"I don't know what to do anymore," she said out loud. "I won't risk going to prison, and I can't kill myself. What do you want me to do?"

You will suffer no consequences. I will take care of that.

She scoffed at the thought. There were always consequences whether they were immediate or not. She ran a hand over her tangled hair and began pacing again. This was going too far. She stared at herself in the mirror. She wasn't a killer. She turned away, toward the bed, deciding that she should at least try and get some sleep. Tomorrow, she'd take the tablet to the office, so she wouldn't have to deal with it for the time being.

The next morning after getting the kids to school, she went to her office. She set the tablet down on the desk. She had woken up in pain but less groggy. With a little more energy than she'd had the other day, she felt she could at least get a few things done. Placing her hands on her hips she decided she needed to clean the place up. Papers were strewn about, along the bookshelves, table, and even the floor. She spent an hour or two organizing and then got lost in some old papers—notes Aiden had written about their travels. By the time she checked her phone, it was nearing seven in the evening. Will had sent her a couple of texts letting her know they were all home and asking if she needed any help.

She jumped at the sound of someone clearing their throat behind her. Spinning around she found Aunt Liv at the door with a bag of fast food in her hands. Will must have told her she wasn't home yet. Thea waved her in. Aunt Liv began piling the papers on her desk in a neat stack and placed the tablet gently on the floor, making room for them to eat. They dug in, reminiscing about Teddy and Aiden, when Thea felt the familiar tug in the forefront of her mind.

You cannot avoid this final task. It's too late to stop now.

She shook her head trying to ignore the voice and to focus on what Aunt Liv was saying.

"Teddy always had the biggest soft spot for you. When you were young, you had him wrapped around your little finger."

"I had a pretty big soft spot for him too."

The plans have already been set in motion. You will not be able to stop now.

Once again, Thea ignored the voice, giving Liv a strained smile.

You would take the only chance your children have to see their father again from them? You want to let your children grow up without a father?

"Thea, dear, are you alright?" Liv asked hand reaching out to grasp Thea's.

"Yes, sorry, I've got a headache." She stood up, stretching out her muscles as she walked around the table. Liv stood up too.

You told yourself you were doing this for your family, your children, but that wasn't the truth was it? You did it for you. You couldn't imagine living without him, continuing on without him.

"Please stop." Thea gripped her head as it began to pulse, not sure if she was talking to the pain or to the voice.

She knows. She knows that you're crazy. Talking to nothing but thin air. She'll go get help, and you'll be taken away. Away from your family that you've been trying too hard to keep together.

"Shut up, shut up," Thea groaned, dropping to the ground. Liv placed a hand on her shoulder, worried. "I'm not going to do it. I'm not."

"Who are you talking to?" Thea ignored her. "Wait here. I'll get someone to help you." Fear surged through Thea. She didn't want to be taken away.

No.

"No."

She grabbed Liv's arm pulling her back with more strength than she realized. Liv stumbled, tripping over her own feet and was unable to catch her balance as her body twisted sideways. Her head slammed into the corner of the desk, a loud crack resounding through the room as she fell to the floor in a heap of limbs. Thea gasped, grabbing Liv and turning her over. Blood spilled from her temple, pooling onto the floor.

"Wait. No. No, no, no. This isn't right. This wasn't supposed to happen. Please no. Not Aunt Liv. Anyone else. Please. Anyone else," Thea sobbed, pulling the body closer to her as she sobbed. She didn't want to lose anyone else. She couldn't lose anyone else.

It's time.

She cried out in desperation and anger as the blood that surrounded her touched the tablet, sinking into it. The tablet split apart, straight down the middle. She ducked her head as a bright light glowed from the opening. As the light dimmed, she was able to make out two figures standing where the tablet once was.

· CHAPTER THIRTY-EIGHT ·

Finn

This will be my final entry. I've hidden the knife where nobody will find it for the time being. I pity the man who eventually will. This body is bruised and broken. I can't live in it anymore. Please let this be the end.

WILLIAM'S JOURNAL DATED NOVEMBER 2059

A couple weeks later, Finn stood between Declan and Celeste, hidden in the cover the forest provided and waiting for the signal. He ran a hand over his chest and down to his side. His wounds weren't fully healed, but they didn't hurt as much either.

The army stood behind them, quiet and ready for a command. Finn had been expecting more noise, remembering the rushed way soldiers flocked toward the camp when the general sent his troops to attack. There was no time for quiet while the entire camp was scrambling. Now the silence settled around them, heavy with the knowledge of what lay ahead.

Time seemed sluggish when there was nothing to distract Finn from his thoughts. He didn't dare speak a word, afraid of breaking the tension that lingered in the air. Liam, Senna, and a small team of extractors were behind them, ready to start escorting out the untouchables. Senna stood close to Finn's back and every time he became restless on his feet, she reached out and squeezed his arm. It was enough to remind him to take a deep breath and relax. She had been far quieter the past few weeks than he'd ever seen her and a haunted look crossed her features whenever she thought no one was paying attention. He'd remained close to her, trying to make her smile like she had before. Not even Henry could bring her back to her former self. He wanted to let her stay at the camp, but she was needed here. He promised that she never had to get involved with the fighting. She was just there to help the untouchables.

He thought of Henry back at camp, just waiting to hear news of the battle. He had cried when Finn explained that they were going to leave, afraid he wouldn't come back. It had broken Finn's heart because he knew Henry was thinking about his mom. Once they were split up, he never saw her again. Finn could understand where the fear was coming from. He let Henry lean his frail body against him, shaking with sobs as both he and Senna tried to comfort him.

Henry begged them to take him and was more than disappointed when they said no. Finn, being as gentle as possible, explained that he couldn't bear it if something happened to Henry and that without training, there wasn't much he could do. Henry only calmed down when Finn promised they would come back to get him when the fighting was over.

He would have done that anyways. Henry was his family and had been since they'd brought him to the rebellion camp and Finn made sure he knew that. A shy smile broke out on the boy's face then. He was still sad but was more willing to understand.

The battle was going to be a bloodbath.

They had been waiting for almost an hour and despite knowing it may take a while for Lucian to check the perimeters for every exterminator and officer, Finn still felt the anxiety constrict his heart. This was real. The place he had once called home lay just ahead. It felt like years since he had walked through his front door with his grandma telling stories, his mother humming while she cooked, his father's deep sigh of relief to be home for the day, Liam muttering to himself as he jogged down the stairs, and Declan's teasing laughter as he won another game.

He was back. He was going to save his family.

Lucian's hawk flew overhead, a bright yellow string attached to its foot. Finn reached into his pocket to give his little sky-scraper a squeeze, hoping it would give him strength. He rolled his shoulders back taking in a deep breath and nodding at Declan, who let out a low whistle. The brush in front of them rustled until Lucian came into view. His towering figure looked solemn and for a moment Finn thought things hadn't gone well, but then a slow smile spread across his face.

"We've got the area covered. Took less time than I thought. Exterminators might be big, but they sure don't know how to fight." Lucian tried to keep his voice low but the excitement behind it was hard to miss.

"Finn." Declan nodded forward. He stepped up offering his hand to Lucian, thankful nothing had gone wrong. Lucian grasped his arm tightly for a moment before turning and lead-ing the way back into Essex. Finn swallowed seeing the giant doors open. The untouchables stared at the mass of them with confusion and fear, just like the day they were rounded up to go to the pit. He had been a different person then—terrified and worried only about his family and himself. He was still scared, but he also wasn't going to turn his back on the world, not anymore. He was no longer just fighting for himself, or even his family. This fact cemented in his mind as he heard the steps of the men and women behind him, who were will-ing to accept everlasting suffering for a chance at regaining control of the region. He needed to fight as much for them as they were willing to fight for him.

"Lee, Senna, take your group and start getting these people out of here. We'll direct as many people as we can to come here, so they're not caught up in the battle," Finn said. Liam turned calling the extractors toward him, coming up with a quick plan. Senna threw her body at Finn, wrapping her arms around his waist and squeezing him tight. She paid no mind to the fact that there were soldiers watching them waiting for Finn's next orders. Despite his embarrassment, he returned her affection.

"Come back in once piece, Hero or I won't forgive you," she mumbled into his chest before letting him go and joining Liam.

"Send the signal." Finn tried to compose himself, but found it hard to ignore the heat in his cheeks. Lucian held up his gloved hand towards one of the trees. It was less than a minute before his falcon had flown down from its perch onto its master's arm. He whispered a soft command to it before jerking his arm up and letting the bird take flight again.

"We've got disguises for you over here." Lucian led them to a small pile of clothes. Declan called over three of the soldiers. They had been infiltrators once, ones who had worked inside the capitol building. They weren't there long before they had been called back to camp.

The three of them were going to be disguised as officers, escorting a couple of troublemakers, Declan and Finn, from the district to the capitol building under the guise that they themselves might be infiltrators working for the rebellion. Finn and Declan would, of course, make themselves look the part. Tearing at their clothing and covering themselves in dirt and grime. Celeste and Lucian would lead the army through town, to the front gates, surprising the general's troops from behind.

"Declan, what are the real chances Mom and Dad are okay?" Finn ran his hands over his cheeks, smudging them with mud.

Declan didn't speak for a minute. "They're probably beat up pretty bad. They may be seriously injured, but since they knew you had the knife, I would say they're still being held prisoner. Having them as hostages is too great of an advantage over you." Declan released his hair from the neat ponytail it was in, shaking it out. "Ready?"

"There's not much of a choice now, is there?" Finn noted as the other three men finished putting on the officer's uniforms. The group made their way to the Beggar's District, trusting in Celeste and Lucian.

There was no one outside in the Beggar's District. For the first time, it was barren and quiet. Finn wasn't surprised. Most of the Beggar's citizens hid inside their homes when they caught sight of officers, afraid of the abuse that would follow if they were considered in the way.

"You need to push us around if you want to be convincing." Finn sighed, pausing to look at one of his men. There was a brief moment of hesitation.

"Keep moving, scum." He was pushed forward, stumbling over his feet. Declan gripped his shoulder, helping him stay balanced.

"Great. Perfect." He groaned when a foot collided with the back of his leg. Declan sent him an amused look before dropping his head to stare at the ground again. Finn's nerves continued to heighten as they made their way closer and closer to the center of town. Still, there was no one. There should have been people using these paths. The Beggars District always had people coming and going. He'd never seen Essex look so empty before.

"Shouldn't you be at the gates?" Two officers met them on the path, coming from the farmer's district. One was a lean man with broad shoulders and a crooked nose. The other was small with a receding hairline.

"The general was given intel that there were more rebel spies in the Beggar's District. We were sent to round them up before they had the chance to escape." Both Declan and Finn received a sharp kick to their backs.

"Scum. You should've just escorted them to the pit," crooked nose sneered. "After today, we won't have any use for them."

"We're just following orders." One of their men shrugged.

Then added, "They may be able to tell us where the other rebellion camps are working from within Leander's region."

The small man stepped up to Finn, who kept his eyes downcast. Acting submissive still wasn't enough to stop the man from punching him in the gut. He doubled over. The breath had been knocked from him. An elbow to his back sent him to his knees. Declan moved forward on instinct.

"Oh, a brave one? Know your place, trash." Crooked nose went to punch Declan, but he dodged, only to be caught in the back by one of their soldiers, sending him to the ground too. "Nice hit. If he wasn't so squirrelly, I could have messed up that pretty face of his. Bet I still could."

"I'd rather get this done and get to the gates; take as many of the rebels down as I can." Finn was pulled up by his hair, still trying to catch his breath.

"That's where we were headed. Escorted everyone about halfway to the farmer's district and turned back. Can't believe we had to waste our time doing that. Like anything's going to happen to them." Crooked nose shrugged.

"Head on to the gates then. We're going to lock 'em up, and then we'll be there." Finn had to give credit to their men. They thought fast on their feet.

"Be quick or you might miss the beginning of the fight." They turned around to leave.

"You okay?" Declan questioned looking him over.

"Sure, I'm great." Finn rubbed his stomach

"Sorry, man. Had to make it look believable." The guy who had hit him patted him on the shoulder, a quick apology.

"It's fine; we knew this might happen," Declan assured him.

"Knowing it and living it is completely different," he replied.

Finn shuffled forward, leading them to the capitol building once again.

They walked down the main road, the same one Finn used to run every day. Six months ago, he would have never guessed that he'd be walking this same path, undercover and facing the largest battle he'd yet been a part of.

· CHAPTER THIRTY-NINE ·

Finn

> *They have started building trenches in the ground to dump those who have been injured in battle. They pile one after another on top of each other and once that gets too high, they pour concrete over top of them. It's horrifying. I can still hear the screaming and begging. They are trapped and will suffer forever. This is Hell.*

FROM A LETTER WRITTEN BY A US SOLDIER, DATED 2023

The capitol building stood tall in the very center of Essex, as if all other buildings had been built around it. It was one of the largest landmarks that still stood. It wasn't as tall as an actual skyscraper, but it was the closest thing Finn had ever seen to one. Before, whenever he had to pass the building, he stared at the ground until it was hidden from view. It always felt like he was being watched.

Officers stood in front of the large, wooden doors. There were eight of them. None of them were from Leander's elite force. Finn took a deep breath, nodding at Declan. They would try and sneak in first and resort to violence if need be.

A part of him still couldn't believe Declan had ever worked

in the building. Declan had worked on the upper floors, lacking the gumption, as Leander called it, to do the work that the lower floors required. What he meant was that Declan lacked the cruelty.

Rumors had always floated around town that Leander was the best interrogator out of all the generals. It was why prisoners were so often transferred to his section of the country. He would get the information he needed. Always. Torturing was his specialty, not surprising for the demon of War.

They moved forward. Finn and Declan lowering their heads and slouching their shoulders. At least they didn't have to fake the aches and pains they felt since their run-in with the other officers. The guards eyed them, becoming more alert the closer the group got.

"Spies. The general had us apprehend them to be brought here." One of their men sneered as he shoved Declan forward by the shoulder.

"We never got word of those orders," an officer said as he stepped forward, looking them over.

"I'm not surprised. They were hiding in the Beggar's District trying to escape and warn the rebellion what was happening. We had to act fast." Their men remained steadfast.

"See, the thing is, I know that boy," the man replied. "Don't recognize me do you? I was one of the men sent to grab you before you escaped." He was already pulling out his sword. "The general wasn't real happy about the fact you got away. I spent weeks being a punching bag, being whipped. You won't get away a second time." The other officers followed his lead. Finn and Declan were quick to get out of their make-shift restraints while their men stepped forward.

Finn took the knife out of his pocket. There was a brief moment where he felt like he still couldn't control it, where he wanted to give into the anger and destroy everything. He took a calming breath, keeping his family in the forefront of his mind.

Finn moved right, parrying one of the men's blades, while moving out of the way of another. Two officers worked together, covering each other's weak sides and keeping Finn from finding an opening. He had to separate them. The strength he got from the sword was useless if he didn't have a chance to use it. He dodged another swing, ducking, before he saw his chance. He dropped down and rolled in between them, grabbing one by the arm and shoving his sword into the other's stomach. The man let out a deep groan, stumbling backward. The other took his chance and swung with newfound vigor. Finn jumped to the side. He saved himself from a serious injury but ended up with a long gash on his arm from the shoulder to the elbow. The other man still lay on the ground, gasping and grabbing his side. His breathing sounded watery and blood poured out of his mouth with every cough.

"Don't think you'll get away from me this time. I won't let you win." The uninjured man didn't waste a second before continuing his assault. He was only thinking about winning, about proving that he couldn't be defeated by some boy who should never have been able to escape him in the first place. He was wearing himself out with his wide, forceful swings. All Finn had to do was wait for him to tire.

Finn parried and stabbed the man through the chest before he could recover. He pulled the blade out before using all of his strength to behead him.

Declan was struggling, two of the men had chosen to surround him as well. He maintained a defensive position, unable to get the better of them. Finn ran to his aide, his sword clanging against an officer's. He pushed him to the ground. His sudden appearance made the other man hesitate, giving Declan the perfect opportunity to attack, puncturing the man through the stomach.

"You two go on ahead. We'll stay here and take care of the rest." Finn nodded at his subordinate, tapping his chest, a silent thank you. Declan grabbed his shoulder. He looked nervous. It had been so long since he had seen their parents. He didn't know how they would react to seeing him again.

The interior lobby of the capitol building was painted a grayish white, chipped in some places along the top. To their right were winding steps leading up. A desk was placed in the center of the back wall. A solid, concrete door sat just to the left of it.

"I never realized how eerie this place could be," Declan said. "This way." He led them past the desk and through the door, trying to be quiet. The door led to a long hallway, colored with the same grayish white paint. Nothing hung on the walls. They walked to the end of the hall, past various rooms to another concrete door. Declan pushed hard against the door. It creaked open in protest. This part of the building was left undone. Steep stairs took them to the dungeon of the capitol building.

The door shut behind them with a loud crash, and they could hear faint shouts coming from below. From what Finn could make out, most were calling for help or begging to be released. The brothers shared a look before dashing down the stairs. They each kept a hand along the wall for balance as they descended, eyes focused on the ground in hopes that they wouldn't trip or miss a step. The calling became louder but less intelligible as it was now mixed with clanging sounds.

The stairway led to an ill lit room that smelled of piss and mold. Finn wheezed into his shirt, blinking back tears from the rancid odor. The screams only got more manic when the prisoners saw them.

"We have to find mom and dad." Finn scanned the area, trying to see if he could distinguish their voices from the cacophony of ones around them.

"We need to calm these people down," Declan said. He pulled out the lock pick Liam had made. "Go look for Mom and Dad, I'll start releasing everyone."

They went opposite ways. Finn tried to ignore the inmates pleas as he passed and threats when he didn't stop for them. He swallowed his fear. The cages were filled to the brim with people, so much so that they were pressed right against the bars. Some seemed to be okay—no visible injuries, only malnourished. Others were beaten and broken with faces so swollen there was no way for them to be recognized. Some were missing limbs. Some sat or laid on the ground too weak to get up and groaning whenever someone stepped on them. The standing ones didn't seem to care whether the others got trampled or not.

"Finn? Finn, we're here." Finn looked around, frantic as he searched for his mother until he met her eyes. His father pushed through the crowd to get them to the front of the cell.

"Mom. Dad." Finn couldn't get any more words out, as his throat constricted and tears spilled down his face. They were both very thin, cheeks hollowed and deathly pale. In place of his father's hand was a wrap, only covering a stump. "Oh God," Finn gasped out. Arlette shushed him, reaching her hand through the bars and placing it against his cheek. "I'm so sorry. I took too long. I should have come earlier."

"You're here," Arlette said through her own tears. "This isn't your fault."

"You've done well, Finn. We're proud of you." Winston gave Finn a weary smile, meant to be encouraging but it only dug the guilt in deeper.

"Listen to me, I'm going to let you out, but you need to head to isolation. Members of the rebellion will lead you to safety from there." Declan was yelling over desperate screams as he opened the cells. He had enough forethought to jump out of the way as people scrambled out. He continued this with every cell, trying to make sure everyone understood, but with how frantic they were Finn doubted they were listening to him.

"Where's Grandma?" Finn turned back to his mother, a look of pain crossed her face. "Mom?" His voice broke.

"We tried Finn," she started, fresh tears forming. She looked away from him, as his hand covered hers.

"Once someone is tortured past a certain point, they're taken away. They go past isolation and straight to the pit. I never knew. It was all kept very quiet, what they do to people." His father slapped his hand against the bar in rage. "Your grandmother was a spit fire. She wouldn't cooperate with them at all, and they didn't take kindly to that. They took her Finn. I'm so sorry."

Finn dropped to his knees, ignoring the concern on his parent's faces. He couldn't focus on the shouts or screams around him. He wailed in anger and pain, his whole body bending toward the floor with the force of it. The pain was overwhelming, clawing at him from the inside. He should have come sooner. He shouldn't have even left. If they had just stayed hidden instead of leaving, his grandma might still be with them. He faintly registered the fact that his mom had dropped down next to him, trying to comfort him, but he couldn't find the wherewithal to acknowledge her.

"…going on? Mom? What happened?" It took Finn a couple minutes to register the fact that Declan was kneeling beside him, one warm hand placed between his shoulder blades, the other grasping their mother's. He knew, from how Declan stiffened, that his mother had relayed the same information to him, but he didn't hear the words, couldn't hear anything over the way his heartbeat pulsed in his ears. Declan hauled him to his feet and jerked him to the side, away from the cell door. His back slammed against the wall. Declan opened it, dodging the hands that tried to grab at him.

He, once again, moved out of the way of the stampede that hurdled out. His arm flung out, over Finn's chest, pushing him back into the damp stone. He was still gasping, choking on sobs that were stuck in the hollow of his chest. Before he could process anything else, other than the tightness of his throat and the strong smell of piss, he was wrapped in the arms of his mom. She held him as the agony that had been welling in his gut burst, red hot and searing. His arms wound around her, squeezing her tight to his chest.

Declan and their father joined them as well. There had been a large part of Finn that hoped he would get his family back, whole and safe. A stupid dream. If he had been more realistic, maybe he would have realized that the only way he would get them back was in fractured pieces. He tried not to think of the pit, of the way the cries from within could be heard from miles out, or the way broken bodies wiggled around, like maggots in a rotting carcass. His father pulled them apart, forcing Finn to look at him.

"We need you, Finn. I know you want to break down right now, but we need you. All those people out there need you."

Finn gasped in a shuddering breath, nodding. He pressed his palms to his eyes, trying to stop the tears.

"Liam?" Arlette's voice shook with unspoken fear.

"He's in isolation right now, trying to get people out of Essex. You need to go there. Our team will be able to lead you to a safe place," Declan said.

"If he's not there, wait for him, just for a little bit. He'll be excited to see you guys again," Finn managed to get a few words out, although his voice sounded hoarse.

Arlette's lips quirked upwards. It was then that Finn took in her appearance. Besides how thin and how utterly fragile she looked, her long hair was knotted and matted to the side of her head. Grime covered every inch of her. There were scars along her arms, thin lines that crisscrossed against the ivory tone of her skin. They rose in an ugly pattern from her wrist to her elbow and upwards. She seemed fine, at first. He thought his father had taken the brunt of the injuries but that wasn't the case. They had both been tortured, both been forced to endure hell, while Finn was at the rebellion camp, getting meals and sleeping in luxury compared to where they were. Bile rose up in his throat and he swallowed it down.

A man stumbled toward them. He was leaning against the wall, using it to support him. His right leg was dragging behind him. He was covered in dirt and grime, but Finn would have recognized the bright red hair anywhere.

"Neal?" Finn grabbed his arm to steady him. Neal looked at him with a broken gaze.

"Please. Please release me." His eyes were wide and unfocused. "I can't go on anymore. Please."

"Neal what happened? We'll get you out of here." Declan reached for Neal's other side.

"They took all of them. They're all gone, and it's my fault." Neal brought his hands up to his face sobbing in them. "My little girl. My poor little girl."

"What did they do to Deli? Neal?" Finn asked, shaking him. Neal shook his head and refused to answer.

"The pit. If she was taken out of here, they took her to the pit." Declan crouched down to lift Neal over his shoulder but Neal pushed him away, the force of it sending him to the ground.

"No. If you're not going to release me, leave me here. I deserve to be here." Neal kept a distance between them, not letting Finn or Declan get any closer.

"We need to go." Declan was already moving toward the steps.

"We can't just leave him." Finn was still planted in his spot.

"There's no time. We're needed in the battle. Every second we waste down here, is another second someone could turn into an untouchable." Declan motioned toward the stairs. "We'll come back for him"

Finn nodded, glancing once more at Neal, who sat with his head in his hands, still begging to be released. Finn offered an arm to Arlette, noticing the way she teetered from side to side. "We'll have some men escort you guys, make sure you get there without any problems."

· CHAPTER FORTY ·

Thea

"What have you done?" The melodic voice asked. Thea cradled Liv's body against her chest, staring up at the beautiful man. His long dark hair was tied at the nape of his neck, out of the way of his angular features. He sneered at her. "You must fix this. We can't stay in this dimension without being tethered to something for long."

"You've already come this far. Taken a life to set us free. You might as well finish it." The other figure, who's voice she recognized, belonged to not a man but a monster—a grotesque lion who was so thin it's bones stuck out. Six wings protruded from its back, deep red in color dark enough to appear black when the sun wasn't hitting them. Eyes littered its body, all moving in different directions, as if taking in every possible part of the room.

"There is still time to fix this before the world pays for your mistakes." Thea shook her head sobbing. She could barely keep herself together, let alone think to make a decision."No? You can't just say no. You've done this. You need to make it right."

"She's mourning." The lion moved forward, taking a small step toward her. *"I can take that pain away from you. Let me fix this. All you have to do is accept me."*

"You cannot. He is not meant for this. Neither of us are. We are to create balance in the world." The man grabbed the lion, pulling it back. Anger danced across his face as he watched Thea with cold eyes.

"Accept me and I can take your pain away. I can help you bring back those you love." She began to reach out for it, seeking the comfort over the scathing rage of the man.

"You can't do this. He only seeks to help himself, not you." The man went to stop her, to grab her arm, but the lion used its massive, albeit frail, body to shove him to the side, giving Thea enough time to run her hand across its mane, to look at the monster that stood before her. She just wanted to be rid of the pain. She didn't want to deal with her actions or the consequences. She wanted to be free—to be numb.

"You must say it, child. Say that you will accept me and my help." It's mane was soft. She hiccupped, her sobs subsiding.

"I accept you," she whispered. Dark red smoke enveloped her and the lion. It seared her skin. She gasped, a scream getting caught in her throat as her skin began to burn. It felt as if her blood was boiling. She clawed at her arms, trying to make the feeling go away, tearing the flesh open.

"What have you done?" The man reached for her and she jerked backwards. The pain was lessening, but she was so tired. Her head felt heavy, full of thoughts that weren't her own. The lion's presence was coming to the forefront of her mind, and she didn't have the will left to fight it off.

"She did what she thought she had to. Humans are so easy to manipulate." The voice that came out of her mouth was not her own.

"You cannot do this. You're going to disrupt the balance." The man's face contorted in horror as the monster, as *she*, reached for the knife that sat on the bookshelf. It had been Aiden's. One that he gave to her for protection a long time ago. She'd never even carried it on her person, despite his pleas. She kept it in the office to appease him when she was working late nights.

"I think it's time that I have some freedom, don't you?" She, it, stepped toward him. Blood still poured from her wounded arms.

"I won't let you do this." The man stepped back. She wanted to stop all of this, to redo everything. She would comfort her children instead of fighting a losing battle to get her husband back. She would never accept the lion. She was still too exhausted to fight against what the demon was doing.

"You have no choice. You're weak, Mathias. Without being tied to someone in the physical realm, you'll never be able to defeat me." It laughed, a deep croaking noise *"You're too weak to use your powers."*

"I'm not too weak to fight." The man lunged forward, grabbing the hand that had the knife. Thea had never thought of herself as strong before but the demon had no problem fending him off.

She wanted to stop the fight, to control her body, but the demon's will was stronger than her own. Mathias and the demon were battling for control of the knife, trying to overpower each other. The demon let go of the knife just long enough to barrel their shoulder into Mathias's stomach. He stumbled back, his grip on the weapon loosening. The demon ripped it out of his hand as he struggled to breathe and plunged it into his stomach.

"Et hanc ferro signati iuberentur." The demon twisted the knife and Mathias cried out in pain. Red smoke, a bright scarlet, once again enveloped the room. When it cleared, only Thea was left in it. Grief once again welled in her. She wanted to scream and cry, to throw some kind of tantrum. Shock filtered through her body but the emotion wasn't her own.

You're gaining strength faster than I had anticipated. It was no longer words being whispered to her but thoughts invading every part of her mind. It felt wrong. The monster chuckled at her unease. *We need to take care of the woman now.*

Her body began moving on its own. The monster grabbed the spare change of clothes she kept at the office, in case of any long nights spent there. It forced her to slip out of her blood soaked ones and into the simple black shirt and jeans. Her arms still burned as the fabric settled on top of the scratches. It grabbed her keys, purse, and the knife before walking out the door.

Images flashed in her head as the demon began making a plan. First of her cleaning herself up, getting rid of the blood that remained on her hands. Then to the basement of the building where the gas tanks were located. The explosion that it created in its mind overwhelmed her with fear.

She tried to find some way to stop it as it washed her hands and bandaged her arms up. She tried to regain control in small bouts, starting with trying to move her fingers. She knew there was a fire alarm on the way to the basement, if she could gain enough control to pull it then the fire department may be able to stop anything before it happened.

Would you risk going to jail just to save anyone who might still be here? Your kids will know what you've done. They'll hate you for it.

Yes. She would risk it because she knew that she had lost her children the moment she let the demon inside her. They made their way to the basement, and when Thea saw the fire alarm she doubled her efforts wanting nothing more than to be able to pull it. She was able to take control of her hand, flexing her fingers before she was mentally cut off once again.

You're stronger than I was expecting.

She felt so small compared to the overwhelming and intrusive feeling of another thing in her thoughts. Every sentence that was communicated pulsated throughout her whole being. She wanted nothing more than to get rid of the parasite that clung to her. It chuckled.

You won't be able to get rid of me. To do so would be suicide. You must destroy the host.

As it should be, should always have been, she thought. The monster slinked down the steps and into the basement of the old building. She was powerless to do anything as it went to the boiler and began fiddling around with it. While it was doing that, she put all of her focus into trying to take over again—to make it stop. A few times their hands would freeze and she thought she had won, but each time the demon bested her.

She felt helpless on the trek back up the stairs. A flood of emotion overtook her when they passed her office. Guilt and despair were mixed with anger, raw and overpowering. She hated what this monster had made her do, hated that she let herself be manipulated, and hated that she would lose her children.

The anger bubbled up inside her, needing to be released. The demon chortled at her distress. The rage soon became a rush of adrenaline and finally, *finally,* she felt herself moving into the front of her mind. The demon was surprised as it began to be suppressed. Thea stumbled forward, feeling the full force of the pain in her arms. The dull ache she'd felt before turned into a searing sensation. She needed to make sure no one else was in the building. She jogged to the fire alarm and pulled it. She heard the demon's scream as it fought her with new vigor.

Her vision became blurry as it began to overtake her once more. She stumbled, the demon's presence overwhelming her. She should have known she wouldn't be in control for long.

Now that her adrenaline had worn off, now that she was no longer in control, she couldn't help but feel even more tired. The last thing she would remember from that day was that the demon began making its way away from the building, already planning to search for the next tablet. To begin releasing its siblings.

· CHAPTER FORTY-ONE ·

Finn

It's time. The guards will be coming any day now. Lillian tries her best to act like it's no big deal but I see the worry in her eyes when her mask slips. I hope the rebellion will intervene before I'm thrown into the pit. I would rather be burned at the stake than left in the pit to rot, squirming around with the other broken bodies.

FROM THE LAST PAGE OF FINN'S GRANDFATHER'S JOURNAL

The group had to take a break halfway up the stairs for their parents to rest while Declan and Finn explained what had been happening during their time in captivity. Winston leaned against the wall, his head tilted back, a grim, sarcastic look settling over his features.

"I knew one day I was going to reach a point where I needed breaks going up stairs, I just didn't think it would be this soon." Winston settled Finn with a look of frustration.

"You were also kept locked in a dark cell for a few months. I think that would knock anyone on their ass." Finn shrugged. His mother shot him a fiery glare, but his dad just let out a surprised chuckle.

"Finley James, don't use that language." Arlette's hands were on her hips in record time.

"He's one of the famed horsemen, my dear. I don't think scolding him will work"

"If you think for one second your new title makes you exempt from being scolded—" her sentence was drowned out by their laughter which she soon joined.

"Alright, I think I can make it the rest of the way now." His father nudged them forward, giving them no chance to protest. He did make it but when they reached the top of the stairs, he was bent at the waist, hands on his knees, wheezing. Their mom was faring somewhat better as she leaned against Finn.

They could hear the fighting now that they were on the ground floor. Clashes and shouts reverberated through the building.

When they got outside, they found themselves surrounded by the battle. One of the men who escorted them was still waiting by the door, shifting his weight from foot to foot. He went unnoticed by the men who were locked in battle maybe twenty yards away.

"You released a lot of people. Most of 'em took off, scattering in every direction. Not much we could do." The man had his hand on his sword. "Our troops came in from the back, just like planned. I think we gave the general a real shock. He's powerful. I never realized just how much until now."

"Leave him to us." Finn took in a deep breath. "We need you to do one more favor." Finn motioned to Arlette and Winston. "These are our parents. Please get them to safety. If something happens—" He swallowed hard. "They need to be safe."

He could see that the man wanted to fight, but he also didn't refuse Finn, giving him a firm nod. He craned his head toward the paths. Arlette threw her arms around her sons, squeezing them in a tight grip.

"Please be safe. I know it's a silly request but please try." She gave them one more squeeze, pressing a quick kiss to their cheeks. Winston hugged them next, not as tight or as long. They watched them walk off, sending quick prayers to the universe that nothing would happen.

They set their gazes to the fight. Declan clapped Finn on the back, his hand lingering for a moment. He wouldn't be able to protect him this time, not from Leander. It would all come down to Finn. It was his responsibility.

Finn wondered if Leander could kill him. Death wasn't something most people worried about. It was the eternal pain or the rotting your body could go through that people feared. He wondered if this would be the last time he saw his brother before something unthinkable happened.

Finn shook those thoughts from his head. Leander was in the middle of the fight and that's where Finn needed to be. He pulled out the knife, channeling the anger and the pain from everything—seeing his parents so broken, knowing that his grandma was forced into the pit. Leander wouldn't get away with that. He would make him pay somehow. The knife grew into a sword, and the familiar weight of it brought him comfort.

Declan and Finn were quick to be noticed once they breached the fighting. Whispers of the horseman arriving spilled across everyone's lips, whether they were friend or foe. It was as if the entire fight had paused like a spell had been cast over the battlefield. The spell was broken when someone let out a yell, charging at him. A frenzy followed. Finn flung away man after man who tried to stop him from reaching Leander, all of them wanting the glory of taking him down. He crossed swords again and again with Declan and other rebellion members watching his back, but he was hesitant to actually hurt the people of Essex. His enemies had once been his neighbors.

People started attacking him in groups. Men and women from the rebellion rallied around him, not allowing anyone from Essex the chance to catch him off guard.

"Shit, here comes Commander McDonnell and one of Leander's guards," Declan said. Leander's guards were the best fighters amongst the officers and, if the rumors were true, some of the cruelest. Mercy was a foreign word to them. There were seven of them in total and all of them were large men, both in height and width. They traveled with the general everywhere. Not even Lydia McDonnell could control them. They reported to Leander alone. Finn had only ever seen them in passing and always averted his eyes when doing so. You didn't want them to take an interest in you, for any reason.

The one that lumbered toward them now had a neck thicker than his head. His hair was trimmed closely to his scalp same as the others. Lydia was following close behind him. Finn stepped forward, sword held in a defensive position. The guard swung at Declan, much to Finn's surprise. Lydia took advantage of Finn's surprise. She was quicker than Finn expected from a person her size. He had never seen Commander McDonnell fight in person before, but he now understood why Leander had picked her. She was quick on her feet and strong; not to mention that she'd do whatever was asked of her.

Declan had started a rapid assault on the guard, trying to gain a fast advantage.

"I'm going to tear you apart, piece by piece," McDonnell's voice was gruff and full of malice. Finn didn't reply, but rather doubled down his effort. Block, block, swing, block. His eyes traveled down after noticing McDonnell favoring her left side. She wasn't putting much pressure on her right foot. Finn dodged the next blow, dropping down and lunging. His shoulder connected with her side, throwing her off balance. She let out a yell of frustration as she landed on her back. Finn, who had managed to stay on his feet, plunged his sword into her chest. She gurgled, blood bubbling up between her lips. Her breathing was becoming wet and labored. She was still trying to stand.

Finn was quick to behead her, turning his attention to Declan who was still locked in battle. They seemed to be at a stalemate. Despite the brute having significant bulk over Declan, his brother was smart. It was as if he was reading the man's movements before he made them. The guard's back was facing toward him and Finn stepped forward, unnoticed. Finn came up behind him with his sword raised and swung with as much force as he could muster, beheading him as well. The man collapsed. Declan sent him a knowing glance, and they wasted no time, pushing forward into the battle once more. They could hear Leander shouting, "Where are you Horseman? Do you really think you can beat me?"

Leander was an easy target to spot. He laughed in the middle of the chaos, reveling in every bloody swing of his blade. For the first time, Finn looked at the man, who was broad shouldered and massive. He'd always been intimidating from the short glances Finn had seen of him, but face to face, he was a monster. There was nothing less than absolute joy settled into his smile.

Leander turned, locking eyes with Finn as if he had felt him there. He had been expecting to see anger sizzling behind his eyes—the same kind of anger Finn felt when he was holding the sword. Instead, anticipation and excitement danced across Leander's features.

"No one touch him, he's mine." Leander raised his sword pointing it at Finn. A hush came over the battlefield. People stepped away from both of them. Leander wasted no time in sprinting toward Finn. Finn moved forward, at a much slower pace, steeling himself. He was aware that Declan's presence was no longer next to him.

Their swords clashed. Leander didn't seem fazed by Finn at all and looked to be rather pleased that the boy in front of him could withstand his strength. The general let out a feral laugh.

"You're stronger than you look, boy. I was afraid I'd just snap you like a twig." He swung again. Finn had a harder time blocking it, and he was forced to take a couple of steps back. Panic settled into the outer corners of his mind with the suddenness that this was real. It almost took him off kilter when it hit him that this was everything he'd been working up to. He tried to focus but the panic remained. He couldn't get across any offensive strikes, but was just blocking Leander's flurry of attacks, each one throwing him off a little more.

"Not as good with a sword as I was expecting." Leander lunged forward. "Soon you'll be begging me for mercy, just like your grandma did."

"Don't talk about her." Finn gritted his teeth.

"Why not? You don't want to hear about how she cried? How she was too broken to even stand?" Leander's callous words were punctuated by a shallow slice to Finn's lower stomach. "You won't find her. We made sure to torch up the pit after throwing her in."

Anger exploded in Finn. The sword seemed to pulse with power. He wasn't in control, and he wanted Leander's head. He wanted him to suffer. If he could, he'd drop Leander into the pit and let him rot there for the rest of eternity. He wanted the same fate for anyone who had a hand in his family's suffering. Leander's attacks were no longer forcing him to retreat, and he swung his blade with only one thought—revenge.

He began pushing Leander back, not feeling the pain from the gash in his stomach or the ache from his old wounds. His new found urgency caught Leander off guard, if only for a moment. The rage he had expected Leander to have when they first locked eyes was there now, simmering just beneath the surface. He was, by far, bigger than Finn. He was faster than what Finn had expected from a man his size, but his wide swings weren't as swift as Finn's controlled ones. Finn took a deep breath, focusing on quick, unexpected strikes to wean Leander down. He was holding his own but felt relieved when Declan broke through, fighting by his side once again. His brother didn't have the strength to fend off the general's blows, but he was able to distract him, keeping some of his attention off Finn. The general's anger rippled off him. He let out a growl of frustration, turning his attention to Declan and rushing him, grabbing his arm and flinging him back into the fray. Finn used that moment and plunged his sword through Leander's side, feeling it scrape against his ribs in protest. Leander stiffened and Finn pulled back, ready for another attack.

Finn wasn't prepared for the red smoke, a deep all-consuming red, to pour out of his side as Leander crumpled to the ground, body folding over and head slamming against the ground with a sharp crack.

They body started to deflate as the smoke congealed into another form.

Finn was no longer staring at the general, but the demon who had taken the man over. It was a lion. Six burgundy wings sprouted from its back, jagged along the ends. Eyes littered its body, dancing in every direction, protruding from fur and muscle. Hysterical laughter rang through Finn's head.

You can't defeat me. The host must die before I'm gone. You'll never find my true vessel.

The words weren't spoken out loud though they seemed to be coming from inside Finn's head like a thought he had no control over.

The battle around them ceased with soldiers looking at the beast with amazed horror. Finn felt the same way, eyes locked onto this grotesque creature. It was real. Before he'd still looked at Leander as a man. There was no way he could have imagined the creature before him.

"Finn, move." Declan shoved him. He stumbled to the side, tripping over his feet and then catching his balance as one knee hit the ground. He heard the blade puncture flesh, heard the gasp of pain before he saw it. Declan was hunched forward, his back toward Finn, and the end of a bloody blade driven through his chest.

· CHAPTER FORTY-TWO ·

Finn

The walls aren't meant to keep our people, the American citizens, in. They are designed to keep out the horrors of our new reality. Each city or town that has a wall around it is led by a commander hand-picked by one of the four generals to keep things running without a hitch. We are only ensuring the public's safety. We are not trying to take away any freedom.

MESSAGE DISPLAYED ON EVERYONE'S
PHONES A FEW MONTHS AFTER THE
PRESIDENT RELINQUISHED HIS POWER

Finn felt like all the air had been knocked out of him. Everything was wrong. He should have been the one on the end of that blade. Not Declan, who's limp body hung in the air, hands twitching, chest heaving with wet coughs. He wanted to call for his brother, but the words were caught in his throat. His brain kept stuttering over the image before him.

Declan. Stabbed. Untouchable.

Declan.

Not Declan.

Please.

He reached for him but was stopped by one of the lion's giant wings.

I'm not done with you yet. Finn raised his sword as the lion moved in front of him, cutting off the view of his brother.

"I'll send you back to wherever you came from, you filthy fucking beast," Finn yelled, charging it. Laughter bubbled into his head.

I hope you got a good look at him, broken body and all. You'll never see him again. It raised on its haunches, wings spread apart, beating against the wind. It's new position allowed Finn to get a glimpse behind it, to see Declan being carried off, struggling. Arran. It was the same body he saw in his dream.

The beast dropped back down, swiping at Finn with sharp claws, a growl ripping through the air. Finn tightened his hold on the sword, his thoughts repeating over and over in his head.

Kill the beast. Get to Declan. Kill the beast. Get to Declan. Don't lose him. Not again.

The lion pounced. Finn retreated a few steps, trying to keep the monster at a distance as he blocked the claws from touching him. He had been prepared for a fight, prepared for the fact that he might lose said fight, but no one had prepared him for this. He had assumed Leander was the demon, not just a body for it to use.

The demon's teeth snapped at him, powerful jaws aiming for his throat. He moved back again, dodging the teeth but not the claws that sunk into his lower stomach. The same place he'd already been injured. It tore deeper into the skin, even as he stumbled back. Pain blossomed in his abdomen as he let out a choked hiss. The wound throbbed but it helped bring him out of his shock, out of his head. If he didn't focus now he would lose and all the sacrifices that were made would be for nothing. Declan's sacrifice would be for nothing.

He let the pain fuel his anger as he thought about his family—his parents, his grandma and Declan, who he would never see again unless he won this fight. The sword's power surged, and instead of the pain, he felt numb. He attacked with renewed vigor, focusing on the beast in front of him and ignoring everyone else around them. He dodged the lion's attacks as best he could, but neither one of them were able to land another serious hit.

Finn found it hard to avoid a flurry of claws and sharp teeth, so maybe he shouldn't be trying to dodge everything.

He sucked in a deep breath, once more retreating a few steps, knowing the demon would follow. As predicted, it did only a moment later, using the new space between them to leap at Finn. Finn didn't try to block or run from the attack, instead he angled his sword up at the last minute, thrusting it between the beasts teeth and out the back of its skull. He was knocked down by the full force of it as one set of its claws pierced his right shoulder, settling deep into his skin. The other set grazed his left side and he inhaled sharply, crying out with both pain and fury.

The beast's voice intruded in his mind once more.

You've sacrificed yourself for no reason. I will come back. You'll never be able to beat me as an untouchable.

"I'm going to finish you off before you have the chance to come back."

The same dark red smoke began leaking from the lion, completely surrounding them until it was no longer visible. Finn couldn't see it disappearing, but he felt it. He pushed himself off the ground and stumbled forward, gasping and clutching his shoulder. Black spots were already dotting his vision. He held onto the knife which had shrunk to its original size. The smoke started to dissipate around him, and he realized the sound of clanging metal had all but stopped.

The world around him blurred around the edges as he slipped the knife into his pocket and careened forward toward the path Declan had been taken. The men around him were still, not quite believing that the staggering, wounded boy had bested the demon.

Finn was aware of his name being called but ignored it. His good shoulder was grabbed and he was spun around to face Celeste. She was talking to him, rushed and panicked but he couldn't make out what she was saying, too focused on the way the world seemed to spin around him.

"Declan's. Gone." He managed to slur out before giving into the painful protesting of his body.

· CHAPTER FORTY-THREE ·

William

Will finished tucking Zoey into bed, trying not to wake her. He set down the book he had been reading to her and flipped the light switch off as he left the room. He checked his phone. Still no messages from their Mom or Aunt Liv. He tried to push back the anxious thoughts he had, but he couldn't get it out of his mind that something felt wrong. He peaked in his room, checking on Ben, who was concentrating on building a model plane.

"Will?" Eleanor called from the bottom of the stairs. She sounded on the verge of tears. Ben was too absorbed in what he was doing to notice. He jogged down the hall.

"What's wrong?" he asked as she met him halfway up the stairs.

"I got a text from Hannah asking if our mom was okay." There were tears running down her cheeks. "The building blew up."

"What?" he asked, not believing what he heard. That couldn't be right. Buildings didn't just blow up. Not in real life.

"The building blew up. Look." She showed him her phone, and he read through the messages. "I tried to call her a couple of times, but she didn't answer."

"Shit." He ran back up the stairs. "Ben, keep an eye on Zoey. Elle and I need to check on something."

"What's going on?" Ben asked, standing up and knocking over his plane in the process.

"Please, just listen to me. We'll be back soon to explain everything. We just don't have time right now." Will didn't wait for a response. He hurried through the house, grabbing Elle and dragging her along. He grabbed the car keys from the entryway table.

"She's going to be okay. Right?" Elle's hands were shaking as she buckled her seatbelt. It took her three tries. He ignored her and flipped on the radio as he pulled out of the driveway.

Right now, authorities are still looking into the cause of the explosion. It's very likely this could have just been an unfortunate oversight as the building is very old and maintenance on it may not have been done to regulation. It seems that most people were able to get out of the building. However, the explosion has seriously injured more than twenty people and killed two.

He switched the radio back off.

"Will?" Elle asked, her voice small and weak, on the verge of cracking. He didn't reply but grabbed her hand instead. He didn't know what to say and he feared that if he opened his mouth all the fear he was feeling would pour out. He needed to be strong right now.

Elle's breaths came out in shallow gasps. Will kept a tight grip on her hand, hoping there was some comfort there. He wanted to tell her that everything was fine, their mother hadn't been in the building, but he was afraid the words would be a lie. He chewed on his lip until he could taste blood, a habit he picked up from his mom. None of them could handle losing their mother too. Not when it felt like they had just gotten her back.

The light in front of them turned red, and Will slammed on the breaks.

"Come on." Will smacked his hand against the steering wheel in frustration. It was the third red light in a row. Elle jumped in her seat, a few tears slipping down her face but said nothing.

The closer they got to the building, the slower traffic was until they were almost stopped.

"We should have realized the roads would be blocked off." Elle leaned her head against the window. Will hummed in acknowledgement, knowing that if he spoke he would snap at her. He let the other car move forward a few inches and, instead of following it, used the extra space to do a U-turn. There weren't any cars coming from the other side of the street anyways. Elle shot him a confused look.

"I'm going to park in the CVS parking lot, and we're going to walk the rest of the way. It's a couple of miles at most." He jerked the car into the lot, tires screeching. He jumped out of the car, not listening to Elle's protests.

"I can't walk that much in these shoes." She gestured down to the small heels she was wearing.

"Why didn't you take them off earlier?" he questioned, not slowing his pace. Elle huffed.

"Because I didn't want to." She grabbed his arm, jerking him back. "Will."

"What?" He turned on her. "We have to go, Elle. We have to see what's going on. It's not my fault you wore those stupid shoes. I'm not going to wait for you."

"Don't you think I know that? Don't you think I'm just as worried as you are? Just give me a minute to take these off." She was already bending down, using his arm to keep her balanced as she unbuckled them one at a time and slipped them off. "Let's go."

She started to run and Will followed. Will wasn't in the worst shape. He was part of the school's hockey team, but Elle was a cross country runner. She was swift and her stamina was better than his.

He began to get winded after the first mile but ignored the burning in his lungs. He concentrated on his breathing. A deep breath in. A deep breath out. They were almost there when they were once again blocked; this time by people trying to see what was going on. They were still a block or two away. Will grabbed his sister's hand pushing through people despite their protests and the dirty looks they got. The sidewalk was closed off and a couple of police officers were calming down the crowd.

"Hey, officer. Over here. We need to get through," Will said, waving his hands at the man. The officer heard him but chose not to respond. "Please. Our mom works there, and we need to know if she's okay." That caught the officer's attention and he made his way over to them.

"Sir, you need to calm down. Nobody's getting any closer while an investigation is in process." The officer took out a small notebook. "What's your mom's name?"

"Thea. Thea Pierce." Will tapped his fingers impatiently against his leg.

"Okay. If we find anything, we'll let you know. Is there a number to best reach you at?" Will stared at the man.

"Our mom might be hurt. You have to let us through. We need to know if she's safe," he began to ramble.

"Son, calm down. We're not letting anybody through right now. I promise you, as soon as we know anything about your mom, we'll let you know." Will clenched his jaw in anger.

"Thank you, officer," Elle was quick to respond before Will could get them into any trouble by opening his mouth. She gave the officer her cell number. He nodded as he walked off, speaking into his radio. "Maybe we should check back at home? She could have left before everything happened."

Will gave her an incredulous look.

"What else can we do? I don't want to be here anymore. I don't want to think that she could be, that she's—"

Elle broke off in sobs. Will pulled her into his chest. His eyes burned as he tried to hold back tears of his own.

He took her hand and made his way out of the crowd. Elle was right. There was nothing more they could do right now, and they needed to get back to the house to watch Ben and

Zoey. Neither one of them said anything as they walked back to the car. They sat in silence on the drive home too afraid to turn on the radio—terrified that it would confirm that their mother was dead. Elle sat up straight when they got to the house, slamming her hand on the dashboard.

"Look, her car is in the driveway. Will, she's here." Elle had her door open before he even stopped the car. She was already to the front door by the time he was stumbling out of the vehicle.

"Mom? Mom, where are you? Mom?" They both called for her. Searching every room downstairs.

"What are you two doing?" Thea came down the stairs, drying her hair with a towel. They both rushed toward her, wrapping their arms around her.

"We were so worried. Why didn't you answer your phone?" Elle asked tears streaming down her face.

"I left it at the office. I was about to go back and grab it." She was hesitant to wrap her arms around them. "I went to the grocery store after work to pick up a few things for dinner tomorrow. I was thinking hamburgers."

"You'll have to get a new one. The office building blew up. They think it was because of how old the building was." Will rubbed her back, not believing she was really there. She was okay.

"Oh dear, that's terrible, but there's nothing for you two to worry about. I'm fine." She pulled them in a little tighter. Will was surprised by how untroubled she sounded but the feeling didn't last long. "Where are Zoey and Ben?"

"They should be in their rooms," Will answered. "Did Ben not notice you come home?"

"I guess not. You know how he gets when he's concentrating on things. I'm going to go and check on them." They let go of her but not before giving her another tight squeeze. Neither one noticed the way her eyes flickered red, just for a moment as she walked up the stairs.

· EPILOGUE ·

Three weeks later

Finn stood at his old post by the gates, leaning back against the stone wall. He waited out there every night for a couple of hours, waiting for Celeste and her team to come back, while he healed from his wounds. Sometimes, he would get letters from her, updating him in messy, hard-to-read scrawl about anything she heard about Declan. There had been very few of them. She had waited for him to wake up before saying she was going to go look for any signs of Arran and Declan. The only reason she had waited was because she wanted to make sure he was okay first.

He sighed and slid down the wall, being mindful of his shoulder until he was sitting. He had woken up three days after his fight with Leander. His father and Lucian had been working together to unify the rebellion and the townspeople. They were all very distrustful of each other. The only things they seemed to agree on was the fact that Leander had been evil and that Finn was the horseman. With Lucian and his father working together though, a bridge of trust was being built one small step at a time. They had come to Finn with a plan to get rid of the districts, to make sure people in the Beggar's District would be treated better and that untouchables would no longer be forced into the pit. They wanted his approval. It was his choice because he was the one in charge now.

The thought made him uneasy. He didn't know anything about how to keep a town running. Why would they trust him to make such important decisions? Of course, he signed off on it. The way Essex had treated people from the Beggar's District and the untouchables was horrific.

Liam was more than happy to work with the carpenters and builders to create more comfortable places for these people. He was also working on expanding the wall to create more space for everyone in town.

The wealthiest people in Essex had the biggest problems with it and often came to Finn to spit out vile words about the situation. He told them if they didn't like it they were free to leave. None of them did. Lucian and his father were often at his side when these people came and did more to appease them than Finn could. They were the true leaders of Essex.

"Hey, Hero, up for some company?" Senna sat down next to him before he could even respond. He smiled at her. She had a bowl of fruit in her hands.

"Do I have a choice?" he asked as she handed it to him, taking out a strawberry and popping it into her mouth.

"Of course not," she said around a grin and a full mouth. He laughed, taking a strawberry for himself.

"Anything tonight?" she asked.

"Not yet."

She hummed in response, taking another piece of fruit. This had become their routine. He had snuck out of the town's infirmary before he was cleared to leave, much to the chagrin of Senna. She'd spent an hour or two looking for him until she found him, sitting alone outside the gates. He must have looked horrible because all she did was sigh and sit next to him, telling him to at least let her know where he was going next time. Some nights they were quiet, just enjoying each other's company and others were filled with laughs as they tried to keep each other awake. He had never been so thankful for another person.

"Where did you go?" she asked, pulling him out of his thoughts. She was looking up at him with a furrowed brow that he wanted to smooth out. He smiled at her. She was a girl made of untamed laughter and iron will and he thought he loved her for it. His fingers curled around her cheek and he pulled her to him, drawing their lips together. She pushed closer to him when he tried to pull back, and he wrapped his arms around her waist in response. Her body molded against his, warm and inviting, as she parted her lips. The world melted away until she was the only thing left. Her hands traveled from his neck down to his chest and he let out a hiss of pain.

She pulled back, big eyes apologetic. "I'm so sorry."

He laughed and rested his forehead against hers. "It's okay."

His heart was racing as she leaned in and gave him another quick kiss.

He tucked a strand of her hair behind her ears. It had been getting longer over the past few weeks.

"We should probably stop for now. I don't want you to become an untouchable because you moved around too much and caused an infection." She settled down next to him again. Her cheeks were still flushed and a small smile remained on her face.

He took her hand and gave it a squeeze. He wanted to tell her just how much she meant to him but was stopped by a loud chwirk. They scrambled up as Celeste's hawk came into view, landing in front of them. It didn't have a letter for them.

"What does this mean?" Senna asked, bending down to pet the bird. It puffed up its feathers and shook its head.

"It means I'm back." Celeste walked out of the brush, a few scouts following behind her. She looked rough. Her hair was a tangled mess, tied at the nape of her neck, and she was far skinnier than she was when she left camp. Senna ran to hug her.

"We need to check you over." she said, pulling away.

"I promise, I'm fine." The purple like bruises under Celeste's eyes told a different story.

"I don't care if you think you're fine. We still need to have you checked out." This was something Senna would not let go which was made obvious by the defiant tilt to her chin. Celeste gave a small nod.

"I'll get checked out, but then we need to talk," she said to Finn.

"Have you found anything important?" he asked, stepping up and giving her a quick hug of his own.

"Just rumors but there's a lot going on out there with the General gone."

"We can talk about this after you get looked at, come on." Senna led her sister into Essex while Finn and the rest of Celeste's group followed behind. The scouts broke away to get a hot meal and Finn followed the girls back to the infirmary. While Celeste was getting checked out, he sent an apprentice out to fetch his parents, Liam, and Lucian. He waited in his hospital room for them to arrive.

His mom came first, pushing Henry in his wheelchair. She had put her counselor duties on pause and started to help out in the infirmary because it was where she felt she was most needed. She had also opened their home to Henry. He slept in their Grandma's old room because it was the most accessible. He seemed to thrive under the new conditions. His body was still weak but he was able to take a few small steps at a time now.

"He couldn't wait to see Celeste again." Henry's cheeks colored at his mother's words and bent his head toward the floor.

"I'm sure she'll be excited to see you too," Finn said.

Liam was next to arrive, covered in wood shavings and muttering to himself. Henry was quick to pull him into an animated conversation about whittling, something Liam had been teaching him how to do.

Lucian and his father arrived at the same time Celeste and Senna did. Lucian pulled Celeste into a hug before she could do anything to stop him. She ruffled Henry's hair as she came into the room.

"I'm guessing you didn't bring good news." Their mother sounded resigned. For the first time, it looked like Celeste was about to fall apart.

"I couldn't find him. I'm so sorry. I couldn't do it." Her voice cracked. Senna pulled her into a hug. Celeste all but collapsed into her arms.

"It's okay. We will," Finn assured her. "I know he's out there somewhere."

"I do have some information on where he might be. There's rumors that Arran's traveling to Washington DC. That's where he suspects the host is at." She started pacing. "That and the other members of the rebellion are still having a hard time getting the other cities to work with them."

This was something Finn already knew. He and Lucian were in frequent contact with the other rebellion leaders. Leander might be defeated, but it didn't mean that everyone was willing to accept it. "I know."

"I think you need to be there, Finn." She came to a sudden stop, looking him over. "They need to see the horseman. You need to be there to lead them."

He knew she was right. He had spent the past couple of weeks healing, but he knew that soon he'd have to start repairing the relationship between people in cities and the rebellion. "I'm almost ready. As soon as I get cleared, I'll leave."

Celeste gave him a relieved smile. "I'll go with you, of course. You'll need a few trusted people as guards. Most of the rebellion is willing to follow you, and I think the free people will be too."

"I'll come too." Lucian stepped up.

"Actually, I think someone who's trusted needs to stay here and be in charge. I'd like it if you and my dad worked together to keep things moving forward here," Finn said. Lucian looked shocked.

"You want to put me in charge?" he asked. He didn't seem offended by the fact Finn was asking him to stay behind. In fact, he seemed almost elated.

Finn nodded. "The people in the rebellion already see you as a leader, and the townspeople are starting to trust you. I can't think of anyone more qualified."

"Are you sure, son? You're the one who's in charge." Winston looked between them all. He had never been trusted with so much power either, but Finn knew his father. He would make sure all of the little details would be taken care of under his command.

"I'm sure. The war isn't over yet, and there are still a lot of places in Leander's area that need to be reformed. I'm going to take some of our soldiers and work on uniting the towns and the rebellion camps while we search for Declan." He turned to Senna and Liam. "Will you guys come with me?"

He knew the question was selfish. Neither one of them liked to fight but he couldn't imagine going on without either one of them.

"You can't get rid of me that easy, Hero." Senna slipped her hand into his. Liam hesitated a moment.

"As long as I don't have to fight, I guess I could come." He shrugged.

"We'll start to get the supplies ready. Once you're good to go, we'll head out." Celeste pulled herself together, determination flickering in her eyes. "We'll find him."

"I guess we better start getting ready then." Finn pulled Senna closer, wrapping an arm around her shoulders. Everything he had was thanks to these people who had worked so hard to help him. It was a debt he'd never be able to pay, but he would do everything in his power to try.

There was just one person missing—Declan. Finn was going to find him, and he would figure out a way to save him. There had to be a way.

Until then, he would start putting the world back together, piece by piece. It would take time, and he would need help but he knew he could do it. He wasn't just Finn anymore. He was the horseman. He was War.

· ACKNOWLEDGMENTS ·

When I first started writing this book, I thought the process would be easy. You're sitting down and putting thoughts on a page. I found out just how hard writing it would actually be when I sat down to do just that. This book has overcome many obstacles, most of them being of my own making. It's gone through a complete overhaul when I realized the entire outline needed to be changed halfway through and all but the first two chapters would have to be rewritten. There were many cases of writers block and times of transition. I've moved five times since I first started writing and that led to many weeks where I felt too busy or stressed to actually sit down and write. It's finally finished though and that is largely in part of all the support I've received while writing it.

First, my biggest thanks goes to my Mom, who has never once in my life discouraged me from being an author when it's the only dream I've ever had. When I was little, before I knew how to even hold a pencil, I would make her write down my stories in her notebooks. She always did, no matter what weird, little thing my brain had come up with. When I started writing down my ideas by myself, I would hand her the pages and make her read them, which doesn't sound like a lot of work, but I would also then make her detail her every thought about it. She never once complained, though she did joke that I'd demand three page book reports from her. I probably would have if I thought I could actually get her to do it.

To my Uncle Dwayne who has spent thousands of hours talking with me about books and sharing all his favorite reads with me. I'm lucky to have grown up with someone in my life who has loved books as much as I have and is always excited to talk about them. He let me borrow any book I wanted from his personal library growing up; starting with Stephen King's *The Shining.* He was one of the first people who read this book, after my mom, of course. I was most nervous about them reading it because I wanted desperately for them to like it. One of my favorite memories is my uncle telling me how proud he was of me for writing this book.

To Shelby, one of my best friends that not only read the book and offered insights to make it better, but has been with me through the whole process of publishing it. She has sat down and talked to me about the ideas I have for future books and the best ways to market this one. I am so grateful that I got to meet her. We clicked instantly and I just knew she was going to be an important person in my life.

To Karra, who has been my best friend for nineteen years at the time of me writing this. She has probably seen every embarrassing story I've ever written. She sent me every mistake she noticed in this book while she was reading it so I could edit. She caught little edits that no one else had and made a list and that made my life infinitely easier. Her friendship has made my life infinitely easier. It's hard to put into words the amount of support she's given me with my writing and my life. I'm so lucky to have such a long standing friendship.

To Ashley, another best friend I've had forever and my loudest supporter. She has always been excited to read anything I've written and this book was no exception. She's sat down with me and has helped me work out ideas and plan future books. She has never once tired of me telling her my ideas and she's helped me expand on so many that I've lost count at this point.

To Bre, who is maybe a bigger reader than I am and has been the rock in my life for so long, I'm not sure what I would do without her. She's also listened to me talk and talk about this book and the one that will follow it and has always supported my ideas. She's been the sounding board I need when I have a half-formed idea or character I can't quite get right.

A special thanks to both the editor and designer of this book. I never would have been able to get this published without their help.

And finally, to my Grandma, who this book is dedicated to. My dreams of becoming an author started with her and her floor to ceiling bookshelves. My love of reading came from spending quiet days in her house surrounded by books. I wish she was still here to see that I wrote my own.